BRIARBURR BLACKMANE

AND THE

UNICORN HOLD

Book 1

G. D. Hanson

ISBN 13: 978-1-7340049-2-2
Library of Congress Control Number: 2017919563

This is the first part of the Blackmane Unicorn story, that takes four more parts to tell.

Briarburr Blackmane and the Unicorn Hold

Naythorn Blackmane Unicorn and His Animal Band

Naythorn Blackmane Unicorn and the Gift of the Winged Horse

Naythorn Blackmane Unicorn and the Seventh Prince

Naythorn Blackmane Unicorn and the Ghost Wolf

Historical Note

Found in Lebanon, Byblos is a UNESCO World Heritage Site. Once the religious capital of Phoenicia, the ancient city was known for its ship building and the craft of its sailors, and gained much wealth through trade with Egypt. For the fame of that historical city's high quality manufactured paper, the Greeks called books made of papyrus, Byblos. The *Biblia*, Bible in Greek, is made of many books (Genesis, Exodus... Mathew, Mark... Revelation).

Prologue

While the dwindling numbers of horned horses in the nine clans of unicorns searched anywhere and everywhere for rescue, a young blackmaned outcast from the magical white herd was drawn to the plight of two orphan children hidden in a forest. In that before time when the horses of haughty overlords trampled upon innocent hearts, the magical gifts of Blackmane Briarburr and the winged horse interwove with wondrous gold that shimmered blue.

with the horns of the unicorn he shall push the people together

Deuteronomy (Authorized KJV)

Chapter 1

Children in a Tree

"I just know I will see him. I have to!"

"I want to see him as much as my sister does!"

As they ran after each other, two fit children had breath to talk easily.

"You do *not*, Lyons. I want to see him more than... *ohhhh!*" After picking herself up as fast as she had fallen, Maryeta ran to catch up with her brother. "Early morning is best to see him. He will be hungrily chomping grass so that he does not notice us spying on him."

"You said the same thing yesterday, Maryeta, and we spent the whole morning *seeing nothing!*" The spontaneous chortling that followed in response to that comment sounded more like a fast running brook than a fast moving seven-year-old girl.

"Today will be the day... it just has to be! Stop twirling about as you run! It makes me dizzy. Lyons, stop... your... dancing!"

Paying no mind Lyons took three steps more and twirled again so that his unkempt dark hair swirled freely. Lyons looked back and held a finger to his lips as he whispered, "Shhhhh." He shifted his feet in another quick circle. "If we make noise we will scare him away." He circled again. "Remember Maryeta, we move quiet like rabbits. Ow! What was that for?"

"That punch is for twirling more. You are a boy, not a dancer."

"I wish Grandfather had *not* told me that because I am two years older I cannot hit you back."

In the gray light of brand new day Maryeta's favorite tree stood in wait, its limbs outspread in welcome. With the agility of monkeys the two children climbed up and hid themselves in low branches, certain that the thin flush of leaves in front of them provided impenetrable camouflage.

"Do not this time fall to sleep up there," admonished Lyons craning upward his neck at his little sister whose legs dangled down on each side of the tree limb she was seated on. "You have to mind me... because I am almost ten years old."

"Why is he not already here?" fidgeted Maryeta. "Yes, I promise I will stay awake."

"Remember sister, you said today would be the first time we would see him up close. Until now we have only seen flashes of something big moving through trees. Shhhhh... now you be quiet."

"I know he is coming," responded the girl disregarding her brother's instruction. "Because he woke up too late, we got here too early."

"Just as much as my sister, I really, really want to see him today."

"Psst, Lyons, I did not fall asleep," said Maryeta yawning and rubbing her eyes. With both hands she brushed tangly tresses of auburn hair away from eyes more green than blue. Hair pulled back and bearings regained, the girl leaned forward and stared toward the place of the waterfall. She again rubbed her eyes, harder this time.

"Psst, look Lyons. Something is coming. Ohhh... myyy. See, just like I told you, he is white with a black mane. And he is a boy horse. Ohhh... myyy. A winged horse is floating down to land beside him, and sniff him. She is a *girl horse*."

"Her stubby horn is not long enough to be a true unicorn."

"Brother, I am so excited that I can hardly say... *anything*."

"I cannot believe that a unicorn and a winged horse are standing so close together," whispered Lyons.

Maryeta put her hand to her mouth and muffled her tone, "The way they whinny and shake their manes shows they are just getting to know each other."

"The unicorn just... *nipped her*," whispered the boy with his eyes widening. "Why did he do that? I thought he liked her."

"She kicked him back! That serves the blackmaned unicorn right. Oh, oh. The winged horse just turned herself around to look at the waterfall. See how her ears stand up. I think she sees something. Maybe there is something behind all that water that crashes down."

"Do... not... move... Maryeta. The unicorn is looking up at us."

Stretched large, the eyes of two children did not so much as blink. Not a muscle in their bodies moved. Then, nothing sudden happened. The unicorn studied them, and in return permitted Lyons and Maryeta to study well him.

"He stands so straight," whispered a reassured little girl, "and his neck is so strong. His horn is perfect. You know what? He is not yet full grown. Still, there is something sad about his eyes." Exactly what occurred to the little girl's mind had to be said. "Lyons, since he came here alone, I think that he is an orphan just like us. Does he have a name? And, does the horse with wings have a name? She is the most really beautiful horse that can ever be. I want to ride on her back and feel her soft feathers against my legs. Her feathers would warm me at night, like a soft starry blanket."

"My little sister does not know how to ride a horse."

"I just know I can ride her... I know I can."

"I cannot believe that my sister and I are looking at a real live unicorn, even if he is a skinny one with a black mane. And we are doubly lucky to see a horse with wings. They both stand so still. It is as if they do not know what next to do... except to breathe."

Maryeta leaned out to get a clearer view of the two special horses.

"Look close, Lyons, the coat of the unicorn is matted. He is dirty, scraggly, and looks to be all legs. Ahhh, I do not care at all that he needs a bath and is as skinny as we are." Her eyes sparkled as she added, "I want to comb his black mane with my fingers." She stretched out her arms and made motions of combing the mane of an imaginary unicorn standing quietly up in the branches with her. Stretching too far out from the limb she lost her perch. "Ayyyyy... noooo!"

Lyons lurched himself out to catch his sister as she tumbled down. Catching hold her brother's arms, Maryeta pulled him after. The boy's legs lost their hold of the limb he was seated on, and in descent unplanned he followed his sister. They landed in two separate heaps of compact arms and legs. Fortunately, a cushion of leaves at the base of the tree spared them hurt. Two children quickly scrambled to their feet.

"Lyons, we scared them! The winged horse is flying into the waterfall! And the unicorn is running into the forest!" As tears watered rosy cheeks the little girl turned to grab hold her brother. "Hunnh... hunnh... will we ever see them again?" Maryeta could do something that her brother could not. She could sob and talk all at the same time. "Waahh... I want to... hunnh... see them... hnmmhmmnh... again. Waahh... my fall... hunnh... scared them away."

"How many times have I told you not to talk while you cry? When you cry at the same time that you talk, I cannot understand anything you say."

"I want to see them... hunnh... standing together by the waterfall. I want to see them... hnnhmm... play with each other..."

"No more tears from you," ordered Lyons as he hugged his little sister. "Do not cry any more. Just think! We are the only two children in our whole valley, maybe even in all the land of Phoenicia that have had the good luck to see a unicorn standing beside a winged horse."

"And Lyons, we saw them both at the same time." Tears quickly dried and the girl's eyes brightened. "I should be happy that I saw something so *wonderful*. I will bet that no one else ever saw a unicorn with a black mane, and a horse with wings, meet each other for the first time by a beautiful waterfall."

"I promise my sister that we will see them again." Lyons patted her shoulder and added, "You will see that I am right about that."

The two orphans slowly made their way back into the forest. When they finally reached a pocket of trees and shrubs that inside dense leaves and vines hid them, the children found exactly what they hoped to find. Laid out for them was a small loaf of bread and a wedge cut from a round cheese. Their teeth immediately began to tear at bread.

"Thank you, Grandfather," said Lyons. "If he were here he would like that I am so polite to him."

"Shhhhh," answered Maryeta shaking her finger at her brother. "You know we have to stay quiet until dark."

The seven-year-old girl was that afternoon transformed into a fairy princess. Leafy branches woven together with strands of long grasses became a princess cape. Stems of wild flowers were made to stick in her hair.

Red berries sprinkled onto the shirt of Lyons.

"Look, red blood stains his shirt," she whispered. "It is so terrible that Prince Lyons was wounded when he saved the blackmaned unicorn from the mean soldiers. Only my magic stick will stop his bleeding." Maryeta poked gently her napping brother. "Oh, no! The bad men sent an arrow into the wing of the horse that flies. But do not worry. My magic stick will make her to fly again." With one wave of her wand the arrow vanished from a bush that to the mind of Maryeta looked exactly like the winged horse.

"Prince Lyons!" The magic stick poked at the belly of her brother, this time to on purpose awaken him. "My reward for healing the deep sword wound in your chest, and for saving the winged horse from the bad soldiers, is that you have to *play princess* with me."

"Aw, do I have to? Again?"

"Granpaw says so! Do you know what, Lyons? For a little girl I make a perfect fairy princess."

CHAPTER 2

GRANDFATHER FAHSEED

Twilight hastened the close of the same day that a fairy princess saved her brother and a winged horse from villainous but imaginary bad men. In a village found close to where the forest began, seated outside the doorway of his small house sat the disgruntled grandfather of two orphaned children.

"On their own Lyons and Maryeta left before the light of day," muttered Fahseed. "Poor things, they did not want to spend another day cramped in my little cellar. Where can they now be? Since my two orphan *briarburrs* have come to know the exact places of tall trees and thorny shrubs, I am confident that they are not lost in the woods. Hmph. I thank the heavens that from out those woods are no more heard the howls of wolves."

Fahseed's thoughts were interrupted by the clip-clop of horse hooves growing louder. A soldier of the valley's overlord reined to a stop in front of the house of a man not especially tall, with a carelessly trimmed reddish beard, thinning forehead, clear eyes, and sturdy shoulders. While maintaining his gaze at the horseman, a hand of Fahseed moved as if he were shooing away a fly buzzing about his ear.

"Hah! So little Lyons and Maryeta are not about the house today?" snickered the horseman in response to the mild rebuff.

Long moments passed while two men stared hard at each other. The leer on the face of the horseman suddenly transformed into a loud laugh intended not only for Fahseed, but also for the benefit of any of the seated man's neighbors that might be eavesdropping. When the heels of the horseman signaled his steed to move on, the horse of the arrogant soldier trotted past the sharp turn of the street and became gone from sight. For more long moments the grandfather of two orphans fumed.

"It is not right!" exclaimed Fahseed rising to his feet. He did not care if his neighbors heard him. "Those that dwell peacefully in the humble village of Byblos stand helpless before the tyrant who rules this valley. We scarce possess the stones walling our houses. Who gave the overlord the right to take anything he wants? When in the heat of day a woman dries clothes on her rooftop, she cannot know that come evening that roof will still be hers to command." Bowing his head in resignation, Fahseed re-entered his little house.

Upon closing it shut, Fahseed addressed the door, "The worst of it, is that in this village dwell turncoats who for the gain of a pittance would give over my little runaways to the tyrant Baltric. When hidden in my little cellar at least the two castaways... *have a floor over their heads.*"

Beneath the floor of Fahseed's one room house was the place, more a den to fit two lion cubs than a proper room, from which Lyons and his younger sister Maryeta had before dawn slipped away. It had become harder for the grandfather to keep two fast growing and energetic children hidden in the confines of a windowless cellar. The two waifs found the forest with its river and twin waterfalls to be more exciting.

Lyons and Maryeta were now old enough to scavenge for themselves. Every day or two Fahseed left something, whether bread, grapes, cheese, or fruit for them in places where the food would be found. But, he had to be careful to keep his contact with them undetected, especially during the light of day when curious eyes saw far and wide.

The grandfather was thankful that with little protest, except regarding the too-close confines of his cellar, the two orphans accepted their lot in life. Lyons and Maryeta each knew that about that they had little choice.

"While so precious to me, their barely begun lives are worth so little to the world," said Fahseed as he sat down on his cot. "The price for children in the market is two or three gold coins apiece. But the love I spend on them is worth a thousand times more than a thousand gold coins." The one thing in the world wanted by Fahseed was that Lyons and Maryeta should one day know lives unhunted.

After night came to the village of Byblos the door to the house of Fahseed creaked open, and then creaked shut.

"I have a big secret to tell my Granpaw," whispered Maryeta. "Before I played princess we saw them, this time we *really* saw them."

"The unicorn had a black mane," added Lyons. "And his hide had dark markings."

"Shhh," whispered Maryeta holding a finger before her lips. "Do not tell anyone, Granpaw, but he looked right at me. And I have one more secret to tell you. A winged horse landed right beside him. She stretched out a wing to cover the unicorn's back."

"It was like she was protecting him with her wing," offered Lyons.

"Mnmmnnmm... hunhmmnn... then I ruined everything," whimpered Maryeta. "I fell out of my favorite tree and scared them away."

"Grandpa, when I could not catch hold of Maryeta I fell after to the ground."

"Thank goodness neither of you were hurt."

"I will never ever forget seeing the unicorn and the flying horse standing together," added the little girl squeezing tighter the fingers of her grandfather's hands. They were watching over each other, just like Lyons watches over me. Granpaw, seeing them together was like... *real magic!*"

The Greed of Lord Baltric

After smiling wide at the little girl on his knee, Fahseed pulled Lyons to his chest.

"I have never seen a unicorn or a flying horse, and I am more than forty years old. I cannot believe two forest urchins, one with a faded blue dress and the other with shirt and sandals in tatters, had the extraordinary good luck to see two magical horses. If I had gold coins in my pocket, for the benefit of your brand new friends the unicorn and the winged horse I would have Lyons to be dressed in a nice shirt and good shoes. With enough coins I could make the ruler of this valley to forget completely about this little boy and his sister."

"And I want a new red dress, Granpaw!"

"I promise, darling girl, that someday you shall have a brand new dress. But the way things go now, in this village it is not safe for a boy by the name of Lyons and a girl called Maryeta. Even so, when you two disappear into the forest I cannot help but worry about you. By heavens, I do not know what to do with you two." Fahseed embraced more tightly his grandchildren. "My worst fear is that you will be taken away, and never be returned to me. Ay! That would break my heart into three pieces, each part forever unable to beat with the other two."

The emotion carried in the words of Fahseed got the best of the little girl. "Hmmhunn," she whimpered. "Why does the bad man... hmmhunm... hate me? I did not hurt him." She crooked her arms at the elbows and brightened. "Just look! My muscles are not big enough to hurt anyone. And why did soldiers have to take away my mother and father?"

"Your arms are stronger than they look," replied Fahseed. "But, Maryeta, you are right. You are too small to hurt anyone. And because he does not know you, the overlord does not really and truly hate you. The ruler of this valley did, however, know your parents. He quarreled with your mother because she would not hand over all her chickens, goats, sheep, pigs, and calves to him. Did you know that your mother, my daughter, knew *all about animals?* Because she understood them like no one I have ever seen, your mother raised more lambs and piglets than any of her neighbors.

"Lord Baltric's love for money turned him into a bad man. Even now he insists that he needs more gold coins. He wanted all of your parents' livestock for himself so that he could sell them. When your mother and father defended their right to the work of their hands, Baltric and his men carried them away, along with their animals. Against fifty armed men I could do nothing to stop his wickedness."

"Where were you when they took away my parents?" inquired Lyons.

"When the bad men came they found me laboring in your father's vineyard. Ten soldiers broke off from the other forty. They grabbed me, dragged me toward my daughter's little house, and bound me to a tree. I could see and hear everything that next happened, but with my arms tied around a tree trunk I was powerless to save your parents."

"Tell us, Grandpa, about everything that happened on that day."

"Well, Lyons, since on your next birthday you are going to be ten, and your sister is soon going to be eight, you are both old enough to hear about all that I witnessed on that terrible day." On his lap Fahseed made comfortable Maryeta and Lyons. As the story of their parents' abduction began to unfold, Maryeta leaned her head into her grandfather's chest.

"While his soldiers went about gathering all your parents' animals, Lord Baltric had your parents brought before him with their hands bound. Fortunately, the short-necked duck and the long-necked goose fluttered out of the clutches of the soldiers. Not so the chickens. Fifteen chickens soon roasted over a fire.

"Because the animals of your mother were every day treated with kindness, they were very tame. When I came to visit I would hear your mother talking to the animals as if they could understand her. She would have surprisingly long conversations, with her animals paying close attention to her words. At times they would groink, baah, quack, cluck, or moo back in agreement with what your mother said. Because they were brought to stand close by your parents the two cows, ten mama sheep, five mama goats, and the four mama pigs that we call sows, did not fuss at the soldiers.

"While he feasted upon roast chicken, Lord Baltric amused his soldiers with frivolous talk. Because the animals were each and every one her friends, your mother pleaded for them. She thought that if Baltric would see how much she loved her livestock, he would relent. She told the overlord the name of each cow, pig, sheep, and goat." Fahseed wiped at something in his eyes.

"Errhrrm. Baltric asked your mother if what the villagers said about her was true, that she understood the sounds spoken by her animals. She answered *yes*. The overlord next ordered your mother to ask the pigs whether they liked to eat barley. When your mother asked the question of the pigs, they grunted back in pig talk while nodding their heads. But the grunting was not good enough for the mean overlord. He said he had to hear the pigs say the word *barley*.

"Baltric then called your mother a liar, and said she could not and did not talk to her animals. That pained me, for in this village our honest name has always been worth much. Before that day your mother had never been accused of not telling the truth, not even when she was a little girl like this Maryeta sitting on my knee."

"Someday, Granpaw, I am going to ask the winged horse if she likes to eat barley," responded Maryeta. At that comment two children were lovingly pressed to the breast of their grandfather.

"What happened next?" asked Lyons.

"Baltric lost his temper. The overlord shouted that your mother owed him back taxes. Both your mother and father insisted that they had always given half of the calves, lambs, goat kids, and piglets to the tax collector. Baltric said that was not so, and could not be so, for if they had paid their taxes in full they would not have so many more animals than their neighbors."

"In the distance Baltric spotted two little children returning from a time at play. Do you remember your father yelling for you to run away?"

"I remember that," answered Lyons.

"I cannot, because I was too small."

"You are right Maryeta, you were very small. Well now, you two cannot know how happy your prompt obedience to your father made me feel. You knew where to find crawl spaces into thorny bushes where the soldiers could not follow. I was *very thankful* that the bad soldiers never found you.

"The most amazing thing, a big commotion, happened next. All at once, and all together, the pigs ran over Baltric and tumbled him down. Dirtied, and with his pride damaged, the overlord told his men to forget about two escaped urchins. He said that the price of a newborn calf was more than what he could get for both of you put together, and that soon enough his tax collector and his guards would apprehend you two.

"For one thing only am I thankful. No soldier beat your mother or father. With so many soldiers about them escape was impossible, so no escape was attempted by your parents.

"Lead ropes were tied to the cows and to your mother and father. Walking in the midst of their animals, your parents were herded back to the fortress of Baltric. I never again saw your mother or father." Fahseed paused to hug more tightly his grandchildren.

"Do you know that you two are all that I live for? Hmph. Now, there remains one thing more that you should both know. It is a very serious thing. The day that your parents were from me taken away, I made a vow. I promised to myself that I would never forget the crime committed by Lord Baltric against your mother and father. I promised that someday I would do my part to destroy the wicked man that rules over this valley. I now repeat to you that vow. Somehow, in some way, I will know revenge for my daughter's terrible fate. But until that time comes you two little briarburrs must move only in the shadows."

No one, for a while, said anything. Suddenly the expression of Maryeta changed as quickly as the direction of a swallow in flight.

"Granpaw, is this the real color of my hair?"

"Your hair is... yes, it is a mixture of red and brown just like the color of your mother's hair."

"Lyons says that because I am always outside my hair gets burnt red by the hot sun. But his dark hair never turns red. Tell me again, Granpaw, about my name."

"Well, your mother gave you a name that *means little sea*. I think the reason for that, Maryeta, is that your mother always wanted to see the sea and never had that wish fulfilled. She wanted that her daughter would someday walk on the seashore."

"Since Lyons taught me how to swim in the river, I can also swim in the sea!"

"And Lyons, I have before told you that your mother was the only one to ever see lions at the place of the waterfall. She was about your age when she saw two of them sitting behind the falling water. She became very excited at the sight of real live lions. Even though I was with her at the waterfall, I did not see the lions. But of course I knew she was telling the truth. Because she never forgot the lions that she that day saw, she named you after them. Hmm... I just remembered something more. Your mother also told me that when she was about the age that Lyons is now..."

"I cannot wait to be ten years old," interrupted the boy.

"That... she once fell asleep close to that same waterfall. And while sleeping she dreamt that a gentle unicorn touched his horn to her head, and then talked to her. Now, speaking of sleep, it is time for you two to hit the hay."

Threading fingers through her hair the little girl shrugged shoulders and expelled what for her was a very big breath. "I still do not understand why I cannot stay openly in the house... of my Granpaw."

"We have to mind Grandfather," said Lyons yawning. "Good night, Grandpa."

The two children moved to the corner of the room and pushed a large basket out of the way. Lifting up a few loose boards they slipped down into the tiny fruit cellar. A stub of candle was handed down to them.

"Thank you, Granpaw, for telling us about that awful day," said the little girl.

Two children curled up together under a blanket, and then together blew out the candle flame. Shortly after, a knock was heard at the door. A man entered, spoke a few words to Fahseed, and left.

When two little hands pushed cellar boards to the side, through the floor emerged a girl's head.

"What was the man whispering about *candles* to my Granpaw?"

"So, Maryeta, not yet fallen asleep you heard something about candles," replied Fahseed moving to sit on the floor by the opening to the fruit cellar.

"Because I do not want to miss out on anything, I learned to sleep lightly."

Lyons popped his head out of the hole in the floor.

"And Maryeta woke up her brother. Well then, I shall explain to you both. That man, his name is Jomain, is a very good friend to me. He knows that somewhere within the confines of this little house are harbored two small fugitives. Perhaps he before glimpsed you two crawl through the wall to enter the village. My friend told me that should Lord Baltric's men ride past his house, he will immediately pass his hand back-and-forth in front of a candle flame. If either of you children see a candle flicker on and off in a window up the hill, you must quick as a wink get to the forest. Go to one of the hidden places that I know about, and hide there until I come to you." That said, Fahseed hit his hands together.

"I hate that I must instruct my two grandchildren to run away and hide! Hmph! Let us right now make together a pact. Someday we three are going to stand up to the overlord, and reclaim our right to live in peace. I do not know when that day will come to happen. But I swear to you that right here in this little house, or maybe in an even bigger house in our village of Byblos, there will come a time when Maryeta and Lyons shall laugh as loud as they want to."

"Take my hands in yours, Granpaw" instructed the little girl smiling. "I promise that we will someday be *a real family.*"

"I promise too, Grandfather," said Lyons extending his hands through the cellar opening. "I am sure that will happen, someday."

"Do you know what?" answered Fahseed grasping in his grip the hands of the two children.

"What, Granpaw?"

"What, Grandfather?"

"When your mother was small she had a real home, playmates, and a loving father. Still, in spite of my not giving you a safe home, I am very glad that I have hugged you two little briarburrs more than I ever hugged your mother when she was your size. Having you two close to my heart means more to me than living in a big palace."

Past the dark of middle night Maryeta mounted dreams of an extraordinarily lucky little girl riding through fields of golden barley... on a winged horse.

CHAPTER 3

LORD BALTRIC'S CORPORAL

Seated at the table where burned a slim candle, Fahseed heard a thin breeze to rustle and whirl leaves about the street in front of his house.

"I heard a door slam shut," alerted Maryeta running to the little back window. "Granpaw, a candle flickers on and off where you told us to watch for it."

"Damn! Jomain signals that they come for you! Slip like foxes through the village wall and run as quick as you can into the forest!" Four bare feet pitter-pattered into darkness. Sounds that mixed of horse hooves and grown-up feet were soon heard outside the squalid house.

"Get out here at once!"

Fahseed found ten soldiers clumped before his door. At the front of the platoon stood a short, swarthy, thin-haired man with hands clasped behind his back. Beside him and for him was held a thick candle.

"We know that you are hiding them," spoke again the short man. "Bring them out to us and you will not be harmed."

"What can you want at this time of night?" answered the man whose shoulders filled the door frame. "Come back tomorrow morning when there is light to see who you are."

"You know me well enough. You cannot have forgotten that I once tied you to a tree."

"Hmph. I remember that a sergeant once tied my hands. It was on the awful day that my daughter was from me taken. I also remember that while he bound my hands, men larger than the sergeant restrained me."

"This is not a game, Fahseed. Your neighbors spy on you. Last night in the darkness they saw the two outlaw children enter your house. And my spies confirm that your grandchildren did not today leave your house. Have Lyons and his sister Maryeta to come out. They will be the worse for wear if I have to go in and pull them out."

"Sergeant, in my mansion dwell no children. Go ahead and post a guard outside my door. Come back in the morning, *Sergeant*, and you will have light to give my grand abode a thorough search."

"Do you see what he is doing?" inquired the platoon leader turning to his men. "Having heard that I was demoted from sergeant to corporal, Fahseed goads me. So what if I now make less pay? I like that a corporal has less responsibility than a sergeant. It is a small task for me to go and fetch two wanted children; that kind of duty exactly suits me. Fahseed dares to imagine that he can delay the one and only corporal of Lord Baltric in order to give his grandchildren time to burrow deeper into his cellar."

More candles were lit; the leader of the armed men stepped back from the door. When the corporal flicked an index finger three soldiers scrambled past

Fahseed into the little house. The sound of men throwing around a table and chairs was heard. Clay plates and cups were flung out the doorway.

"Corporal, we found the hole in the floor!" The same voice sounded again, "Come out before I come down and get you! My knife is drawn! If I cut off an arm your little lives will be worth nothing!" From out the cellar came no answer.

"One... two... three!"

With a candle in one hand, and knife in the other, the smallest of the three men that had mistreated the furniture of Fahseed reached into the cellar. His two bigger companions grabbed hold the legs of the small in size ruffian, and fitted him head first into the small opening. The sounds of pieces of boards being tossed about were heard, and then came the thumping sounds of a fist striking dirt walls. A head thrust back up through the hole in the floor.

"There is nothing here but straw, a few dried fruits, a ratty blanket, and some old sandals to fit small feet. The young fugitives escaped." By his arms the small soldier was pulled back into the room that served as kitchen, living room, and bedroom.

The former confidence and aloofness of the corporal had curiously managed to depart him. He grabbed hold the shirt of Fahseed, and stretching high on tiptoes brought his face close to the face of the master of the great little house.

"They were here only a short time ago! They... were... *seen!* Where did they go?"

"Sergeant, err... that is corporal, I have not the faintest idea what you are talking about. Since your leader took away my daughter, I have been unable to be a grandfather. Are you seriously trying to tell me that Lord Baltric did not, as he promised he would quickly do, as well steal away my daughter's children?"

"Arrest Fahseed! I will make him to talk. I have my ways to make people tell the truth."

"In my house there is an empty cellar," sounded a loud voice from out of the night's shadows. "Are you to arrest me as well? What is the charge for arresting Fahseed? Is it because his cellar is empty? My cellar is empty because you and your men have taken all my wheat and left me with nothing this winter to eat."

"Aye, my cellar is as well empty," came a second voice out of the darkness.

A rock thudded against the side of Fahseed's house. The sight of ruffians blindly waving swords to cut the darkness provoked more stones to be thrown.

"We have more rocks than you have swords," yelled a third voice. "There are only ten of you. Be gone from here!"

The first voice that had spoken from out of darkness was heard again, "The next rocks thrown will have jagged edges and be aimed at your heads!" At that warning, soldiers lifted forearms to shield faces.

"Do you really dare threaten me? I have paid spies in this village. They will find out who you are, and when they do Lord Baltric will take everything from you. Your empty bellies will not last out the winter. You villagers are nothing more than *sheep* to me! From this moment on your fates are sealed! The next time I come back it will be with fifty men. The big lieutenant with the shaved head and the ferocious look will make Fahseed regret even more what happened this night. After we seize the two waifs we will drag off Fahseed in chains."

Mindful of the shadows where lurked villagers armed with stones, soldiers backed slowly away from the thoroughly searched little house. Night soon swallowed the departing horses of the corporal and his platoon of soldiers. Without the walls of Fahseed's abode the three shadowy figures that had intervened to speak on their friend's behalf, lingered long.

Fahseed went inside and closed the door of his house. Next to a broken table the grandfather of two orphans sat down on the floor. To quiet himself Fahseed clasped his knees.

"To be sure, that corporal was there when they took away my daughter and her husband. Not he, but four of his men tied me to a tree. I wish I had throttled the little villain. Now he will take from me my innocents, the two children who are all that I have left." A despondent Fahseed slumped shoulders and drooped his head.

"Maryeta will now have to drink from a... *broken cup.* Like my few belongings, for too long I have been smashed and broken. My life to me matters little. I do not even feel like a man. Still... their grandfather matters much to the safety of Lyons and Maryeta."

With a vacant look on his face and in a manner strange the grandfather spoke again, as if he were talking not about himself, but about another man in the village.

"Fahseed must for now keep himself alive to protect the two briarburrs he loves so dearly... and... Fahseed must someday destroy the one true villain, the overlord Baltric. After tonight Fahseed's cellar is no longer safe for his grandchildren. He must make a new place for them in the forest. Where can Fahseed find a place that will stay ever hidden from eyes paid to spy?

"But at that, Fahseed did tonight learn something. He recognized the three voices that spoke for him. Fahseed knew that Jomain was to him loyal. Now he finds that Colyado and Elyeazar were also willing to take a stand for their friend. Perhaps the lowly grandfather will one day make something of the courage shown tonight by his three blacksmith friends.

"Hmph. They are poor as a... but even temple mice are not as poor as Fahseed's two little ones. And their lively hope is Fahseed's only possession."

CHAPTER 4

THE PLACE BEHIND THE WATERFALL

Since the morning that two orphans saw a unicorn and winged horse come to stand before the twin waterfalls, five years had come and gone. The still welcomed presence of that memory was why again on this day an almost thirteen-year-old girl, and an almost fifteen-year-old boy, reposed in a favorite spot watching swirling waterfall mists perform a subtle dance of intricate pirouettes.

Sitting cross-legged Lyons and Maryeta inventoried hands, arms, and legs that bore too many scratches from thorns, briars, and burrs. For wearing so many scratch marks their grandfather, with affection, called them his briarburrs. Upon seeing them for the first time in five or six days, Fahseed would inform his grandchildren that they had each scratched their bodies taller.

"Soldiers keep coming after us," said Lyons crossly to his sister. "We are nowhere safe. Our chances that never were good, worsen. We make a new hideout in the forest, and within ten suns they have found it. Baltric's ruffians will not stop searching for us. We half starve living on a few snared rabbits, nuts, berries, and fish. It has become harder and harder for Grandfather to get away to bring us cheese and bread. By village spies he is all day watched."

27

"Brother, remember that time Granpaw brought us meat porridge? It was *soooo* good. Oh well, no more porridge for me." Slumping down shoulders she added, "I too am tired of running from the soldiers of Baltric. By myself I would not know which way to turn. Only because my older brother is my leader, do I go on."

"What, Maryeta, can we do? If only we had a place that could not be found out. A real lion's den named after me."

Lyons stared at the waterfalls, for there were really two of them separated from each other by a forehead promontory rising out of the middle of the river. On the sides of the promontory, the halves of the waterfall formed a forward bending V.

"*Haha*! Got you!" yelled Maryeta splashing water at her brother.

"Today I will not splash you back. How can I be in the mood for fun when too many bad men are looking for us? As things now stand, they will soon catch us."

After giving her brother a big hug the girl said quietly, "Grandpaw placed me in your care, and you constantly fret about soldiers one day capturing me. For that I am a burden that weighs on your shoulders. Sometimes I think it would be easier for you to dwell in this forest... alone."

"Never say that! If it were not for you I would give myself up. As the older brother I know my job, and it is to keep you free and to keep me free."

"It was in this very spot where once stood the unicorn and the winged horse," said Lyons with his forehead seeming to relax and brighten. "When he glimpsed us up in the tree, the unicorn did not mind being seen by two children. It was as if he... kind of... liked us."

"But I fell and scared both the blackmaned unicorn and the winged horse away. I interrupted her stare at the waterfall."

"She was much taken with the waterfall. Sister... what if... there was a reason the winged horse turned herself about to stare at the waterfall."

"Brother, we have ten times looked behind that cascade of water. There is no place there for us to hide. There is only a little ledge to stand on, and water drenches down all around." The face of the girl grew animated.

"Come with me! One more time, Lyons... *please?* I want to go behind the falls and check every little crevice. Maybe there is rock handle that opens a magic door... just like in a fairy tale."

"Because you were very little when they took father away from us, I remember him better. It was at this very spot that he taught me to dog paddle. Since then this has always been my side of the river."

"Lyons, you once told me that the rock cliff on the far bank of the river anchors straight down. Who knows how deep the water is over there? You know what? I have never swum all the way across the river. If we are going to one more time look at the falls, let us do it from the other side of the river. I am grown big enough to swim all the way across. Come on! Today we are going to explore!"

Getting the jump on her brother, Maryeta plunged first into the river and beat her brother to where water from the second falls, the far falls, cascaded down. Seating themselves, they watched water plummet out over their heads.

"Where we sit, sister, is wider than the ledge behind the falls on our side of the river. The winged horse could easily fit here. In this place she could hide and no one would know it. You know what! I think this is where our mother saw the two lions when she was a girl."

A boy and a girl began to explore the hidden ledge.

"The falls on this side of the river are different. Just look how much water pours through the cracks at our ankles."

"That, Maryeta, means that a lot of water is held behind this rock wall."

"See that, Lyons? Three birds flew out of the ledges above us. Can birds nest under a waterfall?"

"I counted five," answered the boy. "But it is too wet to build nests under so much falling water. Bird nests... umm... I have it! The birds we just saw fly away, make nests inside a cavern found behind this waterfall. Somewhere above our heads is an opening for birds to go behind this rock wall. I am going to climb up and see where go the birds."

"Be careful! Do not fall and crack open you head!" Maryeta watched her brother find places in the wet rock wall where hands could grab hold and feet could plant. "Hey Lyons, the winged horse was not looking at the mists. She knew there was a cavern behind the falls."

"So, Maryeta, when the winged horse stared at the falls she was looking at the second, and not the first cataract? Wait! I see an opening above me. I am going to squeeze-in."

"Do you want me to climb up after you?"

"No sister, stay down there until I come out from the cavern. If a wild beast is trapped in there, if it is a real lion's den, then you will need to bring help."

"Do not scare me like that!" Maryeta's chin sank into her hands. "I do not like being here alone, and I am soaked all the way through."

Lyons brought himself safely back. After once more swimming to their side of the river, the two were soon perched in the branches of Maryeta's favorite tree.

"So, brother, tell me what you saw inside."

"Well, sunlight enters through cracks in the roof of the cavern. A crystal clear pool that covers the middle of the floor is fed by river water that gushes into the far end of the long cavern, the end opposite the cataract. The water that filters out through crevices in the cataract wall matches the water that enters the cavern. On the edges of the pool driftwood piles high. The part of the cavern closest to where we now sit is layered in rock ledges. There you and I could camp, build fires, and sleep. You know what else, Maryeta? With a rope we could let ourselves down through the big hole where river water funnels into the far end of the cavern."

"I know where we can get our hands on a rope."

The next day found two orphan renegades trespassing the raised and elongated rock shelf that separated the two falls of the river. The place where water flowed into the cavern was at the low point of a shallow basin. Spaced apart by the width of five adolescent hands, gripping knots were fashioned into a piece of rope. One end of the rope was tied around a rock protruding out of knee-deep water; the other end was fed into the water funnel.

"It is my turn!" Maryeta's eyes lit with excitement at the prospect of being a cave explorer. "Since you are stronger than me, you can pull me back out."

"Aww... all right. Tug twice when I am to pull you up. Do not fall and get bloody. Remember Grandfather made me responsible for you."

"That brother, I will never let you to forget."

"She let go her hold of the rope; she is inside. When she is with me, I fret. When she is gone from me, I worry. And now until she is back to me, I am to feel alone." Lyons finally felt tugs on the rope.

"You were inside so long that I began to doubt you would ever re-emerge."

"The cavern is a lot bigger than I thought it would be," answered the short of breath girl. "The crystal clear water in the pool reaches to my waist. As I walked in the pool my hands touched fish. Did you see the cave opening that looks to tunnel into the mountain on the far side of the river?"

"I saw it, but I was too scared to enter that dark place."

"Guess what else, Lyons. I saw birds fly out from two places behind the waterfall. The second crawlway, not the one you used, is higher up and larger."

"I did notice one thing that was curious," added Maryeta with her features made serious. "A layer of sand below the pool glitters golden. It is not the top layer, but a layer more deep. Do you want to know how I found that out?"

Lyons nodded yes.

"Walking across the pool I scratched my leg on a branch sticking out of the sand. Since my legs do not need more scratches, that made me mad. When I pulled the branch from the sand, bright colored grains swirled about. And that made me curious. So I held my breath and with both hands scraped at the sand. Down one hand deep, the sand changed to a blue and gold hue."

"Take my pouch, Maryeta, and fill it with the shining sand. Back down you go. Grandfather will tell us if it is... real gold."

Stand therefore, having your loins girt about with truth, and having on the breastplate of righteousness...

Ephesians (Authorized KJV)

CHAPTER 5

NUGGETS OF BLUE GOLD HOPE

"You saw our signal!" exclaimed Maryeta.

"We only lean the big white limb against the tree... if it is something really important," added Lyons.

"I came as soon as I could get away from the village without my departure being noticed."

From a pouch slung over her shoulder Maryeta pulled out a handful of grains and flakes that glittered. "Granpaw, is this gold?"

"Let me look closely. I would have to say... hmm... yes it... has to be. Wait a moment... its color is not just golden, it also glitters blue. Where did you find this?"

"Behind the waterfall. Lyons found the cavern, but I found the gold colored sand beneath the pool."

"This, children, must be closely looked into." Seriousness took command of the grandfather's visage. "Wait for me tomorrow. While I tell my neighbors that I go to gather branches for the fireplace, I will instead sneak away to join my grandchildren at the waterfall.

Just maybe... just maybe... this gold colored sand can change things for all three of us."

"Lyons and I will here collect a big pile of branches for you to bring back to the village tomorrow. No one will even know that you went to the waterfall."

"Maryeta will soon change her mind about that and insist that someone else will know," said Lyons, "someone that walks on four hooves."

"You do not believe me," responded Maryeta punching her brother's shoulder, "but I just know the unicorn with the black mane still hides in our woods."

With his belt holding a hammer, an iron spike, a chisel, and a length of rope Fahseed began to climb. The larger crawlway behind the cataract was harder to reach than the smaller place through which Lyons had squeezed himself into the cavern. Fahseed found the niche in the rock wall he desired, and there hammered in the spike. He looped one end of his rope to the spike.

"Wish me luck, Maryeta."

"You can do it, Grandpaw!"

"Be careful," cautioned Lyons. "It is a long way down to where we stand."

Fahseed pushed away, swung out, caught hold a protruding stone, and pulled himself into the crawlway. "Children, I am in!"

"I am going to enter the cavern through the hole in the river!"

"Me too!" seconded Lyons.

Possessing an endless source of energy inside their skin and bones bodies two children swam, ran, swam again, and descended the rope that still dangled into the swirl hole.

"Lyons, Maryeta, we will make of this place a secret sanctuary!" exclaimed their grandfather.

Fahseed entered a shallow part of the pooled water, reached down, scraped, and with both hands grabbed at deeper sand.

"My hands hold gold! This can be nothing else!" Moving to the middle of the pool, Fahseed submerged and again scraped hands into the sand. "Hah! Blue hued gold spreads across the floor of the pool! My own grandfather said that blue gold existed. It turns out that he was right to so believe. He claimed that the blue gold was magical. Hmph. I do like that sunlight enters through cracks and crevices in the roof of this cavern. And, I can guess what caused the gold to be here deposited.

"A long time ago a mountain found somewhere upriver held a deposit of blue gold ore. During the passage of countless years bits of the gold broke loose and washed into the river. The current carried some of the gold sand into this cavern pool. The base of the rock wall before the waterfall stops the golden sand from flowing out of here. After the blue gold deposit in the mountains became exhausted, ordinary sand continued to flow into the cavern and so layered over the heavier grains of blue gold."

"It must have taken an awfully long time, Grandfather, to build up so many golden grains on the bottom of this pool."

"My boy, on that you are right. It surely took many thousands of years for the gold to erode and wash down the river."

"Grandpaw, is there enough gold sand to make a girl rich?"

"No, darling girl, we are not rich. My grandfather insisted that magic blue gold can never be used for showy jewelry or personal gain. According to him, the legend insists that the fabled blue gold be used only for swords and armor to guard a country that is worthy and true, a land that treats its people justly."

"Hmph. Now that I think about it, if somewhere in this cavern were found metals and coal to smelt with, we would right here have everything we need to make blue gold swords. In possession of such weapons the people in our valley could defeat Lord Baltric. So I ask you two, can this cavern hold more surprises for us?"

"Look over there," said Maryeta pointing. "That is the cave opening I told Lyons about. If we only had a candle we could find to where it leads."

"See here?" replied Fahseed pulling out a piece of candle and a flint, "Your grandfather came prepared." The blacksmith led into the tunnel opening found in the cavern wall.

"Stay close to me children. We do not want to get lost in this cave where there are many ways to go. Because you two are experts at remembering a path in the forest, I know that you can memorize a cave path." As they walked Fahseed held the candle to the rock walls.

"This is... copper," affirmed Fahseed chipping rocks with his hammer and chisel. Further on, more rocks were collected. With the candle more than half gone, the three reversed course and found their way back to the water cavern.

"Children, after I tomorrow consult with an acquaintance, who is not only a blacksmith but a much experienced miner, I will know with certainty if there are useful mineral ores in the rocks we collected. If they contain copper, tin, and iron as I think they do, we shall fashion a forge and make magic swords to protect us in battle."

The children became quiet.

"Lyons, your face tells me you are thinking on something. What is it?"

"Well, Grandfather, we discovered a hideout where no one can find us. Even if someone found us we could escape through the two crawlways in the waterfall ledge, or else depart through the water funnel at the other end of this cavern. You believe there are metals to fashion weapons. Strewn about the rocks and ledges of the cavern are piles of driftwood to build fires. In the cavern pond there are even fish to eat. I cannot believe it, but my dream is going to finally come true. The blue gold swords we fashion will make me and Maryeta to be free."

The following evening Fahseed and his grandchildren were met in a leafy copse located not far distant from the village.

"Tell us, Granpaw, do the rocks from the cave contain copper and iron?"

"The rocks do bear metal ores. Can you believe, Maryeta, our good fortune?"

"So we are not rich in gold... but we are rich in iron and copper."

"There is also silver. But Maryeta, I need you to always remember that we are truly rich only in our love for each other."

"What comes next, Grandfather?"

"It seems to me, Lyons, that the first required thing is to name our hideout after the one who found it. We will call it the Lyons Den."

Maryeta frowned.

"I know that it was you, Maryeta, that found the blue gold sand," said Lyons noticing his sister's sullen look.

"Aww... I suppose the Lyons Den is the best name."

"It is just fine, sister, if people think that the name refers to real lions and not to me."

"I have been thinking, children, on what to do next. To our cause I will enlist three friends I count as loyal and discreet. As it happens, just like me they are experienced blacksmiths. With their help we will build and work the forge. In the passage of three or four moons we shall have made swords with edges tempered in... true magic. Now I have a question for you. Are two young hearts ready to take on the risks of war? If we someday lose in battle not only is my life forfeit, but your two precious young lives will as well be lost."

"We have to do something, Granpaw. Lyons and I are everywhere hunted. Since I know that the hoof prints in the forest belong to the unicorn, I hope he will help me to fight for my freedom."

"Maryeta is right. Unless something soon changes we two will be done for. Remember when we once made a promise to someday be a real family? It is time for all three of us to keep that promise."

The hug shared by a grandfather and two grandchildren was deeply heartfelt.

"Children, now you have to give me some time. The pieces of rock held in this bag will surely prove convincing to men whose help I can count on. I will invent an excuse to leave the village. I and the three men I trust will say we go... on a trading trip. We will double back and join you at the waterfall. For now you will have to be patient. Wait for my friends and me to secure all the things needed to make a forge. In the meantime I have a job for you. Gather a large supply of nuts, berries, and tubers to eat while we work hard in... *the Lyons Den.*"

CHAPTER 6

THE UNICORN WITH A BLACK MANE

"For days and days we have done nothing but gather food. Since my basket is full, this girl deserves a nap."

"Your basket is only half full!"

Maryeta flopped down on the grassy part of a slope rooted in nut bearing trees. She raised herself onto an elbow and said, "Since you have not worked as hard as I have, you need to stay at it."

"I work twice as hard as you," answered Lyons grimacing. "If anyone deserves a break, it is me. I am always covering for my sister." Setting down an almost full basket of tree nuts, Lyons added, "I am going to take my bow and hunt rabbits. Until I get back you stay here and take a nap, or sing your silly songs."

After rolling herself onto her stomach, with her fingers Maryeta began to smooth plucked grasses. She shifted onto her back and next studied the sky progress of cloud patches. Beginning to hum a tune, she coaxed words into a song.

A little lost girl is twelve years old
Soon she will be... all growed up
Her two friends are a Lyon and a horse

A boyfriend is worse than a broken cup

Awaking from a dream where upon fluffy clouds she rode on the back of a galloping winged horse, Maryeta whispered, "I really love that dream." Her eyes grew large. She sat up and exclaimed, "What is happening?" Springing to her feet she ran up a knoll.

"Oh no! They captured Lyons!" Connected by a long rope to a man on a horse, the hands-bound Lyons was being dragged stumbling and falling. He did not stop yelling at his captor.

Maryeta stood frozen. She wanted to run after her brother, except she quickly realized the reason Lyons was making so much noise was to warn her not to pursue him. But... she had to follow her brother.

"No one can hear the soft paws of a rabbit hopping on the ground," said Maryeta under her breath as she darted through the woods. A branch broke behind her. Maryeta's heart leaped into her throat as she muttered, "Soldiers follow me." She slipped into bushes and there breathed as quietly as she could. Another branch broke. Someone had stopped before the bushes that hid her.

"Is that... a... whinny?" Upon hearing again the sound, she was double sure it was the grunting of a horse. The tone of the horse's *hrruummhumm... hrrungghh...* was friendly, maybe even kind. Her heart convinced her that the unicorn with the black mane was standing close to her. Maryeta's fear turned to elation. On hands and knees Maryeta crawled out of the bushes.

"It is... you! And you are grown bigger than any horse I ever saw!" She rose to her feet and without thinking stepped right up to the unicorn with the black mane and pressed her cheek to his. She liked the feel of the unicorn's warm breath on her shoulder.

The unicorn deftly touched his horn to the side of Maryeta's head. The girl saw the horn shaft glow blue, and at the same time felt unburning sparks sizzle into her scalp.

"They have your brother."

"I was sleeping when they captured him." She began to sob, "Hmmmnn... he is... gone from me... hmmmnn... forever." She suddenly realized that a unicorn horse had talked to her. "But, how can I understand the words you neigh?"

"When my horn touched your head you were given the gift of the uniform animal tongue. You now hear my neighs as words in your language, and I hear your words as horse talk. The sparks did not hurt your head?"

"They tingled, but they did not burn me at all." She was amazed that she was speaking not just to a horse, but to a real live unicorn with a black mane and small black markings splotched into his white hide.

"I go to bring Lyons back to you. There is no time to lose. Eleven men carry him off. Wait here, Maryeta, for me and Lyons to return to you."

"You know our names!"

"I have not been so far away. I have been closer to you than you think." The unicorn reared up, waved his front legs at Maryeta, and was gone.

"If anyone can rescue my brother, I know it is that unicorn. He moves so fast. One moment he is standing still, and the next moment he is in full gallop."

The Overlord's Platoon

Forty paces to the rear of the ten soldiers he had brought with him to capture the children, rode Lord Baltric. To the saddle of the overlord was secured the long rope that wrapped tightly around Lyons' arms and hands. Along a wide and open forest path Baltric's platoon of mounted soldiers proceeded at a leisurely pace toward his walled garrison.

"I finally caught the miscreant that for years has vexed me!" shouted the overlord stretching his arms skyward. "In my hands is held the rope that proves Fahseed was lying, and that I was right all along!"

"Today you are made to be again... Baltric the Bad!" shouted back the small in stature corporal to his commander. "Since it was me that today bound the hands of the youth, I now also have my revenge for that long ago night when I searched the cellar of Fahseed and came up empty. I cannot wait to see what Lord Baltric will now do to the liar Fahseed!"

"Heheh! I assure you that *BalTricky* will invent a gruesome punishment for the liar, and as well for the villagers that menaced my corporal not with sharp swords, but with what was it... stones?" That comment brought laughter from the men riding in advance of the overlord.

"Lord Baltric," spoke another mounted man with head turned back, "your revenge will not be complete until you capture the sister. Her name is... uhh... Maryeta?"

"Her capture will now be made easy for me. On Byblos's twisted street I will tomorrow torture the boy and his grandfather. When Maryeta learns that the torture will day after day continue until she gives herself up, she will meekly come and surrender to... Baltric the Bad! Hah! They say that the sister of Lyons is now quite becoming. If she is as pretty as they say, she will at the market bring twenty gold coins." As the laughter from his men came louder, Baltric's spirits rose more.

"The wine and strong drink are on me! The ten of you will tonight have all you can eat and drink!"

"Baltric! Baltric!" cheered the mounted men.

"Hmph? Did I just hear something behind me?" muttered the overlord jerking his head back toward where Lyons was stumbling along the road.

"It is the sound of horse hooves!" exclaimed the corporal. "But that cannot be! All the horses in this valley belong to Lord Baltric!"

"A horned horse!" sounded a chorus of voices.

"A unicorn!"

"He has a black mane!"

"He is in clear view!" yelled Baltric to his men. "Put arrows into his neck! I will add another magic trophy to my collection! From his horn I will this night drink wine!"

Ten arrows whirred skyward at the trotting horned horse. Strangely enough, all ten veered to the right. Another shower of arrows flew at the black marked unicorn. This time every arrow veered to the left of the target. When a third volley of arrows was shot all ten slanted upward to fall behind the oncoming unicorn. Men swore at their bows.

"Shoot one by one your arrows!" yelled Baltric. "At this distance you cannot miss! Do not worry for hitting the boy; the unicorn is worth far more to me." Single arrows were in quick succession launched. Each time the unicorn moved his horn right, left, upward, or downward, an arrow veered to where directed the horn of the unicorn.

"The filthy horse moves our arrows!" shouted the corporal.

The unicorn sparked his blue-glowing horn against the side of the boy's head. The still sparking horn next cleaved in two, as if it were a thin loaf of bread sliced deftly by a cutting knife, the rope that bound the boy.

"Go now!" neighed the unicorn to Lyons. Throwing off his binds the boy ran into thick woods.

"Lieutenant Abel, charge at him with swords!" ordered Baltric.

Following a big framed soldier with a scary look to his eyes, the squad of soldiers spurred horses past their commander. The unicorn turned his head back to face men and horses hurtling toward him.

Baltric's men were surprised that after releasing the prisoner, the unicorn did not flee from them. Instead the blackmaned unicorn jumped hooves toward the charging Abel. Unicorn shoulders and hooves slammed into the head and chest of the lieutenant's horse. Before being bounced off his horse, Abel had no time to slash out with his sword. Separating right and left, the other horsemen found themselves gotten past the fierce unicorn.

The unicorn now stood between the overlord and his horsemen. The unicorn looked at Baltric, swung his head the other way to look at the overlord's remaining mounted men, and decided. The blackmaned unicorn jumped his lean but well-muscled body around to face Baltric's soldiers.

Understanding the whinnies and grunts of the unicorn, the soldiers' horses grasped that the intruder would use his speed, size, and muscular frame to wound them. More afraid than their riders the horses whinnied frantically, and to their mounts became uncontrollable. The head, shoulders, and hooves of the unicorn toppled one horse into another. Before swords could strike down, Baltric's men found themselves flying through the air. Horses fell to pin riders under their flanks. One frightened horse bucked up so high that he fell over backwards on his rider. Ten horses had quickly become riderless; the overlord's line of soldiers had collapsed.

The unicorn turned to face the still mounted overlord who held a sword in one hand, and the end of a severed rope in the other. The unicorn reared and boxed forelegs out at his foe. With tail arched high the unicorn began prancing toward the overlord. Baltric remained frozen in place. The unicorn planted hooves and shook his head about. Guessing what meant the unicorn's signal, Baltric dropped both his sword and a now useless rope. Above a slumped head the overlord raised his hands. After fiercely shaking his mane, the unicorn backed steps away.

The purpose of the unicorn's retreat dawned on Baltric. The overlord was free to seek refuge behind the fortified walls of his garrison. As Baltric turned his horse away from the unicorn, the realization that he would not that night drink wine from the blackmane's severed and hollowed horn, burned Baltric to the core.

The black marked unicorn jumped, kicked out, turned, and snorted. He walked back towards the platoon of soldiers whose horses had run off. Bows and quivers of arrows littered the ground. Limping and straggling soldiers, with one exception, circled wide past the blackmane toward Baltric. With sword in hand and his head still held high, the big lieutenant walked resolutely past the blackmane toward the horse of his ruler.

As he made progress toward his garrison, the mood of the overlord began to improve. He muttered, "The dumb unicorn let me go free. That, he will live to regret."

Stepping out of the forest Lyons ran toward the unicorn.

"When you cut my bonds I heard you say the word *Go!* You talked to me. Peering out of the trees, I saw you fight to save me. But when the tyrant was in your power, why did you not end his despicable existence?"

"It is unnatural for a unicorn to kill. Besides, I preferred the challenge of facing ten soldiers to confronting only one." With a hand of the boy held lightly to a shoulder of the unicorn, the two began to walk together.

"Baltric's men will confess to their comrades what today happened in battle," neighed the unicorn. "It will be remarked that the overlord did not lift a hand in the fight. In the eyes of his soldiers, Baltric will be a commander disgraced."

With the longest hug of their lives two renegade orphans were reunited.

His hide swollen with bruises and splotched with dried blood, the unicorn did not escape the fight unscathed. With her fingers Maryeta curried, as best she could, the unicorn's coat.

"What is your name?"

"Unlike you, Maryeta, I do not have a name. Because my mare used to call me her black marked colt, I think of myself as... Blackmane."

"Because of all the scratches on our arms and legs, our grandfather calls us his briarburrs," answered the girl. "Almost every day my face gets new scratches from branches I run through. Sometimes I get scratched because I punched my brother, and then he chases me through brambles. But the scratches come in fun are all my fault. Because of all the scratches on our arms and legs, our grandfather calls us his briarburrs. Your white coat is splotched with squiggly black marks that are pointed like briars and scraggly like burrs. Lyons! Because the name fits him even better than it fits us, we are going to call this mighty unicorn Briarburr!"

"Because that is how he sees himself, I still think that he should be called Blackmane," objected the boy.

"There is a nice roll to the name Briarburr; it even makes me think of myself as a battle unicorn. In a fight with me, my enemy would be scratched and pricked hard. *Nyeerrheheh!* I have today been given my very own name!"

"They were going to torture me until I told them where to find Maryeta," said Lyons softly as he hugged the neck of Briarburr. "The nicks of briars and burrs scratching my skin are one thing. But the cuts of torture would be a thing too terrible for me to bear. Briarburr, did you before know that you could turn the flight of arrows?"

"Not until today. When arrows flew at me I became incensed. I asked myself how dare they shoot at me? With what right did the soldiers send sharp arrows at a pure in heart unicorn? Without thinking I willed for the arrows to go the way my horn directed them to move. It was something that just happened. Today I found that in spite of my black mane, and the black marks on my hide, I have my own magical unicorn gift. Briarburr can *change* the flight of arrows."

"I wish I could do that," chirped Maryeta.

"If my mind had not obeyed my will, you would now be busy pulling arrows out of my hide."

"Only once before, by the waterfall, did Lyons and I really see you. On that long ago morning you stood beside the winged horse. Then you ran away. Why did you today come back to us?"

"Over and again I saw that just like me, two orphans had been abandoned. I many times glimpsed you lost in these ten thousand trees. I always knew where I was in this forest, but seeing you lost made my heart to also feel lost." After shaking his mane the unicorn added, "Besides, someone had to scare mean wolves away from a little girl."

"Thank you for doing that, Briarburr," answered Maryeta. The girl stretched out her slight arms and looked at them. "I would have made a poor meal for wolves. Hah! At least, for more than one wolf I would have made a poor meal." Her expression became inquisitive. "Was it you who scared away the bear cub?"

"It was for his own good, Maryeta. Sooner or later that bear cub would have come to the attention of the men in the village, and then been hunted down. I liked the little fellow and did not want harm to come to him."

"I wanted him for a pet," answered Maryeta with a frown. "He would have followed me, everywhere. I would have taught him to talk to me, just like my mother talked to her animals."

"Sister, it is better to leave bears alone. They grow to become unpredictable and fearsome."

"The cub and I would have had fun together. He would have never forgotten, even if he grew to stand as tall as a sapling tree, the friendship of a girl called Maryeta."

CHAPTER 7

A CLIMB THAT BROADENS HORIZONS

"I am bored! We have waited here too long for Grandfather to come. Where is he? All we do is hide ourselves in trees and bushes."

"Sister, my escape made nervous the ruler who commands all things in our valley. It may be some time before Grandfather can slip past watchful eyes. I too am bored, but you know that for me it could have ended far worse."

"Worse for you and me both. Had Briarburr not come to your rescue, I would have become the next prisoner. Lyons, can we please go somewhere far away from this river?"

"I know a place beautiful to see," neighed the unicorn grazing close by his two young friends.

"Can we go right now?" petitioned Maryeta. "I want to see a place brand new!"

Bedrolls slung over their shoulders, two youngsters climbed onto Briarburr's back.

"Hold onto my mane, Lyons. Hold tight, Maryeta, the waist of your brother. I do not want either of you to fall into a deep crevice or ravine." The unicorn climbed a long ridge that joined another ridge, and then another.

"Can you believe how fast I learned to ride a horse!" exclaimed Maryeta.

"I have never in my life climbed a tall mountain," commented Lyons. "This must be the tallest mountain in the whole world."

"The mountain we climb is not the biggest," responded Briarburr. "Far to the east are tall mountains with tops always covered in snow." The unicorn pointed his head towards where the children were born. "From this high place your valley looks peaceful. From up here no one can tell that the overlord has of his valley made a prison."

"At the same time that it looks beautiful, a place can be terrible. In our valley it was not safe for my mother and father to be parents, or for Maryeta and me to be their little children."

"Things can change, brother. Someday Baltric will become gone away." Maryeta's face took on an inquisitive look. "I wonder. Can a bleak looking place that is cold and has long winters, all the while display beauty to the children living there?"

Wide Sea and Big World

"Do you see the blue haze far to the west?" Both children nodded that they did.

"There begins the sea. As we climb higher you two will see it better. I have dreamt that on the other side of the enormous sea lies a new land, a sunny place where volcanoes stretch high to touch the clouds. That far place does not bear the scars of incessant war."

"I bet that in the sea live big monsters," said Lyons, "and lots of crawly things with shells."

"Since there are a lot of fish in the little cavern pool, I cannot even imagine how many fish must swim in the sea." Maryeta brightened with a new thought, "Just think on what amazing things can be found in the far land that Briarburr dreams about. Someday I will go there and see new animals, new mountains, new rivers, and new tribes of people that are always friendly to unicorns."

"Grandfather says the eastern tribes are cruel," said Lyons.

"Long ago, all across those eastern places were found unicorn horses," answered Briarburr. "Because bad men hunted them down, there now are left only a few hundred horned horses. I hate to think of the awful loneliness of the very last unicorn left in the world."

"Oh, Briarburr," said Maryeta, "I cannot imagine the world empty of a magical horse so beautiful as yourself. Now that I washed your hide in the river and combed the burrs out of your mane, I especially admire your coat. You are the most wondrous animal that ever came to be."

"You before said that the winged horse was the most wonderful animal," corrected Lyons.

"Well... both she and Briarburr are very beautiful."

"With a unicorn at my side, I will fight to defeat the tyrant Baltric." That said, Lyons hugged the neck of the blackmane.

To show consent with what was said by Lyons and Maryeta, Briarburr began to prance in a slow trot. As the unicorn and his two young riders moved ever higher, the shore of the sea became a well-defined line that extended as far north and south as the eye could see.

Ship Sails

"The white specks close to the shore, are those sails?"

"I count three trading ships," neighed the unicorn turning hooves toward the sea. "They are probably Egyptian vessels. Here are built no permanent ports where ships can safely land. Those dwelling in this land live isolated from the world."

"The people with ships live better than those that cannot afford ships, or cannot keep their ships from being stolen," offered Lyons.

"Who would build a big ship just to have it be stolen?"

"You are right, Maryeta," observed the unicorn. "Because they cannot protect themselves from the corruption of tyrants, the people that live in the valleys below us cannot build ships only to have them be stolen."

"I will someday build a ship to take Briarburr and my brother, my two best friends, across the sea."

"Briarburr and I are not only your best friends, we are the only friends you have."

A boy, a girl, and a unicorn reached the top of the mountain. Upon dismounting, Maryeta began to jump up and down for joy.

"Look out around us, Lyons! I have never seen something so amazing! I did not know that the mountains beyond our valley grew so tall!" For the beauty of the place the girl was overcome with emotion. After wiping tears away, Maryeta grabbed her brother's hand and pulled him toward the unicorn.

"Thank you for bringing us here, Briarburr. I did not know the world was so big to see. You today made me the happiest girl... *anywhere!*"

"I am gladdened to share this place with my only friends. Up here I feel like I have wings, like I am a horse that can fly." The unicorn rubbed the children with the side of his head. "I knew you before to be brave and honest. Today, I find your eyes discern the beauty of nature. And for that I love you two, more."

That evening while Briarburr grazed on the nutritious grass found in the high place, Maryeta gathered dry branches. A unicorn horn sparked to light a fire. A supper of snared rabbit, with ripe berries for desert, was provided by Lyons. By the time two bedrolls were spread on the ground, a thick blanket of stars had rolled out to cover the heavens.

"More stars sparkle above us than I could ever count."

"Yes, brother, the sky looks warm and magical because there are tonight so many stars. Briarburr, how deep and fluffy is the cushion of stars above us?"

"I do not know about stars. I only know to hope that we unicorns someday find a place where stars shine peacefully down on us."

"Just imagine a palace celestial," offered Lyons, "a place that by night draws curtains... made of stars." Dreams came sweet.

The Broken Mold

"Maryeta, I wish you could have seen Briarburr scatter the arrows shot at him by the soldiers of the overlord," said Lyons the next morning as he patted Briarburr. "Then, this mighty unicorn crashed down Baltric's horse soldiers."

"If other unicorns knew how I fought for you, they would tell me I should not have interfered in the ways of men. But I could not let you two to be taken by the deceitful overlord. For the times I scattered forest wolves away from two orphan children, I would also have been looked upon as a unicorn disobedient. When you two crashed down from the tree, from that very moment I knew that in spite of unicorn rules you would someday come to be my friends."

"Why do you not have unicorn friends?"

"I do not know how to make friends. Just consider, Maryeta, how many years it took me to make friends of you two. *Nyeeeaarrr!* Not liking my black marked coat, my mare never told me that I was a handsome foal. Because other unicorns were not interested in what I thought, I learned not to confide in anyone. So then, when my mare abandoned me I went off alone. Until I found Lyons with his hands tied, and freed him, I never had confidence in myself."

"Briarburr, you can trust my brother. See over there? Lyons stands looking out alone at the world. Like you, my brother has a serious side to him."

"It is good for a boy to commune with the beauty he possesses inside."

"I do not like to be all by myself. I am a talker not a communer. Oh, that reminds me of a question that I have for you. Did your black mane break the mold?"

"Break the mold, Maryeta?"

"Grandfather knows a family of quiet people in the village. All are shy except for the youngest who loves to joke, laugh, and play pranks. Since he did not turn out like the rest of his family, Grandfather says that the jovial one broke the mold."

"Because all the other unicorns are pure white, my black mane must surely have broken the mold."

"So, Briarburr, having broken the mold means you do not have to feel guilty about doing uncommon things like rescuing and befriending two children. You did it because your black mane made you different than all the other unicorns. Just like you, since I already smashed the mold I am free to be different. I am the only girl... *like me!*"

CHAPTER 8

MISSION OF RESCUE

Good use had been made of the bows and arrows discarded by Baltric's tumbled men. Following many days of archery practice, both children could hit a slender tree trunk five times in a row.

"I am tired of shooting arrows!" for emphasis the girl stomped a foot. "We need to do something about Grandfather! I want to go get him!"

Positioned on corners of an invisible triangle a girl, a boy, and a unicorn proceeded to stretch themselves down on elbows and stomachs, or horse legs and stomachs.

"When I spied on the village," neighed Briarburr, "I saw two guards ride horses to the house of your grandfather. The change of the guard takes place at noon. Armed with swords only, the attitude of the guards was relaxed, as though they do not take their guard work very seriously."

"Something is here at work that we do not see," offered Lyons. "Baltric knows how strong and courageous are both Grandfather and Briarburr. Surely the overlord knows that one or the other could overpower the guards. It is almost as if..."

"As if Baltric wants Grandfather to escape from his house," interjected Maryeta finishing her brother's thought. "But why can Baltric want such a thing?"

"*Nyyeerrhunhh!* Baltric wants Fahseed to flee, to go far away and to take Lyons, Maryeta, and me with him. The tyrant has come to fear us. Or if not fear exactly, he finds us four to be a costly nuisance and wants no more to be bothered by us."

"That is it!" exclaimed Lyons jumping to his feet. "When Briarburr saved me he beat ten of Baltric's horsemen. With the help of our grandfather, Briarburr could do even more damage to Baltric's cavalry, and to his authority as ruler. After being humiliated by Briarburr, the overlord does not care if our escape causes him to lose more face. With us gone far away he is rid of four thorns in his side."

"So, does Grandfather not escape because he wants us to go...?"

"Of course!" interrupted this time Lyons his sister. "If in middle night Grandfather slinked away, he would lose face with the villagers. Not wanting to be viewed as a coward, Grandfather is thinking ahead. In the coming fray he wants the villagers to be on our side."

"Fahseed wants to depart from his house arrest... in style," neighed Briarburr shaking his mane in agreement.

Return to Byblos

Clutching their bows, Lyons and Maryeta early the next morning climbed onto the back of Briarburr. Upon their arrival at the house of Fahseed, with bows threaded and arrows drawn the children jumped off the unicorn's back.

"Come out, Grandfather!" shouted Lyons. "Have no fear of two half asleep guards outside your door!"

After unsheathing his sword a roused guard threw it at Briarburr's head. The snorting unicorn nodded the sword to fall at his hooves. Lyons shot an arrow to land between the feet of the sword thrower. Knowing that he was helpless to stop Briarburr and the two youth, the second guard dropped his sword to the ground. In the house they had before guarded, two guards were made prisoners.

Fahseed grabbed first in a hug, Maryeta.

"Grandfather... you are... now safe," the girl began to cry smiling-tears of joy. Seeing that, Fahseed squeezed her more tightly.

"My dear Maryeta, I like that you show emotion when you see your grandfather."

"We shall now be every day together," added Lyons joining his sister and his grandfather in a three-way hug.

"My two forest urchins are getting big," said the stolidly built man as he lifted at once both grandchildren in his arms. "Soon enough it will not be correct to call you... children."

Briarburr stepped forward to spark the head of Fahseed.

"Granpaw, this is the brave unicorn that saved my brother from Lord Baltric. The name Briarburr suits this black marked unicorn better than it does my brother and me."

"News of your heroism traveled fast," said Fahseed turning back to the unicorn. "I shall never be able to thank you enough for saving Lyons in the forest. So, Briarburr, on this day Baltric's two soldiers did not put up much of a fight?"

"They did not, and we are not done here. Soon the two guard replacements will arrive. Welcoming their two horses to your side inflicts more embarrassment on the overlord." The ears of the unicorn alerted.

Two sentries rode up to the house of Fahseed, dismounted, and entered the small house. They immediately re-emerged through the doorway, accompanied now by the two previously captured guardsmen. Awaiting the four soldiers of Baltric were their former prisoner, two renegade youth, and a unicorn. Fahseed nodded to his grandson to speak.

"This unicorn recently demonstrated to Baltric and his platoon the damage his hooves can inflict. If you try to remount your horses, this noble unicorn will knock them over with you on them. It is painful to have a stallion fall and crush his rider's limb. Two swords... remain to be dropped." When Briarburr took menacing steps forward, two more swords were laid on the ground.

"Begin the long walk back to your despot ruler! Be gone!"

"For one so young, does not my grandson speak with unusual authority?"

"For a mere boy, he talks *too big*," responded a guard.

The same guard turned to Fahseed and warned, "While you can, you had better flee this valley."

Four guardsmen began walking back the road that had before led to the house of a just man unjustly imprisoned.

Colyado, Elyeazar, Jomain

The house of the liberated man became a people magnet. Children ran to touch the hide of the unicorn. Men cheered for a neighbor now freed.

"You well-know who I am," said Fahseed stepping before the gathered villagers. "You will also remember my two grandchildren that you here and now see grown like weeds. And, you have this day met the noble unicorn Briarburr.

"My daughter and her husband, the parents of Lyons and Maryeta, were by Lord Baltric cruelly and unjustly taken. The time has now come for me to repair that injustice. I am going to wrest this valley out of the grasp of the overlord that from behind the high walls of his garrison every day steals from us. You will soon have to decide freely to join me, or under the rule of Lord Baltric to remain unfree. Some of you have much cause to despise the overlord. Now go home and think hard on what your ears just heard said."

With a welcoming motion Fahseed beckoned three men found standing together, to join him. Each of the three looked to be about ten years younger than Fahseed. Soon four men sat leaning backs against the front wall of the house where until that morning Fahseed had been held under guard. Until the villagers dispersed, the four friends lingered in comfortable silence.

"Well Elyeazar, well Jomain," began Colyado the conversation, "this afternoon we three sit by the side of a good man, made again to be a free man." Elyeazar and Jomain grunted agreement with the sentiment of their friend.

"From worry and long frustration my hair begins to gray," said Fahseed addressing the ground more than his friends. "For years I swallowed my pride, lowered my head, and bit my tongue. As you have no doubt heard, had it not been for the unicorn, Lyons would have been captured and all my hope made undone. Upon making me his prisoner, the overlord forced my hand. To my cause I now enlist... you three.

"This is why I need you. The ruddy-complected Colyado gets along with everyone. He has not an enemy in the world. He thinks fast and finds the right words to express with diplomacy his thoughts. Elyeazar can build anything he sets out to make. So long as his bushy hair does not cloud his vision, while working with tools his dark eyes glow with knowledge and determination. As for Jomain, behind sky-colored eyes his mind is unmatched for hatching original ideas."

"Thank you, Fahseed, for not mentioning my big nose and thinning hair," reacted humorously Jomain. "But, you might have mentioned how much I like to smile and laugh."

"Everyone knows that Jomain is the best storyteller in the village," affirmed Colyado. "Elyeazar and I have enjoyed countless evenings filled with his jokes and stories. In fact, given his love of laughter, he should change his name from Jomain... to Jokemain."

"Errhmm, I was just going to add, Jomain, that by trade you three are expert at blacksmithing. That makes us to be four blacksmiths in number. Friends, what I now say must stay in your confidence."

Three heads nodded in agreement.

"By the river waterfalls my grandchildren found a hidden place of sure protection. In recognition of the one that found the hideout, we call it the Lyons Den. In that place we can become invisible to Baltric. As it happens that well-ventilated lair contains useful things. There is plentiful water. Fish are there to eat. Wood is there to burn. Minerals for alloys are there found. Most importantly, there is a thick layer of blue gold sand." At the mention of blue gold sand, Colyado, Elyeazar, and Jomain turned to look keenly at Fahseed.

"I need your help for the building of a smelter and forge in the Lyons Den. Even as we are there hidden the smoke produced from melting metals from out of mineral rocks, and pounding those metals into alloys, will blend undetected into the mists of the waterfall. Your skill and hard work will result in swords that wield the legendary magic of blue gold.

"With you by my side, and us four men by the side of two brave children and the mighty unicorn, we will someday prevail over Baltric. Let us four men today make a pact to once, and for all time, make end to the cruelty of the overlord."

Asking no questions, the three would throw in with their friend.

"Very good!" continued Fahseed nodding his head. "I knew I could count on you. Now go grab what you will need."

Bags of tools, supplies, and cooking ware were tied to the saddles of the two horses formerly ridden by the sentries. Singly, and in small groups, people watched the little procession prepare to depart the village.

"In my house someone can live rent free!" exclaimed Jomain turning to the curious onlookers. "Make use of my furniture, but do not take my land! On that same plot of ground I will someday build a *grand house!*"

Fahseed pointed toward his house and said to the onlookers, "Take it!"

Turning to his friends Fahseed added, "Jomain is right. As punishment, the overlord would order my property to be destroyed."

"Where are you going?" yelled a villager.

"When will you return?" shouted another.

"After we find gold we will return to settle accounts with the overlord," answered Fahseed.

"You will be rich!"

"I now make a solemn promise to the people of this village; we will find gold," responded Fahseed raising his hammer high over his head.

"The villagers will not soon forget Fahseed's departure from Byblos," said Colyado as he walked from the place that had ever been his home.

"I want our departure to not by them be forgotten. In leaving I would sow doubt, or better said plant seeds of hope. With the help of Briarburr, my two grandchildren, and my three friends, a bold statement was this day made that will soon reach the ears of Baltric. That news will not be to his liking."

The unicorn sparked his horn to the heads of Colyado, Elyeazar, Jomain, and two horses so that everyone in the little troop could now understand the words and neighs of each other. That night the troop of Fahseed camped on the bank of the river. Through the night Briarburr marched guard. Just to be safe, Fahseed marched a second and a third day further up the course of the river. Moving in a circular route, four men, two children, two horses, and a unicorn doubled back to the twin waterfalls and the Lyons Den.

Where Magic Swords Would Be Made

"How did a place so wondrous and so close to our village, remain for so long hidden?" inquired Colyado upon entering the Lyons Den.

Elyeazar dunked his head down into the pool and soon resurfaced holding grains of gleaming sand in the palm of his hand. He exclaimed, "Look how the gold shines blue! Praise the heavens that I have lived long enough to hold in my hand something so exquisite!"

After making and lighting a torch, and with Maryeta tagging along, Jomain was off exploring the tunnel that wound its way into the mountain that stood on the far side of the river. While Jomain and Maryeta were gone, the other men began cleaning the area that was to become the place of their smelter and forge. Lyons took upon himself the cutting and stacking of wood and branches for fuel.

With satisfied looks Jomain and Maryeta emerged from the tunnel cradling rocks against their bellies.

"You were right, Fahseed," said Jomain. "Because seams of copper, iron, tin, and silver thread the walls of the cave, this place was destined to someday smelt ores and forge metals. For the making of weapons and armor, we lack only coal."

"I once mined a deposit of coal not far from here," offered Elyeazar. "With the help of Lyons and the horses, I can provide all the coal we need."

"We will call upon Briarburr to trail with you and make sure the coal caravans are not spied upon," affirmed Fahseed.

The smelter and forge were with stones constructed to stand as high as the waist of a man. Leather coverings kept the arms and chests of two children from being sparked and burned as they pumped bellows propelling very hot draughts of air.

Hard woods made charcoal that produced hot and steady heat with little smoke. The needs of the smelting and forging processes dictated the amounts of wood, charcoal, and coal employed as fuels. With fine pointed tongs the expert blacksmiths grasped bits of metal as small as a grain of sand.

"My idea is this," said Elyeazar. "Rods of copper, tin, iron, silver, and blue gold shall be twisted into sword blades of unsurpassable strength. Providing the hilt of the sword, the rod of pure blue gold will be two hand widths longer in length. The five heated rods will be pounded and twisted until they blend into one alloy. The center of the blade will be grooved, as if hollowed by my thumb. This will make the sword both stronger and lighter. I tell you that these will be the best swords ever made."

"To that way make a sword... will take a lot of time," responded Colyado.

"Grandfather always said that we had more time than money," interjected Lyons.

"Hah! Looking at the pile of gold sand that is now grown as high as my knees, I say that we have more money than time!" exclaimed Jomain.

"Since the overlord goes nowhere, we have all the time we need," interjected Colyado.

"Elyeazar is now in charge of making the best swords in the world," said Fahseed. "He also is the one that will finish each sword to his high standards of perfection."

Concerning the strength of the twisted metal alloy, Elyeazar was right. Once made, the sword blade was unbreakable. In various stages of completion, four swords were worked on at once. One hundred days after having completed the smelter and forge, twelve swords that maintained fealty to the color of the blue gold ore, were finished.

"The small amount of blue gold that remains ought not to be wasted," commented Elyeazar.

"Do you think that the best archer in Byblos, that being you, might make arrow heads with what remains of the magic ore?" inquired Jomain.

"Exactly what I was thinking," responded Elyeazar with a big smile.

CHAPTER 9

BATTLE PLAN HATCHED

Four men and two youth were gathered where forest met the fall of cascading water. Close by grazed Briarburr and two horses.

"Having completed the making of twelve blue gold swords," said Fahseed, "we next need a strategy to triumph over a force of more than one hundred cavalry. Our gallant force is by twenty to one outnumbered."

"But, Grandfather, we possess uncommon strengths and virtues," offered Lyons who so it seemed gained each day more confidence. "With great magic in his horn, Briarburr is a horse stronger than any other. Colyado, Elyeazar, and Jomain are each one fearless. Blue gold magic makes our sword bearers, including Maryeta and me, stronger than any soldier of the tyrant."

"People are compelled to obey an overlord that marries cruelty to power," responded the always diplomatic Colyado placing a hand gently on the shoulder of the boy. "But since the villagers that do not like your grandfather still respect him, they will be reluctant to cross our leader."

"My grandpaw is a ten times better leader than Baltric!" exclaimed Maryeta.

"Not just yours, he is *my* grandfather too."

"Giving license to his huge ego," offered Colyado, "we can count on Baltric to act with arrogance. He will surely underestimate us."

"But although Baltric thinks us to be weaker than we really are," responded Elyeazar, "that does not change the fact that the overlord's army still greatly outnumbers us."

Gesturing with his hand, the leader directed to Jomain. "Some time ago I asked our most original thinker to develop a plan of attack."

"Fahseed specifically asked me to... *hatch a plan*," corrected Jomain arching one eyebrow. "I once had a laying hen, that come what may, never gave up on her nest of eggs. That dedicated hen always came through for me with more chicklets than any other nesting hen. While the task petitioned by Fahseed was not easy, like my favorite hen I did not give up. Here is what my mind finally hatched.

"Our best hope... *is an ambush*. The crooked street of our village can be made to be a closed box that leaves no exit for the overlord's men. Our one village street will become the trap into which Baltric's men unknowingly ride.

"Here is how it can be done. With a barricade of stones and timbers we close the north end of the street. Past the elbow where the street changes direction, suits that purpose. From the south, the direction from where they come, Baltric's men will be lured into the one street of Byblos. Once the enemy cavalry is inside the street, with the help of the mighty

Briarburr we prevent any escape from where the enemy entered the street.

"The next step is to enlist the fighting help of a few stalwart villagers. Arrows sent from a dozen archers set upon house tops will devastate mounted men trapped in the street. Thinking that the fighting will be house to house, Baltric's cavalry will be reliant on their swords to vanquish our gold swords. For that, shooting arrows at them from above will be like shooting fish in a barrel."

Expectant looks directed to their leader, who rubbed his unkempt beard as if trying to erase subtle streaks of gray.

"I do like... where you go with this idea," replied Fahseed turning to Jomain. "More than half of the houses that line the one thoroughfare of the village were built with shared walls, with no gaps between one house and the next. We can block shut the empty spaces that remain between houses. Fortunately, windows are built so small that a thief cannot enter through to do mischief in the night. Front doors will need to be barred to allow no departure from the street through back doors."

"Exactly," answered Jomain. "However, one problem remains to be solved..."

"Only one?" interrupted Colyado. "That is indeed good news to my ears!"

"As I was saying... how do we lure the enemy to ride en masse into the ambush?"

"Any ideas on that score?" inquired Fahseed turning to the most quiet of the three blacksmiths.

Before answering it became Elyeazar's turn to scratch for long moments what was in his case a carefully trimmed beard.

"Your plan is smart, Jomain. That said, it appears to me that our tactics require two phases. The first part will be to defend the village wall. This is more than anything a diversion, a feint. We must deceive the overlord into believing that the defense of the wall is our whole strategy.

"After fighting hard to defend the wall, we suddenly fall back into the one street of our village, and bring the enemy close after us. Baltric's soldiers must be so convinced that we are on the run, that they forget caution and fly to cut us down in the street. Then like Jomain said, we deploy onto the rooftops. Once entered after us into the street, we can permit the enemy no withdrawal from Byblos."

"Hmph! Elyeazar hits the mark with his idea to begin the battle with a defense of the wall," responded Jomain. "Still, the plan will not be easy to execute. The rickety and tumbledown wall of the village, and its dilapidated gate, will need to be reinforced. As it stands now the wall is riddled with holes where foxes pass through."

"Not just foxes... me and Lyons too!" added Maryeta.

"We must make the wall appear to be a convincing defensive position," concluded Jomain.

"How do we recruit men from the village to join us?" asked Lyons.

"Good question to ask," responded Fahseed. "There are now six of us with swords. So that the number of sword bearers matches our twelve magic weapons, Colyado, Elyeazar, and Jomain will each join to our cause two men that they trust."

"Grandpa," spoke Maryeta, "What if some of the bad men bring their bows to the battle. I am worried about how I can all of a sudden retreat from the wall, and run to enter the street, before an arrow punctures my back."

"As Elyeazar suggested," answered Fahseed slowly nodding his head, "in the first phase of the battle we defend the village wall and gate. When the gate is about to give way, Briarburr will neigh loud for us to retreat. Those of us fighting farthest away from the gate will be the first to break for the street. Those next farthest away will break after. Lastly, those closest to the wall gate will break away in retreat. The broken timbers of the violated gate shall become both a magnet, and a bottleneck that clumps and slows our enemies. Briarburr will be called upon to deflect arrows and spears away from our backs. The blackmane and I will be the last to enter the street.

"Maryeta, you and the rest of our platoon will rush to mount the rooftops. A bow and a supply of arrows will be found at the place on the rooftop where each one of us is to stand and fight. When Baltric's cavalry has rushed after us into the street, Briarburr and I will double back and block the one open entrance. It will be time to shoot many arrows at the enemy."

"What if the enemy horsemen do not fall for our trap," inquired Colyado. "What if they decide not to, all and entire, rush after us into the street?"

"That question also *needed* to be asked," responded Fahseed clapping together his hands.

"I know! We will make a show of flashing our blue gold swords!" exclaimed Lyons. "The enemy soldiers will be captivated by sun reflections of the blue gold. Baltric's men will want to capture a magic gold sword and become rich!"

"Lyons is right," offered Colyado. "Human greed, a thing that causes terrible things to transpire, will be the undoing of the overlord's men."

"The counsel of all of you has grown and bettered the plan I hatched," concluded Jomain. "My friends, among whom I count these two precious youth, much work now lies before us."

Return to Byblos

Into the village of Byblos led Fahseed his platoon of six soldiers, two horses, and a blackmaned unicorn. Upon their return, confident small voices were heard.

"I played twice in the woods with Lyons! I used to be his friend!"

"You and me played tag by the wall! Remember Maryeta?"

A woman with long black hair exclaimed in a loud voice disproportionate to her diminutive size, "So returns the criminal blacksmith wanted by Baltric! The price on his head is thirty gold pieces!" In response Fahseed pulled out his sword and waved it above his head.

"This sword forged of the magic blue gold of legend is worth a thousand times the price upon my head!" At their leader's signal three more men and two youth drew and held high their magic swords. Villagers stepped back from the blinding brilliance of six magic swords flashing sunrays. When Fahseed next nodded three times his head at Colyado, Jomain, and Elyeazar, the men sheathed their swords and with both hands grabbed two more magic swords from their waistbands.

"Look there my friends!" exclaimed Fahseed. "Swords made of the magic blue gold will well-protect true hearts in battle. Colyado, Elyeazar, and Jomain are going to select six more men to join to us, and to the black marked unicorn that has the power of great magic coursing through his horn!

"This is our home! Here grow our children and grandchildren! Too long has it been overrun by men that course wicked blood into their hearts. Because our magic swords are too wonderful to be defeated, I am going to take down Baltric for once and all time!"

Three Days and Battle

"Baltric will attack us not tomorrow, not the next day, but the day after that," said Fahseed as he moved to stand in the center of the one thoroughfare found in the village. "In order to defend this place that we all call our home, there is much to prepare. For the next three days I am going to tell each of you what I require you to do. For three days you will obey me. On the fourth day you will be free of the tyrant, and as well free of me."

In the throng of villagers Fahseed recognized the face of someone that interested him.

"How is the merchant business? It has been too long, years in fact, since we two talked. Your family has long been prominent in our village. Are not two sons of yours soldiers of the overlord?"

"Among us is a spy!" was yelled. Loud murmuring began.

"After hearing me out, I want the spy to go from this village and tell Baltric all that I now say," continued Fahseed. "The spy will tell the overlord that with his own eyes he saw twelve swords forged of magic gold. The spy will inform Lord Baltric that a unicorn with a black mane, one Lord Baltric before met, is my valiant ally. The overlord is to be told that Fahseed fortifies the village wall. Just as I need three days to prepare my defensive line, the tyrant also needs three days to prepare his army for a hard fight at the wall of Byblos."

"What if Baltric does not wait three days but attacks our village tomorrow?" spoke a second time the petite strong-voiced woman. "Am I then to be killed?"

Fahseed shook his head *no*.

"If Baltric were to attack tomorrow the village, his army would not here find the rebels he searches for. I and my soldiers would have slipped away into the forest where in a place impregnable we can hide as long as we choose. Thereafter, every time the ruler of this valley sends out a patrol in the direction of this village, he would fear an ambush. Twelve magic swords and a black marked unicorn would compel incessant damage upon Baltric's men. Because it serves the overlord no purpose, an attack on Byblos will not tomorrow happen."

"But what if Lord Baltric delays for one moon his attack?" continued the same woman. "I will not all summer long disrupt my life just to obey your commands!"

"Listen closely, lady, to what I now tell you," responded Fahseed. "A delay by Baltric for more than three days will be interpreted as cowardice. Inaction by the overlord will bring reinforcements to enlist to my cause. Each further day of Baltric's delay will grow our fortifications harder, and grow greater the number of my soldiers.

"Think on it! A drawn-out war devastates the business of the despot that rules this valley. Baltric takes our crops and sheep because each new moon he needs to meet an expensive payroll. His soldiers have bills to pay. Because Baltric's accounts are always in arrears, the tyrant cannot afford to delay more than three days his attack."

The persistent woman remained still unsatisfied.

"The unicorn could have killed Baltric, why did he not? The unicorn by himself could have saved us from this strife!"

"After his ten soldiers were toppled by the blackmaned unicorn, the overlord was all but defenseless. A noble unicorn does not kill a defenseless enemy simply because... *he can*. Besides, someone even worse could have immediately replaced Baltric as our new oppressor. No, and again no! The overlord's entire army will at the wall of Byblos go down in defeat!

"Baltric will not come tomorrow, nor can he afford to delay for five, for seven, or for thirty days. Mark my words, in three days you will see the tyrant attack our wall! I have one thing more to say, any spy of the overlord's found in this village after today, will into the old dry well be thrown." Fahseed let his gaze to rest again on the merchant he had earlier saluted.

The merchant nodded gravely to the wanted man, lowered his gaze, and slipped away.

Byblos Fortified

The village of Byblos was nestled in a peninsular bend of the river that coursed out of the forest into the valley. A curved wall had long ago been raised to protect the landward side of the town located away from the river. Between the crumbling wall and the village was a common ground where livestock grazed, and at night rested. Beyond the wall the two horses, Lyons, Maryeta, and the blackmane kept lookout. No one was permitted to depart the village and divulge the plan of ambush.

Under the direction of Elyeazar, the largest group of villagers was charged with repairing and raising the wall five more stones high, so that it could not be jumped over by horses with soldiers mounted on their backs. Jomain led another group of villagers instructed to replace a gate that had fallen into a state of disrepair and ruin. The gate was to be rebuilt with thick planks, swing smoothly, and latch tightly shut.

Colyado supervised a third group of village men charged with closing the main thoroughfare at a place past where the dusty street changed course. The workers he oversaw planted in the ground a log barrier made to stand firmly upright. The base of the barrier was reinforced with large jagged rocks.

Assisted by a dozen men, Fahseed reinforced structures lining the main street of the village. Any opening between the wall of one house and the next was filled with stones, brush, or whatever served to obstruct passage. Any roof top lower than the roof line of adjacent dwellings was with boards or stones, heightened. Where needed, board walkways connected one rooftop to the next. House doors were locked and braced.

Reserves of arrows were strategically placed along the roof lines. A safe house on each side of the village's one thoroughfare was marked so that the fighters bearing blue gold swords would not miss their entranceway to the rooftops. Passing through a safe house, Briarburr and Fahseed would double back to block the open end of the street through which Baltric's men entered in pursuit of the rebels.

CHAPTER 10

LORD BALTRIC PREPARES FOR BATTLE

"My spy stands brazenly before me, the lord of this whole valley, and tells me that the outlaw and the blackmaned unicorn have taken control of Byblos... and now raise higher the wall of the village! And to top that, my spy asks me to believe that the usurpers somehow acquired twelve magic swords! So why did not my subjects kill Fahseed and bring me the golden swords? Ahem, my spy is certain that the swords are... *magical*?"

"Of that there can be no doubt, Lord Baltric," affirmed the spy-merchant.

"Blast! They must know that for the whole village this will end in disaster!" Baltric hit an arm to his chest and exclaimed, "I am everywhere known to harshly repay disloyalty! Tarnation! I have had enough of the outlaw... and his two grandchildren! I blame the cussed unicorn for interfering in a matter that was none of his business. The unicorn had no cause to rescue Lyons from me and my men. I swear to you that before I am done, I will devour the very heart... of that unicorn!" Calming himself, Baltric motioned a hand at the spy merchant and muttered, "Be gone with you."

As he turned to address the man seated next to him, Baltric calmed himself. "Abel, what make you of the treason of Fahseed?"

The tall young lieutenant rose and began to pace long steps around the room. Because he had come to highly value the judgment and fierceness of his youthful, mean looking, and powerfully built lieutenant the overlord waited in silence.

"I little like that in this fight the magic of a unicorn, as well as the magic of blue gold swords, are set against you. Sir Baltric, you know that you cannot expect the peasants to support and fight for the overlord that harshly taxes them. That said, the villagers will also be too afraid to fight against you. How well, Sir, do you know this man Fahseed?"

"I know that stiff-necked blacksmith well enough hates me. As you have no doubt heard, some years back Fahseed's daughter and her husband did not approve my taking their goats, calves, and pigs. So... I destroyed them. Until now his two grandchildren have somehow managed to escape my clutches."

"You know nothing more of the man?"

"Hmph. I will admit that Fahseed has a certain presence about him. He can perhaps convince a handful of villagers to fight with him."

"Sir, you have one hundred forty mounted soldiers. Fahseed has the two horses he took from your guards. We cannot lose to a man with only two horses and an unnatural unicorn. Whoever heard of a unicorn mixing in the matters of men?"

The overlord turned to his lieutenant again become seated, and smiled weakly as he solicited, "Give me your advice on how to prepare for this fight."

"You, Sir, have great strengths and advantages. You are merciless. You hit back ten times harder than you are struck. You love to fight, and your soldiers know that."

"I like nothing better than to shed the blood of my enemy."

"Lord Baltric, I can vouch for the absolute loyalty of your men. And until you decide to do battle, you are protected behind these walls. Added to that, you already know the battle plan of your enemy. Fahseed plans to hold the rebuilt wall of the village. To be sure, he has no other alternative but to defend the wall he now reinforces and tightens shut. He may be able to stop an assault by sixty or seventy of your men. But he cannot withstand a frontal assault by more than one hundred cavalry."

"So, Lieutenant, your counsel is to hit hard Fahseed with everything that I have? I cannot keep back one half or one third of my army as reinforcements?"

"To ensure your success," answered Abel nodding his head, "hit the outlaw with every soldier you have. Of course, Sir, when I fight my instinct is to go all out."

"I suppose that if I cannot whip Fahseed with one hundred, the remaining forty will also be unable to prevail on another day. Like you advise... it is best to lead my entire army into battle. Hmph. And what about the defenses of the village itself?"

"After the wall is breached, the village will lie helpless. I ask you, Sir, how can Fahseed, three men, and two youth stop an orchestrated assault by one hundred forty well-armed cavalrymen moving together in unison? That, Lord Baltric, cannot be done."

"Errm, yes, yes Lieutenant you are right. Still, I do not want to overlook some detail that can later prove to me costly. What most perplexes me is how Fahseed can have any confidence of victory. What can he be thinking? Does he have something up his sleeve?" Baltric grimaced and added, "I do not want Baltric to become known as... *BalTricked*."

"The village is nothing more than one mean street lined on both sides with broken down houses," said the lieutenant offering reassurance. "The decrepit street is not even straight. Our horses will trample the village and churn over every garden behind every house. I myself am going to carry off every cask of wine I can find in that rundown place. Those pathetic peasants do not deserve to drink the good wines of your valley. Perhaps, Sir, the renegade seeks to unnerve you. If Fahseed can cause you to doubt yourself, then however remote, he has a chance of beating you."

"Lieutenant, with regard to Fahseed I will stay calm, and think carefully before I act."

"That, Sir, is what I waited to hear you say."

"There is no way on earth that Fahseed can win mind games with me," said Baltric leaning his chest forward. "I am everywhere feared. He is... *a nobody*." As he spoke more to himself than to his lieutenant, the face of Baltric became once more furrowed. "All of this fuss about a... *peasant family*. I will admit that the farm of Fahseed's daughter was surprisingly prosperous.

"The worst thing about this whole mess is that I presently receive no animals from a now deserted farm that once was hers. Aw, I suppose I could have been more lenient with his daughter. They said she could talk to her sheep and goats, and especially to her pigs. Of course pigs *are* the smartest animal. Can you believe, Abel, that she actually made her sows to attack me? They caused so much commotion with my soldiers scrambling to protect me, that her children escaped my clutches." The overlord's face took on a quizzical look. "Can it really be possible that her animals understood her?"

The lieutenant shrugged his shoulders.

"You know I used to be proud to be referred to as BalTricky. Today, I find that I do not much care for my nickname." The overlord exhaled a big breath. "Enough of feeling sorry for myself. I want strong drink. You stay, Abel."

"As you know, Sir, thinking is too hard work for me. I was beginning to doubt you would ask for spirits."

The tyrant and his lieutenant settled in to enjoy a first round of grape brandy. Into the night many more cups were filled. The ruler awoke late the next morning with dull eyes and a head currented by aches. That afternoon the ruler berated his soldiers for, among other things, armor not shined smartly. That evening Baltric called a meeting with Lieutenant Abel and his corporal to talk over the battle plan.

The attack against the village of Byblos would take place on the day Fahseed had said it would.

CHAPTER 11

THE CHARGE OF BRIARBURR

"Y ou waited until dark to come to me."

"You were today very busy, Grandfather."

"No matter how busy I am, what my grandson has to say is *always* important to me."

"Grandfather, do you continue sure that Baltric will tomorrow attack?"

"Of my reasoning... I am sure. Once the overlord's forces are readied they will be impatient for the action to begin. His men want plunder. If Baltric holds them back they will first complain, and then they will begin to shirk their duties. On the other hand, every day that we have not to fight is a day that we build our wall stronger and higher. Yes, Lyons, tomorrow morning we will see two hundred villagers put their finishing touches on our wall. I am as certain as I can be that the fighting will start before midafternoon. My boy, tomorrow you and I shall finally know victory over a tyrant."

"No matter what happens, I will not run from the enemy."

"Tomorrow, Lyons, will also be my first day of armed conflict. It is not wrong for me, for you, or for Maryeta to know fear in battle. In spite of our fear all three of us will fight for each other, for Briarburr, and for our friends. Remember Lyons, the magic of a blue gold sword responds to trueness of mind and heart. By staying true to ourselves you, Maryeta, and I will

87

prevail. Still, in a fight against a battalion of soldiers, I will confess that I worry most about the safety of my two grandchildren."

The boy began to thrust his sword at targets invisible.

"Grandfather, now that I carry a blue gold sword, I will be sure to always tell the truth. Since my arms are only half as strong as yours, for that I can *truthfully* say that I am glad my blue gold sword weighs lighter than yours." After sheathing his sword Lyons added, "Being truthful, Grandfather, you will admit that you worry most about Maryeta. I know you love my sister more than me. But, nothing you can do will stop her from tomorrow wielding her blue gold sword in battle."

"It is that your sister reminds me of my daughter, my only child lost to Baltric. I cannot bear the thought of losing a *second time,* my daughter."

Early the next afternoon Lyons to the wall galloped fast. "Grandfather, your words last night were not wrong. In the lead of a column of horses rides Lord Baltric."

"I have been wondering about something, and I want your opinion on it."

"Certainly, Grandfather," answered the youth straightening his shoulders.

"If you were the overlord, would you personally lead the charge of your men against our wall?"

"Hmm. It is a sign of leadership... to lead troops... into battle," responded the youth after taking a few moments to think on it. "Baltric's leadership in combat would instill courage in his men. Still... he knows that our magical swords can do his person much harm. If Baltric were to early fall in battle, and because of his soft life he is not very hard muscled, his troops would give up the fight and flee."

"Good thinking, Lyons. What else might cause Baltric to think he should wait it out and let his troops do the fighting for him?"

"Well... from the hill that overlooks our wall Baltric will see before him develop the battle. From that high vantage point the overlord can react to the ebb and flow of the conflict, and order one side or another of his force to maneuver, one direction or another."

"In that case he would need someone to stay behind with him, or to return to him to bring forward his orders."

"Yes, Grandfather, that is so. For more than one reason Baltric can think the right thing for him to do is to not risk his life on the front line."

Clash at the Wall

Turning about his horse the ruler of the valley raised an arm signaling *halt*.

"My valiant soldiers!"

"Baltric! Baltric! Baltric!" answered in unison enthusiastic men intent on plunder.

"Only ragged farmers defend that poor excuse for a village. Do I fear a few dirty-clothed men little better than slaves? No! And I never will!" The overlord stiffened his legs to position himself higher in his saddle. "My loyal soldiers will attack all along the length of the wall. After we have softened them up, at the right moment I will order you to shift full to the gate. Once the gate falls, the town is defenseless. Victory will be mine, and the village will be yours... *for the taking!"*

"Baltric! Baltric! Baltric!" came again the chorus from the overlord's soldiers.

"Lieutenant, on my signal be prepared to lead the final charge. We will destroy the traitorous..." The overlord's words were interrupted by sunrays reflecting the brilliance of blue gold swords swung threateningly by those defending the wall.

"Gold! Gold! Gold!" shouted Baltric's soldiers.

Baltric laughed. "So the gold got your attention? They have fashioned twelve gold swords that are to be mine. Whoever of you brings me a gold sword will be richly rewarded with lands taken today by me!"

"I heard those swords are made of the blue gold of legend!" shouted a soldier.

"That is a lie... a ruse!" answered Baltric. "They are made of ordinary gold, with silver blended in to make them shine more. Not a single one of you will be taken in by the preposterous lie that such a poor and humble village could come to possess magic. Fahseed and his dozen men are nothing but filthy swine! Many orphan children will this night walk barefoot in the debris of a destroyed village! You... each of you... are worth ten of my enemy!

"The lieutenant carries my orders to you. Obey him as if he were me!" The tyrant's sword chopped three times for emphasis as he shouted, "Bring me the head of the outlaw Fahseed! Bring me back the gold swords! Bring me *victory!"*

Baltric's column of soldiers charged toward the defenders at the village wall. At the lieutenant's signal the column changed form to become a wide line of men riding side by side in a frontal assault. As the overlord's army closed on the wall they were met by volleys of arrows. Bows, some previously captured from Baltric's men, inflicted only meager punishment.

Upon gaining the wall some of the soldiers flung themselves over with swords raised high. They found that the swords wielded by Fahseed and his friends swung more true and more fast than could be scarce imagined. Still, without the speedy hooves of Briarburr that neutralized enemy soldiers not confronted by a blue gold sword, the defense of the wall would have been short-lived.

Against the first surge of the cavalry, the wall held. Still, with an overwhelming advantage in numbers Baltric knew it was only a matter of time before the wall would be taken. The swarthy commander muttered to himself, "How could Fahseed think his light defense of the wall would hold? He is even more *dense* than I thought he was."

"Sir, the gate weakens!" offered Lieutenant Abel returned to where Fahseed quietly watched the battle unfold.

"It cannot much longer hold. Shift the main attack to the gate, *now!*"

Approaching once more the wall, the lieutenant raised a horn to his lips and blew a sequence of notes as loud as he could. All along the wall the heads of cavalry horses turned toward the gate. Abel also charged the gate.

The gate began to give way to the relentless axes wielded by soldiers with strong arms and shoulders. Planks splintered.

"It falls!" shouted the tyrant drawing his horse closer to the collapsing gate.

"Gold swords! Gold swords!" came the exultant shouts of soldiers.

All together, and at the same time, the entire column of soldiers attempted to wedge their horses through the gate. The collapsed gate became a bottleneck that slowed Baltric's men and so facilitated the safe passage of Fahseed's platoon of running men and one girl, with flashing gold swords raised high, into the street of the village.

Baltric smirked at the thought that to call the village's twisted dusty path a *street*, was far too generous. Upon worrying a new and unexpected thought, the overlord's smile froze. No one listened as Baltric yelled, "Not everyone at the same time! I do not want all my men to ride as one body into one pitiful street!"

With the benefit of hindsight the ruler reflected that once his men had violated the wall it would have been a surer tactic for them to divide, and from all sides overwhelm the miserable village.

With a start, Baltric realized exactly what had happened. His men were each and every one in a *rush to claim gold*. In fact, his burly lieutenant had himself led the charge after the gold swords.

"How can my lieutenant order soldiers right and left to where they are needed in battle, when he is riding at the very front of my battalion?"

The horse carrying the overlord walked through the gate of the breached wall. Again and again Baltric told himself not to worry. Against only a dozen defenders he had well more than one hundred soldiers. With such odds in his favor... *what could go wrong?*

Time to Worry

"What in blazes!" exclaimed Baltric reining his horse to a stop. The blackmaned unicorn had emerged from out the village, and instead of running away, ran toward the entrance of the street into which Baltric's army had now from view disappeared. On the unicorn was mounted Fahseed.

"Damnation!" The overlord whipped the rump of his horse, which made the beast jump about in an excited display of equine displeasure. "The usurper blocks off the very street my men just entered! Well that is too bad for him. From here... I will charge and attack Fahseed." About that Baltric soon had second thoughts. "But there is no need for me to take unnecessary risk. Through the other end of the street my men will soon circle out and return to fall upon the renegade. They will push Fahseed, and the unicorn, back into the village street to be there trapped with the rest of his rebels."

Baltric noticed newly positioned rebels on rooftops send arrows down to punish his mounted men.

"What on earth is going on over there?" Although he could not by his soldiers be heard, Baltric yelled, "Throw the enemy off the rooftops!" None of his soldiers saw the arms of the overlord waving emphasis to his shouts.

"Where are my soldiers? Why cannot I see them riding out the other end of that cursed street that they all entered. What is *wrong* with my soldiers?" Baltric slapped his chest with emotion and exclaimed, "And I cannot give new orders until I get past the blasted unicorn and Fahseed!"

In the initial confusion of the ambush, Baltric's men found themselves trapped. In desperate need of a new tactic, soldiers turned their horses around and charged at Briarburr and Fahseed. To no horse would the riderless unicorn yield. Briarburr's mind refused to entertain the idea that another horse, not even one, could best him. The unicorn's horn, big shoulders, and big hooves stopped riders mistakenly seized by the idea of departing the site of the ambush. Encounters between the unicorn and the soldiers and horses of Baltric left wounds to all involved. Covered in sweat, Briarburr became bloodied.

The dismounted Fahseed shot arrow after arrow into the soldiers trapped in the street.

"Briarburr!" yelled Fahseed. "Enemy soldiers climb onto the roof tops! Our friends need you!"

"*Naaaayuuurrrrhhhrrr!*" After rearing to pound with his hooves another horseman seized with the intention of flight, in full gallop Briarburr landed front hooves back to the ground.

The blackmane collided a shoulder into an equine blocking his way, knocking the horse and rider to the ground. Bouncing himself off the blow, the unicorn propelled his opposite shoulder into the next horse he confronted. Against two more horses Briarburr threw a side-body-block that toppled them both. None of the cavalry horses were as large as Briarburr. No horse and rider in the cavalry could match the unicorn's quickness and speed. As if the bodies of Baltric's men and horses bled only water the color of red wine, the spilled blood of the enemy came to matter nothing to Briarburr.

For the first time in his life the unicorn felt intense hatred. Borne of fierce battle, abhorrence of the foe took mastery of the unicorn's spirit. The innocence of two children and the honor of Fahseed and his friends were not to be annihilated by unspeakable brutality. Banging his body through Baltric's riders, the unicorn advanced down the street.

When the voice of Maryeta sounded alarm, for an instant of time Briarburr lost focus. Shaking his head he looked up toward a rooftop. A short but sturdy soldier held the girl by her hair. Briarburr saw the sword arm of Baltric's insolent corporal pull back. The corporal paused to laugh brutishly at the girl. With a burst of powerful motion Briarburr shoved his body toward Maryeta. The unicorn's hooves climbed over the shoulders of horses and through the breathing bodies of their mounts.

A second time the corporal drew back his sword to slice Maryeta.

By instinct Briarburr leaped high and lunged forward his head.

Baltric's corporal turned to see why Maryeta's eyes had suddenly grown large. The corporal would see what had suddenly gained the attention of a girl facing a certain death blow. That moment of curiosity summoned the last breath of the man holding his sword to a girl. When the horn of the unicorn pierced the corporal's side, the hand menacing a sword against Maryeta shed its grip. With eyes set in bewilderment final, the corporal crumpled down. His blood spilled to stain the place where only a moment before had stood his feet. Upon an unbreathing belly the corporal's sword came to rest.

Freeing himself from his adversary, Lyons rushed to grab hold and embrace his sister.

"From Baltric's corporal the unicorn has now also saved me!"

"I could not fast enough break away to help you. I do not know how Briarburr moved so quickly upon the corporal. I will, Maryeta, hate that man no more."

"Lyons, since the unicorn has now saved both our lives, we must win this fight for Briarburr." Fighting back to back with swords made magical, Lyons and Maryeta returned with renewed forcefulness to the battle.

Stationed on rooftops lining the other side of the street, Colyado, Jomain, and Elyeazar had seen the unicorn's swift and audacious rescue of Maryeta.

Elyeazar, the man of few words, turned with a fierce look to his comrades wielding blue gold swords and unknowingly echoed what Maryeta had just said. "After what Briarburr just did, we dare not lose this day!"

Elyeazar ran off the roof, cushioned his fall on the shoulders of an enemy rider, and so knocked Baltric's horseman to the ground. Elyeazar grabbed the reins and remained the horse under him. Colyado and Jomain followed suit. Three mounted soldiers wielding blue gold swords formed a line with the unicorn, and together swathed through the riders of the despot. The resolve of Briarburr and three allied horsemen could not be dissuaded by any enemy on horse or on foot.

Baltric's men that were yet sound of body dropped their weapons, and in defeat knelt down. Riderless horses that had run past Fahseed were by the unicorn's two horse friends herded toward a far corner of the village wall.

At the entrance to the village street Baltric halted his horse, and sat with his gaze frozen. He beheld a street littered with the broken bodies of what had been his army. Upon finding Baltric come close, the ring leader of the rebels smiled and motioned a simple wave toward the tyrant. By Fahseed the tyrant was paid no more mind.

The rebel commander walked into a street turmoiled by groaning soldiers and gasping horses collapsed on their sides. Fahseed gained the place where awaited him a blackmaned unicorn and eleven bearers of blue gold swords.

"My captain, we give you victory over the hated overlord," said Colyado matter-of-factly.

"That news is to me most welcome. Even so, Colyado, I can scarce believe that we accomplished what we set out to do."

"More than anyone it was you, Briarburr, who won this day," observed Jomain turning to the unicorn. "Your charge through the street was magnificent; your rescue of our precious Maryeta was the most heroic thing that I have ever seen."

"In this place that we call our home," offered Fahseed with solemnity in his voice, "in this lowly village of Byblos will long be remembered the *Battle of the Crooked Street*."

CHAPTER 12

A SECOND WALL FOR BYBLOS

More than with celebration, the victory of Fahseed was greeted with... astonishment. Damage to the houses in the village was acknowledged with frowns.

"I warned you that this would happen!" Remonstrated the petite outspoken woman graced by long dark hair. "You to us brought disaster! Our street is wrecked! Because of your rebellion we innocent villagers will come to be hunted and destroyed!"

"I ask you lady, to look at this unicorn," said Fahseed calmly as he motioned Briarburr to his side. "Possessing not only courage, but also virtue, his great heart is worth one hundred weak and doubting hearts." The truth of these words that could not be argued with, served to quiet the woman and those with her.

"But about Byblos being a mess... the lady is right," observed quietly Colyado standing at the side of his leader. "Our village has never been much to look at. But I have to ask you, can Byblos ever recover to become more than what it is right now?"

"Byblos has always been a community where people were jealous of one another, stubborn, clannish, and quick to reproach," responded Fahseed.

99

"In this village we make life harder for our neighbors than it has to be."

"About that you are not wrong," responded Colyado nodding slightly his head. "However, I am talking not about our hearts, but rather about our houses."

"My friend, on both counts I want for us to be more. Of course I want this street and its houses to be rebuilt and made better than before. But it is even more important that someday this humble place become accustomed to truth instead of falsehood, and purity of heart instead of jealousy. I want the people of Byblos to someday value mercy and love more than money and power."

"All right, Fahseed," the face of Colyado relaxed, "with you I will hope that Byblos will become a worthy city, a peninsula that for the shine of its welcoming lights is loved. Hah! But for that transformation to come to pass it will take a miracle, like making a blind man to see, or making our crooked street to be renamed *Straight Street.*"

With Briarburr still at his side, Fahseed turned to address defeated soldiers seated on the ground with looks dejected.

"Beginning tomorrow you are going to redeem yourselves through hard work. The soldiers that fought for Lord Baltric are here and now sentenced to build a moat and an outer wall for this village. The moat is to be dug beyond our present wall. Twenty paces past the moat you will build a new wall equal in height to the one that now protects us. Enemies that penetrate the outer wall will find themselves trapped between the wall crossed, and the combination of moat and wall that remain in front of them. Before or within the moat, shot arrows and hurled spears will make to fall the next army that attacks Byblos.

"This magnificent unicorn will hunt down and trample beneath his hooves any soldier of Baltric that deserts before stands finished the second wall. From your new duty there will be no transgression. Once the moat is made deep, and the new outer wall is made high, each and every defeated soldier of Baltric will be given leave to depart this valley. On that welcome day of your release, you must swear an oath that you will never again raise a hand against Byblos. Do you agree to my contract?"

Fahseed was answered by discouraged men with bowed heads mumbling *yes.*

"I do not well hear you!"

Defeated soldiers this time spoke loud their assent to the conditions set forth by the victor to build a moat and second wall, and then to depart the valley.

"Because Lord Baltric now commands no army," said Fahseed turning to villagers crowding the street, "he will tomorrow abandon his garrison. The stronghold of the tyrant is no more to be a womb that begets tyranny. The men, women, and children that dwell in this valley are to breathe the fresh air of *freedom.*

"I will tomorrow have you help me and Briarburr transport the wounded that lie in this street back to the walled garrison. What valuables remain in Baltric's garrison will finance a hospital, a place of healing for those here cut in battle.

"There is one other thing. I will take down the unicorn horns that adorn the corners of Baltric's garrison. In the forest above this village the trophy horns formerly possessed by the overlord will be given proper burial. In this valley unicorns will come to know peace and security."

With their own eyes the villagers saw that a humble man, well-known to them, had transformed himself into a valiant leader. The outspoken petite woman, at least on this day, voiced no more complaint to a changed man she now scarcely recognized.

CHAPTER 13

LIEUTENANT ABEL

Fahseed stood watching men heft shovels, that only ten days before had formed the feared and formidable army of the ruler of the valley. In the midst of the prisoners digging the moat a big man worked twice as hard as anyone else.

"While with their feet other prisoners push the spade into the ground, again today the big man makes his back horizontal and uses his arms and hips to lever the blade into earth. As well as with his sword, with a shovel that man attacks."

When the big man that was unafraid to shovel hard sat himself down to eat the noon meal, the new commander of Byblos joined him.

"You led the charge into the city," said Fahseed quietly.

"It speaks not highly of me that I was the first to fall into your trap. My name is Abel. I was before... Baltric's lieutenant."

"Where does your former master today find himself?"

"Knowing him as I do, I say he has gone to convince a ruler of one of the surrounding valleys to do battle against you. Surely you know that Baltric cannot, will not, let go the idea that he is to again resume his former place as ruler of this valley."

"I happen to have always found Baltric to be mean and heartless. Like you Baltric?"

Abel paused to carefully choose his words. "The former ruler was not displeased that I drank much. He knew that as long as I drank heavily, that with my senses dulled, I would not object to any order he gave. Some of his orders were despicable. With much wine in my belly I more easily complied to do his bidding. Sir, am I to call you Fahseed?"

"You are."

"Then, Fahseed, I will give this to Baltric. He treated me better than most have done. He never refused me strong drink. In spite of my carrying out his loathsome orders, I got along better with his soldiers than did Baltric himself. He liked, no, after this defeat I will say that he *formerly* liked my recklessness in battle."

"Lieutenant Abel, when this wall is completed and you are free to leave, where will you go?"

"To this world I have no ties."

"Would you consider joining my small force of warriors? Lieutenant, you can be a formidable soldier next time on my side. I could come to trust you. When you charged into the street there was no hesitation on your part. While still a young man, make your life to count for something worthy."

During long moments Abel's head did not move. After finally exhaling deeply he said, "You merit an answer. One day I will give you one."

"Take the time that you need."

"Truth be told," said Abel looking Fahseed in the eyes, "I had not ever thought about being more than I am right now. To be sure, right now I despise myself for falling headlong into your ambush. I cannot believe that I swallowed the lure proffered by the gold swords. Sir, this is the second time that I not only failed, but was the first to fail. I am little used to losing on the field of battle."

A few days later Fahseed and the big lieutenant ate again together.

"What do you think about my idea to add an outer wall?"

Setting down his bread and bowl the lieutenant answered, "For the defense of the village, the new moat and outer wall five times exceed the value of the inner wall."

"I am glad to hear that you see it that way, Lieutenant. For too many years the breached and broken down wall left Byblos defenseless. Now again I ask, will you throw in with me?"

"I return to work," answered Abel simply. The big man stood and grabbed his shovel.

"Before you go, tell me how so young a man came to have such presence. In spite of your unkempt beard and shaved head, I feel that something deep and hungry flows within you. Why do you make yourself to be apart from everyone?"

"Fahseed... it is this way. For my age I was always big. That made me a target for older boys, and as well a target for smaller boys my age that wanted to prove they could take down an awkward overgrown mate.

The long attention of bullies toughened both my hide, and my outlook on life. My shaved head, the unsociability of my appearance, suit me and save me further trouble with those of the bullying persuasion."

After Abel had left, Fahseed muttered, "He still did not answer me with a *yes* or a *no*. What can he mean by not answering me? For his great size there is nothing ungainly about him. This tall lieutenant may be the best fighter I have ever seen. Who knows, one day he might have saved my life." A smile formed on the face of Fahseed. "For today I will interpret Abel's non-answer as... *a yes*."

"Bad news, Sir," reported Jomain. "When this morning the prisoners filed out to work on the moat, the big lieutenant and two others were not present. They deserted."

Upon hearing that Fahseed slumped his shoulders, and for long moments said nothing.

"I had plans for that lieutenant. It is strange that Briarburr did not alert to their escape. Jomain, tonight we double the guard."

"Sir, it is not too late to send the blackmane after the escapees. If anyone can track and find them, it is the unicorn."

"No, Jomain. Baltric's lieutenant is gone. He is the kind of man that sets his mind, and once set persists in stubbornness. Upon being found he would not easily return here, if at all. I do not want to see Abel by unicorn hooves trampled.

"Baltric's lieutenant was someone about whom I changed my mind. At first, I thought he was a big oaf, more courageous than smart. I was drawn to watch him day after day as he worked hard. He did twice as much shoveling as any other prisoner. Behind his eyes I glimpsed, or thought I glimpsed, the light of repentance. It was as if through his hard work he did penance for past misdeeds. He despised himself for things he had done in the service of the tyrant. I tell you, Jomain, because he loathed what he was and what he had become, the lieutenant of Baltric before drank hard and then for us worked hard."

"Fahseed has thought much on that lieutenant."

"There was more to him than meets... did you know that he could make to sound perfectly a bugle? I actually thought that young lieutenant would someday become a friend. Hah! That shows you, Jomain, what little I know about the human condition."

CHAPTER 14

A STRUGGLE NOT OVER

The moat was shoveled deep. Along the half completed length of the second wall were piled the stones requisitioned by Fahseed.

In reward for their hard work the prisoners were given a day of rest. Now that the villagers did not pay the former overlord's tax of half the grain, fruit, and livestock they produced, food had become plentiful. On this day the prisoners ate their fill, rested, and with their teeth flashed smiles.

To crown the holiday Fahseed levered open the water gate, whereupon river water filled the moat. Seeing with their own eyes the success of the moat fortification, people in the village came to finally trust the leadership of Fahseed.

Two prisoners lingered as they watched water gush into the moat.

"In that current, a man could be swept away."

"The water is deep enough to drown someone that cannot swim, someone like *me*," responded the second prisoner.

"Digging the moat reminded me of the holes that the overlord had us to dig," answered with marked coldness in his voice the first prisoner that had spoken. "Before was closed the hole, Baltric insisted that four or five bodies be tossed in. Pity the fate of the poor villagers that endured torture only to be dumped into a hole in the ground."

"The dirt-covered bodies included not just villagers," responded the second prisoner. "The big lieutenant had us carry the bodies of fellow soldiers to be as well thrown into the hole."

"Baltric wanted the likes of us to live in fear of him. He much enjoyed making examples of any soldier that disobeyed him, or even looked at him wrong."

The second prisoner threw a rock into the moat. Upon hearing it plunk a soothing sound, he continued, "I suppose that Baltric can now be found somewhere plotting his return to this village. As for me, I will not welcome a return of the coward that hung back and let the lieutenant lead the charge at this village."

"I would that the tyrant had himself led the charge," concurred the prisoner that had begun the conversation, "and had himself suffered the fate of our many friends who fell in the ambushed street."

"Before this year is out Baltric will come to meet his maker," answered the second prisoner. "I feel it shall happen. Of Baltric the world is grown *tired*."

In the Next Valley

The lieutenant took his time in travel. He knew that his return to the fallen overlord would, sooner rather than later, signify a return to heavy drinking and worse.

Abel came to find Baltric where he thought he might. Vylas, the overlord that ruled the valley to the west of the village of Byblos, was the defeated overlord's cousin. With no success Baltric had tried to convince Vylas to immediately restore him to the seat of power wrested away by the traitorous usurper Fahseed. After being stymied by many unpersuasive days, the former overlord was delighted to have his right hand man once again under his wing.

"It is about time you found me! Now that my lieutenant and the two you brought with you are here, we can begin to rebuild my army."

Abel nodded once his head in agreement.

"With you three escaped back to me, that makes us four in number. Soon we will be forty, then eighty, then one hundred and sixty!" Baltric's brow changed to take on an aggrieved look. "On that point, Lieutenant, why did you bring only two of my men back to me? And where is my trusted corporal?"

"Your corporal was runned through by the horn of the blackmaned unicorn. That unicorn fights like a small army unto himself. If more of your captured men had come with us, the blackmane would have discovered our trail and wreaked havoc upon us. I knew that the two I picked would be hard to track." The lieutenant stretched his neck and with two fingers rubbed it lightly. "Emm... errmm... my throat finds itself to be... *dry*."

"Of course, Lieutenant!" replied Baltric transforming his frown into a broad smile. "I see that you are back to your old self. Your big frame requires spirits!"

"Drinks for me and my best warrior!" shouted the defeated lord to a garrison servant. "And this time bring me a flask of the good stuff!"

Baltric turned back to his lieutenant, "Vylas brags that his valley produces the best wines in all of Phoenicia. You shall tell me if he does not more than a little... *exaggerate*."

"You once told me that your cousin had a certain flair with words."

"You will find, Abel, that in my cousin's speech the distinction between now and what before happened, is not always precise."

The next evening found met two overlord cousins, the older one recently dispossessed of power. With each cup of wine their separate worries came to seem less large, that is until Baltric changed the subject.

"Cousin Vylas, I must plead again for your help to regain my garrison."

"Did we not just yesterday go overed this?"

"No, cousin, it was the day before yesterday."

"You knowed that I like you, Baltric, and I always haved. But you must recognized that I have my own problems, seriousness problems with thieves and no-goods. Can you believed that my own men have the gall to stealed from me? Why only yesterday five pigs vanished as if flewed away into thin air, and eight days ago a ram and a ewe disappeared. In my garrison theft has becomed epidemical. Time and again I lectured my soldiers and servants that I, alone, haved the right to steal. So, Baltric, before I sended my army to your valley, I must getted my own garrison resituated to order."

Both men had their cups refilled.

"Besides Baltric, I am tolded that against any force the unicorn is a formidable foe. They say that there is not one thing gentled about the freak unicorn with the black mane. Unfortunately for you, he is very magicaled."

"But cousin Vylas, the consequence of the rebellion is not limited only to my rule. Once in firm control of my garrison, Fahseed will preach hatred toward you as well. His cursed enmity will not be quenched until he overthrows all the rulers of these valleys, or until we together *destroy him.*"

"Get holded of yourself Baltric! Enough of this sillied exaggeration. From Fahseed I have nothing to fear. He is, after all, a mered peasant. Although I must say that to have doned the things he did to you, his peasant blood flows stronged in him."

With more wine Baltric wet his throat.

"Blue gold swords and the horn of the black marked unicorn were to me poison. They can also, cousin Vylas, become to you poison. Let us right now combine our forces and wipe the entire pretentious village of Fahseed off the face of this land. Let us leave Byblos desolate so that not one stone remains on top of another!"

"With only three men, Cousin, you do not possessed a force to combined with mine." Vylas sneered as he added, "You command an imaginaried army."

Shoulders slumped and a tear rolled down Baltric's cheek.

"Baltric, I cannot standed you getting tearied on me. Have patience; in a few moons I will helped my older cousin recovered his dignity."

A woman brought the two men goat cheese and bread, and at that Vylas smiled wide.

"Thank you my sweethearted!"

Vylas turned to his cousin and said, "Is not she prettied? You can readily see that she was borned above me. This lady has real class. I tell her that she is... highly minded. Is not her laced and ruffled robe exquisited?"

Without smiling or saying a word in response to Baltric, the lady wearing the frilly robe departed. As he watched her leave, the fallen overlord smiled weakly in agreement with his cousin's voiced praise of the high born lady.

The Dangerous Idea of Freedom

The captured soldiers had raised the outer wall an arm's length higher than the inner wall. The two walls, one renovated and the other newly built, with a moat dug between them made robust the defenses of Byblos.

Briarburr, the two youth, and the four weapons makers sat at the edge of the forest beyond the second wall.

"I am both satisfied and pleased that the prisoners worked hard," commented Fahseed with his back propped against a tree. "They also behaved themselves. I could not believe that on their own the prisoners selected two additional sites where drawbridges now enable our defenders to move between the inner and outer walls."

"The prisoners had a mind to work hard on the wall," responded Elyeazar.

"It does appear that the tyrant Baltric was more perverse than his soldiers," added Colyado.

"On both counts you two are right," answered the captain. "And to each of you I owe heartfelt thanks. I shall never be able to repay you for the freedom I this day enjoy."

"Hah!" exclaimed Jomain. "I will declare that my freedom is most owed to Lyons, Maryeta, and the blackmaned unicorn. Ahem, now why did you call us here?"

"Grandpa, can I join a game of tag over there by the new wall?"

After nodding approval to his granddaughter, the captain answered Jomain. "We are not safe. Yes, we won the battle and have now newly fortified Byblos. But we number too few to withstand the assault of an army led by many overlords. Unaccustomed to liberty, our people are not sturdy in their desire to be free. Freedom requires taking responsibility entire for what one does, and for what one fails to do. For many that is an uncomfortable and distressing burden. You, all of you, were willing to pay with your blood the price of liberty. Few of the people in this village are so willing. They could again come to be herded like sheep."

"I must say that I for one feel blessed for what we have here accomplished," responded Jomain.

"Of course I feel fortunate as well," answered Fahseed. "But we must make sure that the overlords that rule surrounding valleys do not form an alliance to retake our village."

Laughter was heard.

"My friend, the gaiety of Maryeta is music to my ears," said Jomain to Fahseed. "Look, she is the one girl playing tag with five boys. The littlest boy tries, but he cannot catch her."

"If I recall rightly, years back she played with that boy while he herded sheep," answered Fahseed. "Now his head does not measure up to her shoulders."

"She just let him catch her," commented Jomain. "Now she is *it*."

Maryeta did not run off in pursuit of another boy. The men watched as Maryeta grabbed hold of the small boy she had let to tag her, pulled him to her, and lifted him up in a big hug. As with feet ungrounded he half-heartedly tried to push himself away from Maryeta, the small in stature boy could not stop laughing.

"Her prey enjoys a hug from a pretty girl."

"I think that too, Jomain," agreed Fahseed. Watching his granddaughter spin steps around with the boy dangling in her arms, he added, "Not every pretty girl would deign to hug a ragged little shepherd boy."

"Your granddaughter does not know how pretty she is," answered Jomain.

"When alone in the forest with her brother, no one bothered to tell her that she was pretty."

"I am thankful, Fahseed, that the children in our village did not suffer reprisals from the tyrant," continued Jomain. "Innocents suffer most in war. To the likes of Baltric, children are fodder."

"Aherm." Fahseed gained the attention of the others. "A now unemployed spy recently informed me that two cousins were conspiring. So it is as we suspected. Baltric disappeared into the garrison in the valley to our west. Our former ruler tries to convince his cousin Vylas to invade Byblos. Since our walls now number two and are separated by a defensive moat, the cousin knows that unless his force is much larger than was Baltric's, he will face a long and difficult battle. Nonetheless, we must expect Vylas to sooner or later assemble that large army."

"Fahseed is not wrong," offered Colyado. "The freedom this village has come to enjoy threatens the overlords presiding over these many surrounding valleys. Before the onset of winter we will assuredly face an invasion from a united front of tyrants bonded by their hatred for the liberty secured here to common people."

Elyeazar asked the necessary question. "So how do we protect ourselves from an alliance of the overlords?"

"Before he gathers many allies against us, we must topple Baltric's cousin!" exclaimed Lyons. The weight of these words hung heavy on the strong shoulders of the four men and the unicorn gathered together with Lyons.

"The words of this now battle-tested youth ring true," responded Jomain. "The way to finally defeat Baltric goes through his cousin Vylas."

"I hate war!" neighed Briarburr stomping front hooves and shaking vigorously his mane. "Shedding blood in battle goes against everything a unicorn is born to do. I still have not forgotten the look on the face of the corporal when with my horn I destroyed his side. But, Lyons is right. I will go with Fahseed to once more fight a tyrant. After my bloody struggle in the street of Byblos I cannot let to fall any of you, nor this village."

A Strategy to Battle Overlords

"So, Grandfather, how do we win the next battle?"

"With the help of Jomain, I have thought much on that matter. More than a few of the tyrant's former soldiers, made now to be our prisoners, will consent to with us fight against their former master. We will not take villagers with us. Should we somehow fail in our next mission, all the villagers need to be found here to defend their two walls.

"Here is what Jomain and I have come up with. We will surprise Vylas in his garrison. He and his cousin Baltric will not be expecting us to come to them. Our planted tents before the garrison will be the bait. Our force shall be comprised of forty mounted men and thirty extra stallions. Before the start of the battle, the thirty riderless stallions placed under Briarburr's command will remain hidden from sight. When the army of Vylas emerges out of his garrison to attack us, speaking perfectly the horse language Briarburr will order his stallions to charge the overlords' flank. The blackmaned unicorn's company of horses is our secret weapon. They shall be the battering ram that knocks down the horses of our enemy."

"Will we stand in one line of defense?" inquired Colyado.

"On whatever place of height we claim, our riders will form into a defensive square," replied Jomain. "The ten, eleven, or even twelve mounted soldiers on each side of the square will expand or contract to move where needed. A flexible square will protect our sides, our front, and our back."

"In the last fight the odds against us were ten to one," continued Fahseed. "Since instead of twelve fighters we will be forty or more, in the next battle the odds against us will be less, perhaps only five or six to one. Those odds are good enough for us to stand and fight. Forty or more horsemen formed in a defensive square will be the decoy. Our blue gold swords and Briarburr's stallions will be the equalizers."

"We will need some time to sharpen swords and collect arrows for our bows," offered Elyeazar. "We need to prepare cheeses and bread to carry with us, as well as extra water bags."

Maryeta rejoined Fahseed and his fighters. Become quickly apprised of the issue at hand, her eyes directed toward Fahseed.

"In the next battle Lyons and I will fight at your side. You will watch over us and we two will watch over you. In the last fight Briarburr saved my life. In the battle to come I may need my grandfather to do the same for me." After hugging her grandfather, Maryeta ran to embrace the black marked unicorn.

One Blue Gold Sword Left Behind

The choice presented to the villagers of Byblos was among Colyado, Jomain, and Elyeazar. The villagers selected.

"I commend to you Elyeazar, the new leader of Byblos!" proclaimed Fahseed holding high an arm of the master blacksmith. "In matters of defense you must now obey Elyeazar. He will train well the militia to protect our village. One thing more, treat well the twenty horses you now possess." More cheers followed the comment about the horses to be left in the village than the naming of Elyeazar as leader of Byblos.

The prisoners assembled in a line. Elyeazar, Colyado, and Jomain shook the hand and personally thanked every former soldier of Baltric that had labored digging the moat and constructing the outer wall. That done, Fahseed spoke to the gathered prisoners on a matter of keen interest to each one.

"You will march out with us. Upon leaving our valley each of you will make a decision that may be the most important of your lives. You can depart from us never to return to this valley. Or, you can choose to be a soldier in my gallant army that is soon to win a great victory. Having come to know something of each of you, I hope that the stouthearted among you will help me secure lasting freedom for these villagers. Although dangerous, ours is a cause honorable."

Accompanied by Maryeta and nine men bearing blue gold swords, Fahseed led the procession from the village. Fifty stallions, soon to become cavalry mounts, followed after. The prisoners that would be granted their freedom came next. Briarburr and his company of thirty riderless stallions came last. One magic sword remained behind with Elyeazar.

As the procession led by the bearers of blue gold swords departed, the children of the village climbed the outer wall to laugh and cheer. For the idea that they were at last made safe, some of the men and women standing before the outer wall cried with joy. Others worried that their newfound liberty would be impossible to preserve.

The petite woman with long dark hair that had so strenuously objected to the return of the outlaw with a price on his head, threw clods of dirt at the departing column.

On the second night of their march the battalion of men and horses rested on a mountain looming over the far edge of the valley formerly ruled by Baltric. Upon being granted their freedom the next day, more than thirty prisoners chose to remain with those bearing blue gold swords.

The camp a third night was silent and unlit.

The first light of the following day found Fahseed and his force set before the garrison of Lord Vylas. Word had reached Fahseed that the lord of the valley hosted not only the defeated Baltric, but another overlord by the name of Cavour.

CHAPTER 15

THREE OVERLORDS

" I must, Lord Vylas, have a word with you."
"Be gone sentry. Come back when I amed out of bed... and dressed."

"But Sir, soldiers are encamped below your garrison!"

"I gave no lord permission to bringed soldiers here!"

"In the first light of day their swords flash golden. A blackmaned unicorn prances before the encamped soldiers. He is truly something to behold. The intruders can only be the rebels with magic swords who defeated your cousin Lord Baltric."

Jumping out of his bed the ruler would right away see for himself about the intruders. Accompanied by the sentry that had awakened him, Vylas mounted the wall of his garrison.

"What in tarnation? How dared they come to camp in my valley within sighted of my eyes?" Vylas turned to the sentry who had brought him the unexpected news. "Roused my cousin and bringed him here to me. Make it quicked!"

Two cousins dressed in night clothes soon stood side by side peering out at the encampment of Fahseed.

"Blast and double blast! I recognize the despicable traitor! Like sitting ducks Fahseed and his men are out in the open. They number only twenty... thirty... forty or so. Camped in the open, the outlaw cannot spring an ambush on us. Cousin Vylas, my sword will run through Fahseed!"

"*Please* do not telled me that some of those camped below are your formered soldiers," responded Vylas with a sullen look directed at Baltric.

"Those wretched dogs! Fahseed had no right! Those rogues are mine to command! After we defeat Fahseed, any former soldier of mine that survives will be thrown in a hole!"

Met in Council

An overlord bereft of his army, and a visiting overlord, were met with their host Vylas in afternoon council.

"Bringed Baltric's lieutenant to me. He knowed more about Fahseed in battle than any of us." Vylas frowned at his cousin and added, "And *yes*, that included you, Baltric."

The lieutenant came quickly.

"Yes, Sir Vylas, I led the charge against Byblos. I and those others that survived the battle became prisoners of Fahseed."

"Well, what went wronged with Baltric's attack on the village? How camed you to be a prisoner?"

"I am not proud to admit that I was lured into an ambush."

"How letted you that to happen?"

"It happened because of... *my greed*. I wanted one of the twelve blue gold swords forged by Fahseed. Lord Baltric instructed us to bring the swords back to him. My judgment was swayed by the promise of land in exchange for a gold sword handed over to my ruler."

"At least you are honest about the circumstances of your captured. Twelve magic swords would maked Baltric very powerful. Upon coming to possessed the blue gold swords, what did your master intended to do with them?"

"Sir, as to that I cannot answer."

"I would have shared the magic swords with my cousin, and the other overlords."

"Sure, Baltric, of course you would have doned that!" came the retort laden with sarcasm.

"Telled me Abel, what is Fahseed aftered?" continued Vylas. "Why is he violenced... *against me?*"

"Having come to know something of him, I can say that Fahseed bears a hard grudge against Baltric."

"*What* grudge?"

"Baltric told me that many years past he carried away Fahseed's daughter, and after offered a reward for the grandchildren of Fahseed. Taking refuge in the forest, the two grandchildren continued fugitives. Almost full grown, the two youth now fight alongside Fahseed with magic swords."

"Lieutenant, does the usurper wanted only Baltric, or does he wanted me as well?"

"While I care not to know how thinks Fahseed, I have more than once heard him talk nonsense about freedom for the village of Byblos."

"I do not gived a damnation about a village I never once sawed!" exclaimed Vylas stomping a foot.

"You must, Cousin Vylas, understand that Fahseed is arrogant, grasping, and avaricious. Wanting lands and power, greed motivated the outlaw to come here. He is a sly dog that comes to rob the food from off our tables." Baltric's words did not satisfy Vylas.

"Is not the quarrel of Fahseed with the man who tooked away his daughter? By the way, what doned his daughter?"

"She owed me more livestock!" protested Baltric shaking his fist. "She and her husband did not pay their fair taxes!"

"So now I learn that this vexationed conflict is all on account of a landlord wanting a few more lambs and calves from a tenant? Really, Baltric."

"With only a few guards came I here from the north," said calmly the other overlord rising to his feet. "Only passing through this valley, I am not a threat to Fahseed. Nothing I have just heard compels me to stay and participate in warfare. As far as I am concerned, Baltric can solve his own petty problems."

"Not so fasted, Cavour!" answered a visibly angry Vylas. "I counted on you to helped me! My cousin's problem this day becomed mine. The outlaw has recklessed and malicioused here to harm me. For that cause I am going to defeated Fahseed and joined Baltric's valley to mine!"

Vylas turned to his cousin and said with a smirk, "Since you cannot defended your own garrison, you will be my overseer."

"You cannot take from me my garrison! It is my home... *my castle!*"

"Baltric, you possessed no garrison to be from you tooked away."

"Let the brigand stew out there doing nothing," objected Cavour. "It is impossible for his few men to seize this fort. They have to eat. When Fahseed eventually tires of the game, he and his men will melt away."

"If we do nothing the people in this valley will begin to think we overlords are powerless," responded Baltric. "The peasants are conscripted to fight for us. If given the chance, brash young men will talk themselves into fighting instead for Fahseed. You see what happened to some of my former soldiers now become traitors to me. We have no choice but to quickly destroy the invader."

"All right... all right. With reluctance I will join your fight," said Cavour. "Baltric has finally convinced me. Still it would be better to have more men on our side before confronting a magic unicorn and soldiers slashing magic swords. Hmph, the price for my help in this battle is four of the golden swords."

"No, Sir," answered Vylas. "Since my men bear the brunted of the battle, I keeped all but two of the swords. Cavour, and even you, Baltric, will each earned the payment of one gold sword. That is compensationed enough for your meager helped in this fight. Of course, you will as well gained fame for your part in my victory over the sorried renegade."

"I recall a compact signed long ago," rejoined Cavour. "Other overlords, most of them being our grandfathers or great uncles, agreed to defend each other. If one fell the rest pledged to restore the fallen one back to power. Instead of calling me here to help his cousin, Vylas now asks me to help him take over Baltric's lands. Contrary to our long tradition, my host commands me to help him seize more power to himself alone."

"You had best guarded your tongue, Cavour," threatened Vylas.

On the next day no military action was taken by the overlords. Instead, they met over a late afternoon meal. For his guests, Vylas put on an amicable face.

"Enjoy, my friends, the roast duck. It is saided that my valley growed the best ducks in this entired land." After the meal was finished, wine remained to be drunk. The talk at the table finally turned to the issue of the bothersome presence of Fahseed's force.

"They are formed in a defensive square," began Cavour. "Why not divide our force into three companies, and attack at the same time from three sides?"

"Yes," added Baltric, "attacking straight on the small square of invaders leaves little room for our army to maneuver. One cavalryman will get in the way of the next."

"I am beginned to like that idea," concurred Vylas. "A charged on three sides, at one and the same time, will overwhelmed the stationary cavalry of... "

"With a three-pronged charge," interrupted Baltric, "we do not put all our eggs in one basket. If one company does not break through, another will."

After looking closely at his two guests, the lord of the valley nodded his head in agreement. "We fighted in three companies. While I leaded the center, I will putted my cousin back to work leadinged one of the sides. We will all rided out together, and then the two sides will splitted off from my middle and attacked from the east and the west."

"My loyal guards form a unified and highly disciplined company. With them I will lead from the west," said the visiting overlord.

"Cavour, you finally camed to your senses. So then, Baltric will tomorrow leaded the charge from the east. We rided out to victory when tomorrow's sun is directly over head."

"But why lose the morning by waiting until midday to attack?"

"Do not fret, Cavour. With the helped of your fifteen and the four that Baltric commands, my one hundred eighty mounted soldiers will make a quicked end to the rebel. Before you know it the battle will be overed."

"This time my huge lieutenant will be right at my side," added a smiling Baltric.

Baltric's Secret Plan

On the eve of the coming battle Vylas wanted an excuse to closely observe both Baltric and Cavour plied with wine. Nor did the garrison commander want his guests to grow nervous, have second thoughts, or worse still conspire together about gold swords. To impress his guests Vylas entered the hall dressed in a robe of royal purple fringed in ruffles and festooned with gold lacing.

"That robe, Cousin Vylas, is very frilly."

"Comed here Baltric and feeled the softness of the fabric. This is the most comfortabled robe that can be anywhered found."

"I must get me one just like it. Did you buy it on the coast?"

"No, no. I view it as a present fromed my lady friend. You must remembered her wearing this robe. A little while ago she stormied off from the garrison in a huff... about something or other. In the rushed to be rid of me, she forgotted her frilly robe. Fortunately for me, it fits perfectlied."

"But you liked her," responded Baltric. "You said she was... *classy*."

"She turned out to be too highed minded for the likes of me."

"Hah! Would it not be the other way around," rejoined Baltric slapping his cousin on the shoulder, "that you were too low minded for the likes of her?" At his cousin's expense Baltric laughed loud.

"You seem to be in splendid fit on the eve before battle against your hated enemy."

"Does it show? Well then yes, Cavour, tonight I find myself to be in a fine mood."

"Why so, Baltric?"

"I found a way for me, by myself, to ensure our victory."

"Interesting," answered Cavour nodding his head. "So how can you, as you say *by yourself*, guarantee victory? Not long ago you were by Fahseed shamed. Need I remind that you lost your entire army to the rebel?"

"At the proper time my tactic will be shared with my cousin Vylas, and with him only. I will not have my idea to be stolen from me. Tomorrow Cavour will see play out my tactical maneuver, and I will re-earn the nickname *BalTricky*."

Soldiers in the army led by Fahseed had practiced how they would come to the aid of each other, which mounted soldier would move to shore up a weak corner, and which soldier would go to reinforce the center of a breaking line. With Maryeta and Lyons at his sides, Fahseed would anchor the middle of the line facing the fortress.

"Battle will soon come to us," spoke the leader of the rebellion to those about him. "Vylas wants not to wait longer to restore his authority over this valley."

"So then Jomain, what new things, what surprises will tomorrow overtake us?" inquired Colyado of his friend.

"With courage you and I will brandish our blue gold swords," answered Jomain. "We will count on a successful ambush to be carried out by the black marked unicorn and his company of brave stallions. And I will pray to the heavens that some unanticipated magical advantage comes to favor us."

Chapter 16

Briarburr Fallen

L ord Vylas led his cavalry out of the garrison. In command of fifty soldiers, Baltric was to charge Fahseed's east flank. With the fifteen men in his personal guard, Cavour would attack the west flank. Under the leadership of Vylas the remaining cavalrymen would strike head-on the rebel square.

With his sword Cavour pointed at the saddle of Baltric and said, "I know what *your* sword will today do, but I know not the purpose of the rope you carry."

"You will see that this piece of rope is for me today, *lucky*."

"So, Baltric really has one more trick up his sleeve." Cavour could not help but notice that the fallen overlord had reacquired the swagger he must have shown when many men obeyed his orders.

Two hundred mounted horsemen were soon moving at a canter. The *Battle of Three Overlords* had begun.

"Look! Horses break away from the attack!"

Turning to where Lyons was pointing, Fahseed exclaimed, "By heavens you are right! Leading his bodyguard away from battle, the red haired man sitting tall in his saddle must be the overlord named Cavour. That, Lyons, is very good for us. They say that the two swords Cavour fights with have never met their match."

"Grandpa, a man breaks ahead of the formation and speeds toward us!"

"That man, Maryeta, is the lieutenant that was my prisoner. I do not think he foolishly leads this charge, as he did when he rode into the street of our village. He would not make the same mistake again. His sword stays sheathed. Why... I say that Abel comes to *join us!*"

"Hurrah for Briarburr!" came a shout. The blackmane was galloping at full speed toward Baltric and Vylas. Behind him ran thirty stallions that showed themselves committed to the fray.

The lieutenant turned back his head to see if soldiers had been sent to chase him down. What he saw, instead, was Baltric hand something to Vylas. Immediately, Abel remembered the odd thing he had that morning noticed about Baltric; slung over his saddle was a rope looped at each end. The purpose of the rope presented to the mind of the lieutenant. Baltric and Vylas would use the rope to sweep the hooves out from under Briarburr. The unicorn leading the charge of the stallions would be looking for raised swords, not a low slung rope, and when his hooves were tripped the charging Briarburr would fall hard. Wheeling his horse about, Abel dashed towards Baltric and Vylas.

Running in the lead of his stallions Briarburr was only a few paces away from the cousin overlords. A moment before Briarburr's body was to collide into them, Vylas and Baltric separated from each other. When Briarburr's hooves caught on the rope slung between the saddles of the two men, the blackmaned unicorn crashed down.

"Our square moves to where lies the blackmane!" shouted Fahseed upon seeing the valiant unicorn tumble down. Fahseed waved his sword and yelled, "*Briarrrburrr!*"

Thirty fleet stallions smacked into the horses of the enemy soldiers. Angered at the fall their leader, the riderless stallions brought havoc to the force of the overlords.

Amid the tumult and confusion created by the company of stallions that had followed the blackmaned unicorn into the fray, Vylas and Baltric turned their horses back toward the spot where lay Briarburr.

"Hahah! The unicorn is mine!" yelled Baltric as his horse surged ahead of Vylas.

As Abel closed on Baltric he saw his former master draw his sword and launch himself at the unicorn. Abel threw himself at the moving target of Baltric's body. In midair they collided. As if clasped in an embrace the two fell to the ground.

"You... are... my... lieu..." gasped Baltric gurgling blood. An unbloodied sword was still clutched in Baltric's hand. Gathering himself up, Abel found a second sword in the side of Baltric.

"I did not know I could that far throw my sword!" exclaimed Maryeta jumping off her horse. "When my mind directed where the sword would fly, the blue gold magic obeyed."

"Little lady, you are a very fierce warrior," replied the big man with a shaved head as he handed back her sword.

The lieutenant addressed the corpse, "I will no more throw men into your holes in the ground."

"Your horse flew right past me!" exclaimed Fahseed. "I had not known that my girl could ride so fast."

"I would return what Briarburr did when I was about to fall to the corporal's sword. This man and I, both of us together, saved the noble unicorn from Baltric's vengeance."

"This matter, Fahseed, finally gives answer to your question. You now see where from this day lies the loyalty of Abel. Albeit belatedly, I accept your offer of enlistment."

Around the immobile body of the unicorn the cavalry of Fahseed reformed its square.

"*Do not die*, Briarburr," whispered Maryeta pressing her cheek to the head of the unicorn. "You cannot leave me. I need you to be always with me."

"When I fell... the wind was knocked... from my ribs. I broke my leg."

Upon kneeling to examine Briarburr's damaged leg, Abel confirmed, "It is badly broken. Maryeta, we must well protect him."

"We together will do so, Abel, with all our strength."

The battle settled into a pattern of fierce enemy charges met by the parrying movements of Fahseed and his riders, eleven of whom wielded golden swords, and by the counterattacks of stallions no longer under the command of Briarburr. With the seeming strength of three men, the young lieutenant fought more conspicuously than anyone. Ten of the enemy fell for each casualty borne by the company of Fahseed.

"I did not know so large a man could move so fast!" exclaimed Colyado during a pause in the battle.

"For the first time in my life I fight with all my heart," replied Abel.

"Thank goodness you fight not against us. Your strength gives me heart in this battle. It is as if you were sent to replace the loss of the mighty Briarburr."

"That compliment, Colyado, twice over surpasses any I before received."

Blue Gold Swords Point Skyward

Vylas made time to reorganize his forces. The lull in the fighting gave the men with Fahseed time to consider... their thirst. Upon rushing to reestablish the defensive square around the position of the fallen blackmane, the left behind supplies of food and water had been quickly destroyed by the soldiers of Vylas. As the sun burned down hot on a battlefield where horse hooves kicked up clouds of dust, the throats of rebel soldiers grew parched. Fahseed desperately wanted the clouds above to thicken and darken with moisture.

"You say that I am an idea man," offered Jomain as he drew next to Fahseed. "Well, in that regard a new thought just presented to me. If we all together raise our blue gold swords and implore the skies for rain, perhaps drops of rain will fall down to refresh us."

"Are you telling me, Jomain, that the magic of our blue gold swords can extend so high as the heavens?"

"While none of us know the full power of the blue gold, if we show faith, it just might work. As is often said, nothing ventured, nothing gained."

"I agree!" exclaimed Maryeta having overheard the conversation between Jomain and Fahseed.

"Thank you for that, Maryeta," responded Jomain. "I can always count on your true heart to trust in the magic of blue gold."

Fahseed dismounted and called the bearers of the blue gold swords to gather in the center of his company of riders. He motioned for them to raise skyward the points of their weapons.

Knowing that she was the kind of girl that could brook failure far better than not having tried, Fahseed turned to his granddaughter. "Maryeta, it is your shorter sword that will petition the heavens for rain."

"Join with me, Lyons."

"Generous heavens, your servants require rain to quench our thirst!" proclaimed Maryeta standing with her brother amidst magic swords raised high. "Let rain pour down to wet the blades of blue gold swords!" The swords held by Maryeta and Lyons clanged together once, twice, three times. From tip to hilt eleven swords began to shine.

"From our swords goes upward a blue stream of light!" The boy's eyes grew large as he added, "And the magic light separates out to ignite the sky! Our blue gold swords have lightning in them!"

"Look there, brother!" exclaimed Maryeta pointing. "From the west, dark clouds roll toward us! It is going... *to rain!*"

A first sprinkle of rain fell on the faces of eleven sword bearers maintaining gaze upward. The sprinkles of rain turned to a soaking.

"Huh! And Colyado said that I was the strong one," offered the big lieutenant. "The voice of Maryeta has far more power than the muscles in my arms."

Upon hearing that said, the girl bowed to the man who had so nicely complimented her smartness. Her cheeks soon blushed for the repeated cheers, "Maryeta! Maryeta!"

An Overlord Soaked Through

"Confound this rain! The last thinged I needed *is mud!*" The rain that doused his hair and soaked his uniform had soured the state of mind of Vylas. "I cannot order an attack only to have galloping horses slipped and slided all about and into each other. Blast it all! Soon it will be darked. Although I am on the verged of victory, the fighting for today must ended." The mood of Vylas worsened.

"First, Cavour and his guardsmen lefted me. Then, just when my cousin was backed to his treacheried and trickied self, his very own lieutenant killed him. Imagine *that!* For all his conceited and vanity my cousin knewed how to lead a troop of soldiers. Had Cavour and Baltric shored up my forces, the battle would alreadied be ended in my victory. Now, both overlords are to me goned."

"Established right now a defensive line betweened Fahseed and my garrison," commanded Vylas his sergeant. "Extend the line easted and wested, and I want extra guards tonight. Do not concerned yourselves with Fahseed's open side; the brigand is too obstinated to flee this place.

"A double ration will be sent for the suppered of our troops. Breakfast rations will to you be broughted. Tomorrow morning I ride out from my garrison to winned victory." Pointing toward the position held by Fahseed, Vylas added, "Fighting on empty stomachs his men are tomorrow perished. Then it will be my turned to tortured the last moments of Fahseed."

Once inside the gates of his garrison Vylas found fit to upbraid tired guards. "You there, you looked sloppied! Stand up straighted when you saluted me! No sloughing off! Any sentry caughted napping tonight will be lashed. Past middle night I have worked ahead of me, so tonight there will be no commotioned in the garrison."

Reprimands were next found for the benefit of those that conducted the daily chores and housekeeping of the garrison. Vylas found sufficient reason to upbraid and nag each one of his cooks, stable boys, and maid servants.

"I so loved telling my servants whated to do and not to do," muttered the overlord when done with his inspection. "One day this willed be the grandest

garrison in all of Phoenicia, and all willed fear Vylas...
the Possessed of Twelve Magic Swords."

CHAPTER 17

FLIRTATION AND A FRILLY ROBE

"A word with you, Captain."

"What is it, Abel? Mind not the presence of Lyons and Maryeta."

"At the approach of a most dark night the soldiers of Vylas are bogged down in this, for us, fortuitous rain. Had I a gold coin I would wager that because of the mud and rain, Vylas will not this night return to the battlefield, but will instead continue warm and dry in his garrison."

"A battlefield commander should inspire his troops by staying with them," replied Fahseed raising an eyebrow. "Hmm, there must be some way we can make mischief of the overlord's withdrawal to his garrison. Only... I confess that I do not know what that would be."

"Well, Sir, if the garrison sentries that will have marched guard all night are careless when the overlord rides out the gate tomorrow morning, perhaps a few of us could slip in before the gate is again shut. Once inside, it would not be that difficult to take control of the fortress."

"Hmph. Go on, Lieutenant."

"The loss of his garrison would take from Vylas the bastion of his defense, as well as take away his supplies of food and weapons. Not to mention that he would lose his treasury, the gold and the silver coins that pay the wages of his soldiers."

"Soldiers much anticipate the arrival of payday," replied Fahseed with his face breaking into a small smile. "Thinking on it, Abel, once the walls were taken I could advance our defensive square toward the garrison. With our magic swords and the aid of the company of Briarburr's stallions, the enemy would be hard put to stop my cavalry from gaining entrance to the fortress. Once inside the garrison, my soldiers would have food, and Briarburr could in safety heal fast his wounds."

"Sir, since I am the only soldier found with you that knows the garrison, I volunteer to lead a detail to capture the walls of the fortress."

"Lieutenant Abel, for a man so young you have surprisingly important ideas. By heavens, I may have to shave my head so that I too can come up with such brilliant thinking." Seated at the side of her grandfather Maryeta had, of course, been paying close attention.

"Grandpa, someone slender and fast can hide behind a rock or bush and from there slip quickly inside the gate. For any guard, my blue gold sword makes me more than a match."

"What Maryeta just said goes as well for me," added Lyons. "Playing in the forest we learned to well conceal ourselves. And if my sister hides in a tree and falls out of it, which would not be the first time, I will be there to catch her." Hearing that said, Maryeta punched her brother.

"I am toughed up. That did not hurt me at all."

"I hate at any time to see you two leave my side, and especially so on this night of battle. But if you both pledge to obey every instruction of the lieutenant I will consent that my grandchildren go with him. A stealthy party numbering only three shall early tomorrow capture the garrison of Vylas."

While torrented rain in a very dark part of the night Abel, Lyons, and Maryeta advanced silently toward the garrison. After a day of hard battle the thoughts of tired enemy sentries focused on the unfairness of the life of a soldier that fights all day, and then marches guard all night in the rain. Worrying little that anyone would dare be about on such a wet and blustery night, sentries relaxed their vigilance. If a few soldiers of Fahseed happened to desert through the line of sentries, well then so much the better. Each and every desertion would signify one fewer rebel soldier to contend with on the morrow.

Safe passage rewarded stealth. During the last part of the night Abel, Lyons, and Maryeta huddled hidden together eighty paces from the garrison gate.

A surprising amount of brilliant sunlight had shone down before the gates opened to permit Vylas and his escort of soldiers to depart the garrison. The overlord scowled at the two sentries that opened the gates, but to them no parting words were spoken.

"I will take the man; you two take the boy," said quietly Abel as he motioned toward the sentries.

"Since the arms and legs of those two guards are even skinnier than mine, they will not put up much of a fight," observed a confident Lyons.

"Not so fast," whispered Maryeta. "Let us make bloodless the conquest of the garrison gate."

"Remember, Sister, that Grandfather told us to obey the lieutenant."

"Do you think I am... *pretty?*"

"We are *busy* right now," responded Lyon crossly. "We are in the midst of a battle. Err... yes... of course you are pretty."

"Young lady, you are indeed *fair*. Now, are you and Lyons ready to spring at the youth?"

"Stay here while I do something to save a boy's life." Not waiting to be answered by her brother or the lieutenant, Maryeta stepped out and proceeded to walk in plain sight towards the two sentries standing before the still open gates.

When Maryeta waved, the younger sentry waved back at her.

"Miss, are you lost?" yelled the skinny youth gifted with an affable smile. "Are you not aware that hereabout is waged a fierce battle, one that will soon renew?" For long moments the young sentry smiled at Maryeta. "I would hate to see such a pretty girl get mixed up in a bloody battle. You are... not from around here?"

"The morning began so perfectly that I decided to go for a long walk," answered Maryeta. "Wandering too far, I became lost."

"There is still a little time before the fighting starts below us. If you like I can show you this great garrison. It is built of sturdy construction. Since my commander just left, who is to care if I give you a quick tour?" The youth pointed to the older sentry and added, "My uncle Merlew built so cleanly the two halves of the fortress gate that even a girl can swing them shut."

"I will have you know that when it comes to closing gates, I am a very strong girl. But, I cannot go in with you. My grandfather insists that I do not with strangers enter any building." With one hand Maryeta fussed at her auburn hair. "That does not mean that you cannot come over here and give directions to a girl that finds herself to be unfortunately lost."

"Sure I can. I will also show you what I have been carving. I am a five times better artist than I am a soldier. When I am finished, this carving of a unicorn is going to look... *elegant.*"

"You forget that we are on duty, Elyir. The harsh punishment meted out by the overlord for dereliction of duty is not easily endured."

"No, no, do not for that worry Uncle Merlew. I will do my duty, scout the road, and make sure that this lost and... ahem... *very pretty* stranger is in fact who she says she is. Since we are now beset by a real war, our commander would want us to make sure no danger lurks before our gate. For that, Uncle, you need to come with me." As he approached where stood Maryeta the youth wore a pleasant smile. Walking beside his nephew the older guard, half again Elyir's age, wore a frown.

Once the two guards had strode to where waited Maryeta, the lieutenant jumped up and sped to place himself between the sentries and the swinging gates that the two men were charged to protect. His sword drawn, Lyons was quickly at the side of Lieutenant Abel.

"Look, Merlew!" Elyir motioned with both arms. "The youth's sword shines brightly of the legendary blue gold! Uncle, I must for myself see its workmanship!"

"Forged from blue gold, the blade is *truly* magical," added Maryeta drawing out her own sword from beneath her shirt. "Holding this sword makes me much stronger than I really am. Elyir, my name is Maryeta. For your own good it was best that I deceived you. Because of my trickery no blood is shed here. I would have hated for that to be done to two well behaved and respectful men."

Maryeta turned to share with Abel a sudden inspiration, "Sir, what if these two guards who have just shown themselves to be honorable men, came over to our side in this battle?"

"I remember Merlew and Elyir from the days I spent with Baltric inside the garrison wall. Not coarse and rough enough to suit him, these two soldiers were not the favorites of Vylas." That said, Abel turned to address the two guards.

"Take an oath of loyalty to our leader Captain Fahseed, and to the trueness of our blue gold swords. To the side of freedom enlist yourselves. With us stand against the tyranny of the overlords."

"I hate Vylas," responded at once Elyir. "I have seen him do awful things to those with whom he quarreled. What privileges a man arrogant and insolent to merit power and rule? If *Art* and *Grace* visited him wearing the wings of angels, Lord Vylas would not know to recognize them. He would instead throw them into one of his notorious holes. *Gladly* will I take the oath."

Bent down on one knee with his hands placed to touch not only the handle of the planted sword, but also the hands of Maryeta holding vertically the sword, the youth swore an oath.

"I, Elyir, pledge my loyalty to Captain Fahseed. I promise to uphold and protect the purity of the blue gold swords... *and* to be ever enchanted by the grace of Maryeta."

At that final comment the face of the girl flushed rosy. Still blushing, she turned to Merlew.

"I have, and will always, support Elyir," said Merlew taking a knee beside his nephew. "Of all the artists in our family, and there are many, he is destined to be the greatest. And I also loathe Vylas. Upon the heavens I swear that I now change my loyalty to Captain Fahseed. Like my nephew, I promise to uphold and protect the magic trueness of blue gold."

"Well done, Elyir," answered Abel. "Well done, Merlew. We will right away put two new soldiers to work. We five must take command of the garrison. Are there no more than ten guards inside?"

"They number nine, Lieutenant," answered Merlew. "Of those, three now march sentry duty on the walls. Once Vylas left the garrison the other six would have retired to their cots."

"We can handle those odds," responded confidently Lyons. "Look, a sentry on the wall approaches."

The lieutenant, the two youth, and the two new recruits walked at a casual pace toward the gate of the garrison. The sentry on the wall stopped to observe the approach of strangers.

"Remember me? I am Baltric's lieutenant. I am back with two young soldiers that helped me on my mission. Return to your duty. Soon I will be up there to join you."

"Of course I remember Lieutenant Abel. But... they said you had deserted."

"Hah!" answered Abel the sentry. "That deceit was nothing more than a ruse given to me by my true and brave commander. I remain more loyal to this imposing garrison than even Lord Vylas can guess."

The former lieutenant of the petty tyrant Baltric led his little band into the barracks and roused six drowsy soldiers to stand at attention.

"Lord Baltric is dead," said Abel. "Lord Vylas will soon be defeated. With magic swords these my friends, and I, have taken control of the garrison. I now present an opportunity that I require you to consider well. If you decide to leave here and return to Lord Vylas, he will not be pleased to find that in his absence you happened to lose his fortress. So, those who wish to join to the side of Captain Fahseed and the blackmaned unicorn, step forward now."

Four of the six men stepped out from their line.

"More than once I heard it said, Merlew, that you are a man gifted with the power of acute observation. What do you make of these four volunteers?" inquired the lieutenant.

"They are the best of the lot," replied Merlew nodding his head.

As she did the honors, Maryeta wore a big smile. Each of the four was sworn into the army of Fahseed and the code of the blue gold swords.

The three sentries on the walls were disarmed. Not the caliber of men wanted by Merlew, those three along with their two comrades still loyal to Vylas were by their former companions escorted without the garrison. Behind them Maryeta, by herself, closed tight the garrison gates built by Merlew.

As had happened the night before the cooks, maids, gardeners, and stable boys were gathered to stand together. Upon being informed by Abel that the garrison had come under new management, the expression of not a single employee of the garrison registered dismay. No matter who ordered them about, to the cooks, servants, and stable boys work *was work*. Besides, the next commander of the garrison could hardly be more arrogant, condescending, and difficult than had been Lord Vylas.

Servants were told that with one proviso, a pledge of loyalty to Captain Fahseed, that they were welcomed to continue their duties. Oaths taken, every cook, servant, washer woman, and stable boy promptly returned to his or her chores inside the garrison.

Taken down by Merlew and Elyir, the unicorn horns crowning the four corners of the garrison were covered with the cloak of the lieutenant.

When the banner of the overlord was made to no longer wave above fortress walls, a new standard was required.

"What we need is a piece of cloth that is large, colorful, and light so that our soldiers will immediately notice it flapping cheerily in the wind," remarked Maryeta. The girl went to inquire of a cleaning lady for just such a fabric.

"You know what, young lady?" answered a woman smiling through a face deeply wrinkled. "I just might have the very thing you require," After disappearing into the quarters of Vylas, the servant woman was quickly back clutching a rolled up garment in her arms.

Maryeta grabbed one end of the garment, and with the cleaning lady stretched it out. The girl was impressed. "This fabric is indeed light of weight and very colorful. I have never before seen a garment made so fine."

"I think that this will work very satisfactorily," commented Abel upon inspecting the garment. "We will immediately raise this on the flagstaff. Then we will see how long it takes soldiers, mind you on both sides, to notice that the garrison of Vylas was just to him lost." A sudden gust of wind extended full out the new standard.

The lieutenant with fingers touching his forehead, the two youth with golden swords stretched high, and the new recruits standing stiffly at attention on the walkway of the wall, stood in salute of the new flag representing the bloodless usurpation of the garrison.

Almost immediately a loud rumble of groans sounded from the soldiers of Vylas found not far distant from the garrison walls. Louder and more enthusiastic cheers were soon heard from the more distant, and much more exuberant men standing with Fahseed.

When it sank in that he had lost not only his garrison, but also his coveted store of precious coins, sparkling rings, and necklaces of adornment the heart of Vylas plummeted. His brow furrowed, his lips twisted up in a grimace, and his cheeks reddened.

"Aarrghh! Damn!" exclaimed the overlord kicking out a foot. "I have now losted even my... frilly robe... the most comfortabled robe I ever owned!"

"Can I really believe what my eyes tell me they see?" inquired Fahseed to those about him. "Is that flag what it looks to be?"

Several heads nodded their assent.

Observing the banner to wave energetically in the wind, Fahseed smacked his lips and with a hand threw a kiss toward the garrison. "Hmmuah! That, Lord Vylas, is for you unfortunate. Especially about the loss of your fine purple flag!"

The entire force of rebel invaders surrounded their commander and waited to learn what their leader would do next.

"Last night as you slept your horn glowed compellingly against your broken leg," said Fahseed turning to Briarburr. "My heart was moved to see the healing power authored by unicorn magic. For you I now have a question. Can you make it as far as the garrison?"

"I find myself much healed," neighed in answer the unicorn as he gingerly raised himself to stand on his hooves. "But even on three legs I could that far manage to walk."

"That, Briarburr, is the best news to my ears. Neigh to the horses in your cavalry to provide escort as we make our way to take command of the..." Fahseed was interrupted.

"I bring urgent news that I am afraid is bad!"

"Jomain, whatever has happened cannot ruin the heartening news of the lieutenant's capture of the garrison."

"Far up the valley you see Cavour in the lead of an armed force riding towards us. They must have ridden through the night."

"Well then, Jomain, in that case we had best gain the protection of garrison walls, *while the going is good!*"

With his garrison taken, Vylas himself had little idea how to proceed. He turned to his sergeant and implored, "What... what amed I to do now?" Without waiting to be answered, the overlord had more things to get off his chest. "I still cannot imagined that they were brazened enough to sneaked into my garrison! Baltric was right. The deceit of Fahseed is monstroused. The renegade has no scrupled. The peasant who leaded the rebels does not played by the accepted rules of warfare. But, I still have numerical superiority... and the black marked unicorn is broken legged."

Before Vylas and his sergeant could decide on what course to next follow, a report came that Lord Cavour was approaching with a force of more than one hundred cavalry soldiers. At that news Vylas brightened.

"With the soldiers remained to me, and the many reinforcements broughted by Cavour, we are stronger than when the battle commenced. I will retaked the garrison, and annihilated Fahseed!"

Vylas turned to look toward the position of his enemy. Soldiers on horses, and yes the black marked unicorn, were double-timing toward the garrison. The first impulse of the overlord was to order an all-out attack to stop Fahseed from gaining the garrison. The second impulse of Vylas was... for caution.

The overlord realized that before Cavour and his soldiers mounted on horses spent from their long ride reached his position, his own men were unlikely to prevail over the blue gold swords of his enemy. Vylas decided to wait for Cavour and not suffer needless casualties. The next impulse of the overlord was to fret about the status of his authority. Perhaps Cavour had returned out of concern for his own welfare as a ruler, not out of any concern for the welfare or image of Vylas.

"I canned see it right now," muttered the overlord to himself. "He will not putted his men under my command. In the eyes of Cavour, the same as happened to my now deceased cousin Baltric, I am disgraceded."

Vylas slumped down in his saddle. Without looking his sergeant in the eye he said, "Errhmm, Cavour would want me to waited his arrival. For now the garrison is to me losted." Vylas exclaimed more for his benefit than for that of those with him, "Thunder and lightning! Even more than I hated Fahseed, I loathed the black marked unicorn! Burrbriar thwarts me for no reasoned, inspires the army of my wretched enemy, and does me much damaged!"

"Sir, it is *Briarburr*," corrected the sergeant.

"What? What sayed you?"

"Not Burrbriar, it is Briarburr, which for the name of a unicorn flows more smoothly off the lips."

"Cursed that blasted unicorn's hide!" yelled Vylas striking with his forearm the sergeant. "I will called him whatever I wanted!"

The overlord looked again toward the walls of the garrison that for so long had been his to command. Where his sentries used to walk guard, eleven blue gold swords now flashed brilliant under the sun.

Cavour dismounted. Walking through the camp, Cavour and his men appeared to be in no rush to reach Vylas.

"Sir Cavour, I am mightily gladded that you came back to aided me in this fight. As you see, I now have Fahseed surrounded in a place from which he cannot escaped."

"What is this that I now hear? You let a drunk and two children capture your garrison? Please tell me that is not so, Vylas."

"No, no, Cavour, you have it wronged. When he captured my garrison the big lieutenant of Baltric was not drunked. And the two grandchildren of the outlaw were armed with magic swords. The sly dogs bribeded my guards with the promise of gold treasure."

"So, it *is* true. You really did lose your garrison to one man and two children." To express his disgust with Vylas, Cavour threw up his arms with hands bent back at the wrists. "Which means you as well lost *your treasury!* What? Is that your frilly robe that waves above the fortress? Heavens have mercy on us."

"The traitors tooked my favorite robe... as you knowed it *was* one of a kind."

From a mixture of disgust and amusement formed the smile of Cavour as he remarked, "I do believe you are more upset about the loss of your frilly robe than the loss of your treasury."

"Why did not you telled me that you roded away to bring back more soldiers to fight alongsided me? Had I knowed that, I would haved in the garrison awaited your arrival, and thus not losted my fortress, treasury, and even my frilly robe."

"To make sure we would win, I wanted more men to fight with. And I had to keep secret my plan. If word of it had leaked out, I and my few guards could have been ambushed on our way back to my valley. I tell you, Vylas, this war of yours is not in the villages popular."

"But this war is really Baltric's, may he rested in peace, and not mined."

"Get on your horse," instructed Cavour. The two overlords walked horses toward the stronghold now held by Fahseed.

"Listen, old friend," spoke Cavour in a reassuring tone, "Upon leaving you yesterday I immediately sent three riders to request overlords that are in my debt, to here join us. Each ruler is to bring one hundred cavalry."

"You bringed me the best news I could asked for! With so many soldiers we can stormed the walls of my garrison!"

"We will not storm it; we will lay siege to your lost garrison," corrected Cavour. "Now Vylas, think about this. The enemy soldiers are confined inside four walls. That makes the company of stallions, and their leader the blackmaned unicorn Briar..."

"I prefer to call him Burrbriar."

"What? No matter. As I was saying that makes the unicorn and the company of stallions of no help to Fahseed in his attempt to hold the garrison. In this battle our enemy has relied heavily on the hooves of those riderless stallions. The garrison will now for him become a trap. It may take ten or even twenty days. But day after day, little by little, we will grind the rebels down."

"Fahseed has only forty men, and ahem, a girl at his command," answered Vylas. "We can place fifty ladders up against the walls of my garrison. Eleven golden swords cannot stopped fifty men scaling at once the walls."

"Ten archers placed strategically on the wall can rapidly send sufficient arrows to stop fifty ladder climbers. Did not the outlaw use archery with much success when in a village street he ambushed the men of your cousin Baltric?"

"We... just... have to prevailed," responded the disgraced overlord. "We both knowed that the lives of our soldiers matter little. As long as we suffered no more than eight or nine soldiers fallen for each enemy killed, this battle is as good as wonned."

"Look to the west, Vylas," said Cavour with his face breaking into a smile. "The dust you see is from the many horses of Auldham. As we speak our army strengthens. Before nightfall those horses will arrive here. Now, old friend, do not take umbrage at what I am about to say. Neither I nor Lord Auldham will place our soldiers under the command of someone that lost his garrison walls to a drunk and two children. Vylas, you will not lead our combined forces."

Resigning himself to the reality spoken by Cavour, the disgraced overlord slumped his shoulders. Vylas had to admit that it was true enough. His former prestige had vanished, and with that was lost his high place in the hierarchy of the overlords.

"The lieutenant was... stone cold sobered... I will never forgived him for taking my frilly..." Vylas wiped away a tear. "It was prettied... and softed."

CHAPTER 18

PELICAN OF THE WILDERNESS

Two magnificent wings circled high over the fortress of a tyrant. On that morning she had from far away seen unmistakable flashes of blue gold. Now, in the fading light of dusk, the winged horse glimpsed a sentry stationed on the garrison wall thrust his sword at an invisible adversary. It was the glinting of magic swords like that one, that had earlier caught her attention. The five imposing tents she counted outside the garrison walls were surely the temporary abode of overlords that commanded the many soldiers encamped about them.

Under the cover of a darkening sky the winged horse flew closer to the garrison. What she next saw quickened the beat of her heart. The many horse stallions inside the walls of the fortress were, amazingly, accompanied by a unicorn.

Not so far distant from where her wings now glided, she had once before come upon a special horned horse. That one was young, awkward, wore strange black markings, and had been unaccountably alone. The mane and hide of the unicorn below her had unmistakable black coloring.

When only a few days past the soldiers she had been so anxious about had suddenly left off their pursuit of the unicorns under her protection, the young mares she had zealously watched over were made newly safe. Their regained safety meant the winged horse had been freed, at least temporarily, of her vigilance and guardianship.

The winged horse thought again about what she was doing above the garrison. Attracted to the source of magic reflections of sunlight, she had by curiosity been drawn. She had as well surmised that the blue gold flashes somehow connected to the suddenness of soldiers quitting a raid on the unicorns that she had been protecting. The winged horse also did not find it coincidental that during days past she had noticed the dust of three separate cavalries moving in the direction of this very place.

The presence of blue gold swords, a unicorn, and many unhaltered stallions confirmed to her that the balance of rightness tipped to the side of those besieged in the garrison. Could it be that the horses and unicorn had gained protection from the commander of the garrison? Except that rather than protection and advantage the men, stallions, and the solitary unicorn now found inside the garrison appeared to be trapped. The winged horse decided that a siege conducted by the hundreds of soldiers camped about the tents of their overlords, would end badly for the garrison's occupants.

The closer she found herself to the realm of men, the more vulnerable became her wings to cuts dealt by spears and arrows. Still, her inquisitiveness finally triumphed over her caution. Although it was not something that she had ever before done, at the fall of darkness she decided to alight inside the garrison and hope that if soldiers became to her alerted, the unicorn would protect her. She would count on the men found about the unicorn not to do her harm.

In silence her hooves came to caress softly the ground. Upon finding sound asleep the black marked unicorn, her nose touched to his.

With his eyelids made heavy by somnolence, Briarburr thought he again drifted in dreams with the winged horse that had once, so long ago, come to him. The realization was sudden. It was not a dream. Looking down at him she... *was real!* A suddenly wide awake Briarburr scrambled to his hooves.

"Shhh! I thought that from these valleys you had forever departed. The black marked unicorn that I once before saw, hid himself well. You must now be the only horned horse that hereabout grazes."

"I am... filled with gladness to see... to see you once more. It happened so long ago by the waterfall that I sometimes feared I had seen you only in a dream, but the winged horse really *does* exist."

"What is your name?"

"I never had a birth name. Because of my coat's jots of black markings, I am now called Briarburr."

"Why are you and these many free-spirited stallions found inside the fortress of a tyrant? Briarburr, what terrible thing is... *here to happen?*"

The blackmane motioned for the two of them to move beneath the low branches of the one tree growing inside the walls of the stronghold. They reclined on bellies with the stallion's body concealing from view the winged horse.

"An overlord named Vylas lost to us this garrison. Now it is my turn to know your name."

"The black splotches on the underside of my wings make them to resemble the wings of a pelican. For that I am called *Peli*."

"How did you find me here?"

"Following the sun reflections of blue gold swords, I was to this garrison led."

"I want to know more about you."

"Because I am the only one that I have ever seen, I doubt you have met another winged horse. My unicorn mare died giving birth to me. That was a bad omen. When the other mares found I had been born with wings, that I was unlike them, they cared even less for the foal that in birth had cost the life of their sister and friend, my mother mare." Peli cleared her voice of the emotion she ever felt when she remembered the loss.

"*Nyuhuhrrumm...* if even for a day I wish I had known my mare. Not just because of my wings, but also because my horn is stubby the unicorns say that I am not true. Accepting without complaint their disdain, I think of myself not as a unicorn, but as a winged horse.

"Since the unicorns permit me to protect them, that is what I do. I mount on wings to see where danger approaches. I endeavor to make sure that malevolence does not prevail against magic horses, especially against the young mares and foals. Independent minded young unicorn stallions think that they do not need me to protect them."

"Do you on your wings travel far?"

"My wings have carried me a thousand leagues to the north, and south, and east. For that I am called *The Pelican of the Wilderness*. Sadly, the clans of unicorns that used to live far away from here have been forced to gallop to this land. They fled from fierce warriors seeking to destroy them."

"Over there are four unicorn horns formerly raised on the corners of these walls," neighed Briarburr motioning his head toward the gate. "They now wait burial in a peaceful high place."

"So the man who this night rules here, who cast down the horns, is a friend of the unicorns?"

"For Captain Fahseed the unicorn is the most sacred animal of all."

"How came the blackmane here?"

"Lyons and Maryeta, the two orphan grandchildren of Fahseed, became my friends. I rescued Lyons from the henchmen of an overlord named Baltric, who until recently ruled the valley that lies to the east. In the battle of Byblos, where we defeated Baltric, my horn prevented Maryeta from being killed. We came here in pursuit of that malevolent former overlord. We could not wait for Baltric to enlist the support of other tyrants to overwhelm and destroy the small force of Captain Fahseed."

"Why are these many stallions here with you?"

"Whipped and beaten in the cavalry of Baltric, these badly treated stallions chose to help me do battle against cruel overlords."

"I fear that you are in this fortress trapped," neighed Peli raising herself up on her hooves. "I do not want for you to die. Leave now with me."

"Dear Peli, my horn is become bound to the destiny of the blue gold swords worn by Fahseed, Lyons, and Maryeta. I must prevail so that my captain can, in all these valleys, ensure safety for the unicorns."

"Powerful men lust for the magic horns of the unicorns," responded Peli. "Your leader is *only* a man. Can Fahseed be unlike the human race entire?"

"Trueness courses through his heart. For that reason the magic of a blue gold sword is connective to him, and to his grandchildren. Sometimes I think that the goodness in Fahseed exceeds the goodness found in me. Peli, I promise you that I will not permit my captain to be corrupted."

"I go now, Briarburr." A wing stretched out to caress the blackmane. "After the next nightfall I will return to you. In this dangerous time you must be very careful."

"Wait Peli. I have to tell you that... my ever hope was to see you again... and tonight my dream came true. But Peli, you are with me too serious. I still have not seen you to smile. Someday I will see you kicking up your hooves and running free along the seashore, with me by your side."

Wings extended wide as she trotted to launch herself into sky.

Maryeta in Flight

Moments after awakening to the sound of quickening hooves, she shot from out the shadows. Jumping long and high her hands caught hold the mane of the winged horse. Peli was startled to suddenly, for the first time ever, find someone clung to her neck.

The winged horse turned her head to see that the hands holding her mane belonged to a girl. Before Peli fully knew what was happening the girl had bounced herself upon her back. Gaining the air the winged horse flew many wing spans higher. Upon achieving both speed and altitude, the bucking Peli dove fast to unseat the girl. Tumbling off, the girl fell backwards towards the ground. Instinctively the winged horse dove after her. It took only a moment for Peli to regain the falling girl who again came to clasp hold of the horse with wings.

"You should not be set upon my back! When you jumped on me without even asking if you could... you scared me."

"After you bucked me off, you flew back to rescue me! You saved me!"

"When I glimpsed the frightened look in your eyes, I could not ignore your plight. The fall to the ground would have killed you, and it would have been *all your fault*. You do not know how to ride me. I am going to land back to earth before you fall off me, next time all by yourself!"

"I should not have scared you by jumping onto you without even saying hello. Since that time I saw you when I was little, I wanted with you to fly. Please do not make me to dismount. I always said that you are the most beautiful horse in the world. What is your name?"

"My name is Peli. Since you understand my neighs you must be the one called Maryeta. *Nyaauughhehheerr!* All right, my wings will take you for a little ride. You are not afraid to fly high?"

"With you I would fly all the way to the stars! You need not worry Peli, I will hold on tight. And I have another question for you. I once told my grandfather that I would someday ask if you liked to eat barley. Do you?"

"Barley is tastier than wheat."

The two flew upward and then more upward. Below them the nighttime fortress faded from view. They flew above the mountain peaks that loomed over the western edge of the valley still ruled by Lord Vylas.

"Ahead of us, is that dark shadowy place the sea?"

"It is, Maryeta, where begins the sea."

"On a high place Briarburr once pointed out the coast line to my brother and me. I have never walked by the sea. *Please* take me there. I want to see if the sea really does taste of salt."

"If you drink sea water the salt will make your stomach to hurt. Oh, all right. I will take you there so that you can splash drops of sea water onto your tongue. We cannot stay long, for I have to get you back before you are missed." The wings of Peli spread wide to carry Maryeta to the salted sea.

"Agghhkk! This is... *awful!*" exclaimed Maryeta grimacing. "Can all of this wide water taste of salt?" She ran to the winged horse, gave her a big hug, and said, "Thank you, thank you Peli for bringing me to the seashore. There is so much water in the sea. See that over there? At night the fringes of waves sparkle white as they splash against the shore." Rubbing the neck of the winged horse, Maryeta added, "My mother wanted me to see the ocean, and I may never have the chance to come here again." The girl cajoled, "Please Peli, can we go swimming?" Soon they were.

"A beautiful winged horse swims beside me! And watches over me!" exclaimed Maryeta. Her next request was to linger seated on the seashore.

"All right, Maryeta. The night is still young enough, and a rest would do me well." Wrapping arms about the neck of the horse, the girl let fall her long wet hair on Peli's thick mane. A horse wing moved to cover the girl's legs.

"From before, do you *remember* me?"

"I never forgot seeing you fall from out of a tree. But it is still hard for me to believe that scrawny little girl... was you."

"When I and my brother Lyons spied on you and Briarburr by the waterfall, you were so beautiful to see. Your wings looked so soft. To think that I now rest against the very wings that I long ago saw from my favorite tree."

"Was it you that found the blue gold I sensed behind the waterfall?"

"Lyons found the cave; I found the layer of gold sand below the pool in the cave. We remembered that you looked like you were seeing something behind the waterfall. Only we thought you were looking at the close cataract, when you were really looking at the far one."

"More than the promise of blue gold, I remember Briarburr. Although he looked half starved, his hips were built powerfully. I knew he would grow to be a very fast unicorn. But Briarburr smelled bad. I kicked him because he nipped at me, and also because he needed a bath."

"Hah! I also thought he needed a bath." After giggling and yawning big, Maryeta fell fast asleep.

Peli did not know what to think of the reckless girl that had bounded out of the night to grab hold her mane. She told herself she should wake the girl, but she liked feeling the warmth of the girl's slender body against her neck.

"This girl has known a life hard," rhummed Peli softly. "Although at such a tender age she fights with a blue gold sword, her heart remains wrapped in pure innocence. I would that there were more human persons as pure, brave, and spontaneous as this girl named Maryeta."

The head of Peli jerked up. Her ears flicked forward, backward, again forward. It surely was the sound of horse hooves. To her nostrils carried a scent of unicorns.

"Imagine the good luck this night of Maryeta. She is about to meet young unicorn stallions that unlike

Briarburr and me, have no black markings." The sounds of hooves grew near.

"Wake up, Maryeta," neighed Peli nudging the girl. A sleepy head straightened up. The girl rubbed her eyes, and then her eyes grew large.

"Unicorns! And they are *pure white!*"

Upon finding the winged horse waiting for them, the unicorn stallions snorted in happy surprise.

"This is Maryeta, who this night would look upon the sea. She is doubly favored to meet eight young unicorn stallions. Girl, climb on my back. With these youngsters you and I are going to run the beach!" For Maryeta the gallop was splendid.

Breathing hard after their race over sand, the stallions were curious. Maryeta explained that her grandfather was fighting tyrants to make the seacoast and valleys of Phoenicia belong to farmers and fishermen, not to men that built fortresses and took away the freedom of peasants. Before long all the stallions knew the whole story of Maryeta, Lyons, and Briarburr.

"Even though he has a black mane and black marks on his hide, I know in my heart that Briarburr is a gallant unicorn," neighed the winged horse. "I hope the blackmane and his captain win their upcoming battle. In every part of Phoenicia, Fahseed has promised to protect unicorns."

"We tire of running in fear for our lives," neighed the biggest stallion. "If only there was one tribe of men to procure us safety in their land." The stallion reared high and boxed his front legs at an invisible adversary.

He next neighed to his companion stallions, that in return voiced their agreement and nodded heads vigorously.

"We go to fight with Briarburr," neighed the big leader stallion turning to Maryeta. "In two days our hooves will trod the valley of the besieged garrison." Away from the sea the unicorn stallions were off galloping.

"Maryeta, we must quickly fly back to Briarburr."

As tenuous slivers of light filtered into night sky to paint delicate copper hues into an east edge of heaven, Peli alighted a second time inside the fortress. Briarburr was immediately at her side. Maryeta jumped down and hugged as hard as she could the neck of the black marked unicorn.

"Briarburr, I tasted the salty sea! Can you believe that Peli took me to the immense water? And you will never believe who is coming to join us. In two days you are to meet eight unicorn stallions that are now on their way here to help you do battle. I am the luckiest girl in all this land!"

"Really?" neighed Briarburr. "Eight unicorn stallions? Then, my girl, you have brought luck also to me. I am to meet unicorn stallions whose hides are not like mine. I hope that they are not disappointed in my black markings."

"Noble Briarburr, disappointment cannot attend to one as courageous as you." That said, Maryeta curled herself on the ground and was fast asleep.

A restless Fahseed walked predawn inspection of the garrison. In surprise genuine he exclaimed, "By heavens! I see a... it is the winged horse!"

"Captain," neighed Briarburr, "in two days eight unicorn stallions will join us in our fight. They harbor the lively hope that soon they will no longer gallop in fear. They dare to dream that unicorns found in this land will one day come to know peace."

"Good... better than good... excellent!" Rubbing his unkempt beard Fahseed added, "That means that two days from now we commit to attack the overlords who outside these walls grow daily in strength."

CHAPTER 19

LORD AULDHAM'S CODE

Cavour had had enough of the whining of the three overlords seated with him. The more at their campfire they drank, the less educated and more impolite became the grousing and carping directed at the upstart Fahseed. Cavour decided that new battle was difficult enough without overlaying it with depression infectious, and that the camaraderie of his men was preferred to the dour mood pervading the conversation of Vylas and the other two overlords. For that, Cavour went in search of a campfire more inviting.

"How fares Lord Cavour on this starry night?" greeted a wiry sergeant well liked by his men.

"I will fare better here with you than seated elsewhere."

"Sir, you are most welcome. You caught me, and the members of my platoon gathered with me this night, enjoying some innocent merriment at the expense of our host Lord Vylas. Mind you, no harm was intended."

"Do not stop on my account. You and I both know that it does not suit to wear heavy hearts into battle. That is a lesson I this night failed to teach three overlords."

A cup of wine was brought to Cavour.

"I was just commenting that it was a terrible thing to witness the theft of the robe of Sir Vylas," offered the sergeant. "Theft is bad enough, but when you think about it... the *robe-ery* of a frilly robe is more injurious than the robbery of a man's purse."

"Well," continued Cavour with the spirit of the moment, "to wear something so frilly would for me be... *silly*." Laughter ensued. The men liked that Cavour was willing to poke wholesome fun at a fellow ruler.

After scratching his brow, the sergeant's face lit up. He rejoined, "I say it will be the *jobe* of Lord Vylas to recover his own... robe." More laughter followed with looks to Cavour to continue the merriment.

"And I say, sergeant, that a *robe-ery*... makes a mockery of robbery."

"Let me respond, Lord Cavour, that poverty can lead to robbery but... *robe-ery* is pure snobbery."

"In response to that, sergeant, I say that robbery is chicanery but... *robe-ery* is foppery."

Cavour set down his empty cup, grinned at the men about him sporting wide smiles, and said, "Well, I think the matter is for me now settled. I go to find Lord Auldham. Know you his whereabouts?" The fifth overlord was found seated where Cavour was told he would be.

"Lord Auldham, it is said that you still bear a grievous wound from the recent battles that beset your valley. However, you look well. The other overlords are at the fire of Lord Vylas. How sit you at this fire, alone?"

"Let me assure you that seated on a horse, with a sword in my hand, my wound is of no consequence. As for the other matter, I care little for the company of Vylas or the two overlords with him. Those three disgrace the authority of all overlords."

"Lord Auldham, I did not know you to be so forthright."

"In voicing my opinion I have little to lose, at least not with you. I have tried to model my authority after the rule of your valley, not after the rule of any of those gathered at the fire of Vylas."

"And how has that worked for you, Auldham?"

"Far from perfectly. Every day I am called upon to settle vexatious disputes. In one village an insult leads to bloodshed. I am required in another village to find a remedy for jealousy. In another place there is betrayal to inherit a father's property. I will confess that at the end of most days I find myself discouraged. Rather than settling the quarrels of my people, I would be anywhere else. Of course, Cavour, you know these things; you as well are both ruler and judge."

As the fire began to ebb, shadows borne of diminishing flames changed more subtle.

"Err... hmm. Can I be as forthright with you, as you are with me?"

"Certainly so, Cavour."

"Auldham, why are you now found in this place? From what you just said I find it difficult to believe you came here simply because I requested you to."

"Actually, Cavour, I have wondered about that myself."

"You are not only young, Auldham, you are strong and intelligent. Your clear eyes and wavy hair must have caught the notice of eligible young ladies. Surely you have someone gentle with whom you could be this night sharing your burdens?"

"No Cavour, at least not yet," answered Auldham with his face taking on an open and pleasant smile. "I have, unfortunately, found little time for romance." The face of Auldham changed to wear a look serious. "As you are aware, Cavour, it was not so long ago that I put an end to the strife that overtook my valley. From that rebellion many scars remain still. The worst to happen is when families divide, and brothers come to fight against each other."

The young ruler expelled a deep breath and added, "Perhaps Cavour, the rebellion is the reason I am here. As you know, at my side my father fell in battle. Upon taking his place I slowly turned impending defeat into victory. Having preserved the rulership of my valley, my father would have wanted me come here to defend Vylas. Were he seated now with us, I would hear my father tell you that there is no reason to replace one tyranny with another. It is strange, Cavour. I find that I obey my father's wishes more now that he is dead, than I did when he was alive."

Auldham handed Cavour a piece of bread.

"They say that Fahseed has the magic of the blackmaned unicorn on his side. As for me, Cavour, I believe little in superstition and magic. And I ask you, what if the so-called powerful magic of the unicorns someday turns to evil? Begun well enough, many rulers end badly. The chances are that even if Fahseed prevails upon us in the battle to come, and goes on to rule in the place of Vylas and the fallen Baltric, the conqueror will end up a worse tyrant than the two he displaced."

"I hear what you say, Auldham. In their lust for power I too have seen many supposedly good men turn bad. Do you know that you restore my faith in our system of governance? There is nothing better for this land than that a good man, or woman for that matter, is made to be ruler. By the same token a greedy and arrogant overlord is a terrible thing to befall a valley."

"Cavour, I am finding that the most essential requirement of authority is for a ruler to show compassion. At the same time that my strength and discipline are perceived by my subjects, they should also know that I want well for them. Although this may sound strange to you, I try to see each of my subjects, even the most deplorable as a mother, father, brother, or sister. When I ride my horse through a village, under my breath I say *bless you* to every crippled man, ragged child, disgraced woman, and person unfortunate that I come upon. We both know that life is hard. It is best if we neighbor with one another, help each other, and wish one another well."

"It sounds like you want us each to show love to our neighbors."

"Cavour, love is more procurative of the human spirit than is envy or hate."

"Auldham, I give thanks when in a village work is to be found. Work is restorative of the spirit. It does my heart good to see a whole village to prosper. I too believe in fairness and wishing another well. I too worry that if Vylas is overthrown, the one that comes after will be worse than the one that went before. Hah! Can you believe that this strife was born of a man's love for two orphan grandchildren wanted to be taken and sold by Baltric in the market?"

"What?" Auldham gave a penetrating look to Cavour. "*That...* I did not know. Why on earth would any child be taken to be sold? Let children be only loved. That touches the point, Cavour. Love has to do with how I treat my subjects. When paying my tax they would of course laugh at what I just said. But, think on it. Love of our subjects has to do with you and me being here. From what you now tell me of two persecuted grandchildren, that same idea of love has also to do with Fahseed and the blackmaned unicorn taking here a stand against us."

With both hands Auldham rubbed his wounded leg.

"One thing more Cavour, when we defeat Fahseed I will speak that the outlaw be shown mercy. It seems that at the hands of Baltric he already suffered enough. Let Fahseed and his grandchildren be exiled and not killed. Cavour, I will need you to back me on that."

"Auldham, I commend you for having that sentiment. But you do know that by asking that mercy be shown to Fahseed you, or rather we both will inspire the enmity of Vylas."

"I now look forward to meeting this grandfather that has caused us so much tumult."

"You and I surely shall, Auldham, and soon.

"When this battle is done I want nothing more than to be left apart from Vylas. But mark my words, after the conflict is over an act of generosity and love for our defeated fellow man... can win the peace."

"I had not thought about winning the peace. With all the dreadful fighting that takes place, is not the issue of war already enough complex? Now you tell me I have to not only win battle after battle and stay alive, but that I also have to survive for the purpose of winning the peace."

"You know perfectly well, Cavour, that the issues of war and its aftermath are deeply intertwined." Both men came to their feet.

"Auldham, you limp more badly than I was told."

"My injury does this night seem to worsen. Like I said before, when mounted on a horse my limp does not deter the hand holding my sword."

"May all go well with you, Auldham."

"Let us meet again soon. By the way Cavour, a man better on his horse than I, did this hurt to me. When recovered from the wounds he in return received from me, I put him to work in my stable. My former enemy, now become friend, makes me to be a better horseman."

"A rebel that wounded me would rot in jail!" exclaimed Cavour.

"Consider that my love for that enemy has turned him into a friend."

"Hmph! What you just said about showing love to an enemy, is difficult for me to comprehend," responded Cavour.

Auldham began to hobble toward his tent. He stopped, turned around, and again approached Cavour.

"Before you came to join my campfire, something about the looming battle troubled me enough to write down some names. For that, Cavour, before you depart there is one thing else. Between the burial places of my father and grandfather there is room to dig graves for me, and on some distant day for my younger brother." Auldham held out a scrap of parchment. "Cavour, these four men will see to it."

A young ruler limped haltingly into darkness.

CHAPTER 20

UNICORN STALLIONS

On the night following the return of Maryeta from the seacoast, Colyado came to wake Fahseed from a deep sleep.

"Sorry to disturb your rest, Captain. But you must see this."

The still fully dressed Fahseed straightened to sit on the side of his cot.

"I was standing guard on the walkway, when to my surprise, no more than an arm's length from where I stood an arrow lodged into the wall. My first instinct was to duck down. But when no more arrows came I became curious and grabbed this arrow that I now hold. You see that its point is made of blue gold, and that on the shaft is tied a message."

"So it is of course from Elyeazar. Let me see that. Hmph! The message reads that a company of archers is now hidden on a ledge that overlooks the eastern edge of the valley of Vylas."

"The accuracy of the message arrow was fortunately very precise. Otherwise I would have right now an arrow in my chest."

"Neither you nor I can say how far flew that arrow," replied Fahseed.

"It turns out that as well as a sword blade, an arrow head forged of blue gold is very magical."

"This news, Colyado, is to us advantageous. Elyeazar heard that we had come to be besieged in the garrison of Vylas. He put two and two together, and concluded that we will have to break out of the garrison. He brought a company of archers to provide us a welcome element of surprise against the despot overlords."

"Captain, it appears that Elyeazar used well his time back in Byblos to improve the marksmanship of peasant archers. Some farmers before had difficulty making an arrow to hit the trunk of a big tree."

"It may be," offered Fahseed scratching the top of his head, "that Elyeazar's company of archers has come to include fellows from beyond our village. The news of our capture of this garrison surely spread like a wildfire. Like you, Colyado, our friend Elyeazar is a man that inspires confidence. I want to think that Elyeazar's archers will be more than men from Byblos alone."

"I hope you are right, Captain."

"Although they now surround us, and many times outnumber us, the overlords cannot prevent a resolute charge from out this garrison. We will, Colyado, push the coming battle toward the position of Elyeazar."

Against Five Overlords

Built by Merlew to swing smoothly, the garrison gates opened fast. Ten men and one girl armed with blue gold swords led the cavalry charge from out the garrison. The twelfth magic sword worn at the waist of Elyeazar was concealed on the east side of the valley ruled by Lord Vylas.

The sight of eleven magic swords leading the cavalry charge lessened the resolve of enemy ranks to stand their ground and fight. The surge of Fahseed's soldiers hit hard the center of the overlords' combined cavalry. The stallions running at the side of Briarburr were as formidable as they were on the day when the blackmaned unicorn fell; they made sure that this time their leader would not become ensnared by a trip rope.

Just as Fahseed had said would happen, the blocking line of the enemy did not hold. The charge of the rebel force pushed back the soldiers now found under the command of Cavour. However, the enemy numbered far too many to go down in quick defeat.

Slowly but surely Cavour returned his cavalry to offense. The forces of the overlords began to close on all sides. The badly outnumbered rebel army was about to be surrounded.

"Retreat, retreat, turn back!" shouted Fahseed.

Over ground just won the rebel army fought its way back. However, in retreat their captain led them not toward the garrison they had left. In the lead, Fahseed rode full-out toward a prominent rock rim on the eastern side of the valley of Vylas.

When Briarburr broke to run westward away from the strife, the soldiers of the overlords paid scant attention to the departure of the black marked unicorn that they now concluded to be cowardly.

"Fahseed too easily turned back from his charge," muttered Cavour to himself. "The outlaw leader must have a trick up his sleeve. He wants us to falsely think he is fleeing back to the valley from which he came. I will talk this over with the other overlords." Cavour slowed his mount and held up an arm to signal halt to the cavalry he commanded.

"We have them in our grasp! Follow me to victory!" Waving his arms while he shouted to the cavalry, Vylas galloped past Cavour to brazenly usurp command. Soon finding himself at the rear of what had been his army, no one paid attention to the voice of Cavour warning from behind, "It is a trap! The change in battle was too easy! Fahseed only *wants* us to think that he flees from us!"

Upon reaching the cliffs that marked the eastern boundary of the valley, the warriors led by Fahseed turned and looked to hesitate, as if uncertain how to contend with the onslaught of the fast approaching enemy force.

As he rode with bravado and bluster at the front of the overlords' cavalry, Lord Vylas menaced the wind with his sword. From his vantage point on a ledge jutting up from the plain, Elyeazar watched the enraged face of Vylas come into focus. Finding its mark, an arrow with a head forged of blue gold sliced through the neck of the overlord. The ruler of the valley slumped over; his body rolled off his horse. No matter; the horses of enemy soldiers continued to race headlong at the cavalry of Fahseed. Whirring arrows brought new hurt to the overlords' cavalry.

Upon Fahseed's signal half of his cavalry broke right and the other half broke left. Both halves turned to encircle the oncoming enemy soldiers. The two armies had changed position. The army of five overlords was now penned against ledges and cliffs. Formed by thirty-some cavalrymen and the company of thirty riderless stallions, the thin line of Fahseed would seek to hold before them the still formidable enemy force.

Retaking command, Cavour moved his men to the protective shelter of overhanging rocks, and so beyond the reach of the archers of Elyeazar. Pause came to the fight. Before Cavour would again pursue the rebel force he would have his army to hear him.

"Men, during long years I was careful with my purse. For that, the floor of my treasury room is stacked high with coins. Every man that captures and brings to me a blue gold sword will receive double the blade's weight in purest gold. What think you of the exchange of a hefty bag of gold coins for a captured sword?"

Several times came cheers for Cavour. Mercenaries at heart, the soldiers could not help but approve the idea of rich reward in return for success in battle.

"You will only once be given this opportunity!" continued the overlord as he walked his horse before his cavalry. "What matters most is the destruction of those wielding blue gold swords! Do this, and your valor will long be remembered!

"Since we are many and the enemy is few, do not all attack at once and so get in each other's way. Focus your attack on each bearer of a magic sword. If two soldiers fall, two more will step up and fight on. I want orderly execution of my tactics. Keep the pressure of your swords upon the enemy. Now let us renew a fight that promises you rich reward!"

Absent Briarburr, the company of riderless stallions fought unaccountably inspired. Still, the cavalry of Fahseed and the now leaderless stallions of Briarburr could not for long keep hundreds of enemy soldiers before them. In contested retreat, the bearers of the eleven blue gold swords slowly gave ground.

When Cavour's horse gained entry to the position of Lyons, the youth found he faced a different kind of soldier, one far more experienced and expert that fought with a sword in each hand. The great skill of his opponent offset the magic of the blue gold blade wielded by the exhausted Lyons.

"Help, I need *help!*" yelled the youth. Nor Fahseed nor Maryeta could break away from the engagement of their adversaries.

"Damn! Lyons faces Cavour!" shouted the lieutenant as he spurred his horse to answer the plea. The two-sworded overlord turned to face Abel. When with his left arm Cavour lunged, the right handed lieutenant parried the move. In a motion begun a moment after his first thrust, the sword held in Cavour's right hand shoved to cut deep the left shoulder of Abel. The overlord let loose his second sword to dangle in the sinews of the lieutenant. Cavour whirled his horse about and threw his remaining sword to penetrate the side of a youth momentarily frozen by the sight of Abel wounded. Lyons collapsed down in his saddle. Pulling Cavour's sword from his shoulder, Abel propelled his horse to tumble down and trample a now swordless Cavour.

"I have you!" said Abel grabbing hold the youth. "Do not let fall your magic sword!" Two hands clung to a magic sword made useless to a horribly wounded Lyons.

Maryeta wheeled her horse to approach Abel with Lyons cradled in his arms. As Abel spurred his horse to gallop away in flight he yelled, "Girl, follow me! We must save your brother!" The horses of the lieutenant and Maryeta broke away from the fray.

Behind a slowly retreating line of blue gold swordsmen, ordinary cavalry, and Briarburr's leaderless stallions, Abel carried off Lyons. Unconcerned for his own wound, the lieutenant needed to find a place where he and Maryeta could bandage the deeply cut youth.

Jumping off his horse, the lieutenant gently lifted Lyons down. Quenching the flux of blood, Maryeta began to dress the wound of her brother. While she busied herself nursing, the girl seemed to possess a sixth sense. Without looking up she said, "I have never been so glad to find Briarburr galloping towards me."

Looking to the west Abel exclaimed, "Following Briarburr run not eight, but I count... twenty unicorns in a line!"

"I know that it is a sight glorious to see," replied Maryeta.

"Unicorns... will win... this battle..." With those words Lyons lost consciousness.

At breakneck speed, Briarburr and the line of unicorn horses galloped past where knelt Maryeta at the side of Lyons. The lieutenant raised his horn and blew the sequence of notes signifying the arrival of reinforcements. Combatants on each side of the fight turned heads toward the majestic line of unicorn stallions running full-out toward them. While cheers resounded from the men fighting for Fahseed, soldiers in the army of Cavour grew faint of heart. Unicorn stallions pushed back the foe.

In retreat the soldiers of the overlords were forced toward the position of Elyeazar's archers. When newly sent arrows fell to wound harshly the enemy, the battle became a rout. The trap laid for the army of the overlords persuaded no chance of escape. Having suffered enough, swords fell and hands raised high in surrender. The *Battle of the Unicorn Stallions* came to a sudden end.

Accompanied by two unicorns, Briarburr was soon at the side of Lyons. From three magic horns healing sparked forth.

"Thanks to the charge of unicorn stallions," said Fahseed stroking the mane of Briarburr, "the tide of battle changed to favor us. And thanks to the healing power of unicorn horns, my grandson will live on."

Fahseed turned to address Abel, "I once said the day would come when you in battle would save my life. Because Lyons has three times the number of years remaining to him as do I, what you did is valued by me thrice more than had you rescued... me."

"Harnessed with invisible reins of magic," answered Abel, "the unicorns fought as a twenty horse team. It was a wonder to watch them."

"For the first time in my life," neighed in response the blackmane, "I feel myself to belong to the herd of unicorns."

"Grandpa, we were saved by the unicorn stallions who befriended me on the beach," offered Maryeta. "I do not understand how even in battle they move their legs and bodies with so much grace and beauty. It is almost as if they dance while their hooves do battle."

"Come with me Briarburr, for I *need* you."

Fahseed and the blackmaned unicorn reached the place where Cavour lay bleeding. Understanding what was wanted of him, Briarburr touched his horn to the body of the terribly wounded overlord. The spirit of Cavour walked no more toward the grave.

That night while with unity of purpose unicorns guarded the prisoners, Fahseed sat exhausted by a campfire.

"We came today as close to losing a battle as we could have, without so doing," said Abel seating himself with his captain.

"Without reinforcement or recourse the thin line of my cavalry and the riderless stallions had to hold. Cut off from escape into the mountains, our men were forced to stand and fight. Carrying the utmost risk, that deliberate tactic inspired discipline and unity. Thank the heavens that when my army bent, it did not break."

Fahseed looked to where lay the wounded Cavour. "Hmph, he almost killed the boy I hold so dear to my heart. Still, strangely enough, for that I cannot hate Cavour. We all had heard that the swords of Cavour had never been bested. Abel, today I myself saw that Cavour knows not only how to command his two swords, he knows how to command men. In battle Cavour is worth *ten Baltrics.*"

"And... my archers today did their part."

Rising to stand, the commander grasped firmly the shoulders of his old friend and said, "Welcome, and well done Elyeazar. I would not have believed such marksmanship could come from villagers shooting arrows. Without your archers we could not have remained in the battle."

"And without the charge of the unicorn stallions, we would not have won the day," answered Elyeazar.

At middle night Lyons lay clasped in the arms of his grandfather. An exhausted Maryeta lay beside them asleep. The boy stirred; the look in his eyes suggested that something more than his fast healing wound troubled him.

"Grandfather, I do not understand. You said that the magical power of the unicorns came from their purity and love for creation, and that the magic gold was different for it had to do with verity and truth. I was sure that as long as my heart was true, my hand on the blue gold sword would not falter, but it did."

"You are right. I did say that. I am certain that the power of the spiraled horn weaves from the innocence, virtue, and love found within the unicorns. And my own grandfather told me that truth is core to the power of blue gold, and to false men no benefit from the magic gold obtains.

"So, Lyons, I too could not fathom that your blue gold sword could be vanquished by an ordinary sword. It can only be that the heart of Cavour is strangely true. It came to you to withstand a mighty enemy whose heart and mind are noble. You, my grandson, were very brave. On this night you remain still at the side of Maryeta, and at my side. That is all that matters."

Looking to where rested Cavour in the improvised camp hospital, Lyons added, "The man that wounded me is not like Baltric, who was a bad man. Because someone is my enemy does not mean that he is evil. May Cavour from his wounds, recover."

Maryeta awakened, and when she did it seemed that she was somehow aware of the entire conversation between Lyons and his grandfather. She said simply, "I could not stand for my enemy to be a better person than me."

"That, dear Granddaughter, will not happen for it is not... *possible* to happen."

"I knew my sister only pretended to be asleep. Her ears hear everything."

"I can sleep and at the same time listen. I am a very proficient girl."

Finding himself later to be troubled and sleepless, Fahseed distracted himself by fingering the blade of his blue gold sword. As once before done, he found himself speaking as if from outside of himself.

"The magic Fahseed holds in his hands has to do with trueness and rightness. He has no doubt that the heart of his wounded grandson is better than his own heart. In this battle Fahseed killed brutishly. Can that mean that someday Fahseed's heart will not measure up to the purity required by the sword held in his two hands?"

CHAPTER 21

CAVOUR OBEDIENT

Standing before overlord soldiers made to be prisoners, and a large pile of confiscated swords, Fahseed motioned for Cavour to approach. The miraculously healed overlord came forward and before his vanquisher knelt down on one knee. Cavour laid gently, one could even say tenderly, two beautifully made swords in the hands of Fahseed. They were placed with a look that suggested that Cavour would never again see his beautiful and trusted cutlasses.

"Within our greater numbers my men purposed to trap you," said the fallen overlord looking up at the victor. "We instead fell into a trap by me unpurposed."

"Rise. How hurtful are your wounds?" answered Fahseed.

"When Lieutenant Abel knocked me to the ground the hooves of his horse cut me deeply. I felt something to burst inside; pain overwhelmed me. Thanks to the healing power of Briarburr, I find myself today remade."

"Walk with me," said Fahseed hefting one of Cavour's swords in each hand. "I know it was not you, but Vylas that led your men to fall into the trap I prepared. There occurred to Vylas the misguided thought that I was fleeing battle to return to Byblos. I have formed the idea that you would not so easily have fallen into my trap. Here lie together the bodies of

Vylas and three overlords. While those despots worry me no more you, Cavour, do concern me. You can prove to me useful."

Cavour stepped to where lay the body of Auldham.

"By my sword he died," said Fahseed quietly. "It is strange, but I sensed that my blue gold sword was reluctant to take his life. I could make no headway against Auldham, and I did not understand why the magic of my sword was resistant in the fight. When Auldham turned to see the approach of the unicorn stallions he lowered his sword, and so gave me an opening. I took it."

"The heart of so sensitive a young man as Auldham could not but have been impressed by the grandeur of the charging line of unicorns. He knew then that the battle was over." Cavour looked closely into the eyes of Fahseed and added, "I would that you had come to know Lord Auldham. He told me he wanted to meet you, and so he did. That is, he made acquaintance with your magical sword. I truly hate that Auldham fell. Of the five overlords here, including myself, he was the best. Errhrm... Auldham believed that after the strife of war ended," continued Cavour swiping the palm of a hand at his eyes, "that one could actually come to love a former enemy. That is a difficult idea for me to grasp. Hold you that same belief, Fahseed?"

"Until now Cavour, I cannot say that I do. Perhaps a former foe, one true of heart, will come to change my mind on that matter."

"Auldham gave me these names," said Cavour handing a scrap of parchment to Fahseed. "He said these four men knew where to dig a grave between where lay buried his father and grandfather. If his body were to be tightly wrapped in a thick blanket, Auldham could be carried to long rest with his ancestors."

"Some men know when their time has come. Surely Auldham knew this would be his last battle. Cavour, I will see to it." For long moments the two men continued silent before the body of the young overlord.

"Cavour, I am going to raise a new land, one no longer ruled by overlords that each claim a small piece of this country. I will have to be built a capital city that we can all, every one of us, be proud of. You will see come the day when the ships of Phoenicia own the sea off our coast. I now offer to you an opportunity that you could not expect. Join this day these two swords to the new and triumphant army of Phoenicia. If you join me, I will do something that astonishes your men. I will make you to be a general in my army."

The fallen overlord bowed his head in thought. His lower jaw slowly thrust out. Shaking about his red hair, he nodded slowly up and down his head. Cavour straightened.

"Sir, the time in my life has come for me to do full justice. This former overlord will become to a blacksmith obedient. I accept the terms of your clemency." That said the new general saluted.

Fahseed held out the swords that had shortly before been relinquished. "I now officially return these to Cavour. The day will come that you find yourself to be much renowned."

"Sir Fahseed, a few moments ago I was considering the impact my decision would have on others, and on the shedding of blood that before us waits. To convince the proud Cavour to change sides, is not a small thing. My joining you will cause other overlords, and mind you their sergeants as well, to consider again who really is this Fahseed. My joining you will lessen the resistance that you and I are to now face together. But... the success of my enlistment requires that you leave not goodness behind.

"Auldham journeyed here to support a man he despised. He did that because he had before seen that the overthrow of an overlord most often brings to rule a worse tyrant. In that regard I require that you never betray nor yourself, nor me, nor the ghost of Auldham." Cavour heaved a big sigh and added, "The man whose body lies before us would have wanted me to join you. I do this as much for Lord Auldham, as for myself."

"I promise, General Cavour, that I will not abandon myself. You make perfectly clear that I am not permitted to so do."

The two returned to stand before the pile of confiscated weapons. When Abel's horn sounded, Fahseed straightened his posture to address the defeated enemy soldiers.

"A new start, a second chance is a precious thing that seldom favors the life of a soldier. Cavour will select for my army only those that merit that new beginning. Those of you that join to me will each moon receive pay in silver. In exchange you, the same as me, will obey the laws of the new country we together build. Those not worthy to serve under the command of Cavour and myself are to be led to the coast, and from Phoenicia there exiled."

"To fulfill your request I need the help of your big lieutenant," said Cavour turning to Fahseed. "I do not dislike that he has an intimidating aspect. It takes more than a little courage to stare down Abel." Informed of his new duty the lieutenant began immediately to question one by one the defeated soldiers. Cavour and Abel chose almost half of the prisoners to become new comrades-in-arms. That task accomplished, the two approached Fahseed. Cavour motioned his head toward the lieutenant. Fahseed understood the unspoken question and nodded assent.

"Lieutenant Abel, gather men to go with you and Cavour in escort of the prisoners departing Phoenicia. Return soon. Cavour, you and I have much to accomplish before laying siege to the valleys to the south."

The Former Garrison of Vylas

It was time for Elyeazar and his archers to return to safeguard the village of Byblos. In his arms Fahseed held a farewell gift for his loyal friend.

"What in the world am I to do with this... frilly robe?"

"It might wave over the new second wall of Byblos."

"But what if in middle night someone runs off with this fancy robe... that is no doubt very expensive?" inquired Elyeazar.

"Given that for this frilly robe nothing was by us paid, its theft would not be a monstrous loss to our little town."

"I before told you that if you require us to stay and fight with you, that is what my archers shall do."

"You must, Elyeazar, safeguard the place where the rebellion began. Remember my promise to the outspoken petite lady that scolded my return to Byblos. If more harm came to her village, she would never forgive me."

"Ah, yes. I have come to know her well. From her I have learned that no matter how well my job is done, I cannot please everyone."

The day came for the winged horse to accompany Fahseed, Briarburr, Maryeta, and Lyons in a solemn burial detail. The unicorn horns that had once crowned the corners of the garrison of Vylas were to be laid to eternal rest. The place selected for burial had trees on one side; an open view of far mountains graced the opposite side. Other than fallen leaves, grass, sunlight, and wind, over the grave of the once magic horns no marker was placed to honor their remembrance.

"Grandfather, this land will soon become home to many unicorns," offered Maryeta." I am proud of you for protecting horses so noble, possessed of magic so pure."

"To keep the unicorns safe I will long need the help of you, your brother, the blackmane, and a winged horse."

CHAPTER 22

ABEL'S NEXT IDEA

Whether in offensive or defensive engagement, when Fahseed commanded only forty every soldier knew well each other's position of duty. However, his new army had grown too fast for his soldiers to know how to coordinate together as a cohesive unit. In spite of the drills and training overseen by Cavour, something was lacking. Something new was needed for military prowess to grow. The fortress in a valley to the south, the place selected for the next battle, was known to be an imposing garrison. Fahseed was not yet ready to go south.

"Abel, you find me troubled. Not long past most of these soldiers were my former enemies. When the going gets tough I still do not trust them to fight hard alongside of me. Even as I do not trust them, most of my men do not trust each other. Perhaps worse, the loyalty of the standoffish unicorn stallions is given not to me, but to Briarburr. Of course unicorns do not naturally place their trust in men."

"Commander Fahseed," responded Abel, "In lands near and far unicorns are hunted mercilessly. They are a dying breed of horse. It will take time for your company of unicorns to learn to trust you."

"Since you are far more intelligent than your shaved head and fierce demeanor suggest, tell me how

I can unite our brigade so that we fight more for one another than out of obedience to me. Before we depart this place the men and unicorns must not only be prepared, they must be willing to risk death for each other."

"Now that I consume no more than one cup of strong drink a day," Abel smiled slyly at Fahseed, "my mind seems to work better. Mount the wall with me. I want to show you something." The two men soon stood on the high walkway of the former garrison of Lord Vylas.

"Over there," Abel motioned with his arm, "unicorn stallions chase after Briarburr. At play by themselves the unicorns are all speed, athleticism, and loyalty to each other. Below us along the length of this wall, men cheer on two young soldiers running a race against each other."

"Yes, yes, Abel," replied Fahseed. "Instead of racing those men should be drilling."

"Their sergeant would say that they earned a well-deserved break."

"But Abel, instead of playing way over there, the unicorns should be here drilling with my soldiers."

"This is what I propose, Fahseed. Organize something that both horses and men like to do, and also to watch. Proclaim a day of races for the unicorns. The twenty unicorns can run in heats of five; the winner of each heat races in the final. By incorporating into the course obstacles to jump over and posts that the unicorns have to circle, we can make it for them both challenging and fun. The first to return across the starting line will be crowned with garlands. Because speed for them is instinct, organized races will be much to the liking of unicorn stallions. The men, for their part, will be only too happy to cheer on the horned horses."

"We can also, Abel, have horses with riders race against each other. You know what? Your inspiration just might do the trick. Tomorrow my army is given over to... *races*."

A detail led by Abel worked late into the night laying out a course with two separate halves. The return was made difficult by posts, piles of rocks, logs, and branches that unicorns had to scramble around and hurdle over.

Races

Since stallions are nothing if not competitive, each wanted to show that he was the fastest. Soldiers shouted, waved arms, and jumped about as they cheered on their favorite unicorn. Everyone thought Briarburr would win the day. However, on his approach to the starting line he pulled up lame, and so withdrew before beginning his heat. Strangely enough, as soon as he was no more in the competition his lameness cured itself.

For the last unicorn event in which the victors of the four individual heats were matched against each other, the emotions of the spectators ran high. To heighten the drama, for this event the unicorns were to sprint one hundred paces more distant to where a chair was placed for Cavour. After negotiating the return leg beset by many obstacles, the unicorns were to cross a finish line anchored by a chair where sat Fahseed.

Racing off, the four unicorn horses did not slow their hooves until within a stride of Cavour. Crouching hind legs almost to the ground, the unicorns braked their speed while at the same time front hooves pawed a circle around Cavour's chair. After the dust cleared more than one soldier breathed a sigh of relief that both the chair, and Cavour, remained unmoved.

Running again at full speed, at each obstacle they encountered the unicorns fought for the lead. The winning unicorn measured a hand less in height than the other three. Though smaller, the cheering soldiers found his combination of speed and athleticism to be incredible. Hurrahing soldiers surrounded the champion, and as well the three losers.

Unicorns soon joined in neighing cheers for horses with riders racing against each other.

Sporting big smiles Maryeta and Lyons came running. "Grandfather!" exclaimed Lyons. "This is the best holiday!"

"This is the most fun I have ever had!" seconded Maryeta her brother's sentiment. "I just *love* the smell of horses and saddle leather. I will never forget this day!"

"I once saw a girl ride very fast," observed Fahseed scratching his beard in a manner reflective.

"I had to rescue Briarburr after he had fallen."

"Could my granddaughter ride again that fast?"

"If I... *needed* to."

"I think I am catching your drift," said Lyons peering closely at his grandfather.

"Can I and my brother ride horses in a race?"

"You know what?" replied Fahseed still fondling his beard. "That would be splendid. Mind, if you fall off your horses you had better not get hurt. I will need your two magic swords to help win my next battle."

When the race between the two youngsters was announced, a young soldier that had before fought for Vylas, and had just been garlanded as the fastest horseman in the army yelled, "Children *do not* compete in the presence of veteran soldiers!"

Fahseed motioned the complainant to come forward.

"Master Erban, you are a small in frame soldier that stands out bigger than life. You ride very fast a horse. You are also frank and on occasion, even outspoken. I have been given to understand that, for a soldier, you are unusually good at matters of business. So, Erban, you say that as compared to men in our cavalry, my grandchildren are not very good riders?"

"Commander, no matter how good on a horse, children are still... *children*."

"In that case, Lyons and Maryeta will not only compete against each other, but also against a brave warrior on a very fast horse. Erban, you shall race against my grandchildren."

"But Erban won his race. I could never beat him on a horse."

"Brother, you always worry too much. One of us will come through for Grandpa."

"Ready your horses," said **Fahseed** nodding at Lyons, Maryeta, and Erban. "Oh, and Erban if your horse is tired, select a fresh one."

"Sir, for this race against children my horse is *more* than rested."

The Wager of Fahseed

After motioning for soldiers to gather round, the commander proceeded to make the race more entertaining for the rough men in his army.

"Lieutenant Abel, I hereby command you to bring forth the treasury box of Vylas. To our soldiers you are to distribute half of the gold and silver coins contained in the box." Upon hearing that said, hurrahs spread immediately throughout the ranks.

"Sir," remarked Abel cheerily, "it appears that the men unanimously favor getting paid today for their future performance in battle." That said, the lieutenant and Cavour were off trotting. Because the wooden box they hefted weighted very heavy with coins, the pace of their return was notably slower. Abel spread his cloak on the ground, as did also Cavour with his cloak. Men crowded closely to observe the determination of their wages.

The lieutenant grabbed two handfuls of coins from the treasury box. One large hand tumbled coins onto his cloak; the other big hand clunked coins onto the cloak of Cavour. When the wooden box was empty, the mound of coins on Cavour's cloak was transferred back so that the treasury chest contained only half the coins it formerly held.

"Those few men who wish to receive their pay in advance," commanded Abel with a voice made to sound melodious, "are herewith ordered to line up before... *my noble cloak!*"

To each soldier Cavour and Abel distributed six coins. Fahseed was the last to receive his pay. The few coins that remained on Abel's cloak were put back into the treasury box. Cavour and Jomain returned to the fortress a treasury chest made lighter by half.

"Well done, Lieutenant!" complimented Fahseed. "You received not a single complaint about your work. To my mind a proposition now presents. We all recognize the skill of Master Erban with a horse. He is the odds-on favorite to win the race. However, I am going to offer him a generous bet. I will wager my entire salary of six coins against only three of the six coins just given to the champion horseman who is to race against my grandchildren.

"If either Lyons or Maryeta win the race, I gain three coins from Erban. A win for Erban garners him all six of my coins. While from him I can only three coins win, because I win with either of the youth, I have two chances. That makes it good odds for the renowned horseman Master Erban, and also fair odds for me."

Following the out of character example provided by their usually solemn and often ill-humored commander, the idea of wagers spread like wild fire. Dependent upon conviction, the betting odds varied. Six coins on the youth were bet against three or even four coins wagered on Erban. A few men were so confident of the master horseman's equine skills that they went so far as to bet five coins on Erban, against six on Lyons or Maryeta.

The lieutenant was the last to place his bet. He puffed out his chest, extended his lower jaw, squinted his eyes, pouted his lips, and rubbed his shaved head, all to make himself appear even more menacing than normal.

"It comes my turn to make a bet," said Abel combing his full beard with three fingers. "I am so confident of Lyons and Maryeta that I risk my whole salary against only... *one coin!* Understand this well my friends, Lieutenant Abel wagers six coins on the two youth against only one coin against them. While I can lose all six of mine, I can win only one coin. Can there be anyone that will take my bet?"

Hands holding a coin raised up instantly.

"Hahah! I will bet against the man who has arms even bigger than mine!" Upon finding that the arms of the selected young man were not big, but were instead uncommonly skinny, the men hurrahed the humor shown by the imposing lieutenant.

Abel placed six coins at his feet. At the lieutenant's side, Elyir placed one coin before his feet. The slender young man more artist than soldier, that not long before had guarded the fortress gate, seemed to immensely enjoy the attention garnered by his bet of one coin.

For this race of pure speed, Cavour's chair was placed five hundred paces distant from where stood the three horses with their riders. Erban was positioned in the middle spot between Lyons and Maryeta.

"Big Sir," said Abel turning to Elyir, "be you ready to drop your sword to start the race?"

Erban spurred his horse to a very fast start. As Maryeta slowly closed on the leader Lyons did his best to keep pace with his sister. Pushing hard his horse, Erban was the first to circle the chair of Cavour marking the half way point of the race. Hugging with grace and fluidness the neck of her horse, Maryeta continued to gain on Erban. Midway through the return lap the girl made her move. By the length of her horse's head the lead became Maryeta's. Crouched down tightly over his horse's neck, Lyons pressed knees to horse flanks to communicate the need for more speed.

After a too fast start, Erban's horse had little extra energy in reserve. The horse of Erban fell a length behind Maryeta. Lyons made his move, passed the horse of Erban, and slowly but surely gained on the horse ridden by his sister. As they approached the finish line Lyons and Maryeta rode neck and neck. By the length of his horse's nose the race was by Lyons won.

Fahseed and Abel embraced laughing.

Hoisted onto the shoulders of the man he had beaten, Lyons was paraded to accolades of shouting and laughter. A good-natured loser, Erban was accorded nothing but broad smiles. He quipped about the terrible pain he would ever more suffer for losing the most important horse race of his life to not just one, but to two children.

The soldiers that had bet all six coins on the youth carried on with hollers, jumps, and jigs. Those that had lost their wagers did not long complain. The one, two, or three coins that still lined their pockets were one, two, or three more coins than a soldier on almost any other day possessed. The surprise ending to the final race where a boy and a girl bested a great horseman, inspired smiles to glow on the faces of relaxed men gathered that night around camp fires. For the wine made to be dispensed from the cellar of the now forgotten Lord Vylas, the health of Fahseed was roundly toasted.

"That is the best lost wager my brother shall ever know," said Merlew to Erban as they with Elyir hoisted cups at a campfire. "For my part, since I credit Maryeta with saving the lives of Elyir and myself when Abel commandeered the gates of the garrison, I could not bet against the girl."

"So three extra coins now jangle in your pocket?"

"They do at that, Erban. Possessing nine coins makes me feel... almost rich."

"Well then, good for you Merlew," answered Erban. "As for me, the fun I had racing in front of our battalion of soldiers was worth the loss of three coins. And learning now that Maryeta saved the lives of you and your brother, I am even *glad* that the girl bested me."

"If in exchange for my one coin, I and Merlew gained the friendship of the master horseman Erban...

it was indeed worth it. Oh, and here is a wood carving of a horse and rider that I just made for you."

"Elyir, this carving is... *extraordinary*. Thank you. While like you two brothers my frame is skinny, count on my friendship to be thickset. My sword in battle will defend Merlew and Elyir."

On that night new friendships flourished, and unicorns bedded down amongst horses and soldiers.

"How can I ever repay you for the genius of your idea?" said Fahseed before retiring. Placing a hand on the lieutenant's shoulder the commander added, "Your thinking was perfect. Today sport unified us. Everyone ended up cheering for each other. Sore losers are nowhere here to be found. Tonight soldiers, unicorns, and horses see each other as friends worthy to fight for and defend. As I told you before, not only big framed, you are a surprisingly smart young man."

"Sir," answered the lieutenant, "today marks the second time you have complimented my mind."

"True enough. I before praised your idea to slip into the gate of this fortress.

"Telling me that I can think well is more than adequate payment for my humble idea. But, there *is* something you could do... errm... would you call to us Maryeta?" Fahseed sent for his granddaughter.

Maryeta seemed almost always to be a happy girl. On this night her gaiety was irrepressible. "Grandpa, tonight finds Lyons to be *perfectly* content! Is not it wonderful that my brother won the race against Erban?"

"The lieutenant has something he wants to say to you."

"It is just that I saw Maryeta pull up her horse before the finish line, so that Lyons would close on his sister."

The cheeks of Maryeta began to flush rosy. She smiled coyly at the big man.

"Ahh... Lieutenant Abel... you see my brother is older than me. When we were little, Grandfather always insisted that Lyons had to be responsible so that I did not get lost in the woods, or from a tree fall too far down." As she said more the tone of her voice, grew serious. "The sword of General Cavour left more than a scar on my brother's side. I am very glad that the scar before found on his inside, is tonight removed. It was only right that my brother got a boost to his confidence. So if it is possible, I might be even more happy that Lyons won, than is he himself."

"Exactly as I thought," replied Abel with his eyes glinting merrily. "I say congratulations to Maryeta, the real winner of the race. Ahem, your brother will never from my lips hear what my eyes observed. I know it means much to Lyons to be held in high esteem by the soldiers. After all, it means more to him because... *you are just a girl.*"

"How dare you say that!" Maryeta proceeded to punch the lieutenant with her small fists, and for good measure kicked him twice.

"Ouch! Girl, enough of your kicking!" Grabbing Maryeta by her upper arms Abel lifted her off the ground and swung her around. Her feet back on the ground, the lieutenant and the girl who had shown that she loved her brother deeply, smiled wide at each other.

"You must know that I was only teasing you about being a girl."

"Is not this girl special?" said Fahseed reaching to grab Maryeta from the clasp of the big lieutenant.

"Sir, your granddaughter will grow up to be a true princess."

"I used to play at being a fairy princess," responded Maryeta with her face taking on a puzzled look. "I had a stick for a wand. If that is what I someday become, can a real princess climb trees and race horses, or does she need to just look pretty?"

"Of course I know nothing about the idea of being a proper princess," responded Abel assuming a grave look. "But the first princess of Phoenicia, mind you that in my eyes you are already a true princess, can set about her own way to do things."

The next day a small army of men, unicorns, and horses marched smartly southward. With them went two now dearly regarded youth. One could even say that by the hardened men in the army of Fahseed, Lyons and Maryeta were loved.

CHAPTER 23

THE LAST OVERLORDS

B efore the army of Fahseed reached the largest garrison to be found in all the valleys of Phoenicia, the weather changed from sunshine to wet, and then stayed wet. When the rain paused, heavy mists continued to dampen the will to fight.

In the midst of the damp, cold, and gloomy rebel encampment located three hundred paces before the garrison, a fire was by Lyons wanted. The fuel the boy had gathered was drenched through, and try as he might the youth found that his fire would not be sparked to life by one cinder rock striking against another.

The youth gave up on the fire and instead decided to hasten the flow of his blood by practicing moves with his sword. On such a dark day the glow of his swinging blue gold sword seemed to Lyons, remarkable. What he observed led to an idea. From the position where he knew to be found the cloud covered sun, Lyons held the sword so that it would reflect rays onto kindling wood.

"Brother, how did you manage to start a fire from wet wood?" inquired Maryeta with her knack for noticing things quickly. "No matter how hard I tried, I could not do it."

"Take me to the fire you are trying to build, and I will show you." Soon enough Maryeta witnessed what her brother had discovered.

"That is amazing!" The girl began to laugh and pirouette steps of joy. "Even when the sky is covered in clouds, blue gold magic maintains fealty to the sun!"

Hearing the commotion made by Maryeta, the lieutenant approached and inquired, "On such a dreary day, about what can you be so excited?"

"Lyons showed me something brand new. Come with me, Abel, I am going to light your fire!"

"What Lyons today discovered," observed later the tall lieutenant, "will someday prove very useful to Phoenician ships lost in fogs and heavy storms at sea. With such a sword the captain would during both morning and afternoon know where above traveled the unseen sun. Maintaining his bearings, the captain would know which way to sail to avoid weather shrouded rocky shores and reefs."

The Impatience of Briarburr

Through gloomy weather the assault of Fahseed's army several times commenced, and several times failed. Day after day soaked rebel archers shot arrows at drenched soldiers stationed on the walkways of the garrison. The great gate of the fortress resisted all efforts to break through its thick wooden planks made heavier by wetness. The fortress remained stubbornly invincible.

When on the morning of the seventh day of the siege Fahseed's soldiers again failed in their attempt to storm the garrison, the rebels once more trudged feet through mud as they returned to their camp.

In midafternoon of the same day, as the thick cover of clouds lifted higher, a solitary blackmaned unicorn walked toward the wall of the garrison. Briarburr had had enough of a fight where day upon day no progress was made against the enemy held garrison. The unicorn looked to become an easy target for archers on the wall. He proved not to be.

Willed by the combination of great frustration and a spirit indomitable, the unicorn's control of his gift became stunning to observe. With one flick of his head twenty arrows would go the direction his horn commanded them. Jumping his hooves and waving back-and-forth his head, before the long wall of the garrison Briarburr made every arrow to miss, and to miss him badly.

Watching from afar, the unicorn's combination of courage and magic could not but be admired by the troops of Fahseed. One man, then another, was given the thought that by the horn of Briarburr he could be protected before the garrison wall. Without benefit of orders a soldier grabbed a ladder, mounted his horse, and dragged the ladder toward the unicorn. Another soldier followed suit, then another. A growing number of cavalrymen and unicorns came to stand with Briarburr. News of the unfolding movement of soldiers reached the tent of Fahseed and Cavour.

"Commander it is late in the day; when did you order this attack?"

"The order was not by me given, Cavour. And our men should not be attacking without my order to do so. Blast! Am I not in charge here?"

"Then, Fahseed, we must do something or you will lose control of the men, and so lose this battle."

"It is obvious that my men want to fight. If I order them back to camp I will be made to look badly in their eyes. At the same time I do not want this day to end in disaster with many of my men, acting without my orders no less, falling before the garrison wall. Cavour, summon the lieutenant to me. On a field of battle the mind of Abel can be surprisingly creative."

"Sir, I just remembered something," said the lieutenant upon being solicited by Fahseed for counsel. "It is something Lyons discovered, that I saw Maryeta do. It might be an idea we can borrow."

"Out with it, Lieutenant."

"Lyons proved that even through dark clouds the blue gold steals sunlight. If we placed the eleven magic swords together to reflect obscured sunlight against the gate of the fortress, a fire would surely be sparked. Once sparked to life, the fire would grow hot."

"You both remember," interjected Cavour, "that when against the rain-soaked gate we threw spear points wrapped in tar and burning cloth, no fire came to spread."

After reflecting some moments, Fahseed placed a hand on the shoulder of Abel and said, "So long as the heat brought by sword reflections is intense and does not abate, it is worth a try. It will help that Briarburr and the fighters with him keep the bulk of our enemy occupied away from the short wall that contains the gate." So it was to be done. With archers protecting them, the bearers of eleven blue gold swords assembled and positioned their blades to reflect upon the fortress gate the rays of an unseen sun.

At the long wall of the garrison where fought the blackmane ladders were pushed up, shoved away, and pushed up again. Briarburr continued to deflect arrows away from the bodies of those come to fight with him.

"Briarburr, your rear quarters are astonishingly strong," observed Elyir. "And I am very skinny. Like a bucking catapult, your hind legs can bounce me to the *very top* of the wall." Elyir mounted, slid himself back, and rose to stand on the rear haunches of the unicorn. Briarburr's strong rear quarters bucked the skinny young man so high that his hands caught the top of the wall. On the walkway of the garrison wall Elyir was immediately fighting for dear life.

"That is my friend up there!" exclaimed Erban pointing an arm upward as he ran full out toward Briarburr.

"Elyir is my brother!" exclaimed Merlew running at the side of Erban.

In quick pursuit of the example of Elyir, Erban jumped upon the back of Briarburr and was bucked high to grab the top of the wall. Merlew was the next to be bounced upward. The soldiers of Fahseed were inspired to see three of their confederates fighting against long odds on the walkway of the wall.

At the spot where Elyir and two more slender soldiers fought as a team, a ladder was set against the wall. This time the ladder achieved its purpose; soldiers clambered up and gained entry onto the walkway. Elyir, Erban, and Merlew were reinforced. On the high guard-walk the fighting grew intense.

Magic swords traveling rays of closeted sun sparked the birth of flames at the center of the garrison gate. When buckets of water could not dispel the obstinacy of heat inspired by the wondrous blue gold, resolute flames promulgated a fire unquenchable. The burn crept upward to engulf the crown of the gate. Cavour signaled a unicorn to kick at the base of the gate. Whether through cast of magic or sheer will, the stallion braved the heat. His kicks were joined by another unicorn, then another. The planks in the gate began to crack. Hefting a thick wooden ram, the blacksmiths Colyado and Jomain joined to amplify the exertion of unicorn stallions. The gate was at last persuaded to split apart and swing open.

Because the bulk and intensity of the afternoon's fight had prolonged at the long wall of the garrison where fought Briarburr, the few sentries left to guard the garrison gate could not halt the charge into the fortress led by the magic swords of Colyado and Jomain. One after another rebel soldier joined to trespass the intimacy of the fortress. Not long after the gate was breached, enemy swords were unhanded in surrender.

As suddenly as it had commenced with the approach of a lone blackmaned unicorn to the wall of the fortress, the *Battle of Briarburr's Wall* ended.

Mercy Compelled

The ruler was brought outside a garrison no longer his to command. Before the feet of Fahseed, Roward was shoved to the ground.

"Kill the tyrant!" was shouted time and again.

Made testy by many previous days of martial failure compounded by the gloom of dreary weather, Fahseed unsheathed his blue gold sword and prepared to satisfy the will of his soldiers. Reaching high her hands to stop her grandfather's raised arms, Maryeta restrained swift vengeance.

"No matter how bad he is you cannot just... *murder him!*"

"This man Roward is wicked!" came the sharp retort of Fahseed. "His reputation is known by all! The blood of women and children stains his hands!"

"Even if what you say is true this is still wrong of you, Grandfather, and wrong of us."

When Fahseed again raised high his sword to strike, Maryeta felt the pressure of her grandfather's arms to lessen. Standing behind her, the hands of her taller brother had joined to detain their grandfather's will.

"So you are *both* against me!" exclaimed Fahseed with his eyes glaring.

"You act in haste, Grandfather," answered Lyons with a firm voice. "You do not carefully consider your motivation to take a man's life. Both Maryeta and I want you to think about the example that you are setting. It is not right to execute, with no further regard, a man bent down on his knees."

"I suppose I owe you two that much," replied a commander made calmed. "You both have shown genius with your magic swords, making it before to rain and quench our thirst, and now to spark a fire under a wet sky. Still, do not you remember that Lord Baltric carried off your parents, and would have sold you in the market?"

"Roward is not Baltric," responded Maryeta. "And Baltric is no more. The overlord that took our parents is from us forever departed."

"All... right," relented Fahseed. "I promise to control my temper. Call to me Briarburr." The blackmane came quickly to the side of his commander.

"Consider, Briarburr, that trophies of unicorn horns adorn the walls of Roward's fortress. For that alone should not Roward die?"

With head lowered the blackmane jumped several times his front hooves. Upon settling himself he neighed, "Roward's hatred of unicorns is monstrous. It is also said that by the blood and tears of many innocents was built his great garrison. But quick death is not payment enough for what he has done."

"When my father defended the unicorns, Roward had him killed!" shouted a soldier that had from Roward's valley joined the army of Fahseed. "The scoundrel sleeps on a bed decorated with the ivory of unicorn horns! How dare Fahseed's grandchildren stop his execution!"

Fahseed raised his arms again, but this time for calm.

"I will have my say," persisted Maryeta undeterred. "Unicorn horns placed for all to see upon the walls of this now fallen fortress represent terrible crimes, and not just against unicorns. Lyons and I were also told that Roward stole power from another overlord that had done the same to a ruler before that. No laws stopped Roward from seizing awful power. I only ask that my grandfather judge Roward by laws that he shall soon make. His execution today would set a vengeful start to the new land of Phoenicia."

Maryeta turned to look at Cavour, and then at Abel.

"Many soldiers that before followed orders unjust, now fight bravely for my grandfather. If Roward is condemned to death, are not the soldiers that carried out his former wicked orders also to receive punishment?"

After exchanging with Abel a knowing glance, Cavour held out for all to see, his arms.

"In these hands once rested all power. I was a law unto myself. That is how this land was before governed. I ask, why not sentence Roward to hard labor paving streets with stones. When he has paid back the people of Phoenicia for his crimes, then and only then can he be set free."

The defeated overlord was made the first prisoner of the new country of Phoenicia. Still on his knees, Roward held out arms to thank mercy given. Without hesitation Maryeta embraced the fallen ruler.

"Maryeta is not only a good horsewoman, she is unafraid," commented later Abel intent on improving the mood of a dispirited Fahseed. "To top that, a quick thinking head sits on her shoulders. I have never seen a girl to match her."

"She made me to look *bad* in front of my soldiers."

"Not so, Fahseed," answered Abel. "Your soldiers saw today that for all your great authority you were willing to listen to counsel, that you are a fair man. That forbearance is now, and will continue to be admired in you."

"I hope you are right, Abel. Hmph, this reminds me of something. Did Cavour ever tell you about Lord Auldham's code of loving even one's enemy?"

Abel shook his head *no*.

"Auldham believed that merciful acts following battle could help to restore lasting peace. Who knows Abel, after the last overlord is defeated, what Maryeta and Lyons did today will perhaps help me to win... *Auldham's peace.*"

Maryeta found Lyons.

"By holding back the arms of Grandfather you supported me. I tell you that when his eyes flared, I scarce recognized the face of our grandfather. It was as if he did not know me."

"You are more brave than I. Absent your lead I would have said, and done nothing."

"By my side I always had my brother to be brave, if not for yourself then for me. When we were little, all by ourselves and afraid of the darkness, I knew you were there to watch over me. You, Lyons, had no one in the forest to shelter and take care of you. I have only now come to realize that my easy smile came at the price of your earnest eyes."

"In the forest I was more afraid of the darkness than you, but for your sake I could not show it. I would hold you close and whisper funny things to you. Your tears quickly dried. Seeing you calmed made to subside my fears. My little sister made me braver and stronger. Maryeta, you have always meant more to me than you know."

The End of the Overlords

The following battle came to be no battle at all. Winfray, the ruler that found himself next in the path of Fahseed's army, was the most battle hardened overlord in all the land. However, Winfray had heard too many stories about magic swords, magic fires, and a unicorn that could swerve flights of arrows and spears. Upon surrendering without a fight his garrison, the mighty overlord insisted that he be given the same favor Cavour had received, an officer's commission in the army of Fahseed.

"Look at the four corners of your dispossessed garrison," said Fahseed motioning with an arm. "What crowns your walls?"

"You mean... the unicorn horns?"

"Grandfather," interjected Maryeta, "Lyons and I *will not* permit you to kill this man."

"Once again my granddaughter insists that mercy be shown to a very evil man," said Fahseed turning to Cavour. "For that, General, from now on the lord of any garrison displaying unicorn trophy horns will, with no further thought, be made a prisoner."

"So it shall be," replied Cavour nodding his head. Under his breath he added, "It is indeed well that the trophy horn of the unicorn before mattered nothing to me, and so did not crown the walls of my garrison. Else, instead of holding the rank of an officer, I would also be condemned to hard labor."

Summer days began to shorten and fray at their edges. Dismissing tree grip the stems of yellow, brown, and scarlet colored leaves danced whimsically downward.

Remaining despots talked about uniting together to withstand the army of Fahseed that had grown to number more than a thousand men. Unfortunately for them, every ruler was a jealous and independent minded lord. Unable to reinvent themselves by trusting and cooperating with each other, the remaining overlords lost confidence in their ability to oppose the change brought by Fahseed. When the last remaining overlord abandoned his fortress, the army of Fahseed became the only military presence in Phoenicia.

The village of Byblos was at last made safe from tyranny. When Elyeazar came to serve at the side of Fahseed, a twelfth magic sword was with eleven more reunited.

CHAPTER 24

LIBERATOR AND DEFENDER

The capital city was laid out with thick and high perimeter walls, and ample space within the walls for the placement of shops, houses, a wide boulevard, and what would one day rise to be a grand palace. Overlords that had ruled corruptly, thieves, and those guilty of heinous crimes found themselves condemned to the hard toil of public works construction. In the Phoenician corner of a great sea began the building of a harbor planned to one day become the country's crown jewel.

Soldiers every day worked hard their arms, legs, and backs building fortress walls, making weapons, marching guard duty, and drilling in formation. General Cavour preferred fewer soldiers that were well-trained, bodied tough, and well-paid than have more soldiers to join the army... because they had nothing better to do.

Powerful states to the east and north would take advantage of the nascent and newly unified country. The enemies of Phoenicia thought that conquest and victory would come easily to their armies, which were far larger than the army led by Cavour and Fahseed. However, the army of Phoenicia every time held off the invader.

With the twenty young unicorn stallions that had helped make possible the defeat of powerful overlords,

Briarburr organized a scouting brigade. The unicorn stallions not only patrolled the mountains and valleys along Phoenician borders, but also ranged far to the north, south, and east to early on discover threats of invasion. In every part of Phoenicia the magic of the unicorn horn came to be protected. A Phoenicia made convincingly safe and secure became the home of many unicorn mares and stallions.

A respectable country was said to need a king, specifically Fahseed. He thought otherwise. The excuse that he was a peasant of mean origins did not sway the will of soldiers, or that of the people. After all, in Phoenicia peasants were everywhere to be found. The excuse that he was poorly educated, and that his speech was sometimes crude, applied as well to nine out of ten Phoenicians. Nor did the people mind that Fahseed could show bad temper. On one day or another, more Phoenicians than one could count had difficulty controlling their tempers. In the towns and villages one thing could not be forgot. Fahseed had thrown off the oppressive yokes of tyrannical overlords. Common people repeated the refrain *The seeds of freedom were by Fahseed sown.* Reluctantly, and warily, Fahseed found himself made king.

"I am not now, nor ever will be a politician," confessed the new ruler to Cavour. "I am not made to be burdened with absolute power. The only thing I ever wanted was for Lyons and Maryeta to be made safe. If the magic of the blackmaned unicorn swayed the people to believe in me, the people should have made Briarburr their king."

"To your point, Fahseed, people say that the horns of the unicorns brought our people together," responded Cavour.

With their grandfather become king, Lyons and Maryeta were made to be a prince and a princess. That idea held little appeal to youths accustomed to running wild in a forest and unaccustomed to acting formal inside the walls of a royal palace. Maryeta soon discovered that laughing while drinking grape juice, and yelling while chasing after her brother, were especially frowned upon when Fahseed was entertaining important guests. The princess resented being scolded when a costly dress became stained or torn. For the forest girl, running in princess shoes was far less comfortable than running barefoot.

Finding too soft his royal bed, Lyons slept on a lion skin spread on his bedroom floor. New friendship in the capital city came not easily to a newly made prince that preferred to notice not the protocols of his status. The problem was that others too much noticed that he had been made royal. Mounted upon Briarburr and Peli the two royal youths seized any and every opportunity to roam the mountains, valleys, and sea coasts of Phoenicia.

Cavour's dedication to military training encompassed one project particularly dear to his heart. He insisted on sword practice for the royal siblings, with himself as their instructor. It was not long before the fencing skill of the two youths became uncommonly good.

"I am again this day proud of you. I have never seen a soldier twirl about as cleanly and rapidly as Lyons when he parries. My eyes see that when he fights with a sword, Lyons has the balance of a dancer. Not just Lyons bested me this day, Maryeta also proved too fast for my sword to overcome. You two get better, and I only get worse."

"That, Sir, is false!" exclaimed Maryeta. Who then proceeded to give a hug to a man that had become one of her favorites. "Tomorrow it will be *my turn* to beat my brother, and *your turn* to beat me."

At rest after fencing class a lunch of grapes, bread, and cheese was brought to the instructor and his two students.

"I am not as thankful as I should be," reflected Maryeta. "Look how my life has been transformed from when I was an orphan outcast, a waif in the forest. Sir Cavour, tell me something for which you today give thanks."

"All right, young lady. Today I am thankful that a youth I once wounded in battle is now to me become a dear friend. You must know, Lyons, that I teach you swordsmanship so that you will never again receive a cut like the one you once from me received."

"Now it is my turn," spoke the girl.

"You already had your turn."

"Well then, brother, I deserve another one. Remember how thorns and brambles used to scratch our arms and legs? I still today do not know what that little girl full of scratches would have done without having by her side a big brother to dry her tears, and calm and soothe her. So better said, I am thankful that my older brother was always the responsible one."

The eyes of Lyons looked intently at his teacher as he offered, "To of a former enemy make a lasting friend, is for me a blessing singular."

That remark brought to Cavour the remembrance of a poignant conversation he had one evening with a young overlord named Auldham, taken away in the prime of his life.

CHAPTER 25

THE LURE OF BLUE GOLD

"I am Adolfo the pharaoh's ambassador. This is Admiral Boschene. We come in peace."

"It is this king's fervent desire to enjoy long and lasting peace with the mighty land of Egypt. The people of Phoenicia are honored to receive you both."

"King Fahseed," continued Adolfo, "our great pharaoh does not comprehend how a poor and forgotten corner of land bordering the Egyptian sea has in the passage of only a few years managed to become a vibrant merchant state with many barges plying trade. Can there be truth to the saying that Phoenicia is protected by the magic of the unicorn?"

"The unicorn is not here hunted for its horn," replied Fahseed pleased that the tone of the ambassador's voice sounded genuine. "In turn the magic of protected unicorns brings blessings to our land."

"But King Fahseed," the voice of Admiral Boschene sounded crisp, "while disappears the unicorn race, the horse has become a noble beast of burden. We plow with horses, and on them ride into battle. The dangerous sharp horn of the unicorn has no place in the world of men. How long can you protect unicorns that unlike the horse will never be domesticated?"

"Admiral, giving honor to unicorns is not a matter of convenience. It is rather a circumstance of beauty and goodness. Until my dying breath I will in this land protect the noble steeds."

"It is said that the sword you wear is made of magic blue gold."

"So it is, Admiral. Blue gold is a gift secured to the presence of unicorns."

"May I hold it?" responded Boschene taking a step closer to the king and stretching out his arm.

"I will show it to you," answered the king unsheathing his sword. "Since made, this possession has not left my side. After many battles this sword is come to be component to my arm."

"The luster of this most excellent sword is unique," said Boschene sliding the tips of his fingers along the blade of the shiny sword still held by Fahseed. "Who forged it?"

"Three blacksmith friends and I."

"The gift to my pharaoh of such a sword would be viewed as a true sign of friendship," offered Boschene pressing for advantage.

"As you no doubt have been informed, Admiral, Phoenicia has only twelve such swords. Because they were forged from the last blue gold remaining in this land, their full power comes from their fused purpose. The symbol of our strength, the twelve swords combine and integrate as one. With my own eyes I have seen that when wielded by warriors standing together, every one of unblemished heart, the unified magic of the swords is impossible to vanquish.

"Honored Egyptian guests, for the next twenty days you are invited to freely travel about Phoenicia. The guards provided to you will ensure your safety and protection. I shall also send along observers to answer your questions and provide me reports on your whereabouts. You will find that Phoenicia is a place where people build farms and cities, modernize, and fashion goods of trade. Our royal purple dye has come to be everywhere known. Go where you will. From your eyes we have nothing to hide."

After fifteen days the Egyptian tour was finished; the two emissaries returned to the capital. During the planning of a banquet to celebrate the signing of a treaty of friendship between Phoenicia and Egypt, Briarburr and Lyons brought tragic news to Fahseed.

"The brutal raid happened the day before yesterday," neighed the blackmane. "A band of savage warriors killed two unicorn mares. The signs they left make them to be Hittites come down from the north. Because the mares bravely placed themselves as targets before the enemy, their foals escaped unharmed. *Nyeeerrraayy!* Horns were severed from the heads of the unicorn mares!"

"This is a... monstrosity!" exclaimed Fahseed. "We will find the raiders and punish them!"

"Arriving too late, Briarburr and I yesterday lost the trail of the raiders," said Lyons. "Blown sand wiped away all trace of their footprints."

"Briarburr, for this grave loss the white herd of unicorns must not lose heart."

"If not here, then where can unicorn mares find to gain safety?" responded the blackmane.

"Grandfather, we need to reinforce our borders. If another such slaughter should happen, unicorns will no more place their trust in our protection."

"We relaxed our vigil," answered Fahseed. "Seeing our confidence, perhaps the unicorns as well lessened their caution. One thing is certain. This will not be the last incursion into our territory. While fighting an army of invasion is dangerous, it can be more difficult and grueling to fight bands of raiders that travel fast and light. Our mountains offer many places for malevolent assailants to hide."

"Sir, one thing else I must report," neighed Briarburr. "Lorial, an esteemed unicorn matron, told me that she has come to believe that the destiny of unicorns is not to be corralled behind the lines of our army, but to live free and without fear."

"I have told the Egyptian Ambassador that we are sworn to protect the white herd from all enemies, and we will do just that."

"But, there is more to this," continued Briarburr. "I have been instructed to ask miraculous help of you. Lorial has dreamt of a new land far beyond the seas, where warrior tribes know not of the existence of horned horses. If it can bring them lasting peace, Lorial thinks unicorns are now willing to risk their lives passaging the seas."

"Can the dreams of the far land be true?" answered Fahseed.

"I too was visited by the dream," answered the blackmane, "and it has now come to make sense to me. The far place beckons to all unicorns."

"Tell me more."

"Long ago, until it came no more to be, a protected hold shielded in magic the unicorns. A new hold must now be found in a land far from the dwelling place of human warriors that despise the unicorns. The dreams visited upon the unicorns are of a place where all horned horses can live secluded and hidden together."

"That our enemies believe killing unicorns weakens us, is a tragedy," responded the king. "I will, Briarburr, do all that I can to help the unicorns find their new hold."

The king sought out the best mind he knew for analyzing complex things. "I need you, Jomain, to help me solve a new and vexing problem. The unicorns seek a new hold on the other side of the world. So then, how do we transport hundreds of horned horses across immense seas?"

"Phoenicia has barges," answered Jomain undeterred by the strange question. "The problem, Fahseed, is that none are large enough to carry so many unicorns so far. Only the Egyptians possess both the knowledge and the facilities to build barges large enough and sturdy enough to sail upon very distant seas."

"But Jomain, the Egyptians *loathe* unicorns."

"Well then, Fahseed, knowing that the pharaoh cannot be called upon to freely offer aid to the unicorns simplifies our task. We are left to find something that the Egyptians want badly enough to make them risk costly barges on a treacherous voyage.

Have not Adolfo or Boschene mentioned something that the pharaoh covets?"

"Boschene and Adolfo do want one thing, my blue gold sword. From us that is all that they want."

"Hmm, you and I both know that unicorns are markedly drawn to the blue gold. Does not the blue gold protect the unicorns?"

"The layer of blue gold found in the waterfall cavern was covered by ordinary sand," reminded Fahseed. "From that we concluded that the Phoenician deposit of blue gold played out long ago. There is no more such gold left in this land to wash down the river."

"That signifies that in this part of the world blue gold no longer well-protects the white herd. Unicorns seek a place with a rich and untouched deposit of blue gold that will again procure their safety. We can conclude that in the new land sought by the unicorns, and perhaps there alone, is found the magical gold essential to secure a hold for the horned horses."

The unicorn with the black mane was summoned back to the king.

"Briarburr, a thing presses on my heart that I must share with you. Come with me." Two staunch friends, one a man and the other a unicorn, walked out of the city toward the port.

"Look over there," said the king motioning with his arm. "The Egyptian war barge that brought to us the ambassador and the admiral, is in size gigantic. It is seven or eight times the size of our largest vessel. That barge could fit more than one hundred unicorns on board, and enough feed to last them during a voyage of three or four moons. We need to secure large Egyptian barges to transport the unicorns to their new home."

"My eyes see what you say, Fahseed. It is only the enormous Egyptian barges that are large enough to travel long and far over immense seas." Briarburr shook his head. "But, such great barges are costly to build. How can we purchase their use? Unicorn horses possess nothing of value to trade for barge transport."

"Because the Egyptians want something badly... *there is* one way we can purchase the use of great barges. The pharaoh will give anything to secure blue gold swords and armor for his army. I am certain, as are you also, that in the new land sought by the unicorns is found a mountain with rich veins of blue gold. Just as Peli sensed the blue gold found in the Lyon's Den, unicorns will in the far land come to identify the location of the magic deposit. Once found, in exchange for one hundred weights of the precious metal I think the Egyptians would agree to carry the white herd to its new home."

"To pay the passage of the unicorn clans, something has to be given in exchange," neighed the blackmane moving slowly up and down his head. "What in the end matters is that unicorns reach their new home safe and sound. Wherever it is deposited, the blue gold will sooner or later come to be found by inquisitive and greedy men. If finding it sooner secures safety for the white herd, then let it be found now."

"I was afraid you would not keep an open mind about the blue gold," answered Fahseed.

"While I do not welcome the exchange of blue gold for unicorn passage, it is the only solution that presents. It does comfort me to know that the protective power of the magic gold presents only to soldiers that are true hearted."

"Yes, Briarburr. The blue gold is not accommodative to unjust wars."

"It would be a comfort if a Phoenician barge goes with the expedition of the white herd."

"Hmph. Well then, I will send our biggest vessel to accompany the Egyptian barges. In that regard something else just occurred to me. To demonstrate my fealty to you and the unicorn clans, Lyons and Maryeta will provide surety for my promise of safe passage. Though it breaks my heart to have them be gone from me, inform the matrons that I have the confidence to send the two royal youths to accompany the unicorn voyage.

"Understand that I say this, Briarburr, knowing that unicorn magic will summon clement weather for the passage of my grandchildren on the one Phoenician barge that goes with the Egyptian fleet. Once the Egyptians return with their blue gold they will never be able to cross the vast sea again; they will have no unicorns on board to protect and guarantee a second voyage over an impossible distance. So long as my intent in this matter is pure, some benefit will also be consequent to Phoenicia. In matters of great love, and Maryeta and Lyons love greatly the unicorns, good returns good."

Maryeta welcomed the prospect of a voyage of adventure. As was his manner, Lyons accepted with no complaint his new responsibility.

The banquet for the ambassador and admiral was delayed. Briarburr, Lyons, and Maryeta had three days to secure the approval of unicorn matrons for the plan of Fahseed.

Clans in Council

Nine unicorn matrons spoke for nine clans of magic horses gathered on a high mountain. Cavour positioned sentries so that nothing would disrupt their council.

The first day went badly for Briarburr, Lyons and Maryeta. Because many unicorns had in the land of the Nile been slaughtered, the unicorns had ample reason to distrust the Egyptians. The only positive outcome of the first meeting was the acknowledgment by all nine unicorn matrons that blue gold did indeed exist in the far land that was calling to them. The day ended with nervous unicorns abruptly walking out of their conclave.

"This has been a disaster for us. I feel like I could cry."

"Maryeta, we unicorns are cautious herd animal persons. Remember that for many years I dared not present myself to two orphan children dwelling in my forest. Because the prospect of such a long voyage places the entire white herd at risk, I knew that unicorns would at first resist any plan so bold. But, young lady, the talks could have gone worse. Did you notice that at times the unicorns argued more with each other than they did with us? Since by habit herd animals disrupt and challenge their leaders, noisy unicorn division is a sign that a compromise can still be reached. While unicorns think the Egyptians are brutal and greedy, by tomorrow some of the matrons will recognize that all things bear a price in the world of men."

"It may be that some clans will decide to stay behind," offered Lyons, "while other clans consent to face an arduous voyage across unknown seas as a better alternative than being surrounded by strong tribes that hate them and covet their horns."

Sounds of unicorn scuffling reached their ears. Briarburr grinned as he neighed, "When unicorns start to kick and nip at each other, progress is being made."

On the next day it became evident that many unicorns believed that threats from surrounding kingdoms posed an even greater danger than unicorn passage across vast seas. After more contentious disputation on the third morning of the council, Briarburr had had enough of the bickering.

"Unicorns must now decide if they will accept the protection of King Fahseed, Prince Lyons, and Princess Maryeta on a sea voyage to a new land. Remember that time and again the king has shown himself to be our true friend."

With head high and tail extended straight, the matron Lorial pranced to stand by Briarburr.

"This matron and her clan will receive safe passage across the sea," neighed the blackmane. "Am I to tell the king that the other eight unicorn clans are to remain here in Phoenicia? I am sure Fahseed will be happy to know that though you be surrounded by foreign enemies that seek your horns, you are content to here stay with him."

Fahseed gave a welcoming embrace to his grandchildren, and then as was his custom hugged the neck of the black marked unicorn.

"Grandfather!" Maryeta could not wait to share the news. "When I was ready to give up hope eight unicorn matrons agreed to risk the long voyage. Only one clan refuses to sail the far seas." She jumped up and clapped her hands, "And I cannot wait to sail over the great waters! Do you think I will get to see a real pirate?" Grown to be tall as a woman, Maryeta remained still half little girl at heart.

"You must promise, little lady, to bring your brother back to me," responded Fahseed embracing a second time Maryeta.

"We will both, Grandpa, return to you. You see I am almost seventeen, and I can take care..."

"You only just turned sixteen!" objected Lyons.

"And, Grandpa, I made Briarburr promise to escort us all the way back over the high seas to your palace. After all, he still has one clan of unicorns here to protect. Surely we will be away from you for a long time, perhaps almost a whole year. By the time we return I will be... *all grown up!*"

"So with my grandchildren, Briarburr is to return to me!" exclaimed Fahseed.

"*Nyeeerrraayy!* Maryeta is right. If I return not, who will everyday watch over the unicorn clan that remains in Phoenicia?"

"I only wish that you could come with us." Taking the hand of her grandfather, Maryeta added, "But... I know that you are needed here. It is your destiny to well begin the kingdom of Phoenicia." She tilted her head and smiled at her grandfather. "This is the last favor I shall for a long time ask of you. Please send Elyir, Merlew, Jomain, and Abel to go with us. My friend Elyir is a real sculptor. Artist ideas are with him fun to talk about. Elyir's uncle, Merlew, is smart and stout-hearted. He is the nicest uncle one could ask for. Jomain and the fearsome lieutenant will ever protect me. Lyons is grown so tall that he no longer needs someone to protect him."

"I wish that I could send not just Jomain with my darling Maryeta, but as well Colyado and Elyeazar. However, while you are from me gone away I require the counsel of my two trusted blacksmith friends to help me rule well Phoenicia."

CHAPTER 26

THE STRONG ARM OF EGYPT

The banquet table was placed before the outer half wall of the spacious room that opened to the large garden of the palace. King Fahseed and General Cavour sat at the opposite ends of the long table crafted of polished cedar. Behind Fahseed stood Abel. With his guards in tow, Boschene had seated himself at the middle of the long side of the table, with the half wall at his back. There positioned, Boschene could observe the entire banquet room. Opposite the Egyptian admiral sat Ambassador Adolfo. After putting on a large smile for the occasion of state, the king began by raising his cup to the two eminent Egyptians.

"The flood plain of the Nile is farmland most fertile. Great Egypt has the most powerful army in the world. No ships on the ocean can compete with your enormous barges. This evening I toast the continued success of Egypt!"

Putting in place a smile larger than the one worn by Fahseed, Admiral Boschene began to raise his cup.

"But I am not finished," continued the king. "Your royal court is the most distinguished in the world. I toast the two honest and well-intentioned emissaries of the pharaoh found here with me tonight."

"Let us drink to *trust* between our peoples," reciprocated Admiral Boschene.

"Compared to the mighty land of the Nile, Phoenicia is a humble nation dedicated to farming and common trade," continued Fahseed as he put down his emptied cup. "About this corner of our sea young Phoenician ship captains are still learning to sail. That said, we are especially blessed in two ways. The noble unicorn horses are our staunch friends. And the unity of twelve magic swords is bound to the unicorn presence in our land."

Cavour nodded to the guard standing at the door that gave entrance to the banquet room. Colyado, Jomain, and Elyeazar entered. As Abel grabbed a torch from off the wall, the king left his chair to join his old friends.

"With your permission, Ambassador Adolfo, we will demonstrate the magic of not twelve, but four swords."

"Please do so, Fahseed. For too many days I have waited to see this."

Four men touched the points of their blades together and held them to reflect the burning torch held by Abel. When the swords mirrored torchlight toward a pile of logs stacked at a far end of the banquet hall, the wood lit afire and became a consuming flame.

"You before told me, Ambassador Adolfo, that your pharaoh desires blue gold for his army," said Fahseed returning to the table. "I recently learned where blue gold can be found. Unfortunately, the deposit of the magic gold is located very far away."

"Where, where do we obtain this wondrous gold?" responded Admiral Boschene not waiting for the ambassador to answer. Fahseed turned again to Adolfo and waited for him to speak.

"Our illustrious admiral that has won countless sea engagements, speaks aright. I hope King Fahseed does not taunt us with his demonstration of the power of the magic swords. Where can Egypt find such gold?"

As three bearers of magic swords exited the hall, the king walked to where sat Boschene and handed him his sword saying, "I before did not permit you to hold my sword. As you think on things that are pure and true, the love held for you by your mother, you will feel the sword become constituent to your arm." The silver sword glowed briefly blue. With evident reluctance Boschene handed back the sword.

A chair was placed for Fahseed to sit next to the ambassador and across from the admiral. Newly seated, the king continued, "I have welcomed you here as friends. I commended you to see with your own eyes the land of Phoenicia. In all things I have placed in you my trust. Now, I am about to offer you an opportunity to with me save the noble white herd. By so doing you will for Egypt obtain magic blue gold."

Boschene bent forward to listen expectantly to the king. Upon learning the details of the proposed odyssey to the end of the far ocean, the admiral's voice rose in pitch. "You ask us to take the unicorns beyond where any ship has ever traveled! Based only on your words, we are to risk our barges on a trip to... nowhere! What if our barges fall off the edge of the world?" Boschene hit a fist to the table and shouted, "A unicorn is nothing but a dumb animal not worth one tenth of a horse compelled by the reins of his rider!"

At that Fahseed said nothing, but instead looked to Cavour who nodded to the guard at the door entrancing the banquet room. When the blackmaned unicorn entered the banquet room, the king moved to embrace the neck of Briarburr.

"Put this animal to the test, Boschene," said Fahseed turning toward the Egyptians seated at the table. "You will find that along with a magic horn he as well possesses acute intelligence. By this noble unicorn my words are understood. I will relay your questions to him."

"Hah! Have him count with a hoof to four," smirked the admiral.

"Come now, Sir," answered Fahseed. "Do not insult this animal, that as you are well-aware, has proved himself valiant in war."

"Hunh! This is the first time I have seen a unicorn with ivory still shafted to his forehead. Have him singe your beard with the heat of his horn."

"But, Sir, you are our king!" interjected Abel.

"No matter," responded Fahseed. "It seems that my beard is grown scraggly. I will proudly wear a beard trimmed by this noble beast." Before the blackmane the king bent back his head.

Briarburr jumped front hooves and shook his head. After Fahseed made the unicorn to calm, a magic horn sparked and the beard of Fahseed curled smoke upward. The calloused hands of Abel snuffled the small flame.

"That is a first rate trick," responded the admiral. "Hmph! People brag that this unicorn can move an arrow in flight."

After standing and showing his spoon to Ambassador Adolfo, Boschene turned and threw the spoon at Briarburr's head.

Flicking his head, the unicorn propelled the spoon to clang against a wall.

A visibly upset Boschene picked up his table knife and threw it at the unicorn. Briarburr jiggled his horn back-and-forth and then down. The table knife stopped in midair, hesitated, and changed flight. The admiral jumped back when half an arm's length before his face the knife point lodged deeply into the table.

"Admiral, your dangerous actions are an insult to Phoenicia!" exclaimed Cavour drawing his sword.

"Ahh, so the *warlord* has indeed a voice," rejoined Boschene.

"I was an overlord, not a warlord! I now train an army that has strength and might far beyond its numbers!"

"Your games, Sir, have gone far enough," said Fahseed frowning at the admiral. Briarburr neighed to the king.

"So what does the beast tell you now?" asked Boschene.

"Hmph! This unicorn brings to me startling news. Briarburr says that unicorn scouts have seen the approach of your army. From the south march toward us five thousand Egyptian soldiers. Those soldiers are only ten days distant from my palace."

"You do know King Fahseed," answered the admiral, "that Egypt has many possessions. Every year we send our armies on long marches. Conquered peoples must behold the might and power that is Egypt."

Briarburr neighed again to the king.

"Hunh! Unicorn scouts have also found that forty leagues to the east of your first army marches a second Egyptian army. Those four thousand men are thirteen or fourteen days distant from us. Boschene, do you have more information to share in friendship with Phoenicia?"

After Boschene shook his head *no*, Briarburr neighed once again to Fahseed.

"The blackmane now tells me that a third army of Egypt, numbering three thousand soldiers strong, was also sighted. That army follows below and between the first two. Three Egyptian armies are now found on the doorstep of my kingdom."

Once again, Briarburr neighed to the king.

"Well, Boschene, Briarburr has even another piece of intelligence to share with us. It appears that mighty Egypt has war barges to spare. In addition to the barge that carried you to our port, three giant war barges sail toward our land. Each one is filled with heavily armed marines."

"You cannot know these things!" exclaimed Boschene with his face flushing. "You are only guessing!"

"Admiral, unlike some powerful and ambitious people, unicorns do not know to lie. How can I be guessing when you, yourself, know that all that I have said is certain?"

Fahseed shifted his gaze to Adolfo. "What explanation does the ambassador give for what Briarburr has told me? How do you account for three separate armies and three war barges headed toward the place where we now speak? How can this not be a multipronged force sent to conquer my country?"

Bending down his head Adolfo addressed the cedar table. "Worried about the sudden emergence of a united and well-armed Phoenicia, whose vessels begin to compete with ours for trade, our pharaoh wanted to make certain you did not have the magic of witches and demons conspiring against him."

"This land is a threat to us! It must be conquered!"

"No, admiral," answered the ambassador calmly. "During these last twenty days you and I have with our own eyes seen that Phoenicia poses no threat to Egypt. Compared to Phoenicia, your unbridled ambitions for war and conquest are ten times a greater threat to the peace of Egypt. Do not you see, Boschene? We cannot win a war against this land of blue gold swords, magic unicorns, and a winged horse that patrols the seas giving entrance to Phoenicia."

"Listen well, Boschene. While I try to be a patient ruler, I have my limits. My army has never lost a battle, not even when our soldiers were outnumbered by ten to one. Our golden swords and unicorn stallions will prevail against Egyptian marines come by sea, and three Egyptian armies come by land. Fighting in defense of their homeland, Cavour's five thousand soldiers are more than a match for your thirteen thousand infantrymen and marines. If provoked, my upstart country will before the eyes of the world... *humiliate mighty Egypt.*"

"Can you really not understand, admiral?" said the ambassador motioning with an open hand. "When the entirety of your complex plan of attack was by unicorn scouts discovered, the element of surprise that you counted on was lost. This king will not permit your three armies to unite. Strategies will be made to battle each Egyptian army apart and separate. Fighting in their mountains, five thousand Phoenicians will defeat all your soldiers. Moreover, without the entry of your land armies into the walls of the capital, the marines on your barges will be struck down as they wade through the waves.

"To suffer defeat against this small kingdom would be a disaster for which the pharaoh would requite your head, and perhaps mine as well. No, Boschene, it is better to share the benefits of trade with this land than to be by King Fahseed disgraced in war. You will this night turn around your barge and direct it to intercept the three ships that now sail toward us. You will instruct our war barges to return at once to Egypt. You will also this night send couriers to the three armies that march toward this land, and instruct them to turn away from Phoenicia."

Adolfo addressed the king. "The conventional wisdom heard in the palace of the pharaoh is that for all its progress, Phoenicia remains weak. This night you have shown that counsel to be in error. Fahseed, you are a king that Egypt needs to contract... *as a friend*. More than arrogant, you are humble. More than devious, you are wise. As you have learned, as you now know, the mission of the admiral and myself was not diplomatic but preparatory to a war of conquest.

"Upon learning of our deceit you could have had us thrown in a dungeon, or done even worse to us. Welcoming war, you could have made your fame to spread far beyond this land. In a gesture magnanimous you instead chose to confront us this night with a strong argument for continued peace. Not possessing your wondrous golden swords and unicorn stallions, my pharaoh will no more seek harm to come to Phoenicia."

The Irrevocable Tie to Blue Gold

"There remains yet something to show you," said Fahseed to the ambassador.

Cavour again nodded to the guard at the door.

Holding the handle of a sword with one hand, and the flat side of the blade with the other, Maryeta, Lyons, Elyeazar, Jomain, Colyado and six more bearers of magic swords entered the hall and assembled in a line facing the length of the long table. In their center was left a place for the twelfth sword carried at the waist of Fahseed.

"Our two esteemed guests will now see that twelve blue gold swords have more power together, than singly apart. You will also witness the unfathomable correspondence of blue gold to unicorns." That said, Fahseed moved to complete the unity of twelve magic swords.

Maryeta stepped forward and raised high her sword. Behind the girl eleven blue gold swords were raised. The tip of each sword began to glow blue.

"Come and touch sword tips three times to mine!" proclaimed Maryeta.

With the first touch a small orb of light formed above each of the twelve swords. With the second and third touches the orbs grew in size. Twelve orbs, each as large as the hand of the girl, oscillated blue and gold.

The line of sword bearers stepped back to make greater space between themselves and the table where sat the Egyptians.

"Briarburr, now command you the magic light!" instructed Maryeta.

The blackmane moved to face the sword bearers. He swung his head about and jumped up his front legs. Overpowered by attraction, twelve orbs of light moved toward Briarburr. When they transformed themselves to become one large and brilliant orb floating above his horn, twelve blue gold swords were lowered.

The unicorn pranced his hooves in a circle. As if held to the tip of his horn by an invisible cord, the single orb whose diameter now measured the length of Maryeta's forearm, moved with him.

When Cavour motioned for the sword of an Egyptian body guard, Ambassador Adolfo nodded approval for the sword to be given. Repositioning himself by his chair at one end of the banquet table, Cavour raised the Egyptian sword over his head. After bending back his head Briarburr brought his horn forward to slice through the bottom of the orb. From the orb streamed a slivered beam of light toward the elevated sword. Adolfo and Boschene saw light instantly pass through the metal of the sword. When Briarburr shook his head, the stream of light vanished.

Cavour handed the sword to the admiral. Upon inspection of the newly made hole passing through the center of the blade, the face of Boschene blanched. The admiral placed his index finger through the hole in the sword and exclaimed, "This is not possible! By no light can a sword be burnt through! The blade is not even hot to my touch!"

Cavour motioned for an Egyptian shield to be brought to him. Upon receiving it, Cavour raised the shield high over his shoulder. When Briarburr a second time sliced his horn through the orb, a wider beam of light penetrated through the center of the shield.

"Surely my arm deceives me," said Adolfo as he passed his hand through the cut in the shield. "No thing can penetrate bronze metal to burn a hole so large."

"Two magic beams have departed the orb," said Cavour to Adolfo. "Ten remain."

With exuberant joy Briarburr began to buck and cavort as his legs moved sideways several paces and then back again. All the while the orb hovered true to his horn. The unicorn reared front legs high, and so standing shook several times his head. The orb of light separated into ten balls of flame. When with hooves resettled the unicorn nodded once forward his horn, beams of brilliant fire shot out the open side of the banquet hall to light ten corners of night sky.

"Two Egyptians this night witnessed something no man or woman has ever before seen," said the king upon retaking the chair next to Ambassador Adolfo.

"You, Fahseed, saved the greatest magic until last. Nothing in Egypt compares to the power you this night put on display. Even to the doubter Boschene, the connection between the blue gold and the unicorn is incontrovertible and undeniable. King Fahseed, for what I have this night been privileged to with my own eyes observe, I thank you. At whatever cost Egypt must come to possess the magic blue gold. Tomorrow I will learn more of your plan to ferry the unicorns to a far land. But, I must inquire whose genius led to this majestic display of the power of blue gold and its correspondence to the unicorn."

"That was the doing of my granddaughter, Maryeta. She loves deeply the unicorns, and she herself feels deeply the magic of blue gold."

"Fahseed, what you just said is not exactly accurate," corrected Cavour. "Maryeta took her ideas to the three blacksmiths that with you fashioned the blue gold swords. With their help she perfected this powerful display of blue gold magic."

"Cavour, I stand corrected," replied the king. "Step forward Maryeta, Jomain, Colyado, and Elyeazar so that our Egyptian friends can applaud your inspiration." The clapping of hands by the two Egyptians, and everyone else present, lasted long.

"Ambassador," said Cavour, "not you but Boschene has... *a higher look*. I was given the impression that the admiral outranked you. However the words you this evening spoke suggest otherwise."

"Like Adolfo, I am one of the pharaoh's eight brothers," interjected Boschene with what was for him a subdued tone. "There is, however, one thing that favors Adolfo over me. The mother of Ambassador Adolfo is as well the mother of the pharaoh." Boschene lowered his gaze as he added, "The high look I wear, should rather display on the face of Adolfo."

CHAPTER 27

THE LAUNCH OF THE *MARYETA*

"How lucky is that? The biggest barge ever built in Phoenicia bears my name! And just as Grandpa wanted, the *Maryeta* is to sail on the first day of spring."

"By Egyptian standards our barge is too small," replied Lyons who was notably less impressed with the namesake of his sister. "The three Egyptian barges are big enough to hold hundreds of unicorns, not to mention horses for his officers, and cows. It seems Admiral Boschene must have fresh cow's milk for his officers' breakfast, and fresh mare's milk for his own. For cows to freshen into milk also requires Boschene's barge to carry two bulls to breed the cows, one being a backup."

"Grandfather said the holds of the Egyptian vessels each store thousands of bundles of hay to feed the unicorns, and a thousand sacks of wheat to provide bread for the sailors. Brother, can you believe each great barge has two hundred sailors to row the double sets of long oars? And they are not just sailors; they are marines trained to fight on sea and land."

"Hmph, *mare's milk!*" persisted Lyons in complaint. "Boschene needs his luxuries to show everyone that he is better than they. Why does our barge have to be so small compared to his?"

"I will have you know, brother, that by the standards of Phoenicia the *Maryeta* is not small. Our vessel is big enough to hold Briarburr, Peli, Lieutenant Abel, Elyir, Merlew, Jomain, and our crew. There is even room for my five black dogs. Hah! They will bark to warn us that a sea monster comes to attack our barge."

"What if we see no real monsters? Now that I am eighteen years old I do not even believe in sea monsters."

"When you were my play prince you had a good imagination."

"Too bad I became a real prince. Abel declined to be named a sea captain, and so remains Lieutenant Abel. I wanted to stay *not* a prince. Remember how exciting it was to find the blue gold in the cavern behind the waterfall? You and I helped to free Byblos. You and I did brave and wonderful things. Now we are required to wear pretty clothes."

"Since on the *Maryeta* I will have to do my own washing, I am going to wear a set of clothes for more than one day. Hmph! Lyons, we can use our magic swords to reflect a burning beam of sunlight to scorch a monster's nose."

"If it has a nose. Monsters are not like dogs that have soft noses."

"The different sizes of my dogs will make interesting the voyage. Lyons, do you know why I picked black dogs? Upon finding himself surrounded by hundreds of pure white unicorns, I wanted that

Briarburr should not feel so out of place. Briarburr and my black dogs will become fast friends."

Abel, Briarburr, and Peli joined the royal siblings.

"I hope," said Maryeta to Abel, "that the beauty of tomorrow's parade of unicorns will keep me from crying when I say goodbye to my grandfather."

"The only girl to ever cross the far seas is braver than me," responded Abel. "After spending too many days learning how to command a barge, I still would rather fight on hard ground."

"Can your worried look have to do with concerns about my seamanship?" inquired Abel turning to Lyons.

"Not *your* seamanship, Lieutenant Abel. I worry about Admiral Boschene's."

"But the admiral has fifty times more experience at sea than I do."

"If most of the admiral's time at sea was spent in a luxurious cabin, it does not really count as experience," replied Lyons. "Boschene is arrogant. And it is not just me who dislikes him. Briarburr and the winged horse detest the pride and selfishness of the admiral. Why does Boschene need to hate unicorns? He only wants to be the big hero that brings back magic gold to Egypt."

"If it were not for his lust for the blue gold, he would today be anywhere but waiting for unicorns to board his vessel," responded the commander of the *Maryeta* patting Lyons on the shoulder. "And, I will grant you that on some future day Boschene's pride could get our fleet in trouble."

"Horned horses trust you more than the Egyptian commander," observed Peli as she reached wing tips to feather the smiling cheek of Abel, "and they respect that King Fahseed sends his only grandchildren to show his confidence in your success."

"While unicorn confidence is most sure about this smaller vessel," neighed Briarburr, "the magic of the white herd will serve to keep all four barges safe. You, Maryeta, and Lyons will return safely to Phoenicia. And I, the black sheep unicorn, will with you return."

Farewell to the Phoenician Barge

Soldiers lining each side of the league-long road from the capital city to the harbor held their salute while to the sound of drumbeats their king passed before them. Fahseed was followed by white unicorns walking five abreast. Children holding flowers crawled and squeezed themselves through the two long files of soldiers. For the perseverance of the children, unicorn hooves came to be cushioned by soft and colorful petals.

When Fahseed reached the harbor, the patter of drums quieted. The king voiced encouragement to the unicorns as they stepped onto gangways entrancing great Egyptian barges. When the landing ropes of his barge were untethered the proud admiral remained, the same as on days previous, unseen in his sumptuous cabin. Freighting precious cargoes of unicorn horses, three enormous Egyptian barges departed the Phoenician port.

Painful farewells awaited those readying to board the *Maryeta*, the last vessel to embark. His grandchildren came to stand before the king. During the many years that followed the loss of his precious daughter, Lyons and Maryeta had given their grandfather everything to live for. The king did not know what now could take their place to fill the unsmall hole left in his heart.

"I give to you the blessing of the ruler of Phoenicia. I commend safe passage to the distant land where is to be found the new hold of the unicorns." Fahseed set his gaze on Maryeta. "To you I also give the blessing of a grandfather. Let benign winds soon bring you back to me. Until I see her again, may the heavens keep my Maryeta safe." The king hugged long Lyons and Maryeta; tears welled up in his eyes.

"Wahuuhh... Grandpa... you always loved me... hunhhunh... so much," whispered Maryeta through her sobs.

"How I wish that I could share this great voyage with my granddaughter. I fix my heart on the sure hope that Abel and Briarburr will bring you back to me."

"You sacrificed everything for us," said Lyons in a husky voice.

One official act remained to be done. Mounted on his horse, Erban brought two fallen overlords with hands tied, to stand before Fahseed. From within his cloak the king drew out a scroll. "Roward, Winfray, without fault or reprimand you have toiled every day building the streets of the capital. I now charge you to fulfill new duty as crew members of the *Maryeta*. Upon your return, and with the good report of

Lieutenant Abel, this writing proclaims that you will be granted full pardons and have restored your liberty." After studying the eyes of the two prisoners, Fahseed added, "You have my granddaughter to thank for the mercy I this day show to you. Bring her and her brother back home to me. Do not on this voyage fail me."

The two prisoners stepped onto the boarding planks of the *Maryeta*.

"I am surprised that on this voyage of discovery you do not accompany your two best friends Merlew and Elyir," said Fahseed to Erban still mounted on his horse. "Atop a garrison wall you three once formed an incredible fighting team."

"King Fahseed, it is just that... I cannot bear to leave behind my horse. Hah! Did you know that in its entire life this stallion has never lost a race against... *horsemen?*"

"But if I am not mistaken, by two children your very fast steed... was once challenged."

After smiling wide, Erban reined his stallion to depart the king.

Fahseed called for Abel. "Here, take it. To you I entrust my magic sword. Other than to encourage and aid the protector of Maryeta and Lyons, I would not for any reason part with this precious blade. Nor my grandchildren, nor you, nor my magic sword can to me be lost."

"You do not know how much I have wanted to wear at my waist one of the twelve magic swords. Along with this blade, the blue gold swords carried by

Jomain, Lyons, and Maryeta will make safe our voyage."

"Keep a close eye on the two prisoners," added Fahseed tugging on Abel's sleeve. "Both of them were needed to fill out the crew."

"For that charge I shall as well have Jomain to assist me," answered Abel quietly. The lieutenant was the last to board the Phoenician barge that would accompany the convoy of three very large Egyptian vessels carrying eight clans of unicorn horses to a far side of the earth.

As he slowly made his way back to his palace the brow of the king was furrowed in doubt. To a gentle breeze he unburdened his heart.

"All I ever wanted was for Lyons and Maryeta to be safe. It took long and bloody struggle to make them safe. With these very hands were dug the graves of five men who died in the war that I began, men I once called friends. And now that Lyons and Maryeta are made safe, I send them off to the end of the world. With their departure I have lost the grounding and center of my existence. What is wrong with me? What have I done?" In frustration and disgust, Fahseed hit a hand to his chest. "I was not thinking right. I was too hasty when I made the promise that my grandchildren would accompany the unicorn voyage. Still, a man's promise is his bond, and the promise of a king is inviolable."

Walking more, he calmed himself.

"It is true enough that Maryeta wanted to go on the great adventure. And, it was right that Lyons be at her side. Perhaps I should have renounced my crown and joined Lyons and Maryeta on the voyage. Then I could again have protected them. But wearing no crown, my promise to the eight matron unicorns would have carried no kingly guarantee. Now I can do nothing but wait helplessly for their return. Perhaps with this blunder, this terrible risk that I have burdened on my two loved ones, I am shown little fit to be king.

"Without me beside them, my two little briarburrs are now to cross seas unknown. Can I even bear the thought that my Maryeta will return to me changed, made more woman than girl?"

CHAPTER 28

INTO OPEN SEAS

With one small Phoenician vessel trailing in their wake, three very large Egyptian barges cut through ocean waves. With each passing day four crews were made more competent to sail cleanly the sea. Unicorn stomachs gradually calmed; horned horses learned to sanction the motion of rolling waves to rock themselves to sleep.

After fifteen days of westward sail no more trading vessels came to be sighted by the four barge convoy. After ten more days marked by favorable winds, a huge mountain came to trace the far horizon. Abel identified that mountain as the mighty pillar that marked the end of the known sea. Four barges landed at the base of the marking mountain to refill water stores and resupply firewood. Perhaps never before had so many unicorns reveled together in bucks, kicks, cavort, and play. The magic horses delighted in spontaneous races that stretched every muscle and sinew. No unicorn mare knew when land would next be sighted, and when next she would drink at the bank of a river.

Because herd animals fear the unfamiliar and unknown, the matron unicorns had the foresight to station trusted guard stallions to keep the white herd confined together in play. No unicorn was afforded the opportunity to desert the barges. Had the matrons not made restriction, the end mountain of the known sea would have birthed a new colony of unicorns seized by the sudden thought that there they were more safe than on Egyptian barges.

A Sea Unknown

Every night those aboard the Phoenician barge took time to notice the stars that blinked and sparkled above them. Maryeta called the stars that formed a cup and pointed to the fixed star, *The Ladle*.

"I think it is a ladle to store the mare's milk that Admiral Boschene drinks."

"While he may think that he commands the whole sea, not even Boschene can boast that he commands the stars above," disagreed Jomain. "As for me, I say it is a ladle brimmed full with the magic milk of unicorn mares."

"As we sail westward, tiny changes in the night heaven fascinate me," offered Elyir. "I identified last night a star that I had never before seen. Maryeta, did you know that Merlew has memorized all the star formations in the Phoenician heaven?"

"I know of no smarter man than Merlew," answered the girl. "On the other hand I, for one, cannot imagine memorizing all the important stars in the sky. For that I do not have the required patience."

"My memory certainly does not possess the capacity to remember each star," added Lyons.

"The most beautiful stars in the sky will shine down on tall trees and... the waterfall sure to be found in the new home of the unicorns," neighed Peli.

"In spite of the beauty of the stars," whinnied Briarburr softly to the winged horse, "if you were not at my side I would face an unbearably long voyage. Knowing that you shall one day again race with me on Phoenician beaches makes bearable the thought of the long return voyage."

Peli did not neigh back answer to Briarburr, but instead stepped away from her friends. The blackmaned unicorn followed after the mare.

"I know that the white herd does not see me as a true unicorn, or a true friend. Still, I cannot imagine leaving them all behind. Because I care... *so deeply* for the unicorns, I do not know if I can return with you to Phoenicia."

"And Peli, I for you care deeply."

"How, dear Briarburr, does one decide which half of the heart to leave behind irretrievably lost, and which other part of the heart to carry beating into a new life? Either way the tear of one's heart brings pain unbearable."

"I feel your heartbreak." The eyes of Briarburr softened as he neighed again, "Peli the unicorn hold will be a wonderful place of new beauty and safeness. I am certain the white herd will greet your presence as a gift to them."

"Could not you remain with me in the new place?"

"Nothing would please me more than to begin my life anew in the magical hold of unicorns, with you by my side. I would that with them... I were welcomed. But, I am three times judged by the unicorns. My mane is black. My violence in battle has killed, and a war horse is inimical to the cohesion of unicorn purity. Worst of all, I count human persons as true friends. Friendship and loyalty indivisible connect me to Maryeta, Lyons, and Fahseed. It is for me especially unfortunate that unicorns deny all friendship that transgresses the confinement of magical blood. And, the friendship I give to Fahseed carries with it a promise of my return to him. Dear Peli, the unicorns would perhaps pardon one, but they cannot ignore all three of my failings. They will forbid my presence in their new hold."

"It is Briarburr that leads westward the white herd. For that the unicorns must make exception."

"Unicorns neigh that become involved in war, I have lost all innocence. And that because I am no longer pure in heart, I shall not long feel in my body the continued presence of unicorn magic."

The vastness of the ocean could be compared to nothing known. The day upon day participation of the *Maryeta* with endless expansions of water, resulted in boredom. Amidst unabating and overwhelming vistas of sea water, it seemed that only two passengers aboard the Phoenician vessel found profitable leisurely occupation. As they each day imagined the things that one wave would converse about with the next wave, the friendship of Maryeta and Elyir grew.

"That wave is too proud of the elegant line of her crest," said Maryeta pointing. "She strikes me as a very haughty wave. Because of her conceit, the line of her crest will soon become crooked."

"That wave, over there," responded Elyir, "just invited sharks to ride her curl. Because her wave is more moist and luxuriantly buoyant than the waves following her, two sharks gladly accepted her invitation."

"You must admit, Elyir, that the big wave now approaching is the most loyal. She employs the three dolphins that every day keep watch over the *Maryeta* and her crew." Within ever changing formations of clouds the two friends identified palaces, bears, birds, cows, and heavenly beings with delicate wings.

"I think there are few things more lovely than a cloud beset purple and red sunset. What find you more beautiful, Elyir, the sea or the clouds?"

"Maryeta, the sight and sound of waves rippling, breaking, and crashing is to me enthralling. The sea wears countless subtle colors of emerald, gray, and blue. The colors of the sea are ever at play."

The vote was one for the sky, and one for the sea.

Even with their own sails trimmed to perfection, Abel and his oarsmen could scarce keep pace with the Egyptian sails and oars. For his part, Admiral Boschene seemed not to mind if the smaller Phoenician barge trailed far behind his three great vessels. Many times Peli took to flight to find where into the night disappeared the large Egyptian vessels.

Unlike his admiral, the Egyptian captain by the name of Lockshray proved himself friendly to the Phoenicians. Some nights he drew alongside the barge of Abel and made sacks of grain and bundles of hay to be surreptitiously conveyed to the *Maryeta*.

"Again on this night I thank Captain Lockshray for his kindness," said Abel as he saluted smartly. "Without your largess, Briarburr would now be nothing but skin and bones."

Sea Shepherds

"I say that you have made our small barge more beautiful than any of the three large ones," said Jomain to Elyir one afternoon as friends relaxed together at mid-deck.

"Out of a little piece of wood Elyir can sculpt a delicate winged horse," seconded Maryeta the opinion of Fahseed's blacksmith friend. "Look at these blocks carved by Elyir. Can you believe that they individually lock together to build a palace?"

"Hmph!" reproved Merlew mildly his nephew. "Because most of our wood becomes ornamentation for our barge, there remains precious little wood left to cook with."

"Seeing that we have only mere scraps of food left to fry," responded the girl with a mischievous smile, "not having enough firewood is the least of our worries. Anyway, Elyir's carvings are worth a hundred times more than mere scraps of firewood." Pretending not to hear compliments about his art, the modest young sculptor moved to stand with hands hanging over a deck rail. He found that the dolphins that followed the Phoenician barge had multiplied, and become splashingly noisy.

"Over here, Merlew," said Elyir motioning to his uncle. "Just look at all the dolphins that have joined to our vessel. Why do dolphins today cavort so much?"

Both men moved to the other side of the barge and looked out upon many more dolphins. Fore and aft they observed even more energetic dolphins.

"Surely you, the smartest young man I know, can see what the dolphins are doing," said Merlew as he looked closely at Elyir.

As was his habit when he was solving a problem, before his chest Elyir rubbed hands together. The youth's face broke into a wide smile of discovery. "Since my uncle was the first to solve the riddle of the dolphins, he shall inform Abel."

"A moment, Lieutenant," petitioned Merlew. "As we sail ahead a circle of dolphins moves and maintains rotation about us. It is as if the dolphins are trying to herd sheep to match the progress of this vessel. You know how hard it is to herd mindless sheep. But of course it is not sheep that they herd. Come Abel, and see for yourself." The two men walked to the starboard rail and looked over.

"Well, well, Merlew. So it is not just dolphins that surround us."

"Lieutenant Abel, we need a fish net, and at that a big one."

"Merlew, on this side of the boat there are too many fish; when we should attempt to haul in the net it would break."

"Mates, look into the water!" carried loud the voice of the lieutenant. "Fish swim all about us! How would it be if we catch for our next meal some of these eager fish?" The fish were ravenous for the snippets of bait and shreds of food thrown to them. The fish would even swallow a hook baited with a bit of colored cloth.

"Hahah!" Lyons was joyous. "This, Merlew, is the most fun I have ever had! Any fish that is not as long as my arm gets thrown back!"

The sails of the *Maryeta* were collapsed down. The far off sails of Egyptian vessels grew small, and then over the horizon disappeared. No one on the admiral's flagship worried that in uncharted waters the smaller Phoenician barge was left behind.

The next morning the fishing was even better. That the fish were biting like mad, and that they were the best eating fish that anyone had ever tasted, made it everyone's choice to stay put and just fish.

Observing the Phoenician sailors that for so many days had rowed hard, and were now laughing and joking with each other as they fished, Abel allowed, "Merlew, these men *needed* a break."

"We have a unicorn with great pelican wings that can rise upward and relocate the whereabouts of our impatient admiral," replied Merlew. "In a matter of six or seven days we can rejoin the Egyptian fleet. Ermm... Abel, I just had an idea. Let us right now organize a contest. Everyone will want to prove he is the best fisherman," Merlew nodded at Maryeta, "or the best fisherlady."

"To catch fish the men use hooks and lines, stringed arrows, and even lowered baskets," answered Abel. "We will award a prize for the biggest fish by each method caught." Measuring strings made with equally spaced interval knots were soon put to work.

"This will be so much fun!" exclaimed Maryeta upon hearing the rules for the fishing contest. "The best thing about our contest is that I am sure Admiral Boschene has not even noticed that one vessel has to his fleet become lost."

Sailing in his customary rearmost position in the admiral's three barge formation, Lockshray found himself fretting. His admiral would brook no delay to allow the disappeared Phoenician vessel to catch up with the Egyptian fleet. Lockshray knew of no deadline that Boschene had to fulfill. Rains had replenished the Egyptian fleet's water supply. To be sure, daily rations for man and beast had been reduced. But the fleet still had large quantities of food and feed in reserve. On the other hand the Phoenician barge had no reserves of food. Lockshray could only conclude that Boschene had an ulterior motive. The admiral wanted that in the middle of an immense sea the Phoenician barge should be forever lost. Boschene would shed no tears if Abel, his sailors, and perhaps above all the grandchildren of Fahseed died of hunger and thirst.

"I wonder if the mares that supply milk for the admiral had their rations cut in half?" mused the captain of the hindmost Egyptian barge to his first mate.

When towards evening Lockshray slowed the stroke of his rowers his vessel began to fall farther and farther behind the other two Egyptian barges. During the deepest part of the night the captain himself turned the rudder. Aided by a newly propitious tail wind, the vessel of Lockshray sailed back toward where had last been sighted the Phoenician barge.

The deck was everywhere strewn with fish drying in the sun. No matter; the Phoenicians fished on. Abel said to no one in particular, "Befall us what may, the hold of the Maryeta will contain plentiful supplies of salted fish."

"Lieutenant, to the west looms a sail!" Soon again the lookout shouted, "Captain Lockshray comes back to find us!" A skiff brought the Egyptian captain to board the Phoenician barge.

"I now discover that Lieutenant Abel found a splendid reason to vanish from our fleet. You have replenished food supplies with what looks to be half the fish in the ocean. I dare say that these fish could feed a thousand sailors."

"Captain Lockshray, my men were not only hungry, they were exhausted. That man standing over there, Merlew by name, noticed that the dolphins had herded fish to our barge. I decided to heed the will of the dolphins and stop rowing in order to fish. After all, when they are biting who does not love to fish? Come with me and have a taste. Our cooks have learned to fry them just right. Oh, that reminds me, Lockshray. Our cooks complain that precious little flour can now be found on my barge."

"Regarding flour, cooking oil, and firewood your cooks need no longer worry."

Lockshray sent back his skiff with instructions for his men to try their hand at fishing. His sailors were further informed that the ten men that caught the biggest fish would each receive a prize. With sailors dedicated to winning recognition for their fishing prowess, surrounded by dolphin shepherds a Phoenician barge and an Egyptian barge languished dead in the water.

When the fishing came at last to end Maryeta handed prizes to the winners on board her namesake barge. One of the winners, the former overlord Winfray, received as well a special smile from the girl.

"Winfray told me that I remind him of a daughter now gone from him. Can you believe, Lyons, that she would have been exactly my age? I wish she had lived to accompany me on this barge. You and Abel are too quiet. I need some... girl company!"

"Elyir talks to you."

"Yes, but all he wants to talk about is... *art!*"

"My men now sail on full stomachs," commented Lockshray as he piloted his barge westward in convoy with the Phoenician vessel. "Whatever punishment I receive from Boschene for turning back to find Abel, will be worth it."

"Boschene will be unwilling to delay his progress by searching for us," responded his first mate. "Captain Lockshray, what if during the next ten suns you do not worry at all about finding Boschene? Let our admiral instead worry and stew about your disappearance. When you finally catch up to him, for his joy at not losing this great sea craft Boschene will surely pardon your tardiness. Neither worry you about being lost at sea. Just as the unicorn matrons carried on the vessel of Boschene know where they want to go, so also know the two unicorn matrons on this vessel. We may arrive a few days late, but we will surely arrive at the same destination as does the admiral."

While under the command of Admiral Boschene two great Egyptian barges sailed onward toward the set of the sun, one great and one small barge commanded respectively by Captain Lockshray and Lieutenant Abel, sailed apart.

CHAPTER 29

BEFORE THE PAVILION RIVER

Officers on board the two barges under the command of Boschene had every day marveled that their vessels traveled so long, and so far, without facing contrary winds or heavy seas. Then something new, something not having to do with the weather began to be noted. With neighs, head shakes, stomps, and jumps the magic horses exhibited each day more and more excitement. The neighing and stomping annoyed Boschene. Twenty times a day he made comments to the effect that he could not too soon be rid of the horned beasts; their ruckus prevented his napping. To the mind of the admiral it was past time to exchange mindless unicorns for the blue gold that would make mighty Egypt forever invincible, and make the admiral even more famous than his half brother the pharaoh.

A distant line on the horizon marked a place where land was to be found ahead. At the same time that Boschene's lookouts sighted the distant strand of mountains, the sea turned uneasy. Word was brought to the admiral that the unicorn matron named Lorial had identified the land that the barges sailed toward, not as an island, but a mainland.

Lorial directed the pilot of Boschene's barge toward a spot situated before a perfectly shaped volcano. There the unicorns would claim a new home.

Beset by rising winds the two barges of Boschene landed in... paradise.

Each time a unicorn found footing on the beach, four hooves exploded in joy. The horned horses sped after each other jumping, kicking, bucking, and all the while neighing with excitement that could be properly called *a jubilation of horses*. Even Boschene had to admit that he had never seen a sight as triumphant as hundreds of unicorns at play in celebration exultant.

The white sand beach fronting the unicorn hold was backed by a thin fringe of palm trees. It was quickly noticed that the waterfall cascading above the north end of the beach provided not only fresh water, but also concealed the entrance to an enormous cavern providing a place of shelter. Directly to the west of the hold stood the tall volcano crowned with a white collar of pristine snow.

Once the unicorns were safely ashore, rising storm winds dictated that Boschene's vessels quickly depart. With lightened cargo holds, two great barges blew northward. The admiral now desperately wanted one thing, and one thing only. Remaining on the flagship barge, the matron Lorial would fulfill the unicorn pledge to lead the admiral to the deposit of the blue gold.

By the time the ships of Lockshray and Abel sighted the volcano marking their destination, winds had turned violent. The two sea commanders had the same thought; the stormy weather was repayment for having squandered several days of perfect enjoyment catching fish.

"At all cost I land the unicorns," signaled with flags the Egyptian captain to his friend Abel. "Turn your barge back to the sea. Ride out the storm. We will again find each other."

"Briarburr and Peli instruct to sail northward," signaled back Abel to Lockshray. As the *Maryeta* turned out to sea the blackmane paced nervously the rolling deck.

"Briarburr, you and I will soon stand on firm ground," neighed Peli to reassure the big stallion.

"I fret not about the storm, Peli. My heartfelt desire was to gallop, at least once, in the new home of the white herd. It is because of me, because of you and me both, that the unicorns found and gained their new hold. We are the ones that made a pact with Fahseed to protect the unicorn clans. Peli, I wanted the matrons to acknowledge my hard fighting for them, to acknowledge all the sacrifices that I for them made. Now they will never have to thank me for the battles I fought to gain their safety."

"Would you rather have the love of the unicorn matrons, or would you rather have their respect? Perhaps their love does not mean more to you than their high regard?"

"Peli, to *Love* I am little known. My mother mare did not choose to love me. But Peli... you are right. When I consider it, because of my ignorance of matters of the heart I would every time rather be respected than loved."

"I learned to love unicorn mares beset by wolves and black-hearted men. That occupation taught me how to love the unicorn with the black mane."

Winds howled dark and sheets of rain shot horizontal. Amidst towering waves the crew mightily struggled to maintain control of the *Maryeta*. On a rolling deck the winged horse and the blackmaned unicorn huddled side by side balanced against each other. At last the winds left off and the driven rain softened its descent.

On a day when the sun shone clean the Phoenician vessel refound the coast. After three more days of coastal passage Abel's barge came upon Boschene's two barges. That is, Abel found what was left of them. All about the shore barge timbers were splintered and broken. As Abel splashed his legs through the waves he was greeted by the scowls of Admiral Boschene. The glares were poisonous.

"Where in blazes is the barge of Lockshray? Cannot he sail his barge to keep up with a mere Phoenician?"

"It was almost a moon ago, Admiral, that we lost sight of you. You did not sail back to make sure that the *Maryeta* was safe. We at last found Captain Lockshray, of whom you had also lost track. We followed him toward the coast where lies the unicorn hold. When Lockshray insisted upon landing his precious cargo of unicorns, the dreadful storm blast separated us from the barge of your captain."

"But where in tarnation is he? His barge is all that remains to me!"

"Rest assured that Lockshray will arrive here no later than tomorrow… or the day after."

"If Lockshray should fail me, I will take command of your small vessel." Boschene scowled again. "Blast! Your little boat will not freight much gold."

"Sir, there is not sufficient room on the Phoenician barge to house even your officers and ranking sailors."

"Damn my officers! All that now matters to me is the magic gold! I swear by the heavens above that I will not without the blue gold return to Egypt!"

"Who can say," muttered Abel as he moved away, "perhaps the admiral's oath will ring more true than he imagines."

"Look about us on all sides," said Merlew to Lyons Abel, Elyir, and Jomain as they together walked along the shore. "The timbers found everywhere about us are irretrievably rent. With shattered boards the two shipwrecked barges of the admiral cannot be rebuilt."

"How in the name of heaven did the admiral manage to wreck his barges against this benign shore?" inquired Jomain. "The wreckage lies too high up the beach to be explained."

"The admiral was obsessed with his search along this coast," offered Merlew. "He would not have a storm to turn him away from where the gold was said to be found. Having made a bad wager with the elements, the storm at last broke apart the reckless and conceited plans of Boschene."

"That must be so," responded Abel. "Now that I think about it, where is the matron unicorn that was to guide the admiral to the blue gold?"

"I was told," replied Jomain, "that when the admiral's barge was thrown against the beach the unicorn panicked and jumped off. By now, the frightened unicorn matron is from here long gone."

"Briarburr and Peli now offer the only chance for the admiral to find the blue gold," reflected Lyons.

"Boschene is going to have to change the manner of his coarse treatment of the blackmane, and as well his rude treatment of the winged horse," concluded Elyir.

As was foreseen by the lieutenant, in two days the one remaining Egyptian barge found its way to the site of the admiral's wreckage. Standing on a beach by brokenness befouled, the wits of Boschene had become collected.

"Captain Lockshray, thank the heavens your barge is whole. Your arrival today brings me the vessel that will transport the blue gold back to Egypt."

"So, Admiral, you have found the gold? That is the best news to my ears."

"No, no, not yet, Lockshray. Still, it is only a matter of days before the black marked unicorn will lead me to where we shall mine magic gold. Unlike the silly matron unicorn that abandoned me in the storm, Briarburr understands what it is like to obey military orders."

"Sir, with two thirds of your fleet destroyed, how will all your sailors be returned to Egypt?"

"You need not bother yourself about that." Boschene slapped Lockshray on the back and added, "Upon my return to Egypt, I will immediately send barges back to these waters to retrieve my loyal sailors that were necessarily left behind."

"Right, Sir," answered Lockshray.

As he stepped away the captain of the only remaining Egyptian barge rolled his eyes. Under his breath he groused, "Boschene, you are to me well known. Once you return the great hero to Egypt, you will have no further thought for those that risked their lives on this voyage. Your only concern and ambition will be to have the army make of yourself the next pharaoh."

It took time for Lockshray to digest all his thoughts. Because of his commander's recklessness he was now forced to consider that he would forever remain stranded in the new land. Lockshray began to fume. He had captained well his barge. It was Admiral Boschene that had wrecked the most part of the Egyptian fleet. Truth be told, on the return voyage his admiral would likely treat his sailors no better than bilge water to be thrown overboard.

Lockshray decided he had had enough. Barely controlling his temper he caught up with Boschene and said, "You are the High Admiral of Egypt. How is it that the small Phoenician barge survived the storm, and both great barges under your command did not?"

"You should have learned by now that those that question me are crushed beneath my feet," replied Boschene with his face flushing red. After stepping away the admiral changed his mind and stepped back to confront Lockshray face to face. "You steered your vessel to me; for that this day began in your favor. This

day, Captain Lockshray, *does not end* in your favor."
With his guards in tow the admiral turned and in a
huff walked away.

"For too long I have borne the arrogance and
insults of Boschene," muttered Lockshray. "I can with
certainty already know that he intends to abandon me
and my crew to die here. Boschene now surmounts
insult with grievous injury."

CHAPTER 30

THE PLACE OF THE MAGIC GOLD

Fires on the beach frolicked flames, which try as they might were little able to unravel encircling darkness. Undulating flickers of firelight did, however, illuminate the drawn and brooding face of the admiral as he sat in counsel with Abel and his three barge captains Lockshray, Lufflol, and Altber.

"How say you that we proceed?" inquired an uncharacteristically pensive Boschene rousing himself. All eyes turned toward Lockshray and Abel; still having anchored barges to command their status had risen.

"Because the blood that flows in the race of unicorns pulses with a magical attraction to the blue gold," replied Abel shifting long arms forward over his crossed legs, "Briarburr and Peli represent our best and perhaps *only* hope to find the sought after deposit. Wings make Peli a scout invaluable. She can lead us to food, of which we now have very little in store. She can also lead us away from enemy tribes that should roam hereabout. You need, Admiral, to request the charitable help of two magical horses."

The next morning the admiral and Lockshray met with Abel, Briarburr, and Peli. For the purpose at hand Boschene suffered a notable deficiency. Because magical sparks from the touch of a unicorn horn impacted not his skull, the admiral could not comprehend the uniform animal tongue. Nor could Briarburr and Peli understand him.

"Boschene asks your help to find the place of the magic gold," offered Abel relaying the request to Briarburr. "He understands that when you draw close to the blue gold you will feel its presence."

"Peli and I are thankful that the white herd reached in safety its destination," began Briarburr looking closely at Boschene. "That neighed, I have a question for the admiral. Did the matron unicorn that was thrown from his ship, limp onto the shore? From a fall so high did she suffer hurt?"

Informed of Briarburr's question, Boschene turned to Lockshray and ordered, "Find out at once if the matron unicorn was injured by her jump off the barge." After some moments passed the admiral began to fume.

"From here the matron unicorn is long gone. How does that unicorn now matter to me?"

"Admiral, what is your plan?" inquired Abel changing the direction of the conversation. "Will you stay here with your barge, or will you accompany the search for the gold?"

"Of course I go for the blue gold! My long experience in command is essential to the mining expedition. One hundred of my sailors will stay behind to lay up food stores for my return to Egypt. Those one hundred will defend my ship from any enemy that crosses my beach."

It did not take long for the admiral to receive report from Lockshray. "Sir, as she ran into the forest the matron unicorn was seen to limp badly."

"To me, Lorial matters much," neighed Briarburr when later told the full response of Boschene. "To wolves or lions I cannot and will not abandon a lost unicorn. Whether she is badly injured, or only lost and bewildered, I must help her. This is my last promise to the white herd."

That evening Lyons stroked the back of a blackmaned unicorn found sprawled on his belly by a camp fire. At the same fire were gathered Maryeta and Merlew.

"Cheer up, Briarburr," cajoled Lyons. "Thanks more to you than to anyone, even including my grandfather who negotiated well with Egypt, much has been done. When in the forest you cut the rope that bound my hands, you became the first to take a stand against Lord Baltric. Fahseed has said a hundred times that it was because of you... that you were the unicorn that united and brought the people of Phoenicia together.

"It was as well your doing that reunited the unicorn clans in Phoenicia. And, it was you who convinced the unicorn matrons to sail across a fantastic expanse of water to find a new home in a land made a luxuriant garden. For all you have accomplished, you should be smiling. Only two things remain for you to do; find the lame matron unicorn and locate the blue gold. In those quests you will have the full help of Peli and the rest of us."

"I think that Briarburr not only worries about the fate of one lost matron unicorn," observed perceptively Merlew. "The blackmane is anxious about what is to happen to all the sailors that are to be left behind in this strange new land."

"I too worry about that," chimed the crystal noted voice of Maryeta. "With lots of barrels of food supplies, and the gold that weighs heavy, there will be room for less than half the sailors to return on the one Egyptian barge that remains."

The girl rose, crossed her arms, and stomped a foot.

"What exactly is to become of those sailors that are abandoned here? Those men sacrificed much to bring the white herd to their new hold. Before we return to Phoenicia we must help the abandoned Egyptian sailors to secure a home where they can live out their lives in peace."

The next morning Boschene gave final orders to the one hundred sailors remaining on the coast with the Egyptian barge. The men left behind were to first build a defensive fence on the beach. They were to clean, wash, repair, and re-equip the one remaining vessel. Albeit reluctantly, Boschene allowed that little hay needed to be gathered for the return voyage. Excepting for the one he rode, no horses were to recross the ocean. Along with the cattle, their fate was to be slaughtered. Upon learning this, Briarburr neighed a vow that the horses and cattle that had survived the long crossing over the ocean would in the new land establish their race. The horses and cattle could not travel so far only to merit a butcher's knife.

Search for Blue Gold

Following slowly westward an ascendant river valley lush with vegetation, Admiral Boschene led forward the expedition in quest of magic gold. Trees blossomed yellows, reds, and purples. Through myriad branches flitted birds plumed in every color imaginable.

With the five hundred Egyptian sailors that followed the admiral went Lyons, Maryeta, Abel, Elyir, Merlew, Jomain, Roward, Winfray, the blackmane, the winged horse, and five black dogs. For the slowness of their forward progress, it was obvious to the Phoenicians that the emaciated Egyptian sailors had for too long been limited to half rations.

"I climb to a high place of lookout to make sure we march not into an ambush," neighed Briarburr to Abel. The blackmane was off with Peli and five dogs running at his side.

"Who told the unicorn and winged horse that now bear the utmost import to my success, that they could leave my formation?" barked Boschene. "No one leaves without my orders. Send a platoon to bring them back." Glancing about, Boschene complained more. "The formation is sloppy. Order the men to shape up their files of march." No detail of soldiers was prevailed upon to retrieve the quickly disappeared unicorns.

"Sir, because they find themselves disheartened and fearful, your sailors move with timidity and hesitation," said Lockshray drawing his horse next to the admiral. "No jungle in Egypt is so dense as the one we now travel through. The men know not what great beasts are found in this new land. Having lost two of three barges, your hungry sailors also know that two out of three of them will not with you return to Egypt."

"I am the High Admiral of Egypt. My sailors had better shape up or they will feel my lash."

"Unfortunately, Sir, in this jungle your admiralty is less high than in Egypt," continued Lockshray. "It might be advisable for you to tell your sailors that you will find and establish a fortified position that they can well defend, until from Egypt you return for them. It will inspire them to know that your code is never to abandon loyal seamen."

"Hmph," was Boschene's terse response.

"Limping along the bank of the river far below us, the matron unicorn would have come this way," whinnied Briarburr to Peli.

"I agree. If only amidst the confusion of trees and vines we could catch a glimpse of her white coat. As you ahead travel, stay on high ground. I will find and return to you." That neighed, the winged horse mounted a thin breeze.

Trotting onward, Briarburr concluded that exercise was exactly what he needed. During the long voyage the muscles in his legs had notably softened. Shrinking muscles are sore muscles. Accompanied by Maryeta's canines he would give his legs a hard workout.

"I did not find her," informed the returned Peli. "Neither did I find nearby any bands of enemy warriors to threaten us. For now we are safe." Since on its daily path the sun had advanced far, the blackmane and the winged horse turned heads and hooves back to rejoin their friends.

"My sailors, I will offer you tonight new encouragement!" By for once taking advice offered, Boschene surprised Lockshray. "Since light remains to the day, and these trees bear fruit, eat your fill of whatever you find."

When he later stood before his men, Boschene's features were relaxed. "Without the sacrifices made by each and every one of you, we would not be so close to the magic gold I seek." Vacant stares, and here and there a weak smile greeted Boschene's words.

"I will have the unicorn and the winged horse to do two things for me. They are to find the place wherein lies the blue gold. That accomplished, they are to next locate a redoubt that we can fortify as a military outpost of Egypt. For those sailors that temporarily remain behind, I will have quarters built. Fields will be sown to supply food. Until from Egypt I for you return, the very capable Captain Lockshray will be placed in command of your new garrison."

It took time for the words of the admiral to fully register with his dispirited men. The proffered hope of a new garrison, plentiful food, and real beds gradually strengthened the resolve glimpsed in the faces of beleaguered sailors. Perhaps life would go on after all. Still, no shouts of *hurrah* came forth from the men.

"You seamen know me well," the officer to be left behind would have his say. "Like my grandfather before me I am a builder. Like my father, I am a soldier and a sailor. I promise that we will for ourselves raise a strong garrison."

Moving to stand next to the admiral, Lockshray nodded politely his head and smiled wide. Reciprocating the gesture, the admiral returned a grand smile.

"We must thank the admiral for one thing more," continued Lockshray raising his hands for emphasis. "Boschene has generously agreed to gift his horses and cows to those of us that here remain behind. In this land you will have horses to ride and cows to plow with!"

Hurrahs now sounded from men who understood well that the presence of cows and horses much improved the odds of their survival. The captain grabbed a hand of the admiral and raised it high. While for effect Boschene smiled, inside the admiral seethed.

"How dare you presume to speak for me. Those horses and cows belong to me *alone*."

"Sir," answered Lockshray still smiling, "you have made it my lot to make sure the abandoned sailors that are left behind have a fighting chance to survive. We both know that I, the captain of the one Egyptian barge that survived the storm, will nevermore see my father. I say that the livestock, this small fraction of all that you call your own, is to me owed."

Lorial

On the next day difficult terrain and dense foliage slowed the column's westward advance.

"I sense that the unicorn matron is not so far away from here, and that she finds herself desperate," confessed that evening Peli to Maryeta. "I hate that I cannot find her. Some of the brush by the river is so dense that my eyes cannot penetrate the leaves and bushes."

"My dogs and I will tomorrow join your search for Lorial. As you fly close to the ground with me on your back, my dogs will follow after my voice. Five acute canine noses will do the trick."

"While I am not fond of dogs, it is worth a try, Maryeta."

"If my five dogs find Lorial, will Peli begin to like them?"

"I will try, Maryeta."

At sunrise the next morning Peli, Maryeta, and five dogs found themselves on the river bank. After making each dog in turn sniff the scent of Peli, Maryeta remounted the winged horse.

"You are right, Peli, our eyes do not penetrate well the thick cover. But because invisible scents travel far, my dogs will soon find Lorial." Through the morning the search continued futile.

"Peli, what if our column yesterday passed the spot where Lorial now rests?"

"So we have to go all the way back to where we were yesterday?"

"My dogs have energy to spare." Maryeta called her dogs to follow in reverse direction.

The winged horse glided down and spread wings to embrace the blackmane.

"We finally found her! That is, Maryeta's dogs found her. To keep a pack of wolves at bay, Lorial had taken refuge in the far recess of a high-walled ravine. The broken place above her hoof is so badly infected that she can scarcely stand. After scaring off the wolves, Maryeta and her dogs now protect the matron."

"Walking so far on a bad hoof obviously worsened the injury," offered Briarburr.

"Lorial does not understand why within herself she cannot find enough magic to heal her bones. She told me she was ready to give up. Having lost hope, her magic failed her."

Peli led Briarburr to the place where the matron unicorn lay injured.

"Although parts of his hide are unwhite," neighed Peli to Lorial, "the magic of Briarburr is pure. His horn will fix your leg *good as new!*"

Healing sparks flashed into Lorial's broken and infected leg. It was as Peli had said it would be. By the next dawn the leg of Lorial sustained her weight.

"When I saw that Boschene's barge was about to crash onto the beach," recounted Lorial, "I panicked and hurled myself down. Starting today, this unicorn matron will act her age and no more be afraid. After all, I lead one of the eight lines of unicorns that inhabit this new world. With the strength of the mighty Briarburr, and the resolve of Peli's spirit, we three will repay the unicorn debt entire."

"I begin to like canines," neighed Peli with a smile, "at least a little."

"Me too," replied Lorial. "I could not believe how the dogs frightened away wolves bigger than themselves."

"Hah! You are the first unicorn to be by black dogs rescued from wolves!" exclaimed Maryeta.

"Now that the unicorns are three, they will soon find the magic gold," reported that same evening Lockshray with Briarburr at his side. For once Boschene looked with no antagonism at a unicorn. Because the admiral's horse had come up limp, like his men Boschene was now on foot.

Air Scouts

"Please Peli, I want to flip in the air and land back on you. Remember that I am a girl acrobat!" The winged horse bucked hind quarters to launch the slender teenager upward.

"Flying with you is more fun than flying alone. I like the feel of your legs clamped against my sides."

On a high place Peli set down her hooves. After sliding feet to ground Maryeta draped an arm over the neck of Peli, whereupon the winged horse engaged the girl in their mission, "What do you see about us? Tell me where stands the mountain bearing blue gold."

"There is something strange about the mountain tops arrayed far to the west."

"I know that today we are supposed to extend further our search, but Maryeta, those oddly set mountains are too far away. Lorial sensed that the blue gold deposit is not that far distant from the coast."

"Well then, look over there Peli," Maryeta pointed to a new place. "See the unusual mountain to the south? I think the blue gold lies in that strange mountain whose one side climbs upward in three massive steps."

"It is also quite distant, but the day is young enough," answered Peli. In an easy motion Maryeta grabbed mane and swung herself onto the back of the winged horse.

"Look, Peli. We are going to fly over a mountain that for all its length and width is not so tall. It is crowned with many spires that rise up like giant, craggy, stony thorns." Peli wheeled and descended towards a place in the spired mountain where lions rested on the crest of a canyon wall.

"I have never seen so many lions gathered together, and all with muscles so powerful," commented Maryeta. "Those lions are the true lords of their domain. Below them is a beautiful box canyon with a waterfall. It is strange to see so many lions guarding a waterfall."

The winged horse once more straightened her course for the mountain that rose in three immense steps. She and her rider landed at its base to investigate.

"Maryeta, I do not here feel the presence of magic gold. But since daylight remains, let us fly to the other side of this mountain and look there for gold."

When no signs or intuitions of magic gold presented at the mountain shaped by three enormous gradients, the winged horse and Maryeta gave up their search and headed back to discover how far had advanced that day the column of the admiral.

"So *again* today you did not find the blue gold!" scolded Boschene leading on foot his horse.

"I am sorry to disappoint you, but today Peli flew very far," offered Maryeta. "We looked to find the gold in a mountain that rises high in three great steps." Without another word said, the admiral turned and walked away.

"He is once more angry at us," neighed Peli.

"He is once more not courteous," responded the frowning girl.

With Lyons and Lockshray at his side, Abel had overheard the remark of the admiral. The Phoenician lieutenant offered, "You two did your best. The admiral knows that the men are hungry. With each passing day they look more starved. It hurts me, and it should hurt the admiral more to see waste away the bodies of hearty Egyptian sailors."

"More than gold we need to find food," said Lockshray nodding at Abel. "If during the next three days we do not obtain food, we will be forced to stop and do nothing but hunt and gather. Once the column stops its advance, discipline will be impossible to maintain. Groups of ten and twenty men will desert. Our marching days should then be ended, *for good.*"

"The vegetation around us is fabulously lush," said Lyons gliding fingers along the string of his bow. "It is, Lockshray, as if the forest expresses joy for its exuberance. Some of these plants will have big roots that can be eaten. The roots of others are likely poisonous. I wish I knew which plants had edible roots that would not pain my stomach. Hmph, in a forest so full of green leaves and fronds... there must also be deer."

"Take Winfray and the dogs with you," instructed Abel. "More than they obey Maryeta, they mind him."

That evening Winfray and Lyons returned to camp each carrying a deer on one shoulder. The two fires in the camp that soon roasted venison could not begin to satisfy the hunger of five hundred men.

CHAPTER 31

SPIRE MOUNTAIN

"Since my empty stomach quarrels against sleep, I have time on my hands for my sister to tell me everything she saw while seated today on the back of Peli."

"That, brother, I will be glad to do. Now let me see. Peli and I first noticed distant western mountains that loomed high in a strange and irregular pattern. Placed with abruptness, one peak did not connect smoothly to the next. Changing course southward we flew on to a three-step mountain to there find *no blue gold*."

"You saw nothing else?"

"Oh... I forgot. There *was* something else. We flew over a mountain of spires with a canyon that was guarded by the biggest mountain lions I have ever seen."

"Anything about lions, those spelled differently from my name, interests me. Hmph. You found blue gold in the cavern now named after me... the Lyons Den. Our mother once saw two lions guarding that cavern. What if the lions you sighted stand guard over another den of magic gold? Did you investigate what the mountain of spires might hold? Did it by chance have a waterfall? Our Lyons Den in Phoenicia was found behind a waterfall."

G. D. Hanson

"Brother... well... no... and yes. No we did not take the time to look closely at that canyon. But as I recall, it did possess a waterfall."

"Perhaps the mountain of steps was meant to be a diversion, a monument so great that it overshadows the true place of the blue gold, and so confuses any quest to find the treasure."

"All right," said Maryeta patting her brother on his arm. "When Peli musters more strength I will compel her to fly back to the spired mountain to take a closer look. And brother, now that I think on it," she hit the arm of her brother with her fist, "you are not wrong to ask why lions are to that place drawn."

Despite her tired wing muscles, Maryeta prevailed upon Peli to again fly the next day. It was not long before the flighted horse drew close to the mountain of spires.

"Look Peli! Lions still stand guard... over something." As she descended the winged horse glided close above the heads of lions. In vain the huge cats jumped up to claw at the flying horse.

Peli landed hooves next to a brook, gulped water, and exclaimed, "This is the best water I have ever tasted!" As soon as she was done drinking the winged horse began to graze.

"It is so pure that it tastes... *sweet*," answered the girl cupping water to her mouth.

"This grass is delicious! Each bite-full strengthens me."

The girl splashed legs across the canyon's brook and looked closely at the rock that built upward into a canyon wall.

"Peli, in spite of a thick layer of dust this rock faintly glistens." Maryeta splashed water against the rock wall. "Hmm, you know what? Just like the sand I found in the cavern by the waterfall, these rocks have blue and gold color." She walked along the canyon wall pausing to splash more water against the rock. "Yes! Yes! A streak of gold tinted with blue traces along the wall. The vein grows wider than my thumb!"

"Maryeta, the reason the water and grass are so sweet and good tasting is because this place is assembled in magic. I now feel it in my wings. I do not know how I was so dull to not sense this when we first flew over the lions on the wall of the canyon."

"Heheh! The sight of so many great lions distracted you!" Maryeta threw herself down in the grass, and for her joy could not stop laughing.

"There is only you and I in this place, and I am not laughing. How is it that you laugh so long alone?"

"Grandfather told me that I do everything with all my heart. Hahah! So, I am laughing *heartily!*"

Blue Gold Found

In the camp of five hundred sailors shouting came to be heard, and hunger was forgotten.

"The blue gold is found!"

"Hurrah for Peli!"

"Hurrah for Maryeta!"

"Praise the skies!"

"I did it! I found the magic gold!" exclaimed the admiral bounding about as he slapped his officers on their backs.

Every Egyptian sailor knew that by himself Boschene had had little to do with the discovery of the blue gold. But on this day sailors did not care a whit that their admiral once again exaggerated his own significance. Still, more than one sailor reminded another that upon being advised that Lorial sensed the blue gold close by, the admiral had thrown caution to the wind and rushed to land his vessels. Two wrecked barges had been the result of his recklessness.

Briarburr did not have the same reaction as the admiral. The black marked unicorn wanted to be alone with his thoughts. The finding of the blue gold meant hard choices awaited him. His first thought was for the unicorn matron Lorial. She had consented to lead Boschene to the gold. Her job done, Lorial must be escorted safely back to the hold of the unicorns. Her clan of horned horses required the return of their matron. Would Peli accompany Lorial, and if so when? Not wanting to lose forever the winged horse so dear to him, the unicorn stallion fretted at the thought that Peli would stay on in the new land.

Briarburr next thought on his promise to Fahseed. The blackmaned stallion knew that he must again sail across the wide waters and return to protect the one clan of unicorns that had remained behind. The blackmane's one consolation was that at least Abel, Lyons, and Maryeta would with him undertake the long voyage back to Phoenicia.

"Lockshray, this is the news we have long waited to hear," offered Abel motioning for his friend to walk with him toward a declining sun.

"It is the best news I have had since I was ordered to join this amazing voyage. But, I hope that about something I am wrong. My worry is that Boschene will now become even more difficult than before."

"And I know, Lockshray, that your most pressing concern is for the men who will here live on for the rest of their days."

"Hmph. My thoughts just entertained an image of the cows that were freighted on Boschene's barge." The face of Lockshray brightened as he added, "I was just a boy when my father gave me a calf all for my own. With her mother close by, the heifer calf would sprawl herself out in the grass and soak up the warm rays of the sun. Between the cow and her calf existed an unforgettable natural intimacy. The best part for me was that I knew my little heifer calf would someday mother her own calves. That is how I planned to build my very own herd. Abel, to me it is a precious memory."

"One of the few gentle memories I have from my youth was tending sheep," responded Abel. "I will never forget a boy's joy at seeing twin lambs to be born. And, I think I can guess, Lockshray, to where else stray your thoughts. I worry about the same thing. The cows mean fresh milk and cheese for the men who here remain. We have a saying in Phoenicia that a man without a cow is a man without a bride. The cows must be kept safe and secured for those who do not sail on the voyage back to Egypt."

"The horses are to me even more important. With horses to ride, I and my men can here defend ourselves."

"With regard to cows and horses, I will support my friend Lockshray in whatever he finds necessary to do."

Boschene at the Place of the Blue Gold

"Find the entryway!" Boschene was impatient for his own eyes to see the magic gold. "Know that I refuse to mount a winged horse to enter into the canyon of gold."

Lockshray determined what must be done. Hammers and chisels pounded through the back wall of a cave corridor that led conveniently inward toward the canyon of blue gold. As the men fanned out along the walls of the canyon, none could believe the richness of the gold deposit.

Once the sailors gained entry into what soon came to be called *Shining Canyon*, the sentinel lions that had roared their displeasure at the arrival of the Egyptians, strangely quieted. It was if they recognized that the purpose of the intruders was noble.

"We will not waste time smelting the gold into sheets!" exclaimed the exuberant Boschene. "The gold ore is pure enough to take with us as it is."

Sailors were divided into two groups. Four hundred men chiseled ore from veins in the sides of the canyon. The remaining men chipped away impure rock fragments from lumps of blue gold.

"I found it, Abel. This vein of gold is exactly the color of my sword."

"Why so it is, Lyons. Just imagine the surprise of Fahseed if our barge returns to Phoenicia bearing blue gold ore."

"You know what I think, Abel? Our barge could transport enough gold to make swords for a thousand Phoenician soldiers."

"Lyons, our barge could carry enough gold ore that, alloyed with other metals, would supply not only swords for *two* thousand soldiers, but also shields and breast plates."

CHAPTER 32

LOCKSHRAY LEADER

While over the western rim of Shining Canyon began the decline of the sun, a triumphant Admiral Boschene stood watching Roward and Winfray as the two former Phoenician overlords placed gold nuggets into cloaks for transport. Joining the admiral, Lockshray and Abel seated themselves.

"Sir, there are things we must look to, decisions that must soon be made," said Lockshray.

"Did you know that Roward once commanded the greatest garrison in Phoenicia?"

"That was some time past, Admiral," interjected Abel as he reclined to lean on an elbow.

"Hmph? And what is this... *we* business?" retorted Boschene turning to Lockshray. "The one and only job of you two officers is to obey *me*, the admiral."

"Boschene, the day you lost two barges, my status as a captain rose," replied Lockshray regaining his feet. "When you ordered me to stay behind in command of most of your men, my authority a second time rose."

Knowing where the words between him and his subordinate were headed, Boschene drew his sword and menaced his captain. "You, Lockshray, are a dog!" To Boschene's astonishment Lockshray as well brandished his blade. Shouts arose that the admiral and Lockshray had drawn swords.

"You are a traitorous dog!" exclaimed Boschene lunging at his subordinate, whose blade parried the sword thrust.

His sword unsheathed, Roward rushed to the side of Boschene. Quick to take advantage, the former Phoenician overlord thrust his sword to pierce the shoulder of the Egyptian captain. The wounded Lockshray stumbled and fell backwards to the ground. As Roward pulled his sword back a smile grew to engulf the contorted features of his face. With his next stroke he would tear at the heart of Lockshray.

Roward's sword hand fell limp; the intention of a former overlord went unfulfilled. The sword of Winfray, the other disgraced Phoenician overlord, brought end to the life of Roward.

Boschene felt a sharp edge to set against his throat. With hatred firing his eyes, the admiral turned to look at the menacing Winfray. Deciding immediately that armed contention with Winfray was not in his best interest, the hand of Boschene let go his sword.

"When I ruled my valley in Phoenicia, even then I knew Lord Roward to be a scoundrel," said Winfray while extending his free hand to help Lockshray to his feet.

"Roward bided his time," observed Abel come to the side of Lockshray. "He waited for the perfect opportunity to make of himself your replacement. Only when Boschene returned to Egypt, Roward would not have been here left behind."

"Some people do not change," remarked Winfray as he looked knowingly at Abel. "Others of us... *do*."

"You, my friend, and I, have made ourselves to be better men," replied Abel clasping the hand of Winfray.

"Admiral, this day my mouth will not be locked shut!" exclaimed the Egyptian captain with a hand pressed to his cut shoulder. "Your traitor Roward lies dead at your feet. Since surely he was in your pay, his blood is on your hands. Now you, and the men with us, will hear what I have to say." Hundreds of Egyptian sailors gathered with eyes riveted upon two commanders that with swords had come to blows.

"These are my conditions," began Lockshray. "As the future success of Admiral Boschene is at stake, and perhaps also his very life, he will do well to listen... *carefully.*"

Boschene looked about for help from his men; no offer of aid came.

"We are here five hundred Egyptians," began Lockshray to address the sailors before him. "One hundred men, and only that many, will return the blue gold ore to the admiral's barge. The other four hundred that in this land are destined to remain, are too weak and hungry to march down to the beach, and then be made to turn around and march immediately back to this highland. I and the four hundred men I am to command will not deliver gold to the barge and then starve on the beach, or sicken in the jungles of the lowland. I will not freight gold for the admiral only to myself die on the coast. The lives of those who stay with me will from today be built in this high mountain climate."

Lockshray saw that the men listened keenly to his every word. More than that, in the eyes of the sailors he glimpsed agreement.

"Without horses, those four hundred men remaining under my command will not long survive. For that, Admiral Boschene, one horse only will accompany your column back to the barge. The rest of the stallions and mares, along with the cattle, will belong to those of us that continue in this highland."

Lockshray paused to hear objections to his words. None came.

"All of us here present wish to return to the valley of the Nile. Because that cannot be, we that remain will build a fortress and there stay alive as we await a new Egyptian fleet come to rescue us. If the pharaoh wants more blue gold, and he assuredly will, then he will also have us to return home on the next three great barges that sail here from Egypt." That said, the Egyptian captain would extend more hope to his men.

"Admiral, in case you absent yourself from the barges that someday here return, tell the pharaoh that stone inscriptions will be placed to show our countrymen where loyal Egyptians are in this land to be found."

"On one thing I insist, that the winged horse accompany my barge on the return voyage," responded the admiral as he straightened himself to again show military bearing. "Her wings will help me navigate away from storms. She has the mobility and keen eyesight to see where dangerous reefs lie under the surface of the water."

"With her Phoenician friends belongs Peli," answered firmly Lieutenant Abel.

"Then I take with me the Phoenician barge!"

"The admiral has many times brought to my attention the fact that the Phoenician barge does not meet his high standards," replied Abel. "Reckless navigation will not wreck my barge in a storm. My barge returns me to Phoenicia."

"Admiral, why not build small barges like that of the Phoenicians?" inquired a sailor. "That way all of us could return with you to Egypt."

"On its own the Phoenician barge is too small to survive the return voyage to Egypt," answered Boschene. "Nor have we here the tools or facility to build barges to the high standards of the Egyptian Navy."

Lockshray declared that one thing remained to be done. From a pile of cleanings four hundred black rock fragments were gathered. To those were added one hundred nuggets of blue gold. From a cloak formed to be a sack each sailor drew, as chance assigned, either a pebble or a gold nugget. Because some of the seaman dreaded the prospect of long return voyage to Egypt under the command of an arrogant admiral, more than one nugget of gold was freely traded for a black pebble.

For the healing touch of Lorial's magic horn, Lockshray's shoulder began to mend. Joined to sit with his friend, Abel confessed, "Knowing that your sword was more than a match for Boschene, my sword remained sheathed. By Roward's perfidy and deceit I was caught off guard."

"Had you drawn your sword at the start of the fight, it would have been two against one. That would have looked very unfair. The sailors would have concluded that had Boschene vanquished me, he would then face the mighty Abel. No, my friend, Roward should have followed your example and let Boschene handle his own fight."

"Still, I will next time be better prepared to come to your aid."

"For that I thank you. Everyone knows that in a fight Lieutenant Abel is assuredly not someone to be trifled with. Still, I will hope that the sword fights I face in the future are one against one."

"I cannot tell you how thankful I am that my countryman so quickly intervened. Winfray must have known that if given the chance, Roward would again be... *Roward*. I should have hated for your life to be taken by a corrupt Phoenician found under my command."

That evening Boschene sulked alone by his fire. He told himself that he had not verbally assented to any of the conditions laid out by his rebellious captain. But try as he might, he could not pretend that he had not been grievously insulted. Not once in his illustrious career had he been so humiliated.

"I have a request to make, one that only you two can help me with," said later that night Abel to Maryeta and her friend Peli.

"My dear Abel, you have only to ask," replied the girl.

"I need the two of you to fly back to our Phoenician barge. Tell my men that in less than twenty days Boschene will have returned to the beach. Before that happens, the corralled cattle are to be taken to a secluded canyon, and there guarded until the Egyptian barge weighs anchor. I refuse to let Boschene make of the cattle barrels of meat to take on his long voyage home to Egypt. Nor do I want our vessel to be found on the beach to tempt Boschene to steal our stores, or the barge itself. On the same dark night that the cattle are made safe, our barge is to slip quietly out from the bay.

"Before our barge returns to the landing beach, have my men make sure that Boschene and the Egyptian vessel is long gone. As for me, I am compelled to help Lockshray begin a fortress that secures safety for his men. In the intervening time, my men must not grow impatient for me to return to them."

"After tomorrow's fall of darkness, Peli and I will arrive at your barge."

"This, Maryeta, is the best part," continued Abel grinning slyly. "Tell our sailors that we will sail back to Phoenicia bearing blue gold to protect them, their children, and their children's children. Hah! Remember those tabac leaves that the men found? Our return voyage would be made more pleasant if my sailors should happen to find more."

Boschene Wears No More Smiles

Boschene hated that he had been outflanked by the captain that he himself had designated to command the four hundred Egyptians stranded in exile. However commanding only two hundred Egyptian soldiers, with one hundred of those found far away on the coast, the numbers were overwhelmingly against him.

Boschene convinced himself that he knew who was really to blame for Lockshray's treasonous behavior. The culprits were the blackmaned unicorn and the scoundrel Abel.

"I never liked unicorns, or for that matter Phoenicians," muttered the admiral to himself. "And a black marked unicorn is the worst of his kind. Abel, Lockshray, and the unicorn can all rot here." If on some future day an Egyptian expedition sets sail to retrieve the left behind sailors, Boschene would make sure that Lockshray's blood was spilled in the far place.

With backs burdened by heavy sacks of gold ore, one hundred Egyptians walked away from the mountain of spires. Facing the risks of a long voyage begun without the magical presence of unicorns on board, the seamen harbored superstitious doubts. Proof of that benign influence was that the one storm that beset the fleet occurred immediately after the horned horses were deboarded at their new hold.

Seafaring tradition called for the captain to go down with his ship. That meant that having lost the two vessels under his command, it should have been not Lockshray but Boschene that stayed behind. The sailors returning back to the shore with Boschene knew that sea captains in crisis need to think clearly and calmly. However, Boschene in crisis was given to rants, name-calling, and panic. Boschene's motives and actions centered always on himself. Half of the one hundred men marching back to the remaining Egyptian barge came to regret not having exchanged the gold nugget they had drawn, for one of the four hundred black pebbles.

Peli and Maryeta Returned

"How did the men respond to my orders about the cattle and the barge?"

"The cattle will with stealth be removed from the corral the same night that your barge slips away from the beach," neighed Peli in answer.

"The men are loyal to you," added Maryeta touching Abel's arm. "Whenever it is that you return, your barge will be in wait. The crew was very glad to learn that both Briarburr *and* the benign presence of blue gold will accompany them on the return voyage."

"Ahh, I was worried that my sailors would lose heart. It cannot be easy to wait so long for the return of their commander."

"Sir, the sailors manning the barge have coaxed food from their surroundings. Your ship is well-filled with barrels of dried fish, dried roots, and dried fruit. And... the tabac leaves you wanted have already been secured and sun-dried."

"Peli, Maryeta, without your help I do not know what I would have done. Before Boschene would have left my newly resupplied vessel in wait for me, he would have burnt it."

CHAPTER 33

THE WIFE OF OLD CHIEF CALI

Southward followed four hundred Egyptians a babbling stream. Somewhere in the direction of the unicorn hold Lockshray would search out a new home for his stranded sailors. On some future day his garrison might be called upon to provide military protection for the magic horned horses. With the column of hungry Egyptian sailors went Abel, Lyons, Maryeta, Jomain, Winfray, Elyir, Merlew, Briarburr, Peli, Lorial, and five black dogs.

"At least the horses enjoy the grass they eat," said Abel to Lockshray as the two walked ahead of their horses that now and then paused to graze. "To put something, anything into their bellies the men grind grass and bark to mix with white clay. We are become desperate."

"Unfortunately the supply of fish, nuts, and berries in Shining Canyon was too quickly exhausted by five hundred hungry sailors. But Abel, resourceful Egyptians always find some way to survive." Upon hearing that said the big Phoenician was impressed that even when things were most trying, Lockshray's outlook stayed positive.

"For the deliverance of the unicorns I owe a large debt of gratitude," neighed the unicorn matron upon joining the two commanders. "I will prove myself to be of service, and this time I will not depart until you find yourselves newly established in this land."

On the right flank of the slow moving column walked Briarburr and his rider Lyons, and Peli with her rider Maryeta.

"I need to teach you two youth to enjoy eating grass," neighed the winged horse.

"Grass would be better than the earth worms I saw my brother devour for supper last night."

"Yuk. Thank you, Maryeta, for reminding me of those *delicious* worms."

The two unicorns headed to the close by stream for a drink. Slipping feet to the ground, Lyons and Maryeta began to cup water with their hands. Fixating his eyes on something across the stream, Briarburr froze. Peli moved her head to follow the stallion's gaze.

"*Nyerrrummumm*, Briarburr, in the big tree, I see them too," she neighed quietly.

"Remember long ago when you and I first spied two children up a tree?"

"I had just met you for the first time, and then two half wild children suddenly tumbled down from tree perches."

"This time," neighed the blackmane, "you will not fly away."

"My dear Briarburr, from two children neither of us will this time run away."

After splashing through the stream the stallion swerved his body this way and that around trees and bushes. The hooves of Peli and the feet of Lyons and Maryeta followed fast after the blackmane.

"It is happening again," muttered Maryeta as she ran. "Only this time it is not me and my brother that will fall to the ground."

As Maryeta anticipated, in their haste to flee charging beasts two children neglected the requirement for their hands to maintain firm hold of tree limbs. Through leafy branches caromed two small bodies to thump down on the ground.

Peli, Maryeta, and Lyons closed the circle on two young tree spies now grounded and caught. No more than ten years old, the girl began to cry. A couple years younger than the girl, the boy seated on the ground dropped his head and with his hands covered his eyes.

Maryeta grabbed up the girl and pressed her teary face against her chest. Lyons pulled the small boy to his feet. Briarburr deftly sparked his horn to the heads of two native children.

"Why were you spying on us?" inquired Maryeta as she stroked the girl's long black hair.

"Did you hurt yourselves by falling out of the tree?" neighed Peli.

"We were watching the shining warriors walk past us," answered the girl without pausing to think how she had come to understand words spoken by a strangely dressed girl and an even stranger winged creature.

"We meant you no harm," interjected the boy.

"Do you come from up this canyon?" neighed Briarburr.

Two heads nodded *yes*.

"It is dangerous for you two to come so close to an advancing army," neighed Peli in an amiable tone. "Where are your parents?"

With sudden realization that something strange had happened, the girl looked wide-eyed at the unicorn and winged horse and exclaimed, "Big animals talk to us!"

"I never spoke to an animal before," added the boy with the tone of his voice brightening.

"We are not going to harm you," soothed Maryeta. "We want to know about you. That is all."

"Our mother lives in the ledges of this canyon," responded the girl gaining her composure. "Our father was lost in battle. They killed him and his friends out in the plain where your soldiers now march. From this big tree we watched to happen the battle."

"It was terrible," added the boy. "Our father will never come back to us."

Lockshray had sent Abel to find out what the commotion at the stream was about. Maryeta explained that the two children fell out of a tree.

"Well if there are children here, then there must be a settlement, and food."

"Are you the tallest man in the world?" asked the native boy tugging at Abel's leg.

"Heheh! You are right about some men being shorter than me." The big Phoenician grabbed the little boy and swung his light frame around in a circle.

"It has been too many years since my arms swung a child about. I had forgotten how *good* that is to do."

"I used to love to swing little boys around. My turn!"

When Maryeta set down the boy, Abel crouched on bended knees and asked, "Tell me, do your people have food they might sell to us?"

The still smiling boy quickly nodded *yes,* and added, "Our enemies cannot find where we hide our food."

"We always harvest a big crop," added the native girl. "But now there are not enough grown men left to eat all the flatbread our mothers make."

"See here young lady," said Abel raising his forearms for inspection. "Made of precious gold, these braces protect in battle my forearms. I will trade them for food from your village."

Upon seeing Briarburr, with a child on each side, lead the way into the settlement women yelled to their children to run and hide. It took time, but as almost always happens curiosity came to triumph over suspicion. With each tree child pulling one of her hands, their mother was dragged along to meet the new friends. Soon after, gathered villagers stood scrutinizing the foreign warriors and the two horned creatures taller than a bison.

The chief of the village looking dusty and neglected, along with his wife looking neat and tidy, presented themselves. Briarburr gave them the gift of the uniform animal language. It soon became evident that the one that made decisions having to do with the village was not the chief, but his wife. For her part she quickly concluded that the intruders with strange dress, and even stranger animal friends, did not intend harm to befall her village.

Bread was prepared and set before Abel, Maryeta, and Lyons. All three were immediately observed by native bystanders to be ravenously hungry.

"Spread with honey this bread is scrumptious," complimented Maryeta. Accompanied by smiles from the chief's wife, more flatbread came forth along with fried beans and sweet tasting fruit.

"My name is Benilvina. My husband is called Cali."

"I am Abel. We come here from very far away. If our men do not soon eat, they will die of hunger. Will you sell us food so that we do not perish? If our men eat your food today, one day soon they will learn to feed themselves."

Abel held out his forearms to demonstrate the means of payment. After carefully inspecting the braces the wife of the chief promptly disappeared. When Benilvina returned, she was accompanied by women carrying large baskets filled with the grain that for famished Egyptian sailors signified survival.

"We call this delicious grain *maize*," said Benilvina. "If there is not enough maize to feed your men, return to my village and I will refill the baskets for you. Now tell me, were you the ones that found their way past the great lions into the mountain of many spires? And what exactly are the great four-legged animals that stand before me?"

For the benefit of the women, children, and the few native men that had gathered to stare at the unusual visitors, the chief translated the responses given by the strangers.

"My husband is called *old Chief Cali...* but not because he is old. It is because he is not the younger Chief Cali that leads another clan of my people. In my eyes my husband is still young. I tell my husband that old Chief Cali looks younger than young Chief Cali."

Upon hearing the compliment from his wife, the chief held out an arm motioning a salute to her.

"Take away the dust," whispered Maryeta to her brother, "and the chief has the physical condition of a young man. There is not an ounce of fat on him. I like that he is not adorned with anything other than his knife and the pelt that hangs from his waist band."

"That pelt once belonged to a very big rabbit," observed Lyons. "The handle of his knife is nothing to look at, but his rabbit skin is beautifully feathered and beaded. That pelt must be his good luck charm."

Old Chief Cali's wife explained that since the mountains came to be, her tribe had lived within the same canyon walls. They had been content to cultivate maize and to hunt and gather what was to be found in their mountains. Her tribe had never wanted for food. Now, her people's story had turned to grief. Since three years before they had lived in constant fear of fierce northern warriors that raided their village, kidnapped their children, and killed their men.

"Big man Abel," said the chief. "You must help me to defeat my abhorrent enemies that took my youngest daughter from me."

"It is not me that commands the soldiers that march through this broad valley. My captain is the one to offer help to Chief Cali."

The backs of Briarburr and Peli were weighted down by eight large baskets of life-giving maize tied two by two. The sailors in the column greeted the arrival of two equines freighting food with a welcome fit for heroes. It had been far too long since the men commanded by Lockshray had fallen to sleep with bellies full. That night sailors' dreams pillowed soft in newly gathered hope.

"Lockshray, now that your men rest with food in their stomachs, what is it that worries you?" neighed Briarburr.

"So, you noticed. I do not want the cattle to become lost to me."

"They will not to you be lost," neighed Peli. "You worry a lot about every matter concerning your army."

"It is my obligation to worry not only about the battles we fight, but also about every morsel my men must eat. Hmph. I also worry about the poor condition of the shoes worn by my sailors. You do know, Peli, that officers are paid to worry about their men."

"For your many worries you are not well enough paid." Harrumming a horse grunt Peli neighed again, this time with a smile. "Worry no more, Captain Lockshray. At dawn I will fly off and bring the cattle to you. As the cattle pause to eat grass while they walk... it *will* take some time."

"I go with Peli," neighed Briarburr. "Keeping safe the cattle we will find to where Lockshray has newly marched, and to that place bring the herd."

"Peli," answered Lockshray, "it turns out that I need your wings even more than Boschene claimed he did."

Growing Friendship

After Chief Cali and Benilvina finished the next morning their inspection of the Egyptian column, the chief's wife made a decision. She and her husband would accompany Abel, Lockshray, and the sailors as they resumed their march down the valley. Benilvina laid out one condition.

"You will show me how to ride a horse, one without a horn. The horses with horns frighten me." She wanted to learn what it was like to ride on the back of the elegant animal that she had not before imagined to exist.

Upon finding at the approach of evening fresh baked flatbread set out for them, the mood of the column of sailors again improved. Sporting a self-important smile Benilvina motioned to the baskets laden with food and pronounced, "I before sent word to the next canyon that food must be presented to our new friends."

The following morning, as Abel's heart once again gladdened to see curious children perched in trees, he was joined by Lockshray and the chief.

"Those youngsters have never seen so many men with skin colored so light, let alone seen horses and unicorns."

"I suppose you are right, Cali, but my skin is about the same color as yours," replied Abel.

"Hah! But unlike the color of your hair, mine is black as a moonless night." The chief motioned toward a canyon fingering up into the mountains. "Looking at the roughness of that place, one would think that no people live there. That thinking would be wrong. My relatives that dwell in those mountains have learned where maize can be coaxed to grow tall. In a tiny draw no wider than a path for one person to walk on, two hundred kernels of maize will grow fruit to feed for two moons a family. My mountains are the *best* place to live."

"Chief Cali," said Lockshray pointing toward the faraway east side of the plain, "the cliffs over there have an aspect formidable. Have any of your relatives found a way to penetrate those high cliffs and live on the other side of this valley?"

"There it is impossible to dwell. Only lions live above those high cliffs." Because it was the only way he knew to smile, the chief grinned wide as he added, "When I was young I crossed the river that moves fast below the high cliffs. After almost killing myself, I finally found my way up the cliffs. The high place was so full of fierce lions that before scrambling back down I was almost a second time killed."

Heeding the chief's words, Lockshray sent men to explore for ten days not the high cliffs to the east, but the canyons to the west.

All the scouts returned with reports unfavorable. No place in the western mountain canyons could be adequately fortified to withstand the attack of an organized army. The narrow canyons were ambush prone; room for an army to maneuver was too much restricted.

Lockshray remained intrigued by the valley of the great plain where could be found a unique combination of desert sand, grass, and water as well as his new friends Chief Cali and Benilvina. The problem was that defense of the wide valley looked to be next to impossible.

After some days of hesitation the captain shifted the course of his column of sailors. Still accompanied by Cali and Benilvina, the Egyptians marched toward the formidable rock walls that rose on the eastern edge of the wide valley. Lockshray would himself inspect the mountain that loomed high above a fast river, the place so disliked by Cali. On the eastern side of the valley camp was made.

"Cattle! Cattle!" was shouted.

"See there, Abel! As promised, the blackmane brings the cattle to us," said Lockshray. "Praise the heavens we lost neither Boschene's horses nor Boschene's cows."

"Only, where is the winged horse?"

"Look upward, Abel," replied Lockshray pointing. "Before the rock face of the mountain her wings enjoy strong updrafts."

As Abel watched the wings of Peli float before the high rock wall, he decided the sight would make a good subject for a future painting by Elyir.

"We natives do not comprehend that people should own animals," said Cali. "Herds of bison are not by anyone owned. Guard well your cows, Lockshray. There will come a day when natives come from far away will attempt to steal them."

"The cattle bring the welcome prospect of fresh milk and cheese," answered Lockshray. "The possession of cattle that can be yoked to plows will help persuade my sailors to become farmers. In this climate we can each year grow two crops of the delicious maize. As well as my men, the cattle and horses will savor each mouthful of the multicolored kernels of grain."

"Cali is right," affirmed Abel. "The arrival of a herd of cattle means we must redouble our efforts to build a stronghold protective of both men and livestock."

CHAPTER 34

PROW MOUNTAIN

"It is as the chief told you," offered Abel. "The rock walls of this mountain are impregnable. This sheer and imposing mountain permits no entry."

"Over there," answered the Egyptian captain. "That place of folded rock would be a perfect way to enter the mountain. That narrow entrance is wide enough to allow passage of man and beast. And, it would require only a half dozen soldiers to defend that fold in the rock."

"You both know that the folded entrance is a dead end," objected Cali. "That place opens only to solid rock."

"Chief Cali, Abel, this mountain fascinates me," continued Lockshray. "Perhaps it is like the feelings that unicorns have as they approach a place of the blue gold. I cannot help but imagine that behind these high rock walls lies something unexpected. I tell you that if the safety of my four hundred Egyptians was secured, without knowing what I was looking for I would through that folded entrance tunnel into the mountain. Hunh. Can blue gold also be found inside this mountain?"

"There was no hint of gold in the rock walls we inspected," answered the Phoenician lieutenant. "We have all noticed the magnificent look of this mountain. Two towering slabs of mountain fuse together to form a massive rock prow. It is as if this mountain is a stone vessel sailing into the wide plain of this valley. No matter what is to be found or not found inside, the singular look of Prow Mountain cannot be easily forgotten or dismissed."

By an evening fire rested three young people.

"You know to sculpt stone," said Lyons to Elyir. "What make you of Lockshray's idea to mine a cavern behind the natural doorway that opens into yonder cliff side? I myself think it would be a terrible waste of time. The mountains on the other side of this valley have plenty of caverns that are just waiting to be used for something. Why waste time digging into this mountain?"

"Young lady," inquired Elyir turning to Maryeta, "would you volunteer to help me dig a huge cavern into Prow Mountain?"

"That would be too much pounding into hard rock. No sirree, I would rather ride horses."

"I will admit that this place does offer strategic advantage," reflected Lyons. "A lookout placed on top of the mountain wall could detect within the entire valley any movement of armies. The only way to defeat this outpost would be to deprive the soldiers inside the cavern of food and water."

"What if on the other side of the rock wall water could be found?" inquired Maryeta. "During the long rainy season a lot of water must accumulate on top of that mountain. Chief Cali says that during three moons of the year it rains hard in this valley."

"No cataract overflows the high cliffs," responded Elyir. "How is it that no water pours off the mountain?"

"*Yaghnnah...* please excuse my yawning," offered Maryeta. "Now I am curious. Tomorrow I am going to cajole Peli to take me to the top of this mountain so that with my own eyes I can see where flows the extra water of the rainy season."

On the new morning heavy clouds and drizzling rain dampened the moods of sailors. No one had the ambition to do anything other than to eat and sleep. That is, no one except for Maryeta who could be counted on to grow quickly bored at doing nothing. She began to poke Elyir and her brother with a stick. Her shorter legs could out-dodge her brother, and she knew that Elyir would let her win a race against him.

"You and your sticks! Be off with you!" exclaimed Lyons grown tired of the teasing. "Go fly with Peli and see if Chief Cali's lions are still to be found on the top of the mountain."

"Oh, all right," said the girl with a shrug of her shoulders. "I did say last night that Peli and I would do that, and Grandfather says I should always keep my word. But when I come back we are going to fish, or dig roots, or do anything that helps to pass this dreary weather."

It took time and effort for Peli to be made convinced. "Maryeta, today I am sluggish. I feel like my belly weighs twice what it is supposed to. I do not want to go flying, just to pass the time."

"Peli, the cure for your belly feeling bloated, is to stretch your wings. *That...* is exactly the exercise you need. After using up some energy you will be ready to eat some delicious thistles. Hah!"

"I today feel myself far too delicate a horse to eat prickly weeds." When she at last mounted the wind, the winged horse neighed to her rider, "No somersaults. I have today no energy for winged acrobatics."

As if she were galloping higher a zigzag road paved with airy bricks, the wings of Peli wove many times back-and-forth along the cliff side.

"I am short of breath, Maryeta. The first thing I am going to do at the top of the mountain is rest."

"The first thing I am going to do is look down and see if the sailors appear to be no larger than ants."

"Are you sure that just like me, you have not gained weight?"

"I hope I have!" came immediately Maryeta's answer. "Every day I try hard to grow taller and make my muscles bigger."

When the winged horse gained the top of the mountain the girl ran to the edge of the cliff and sprawled herself flat to gaze down at camped sailors.

"Look, Peli, from up here even the cattle look to be as small as ants! Ten, eleven, twelve... from here I can count all the cows."

"Look the other way," neighed Peli nudging the foot of the girl.

The girl pushed herself back from the edge of the cliff, stood, and looked to the east.

"My goodness! Into the middle of this mountain is sunk a gigantic hole!" Maryeta ran about one hundred steps, peered down, and carefully surveyed the sunken canyon. "The hollow in this mountain is enormous. We must fly down and see what lies hidden on the floor below us."

"Jump on quick!" neighed Peli with her nostrils flaring. "If we do not leave here right now two charging lions will be upon us, and then we will never get to the bottom of the hollowed canyon." On motionless wings Peli floated with her rider down to the floor of the hidden canyon.

"The grass here grows very thick," neighed the winged horse grabbing a mouthful. "Mmmmhhh. I did not know I was so hungry."

Maryeta was off exploring. "Right here is where the water escapes! Look Peli, through this big hole the water flows underground. It is only a trickle now, but when the heavy rains come it will be a torrent. I will bet that this underground tunnel leads to the river." The girl ran off to explore more. Before returning to where Peli still grazed, Maryeta had run all the way around the perimeter of the sunken canyon.

"Peli... Peli..." said Maryeta gasping for breath, "I must have run two thousand paces. This hidden canyon is big enough to house an army many times larger than that of Lockshray."

Having satisfied her hunger, Peli walked beside her friend toward the center of the canyon. "Maryeta, you are right. There is more than enough room here to build barracks, food sheds, and even a big plaza for an assembly. We must tell Lockshray that if he tunnels into this mountain he will emerge into a canyon that forever past remained hidden."

Sailors gathered to hear Maryeta and Peli tell and retell what they had discovered.

"I just thought of an important question for you two," said Lockshray. "If from the folded entryway we tunnel into the mountain, will we emerge onto the floor of the sunken vale? Or will the tunnel pass below the floor of the vale?"

"That is a very good question," answered the girl. "What do you think Peli?"

"I flew a long way down. I think we flew down into the hollow mountain as far as we from here flew upward to get to the top of the cliffs."

"Here is a second question for you. Do the walls of the vale plummet straight down, or did the rock walls thicken as you glided down inside the mountain?"

"When I looked up," answered Maryeta, "I remember thinking how strange it was that the walls inside the hidden canyon climb straight upward, just like the outside walls do."

"I have one more question for you two. How big is the tunnel that channels down water from the canyon floor?"

"Within the opening of the water tunnel I could extend full my body from head to toe. And, as I before said, I ran at least two thousand steps around the perimeter of the secret canyon. The hidden place is far bigger than you can imagine." That was all that Lockshray needed to hear.

"As done not long ago in Shining Canyon, tomorrow my sailors will again become miners. We will tunnel inward through the entrance fold of the mountain. If we find the inside floor is higher than is the floor of the folded entrance, we will slant the tunnel upward until we emerge into the canyon that hides within the mountain."

Sailors smiled at their captain as he hopped, clapped hands, laughed, and to himself talked out loud while walking his evening rounds. It was obvious that Lockshray entertained no doubts that the fortress he sought was here to be found.

"This mountain is to become my stronghold!" exclaimed Lockshray upon finding Cali and Benilvina. "From any enemy we will be here protected. Chief, it seems that I am to stay here, and that you and I are to be neighbors." Cali enjoyed feeling the closeness of a bear hug proffered by the Egyptian captain.

"I welcome Captain Lockshray to this wide valley that has ever been home to my ancestors," answered Cali with an air of solemnity. "You and I will be always friends."

"Because our enemies steal anything they can get their hands on, even our children," offered Benilvina, "I was sure that before two moons had passed the warriors that plunder these lands would have stolen all your cattle and horses. About that I just changed my mind. Inside this hollow mountain your animals will be well-protected."

At first light were heard the sounds of hammers striking the heads of chisels. By the close of the day the miners had advanced their tunnel two arm lengths into hard rock. The opening made by the advance miners was barely wide enough for three men to work. A more numerous second gang of miners followed behind widening and heightening. The tunnel passage was gradually made wide enough and high enough for three mounted horses walking side by side, to pass through. However, after fifteen days of hard pounding still was gained no entry.

"If in three more days we do not break through," confided Lockshray to Abel, "I will turn upward the direction of the shaft."

From where worked the miners sounded the next afternoon shouts of joy. A man came yelling as he ran, "Captain, we broke through! Come quickly! You are to be the first Egyptian to enter the hidden canyon!"

Through the narrow cut Lockshray squeezed his body. To accommodate his larger size, Abel had to wait for the cut to be made wider. Behind Abel came Maryeta. The men that next filtered in were soon in shared enthusiasm jumping, hollering, and rolling about the grass that spread over the canyon's floor.

"I told you that this hidden canyon is beautiful!" exclaimed the girl.

"Maryeta, thanks to your restlessness provoked by a day of dismal rain," responded Lockshray, "I found the perfect place to build my stronghold."

Upon entering the mountain Elyir fixated to the left his vision. By something his eyes were drawn to the north side of the sunken canyon.

"Where do your thoughts take you... Elyir... *Elyir*?" inquired Maryeta upon finding the youth seemingly lost to the world.

"Oh! It is you, Maryeta. I was just thinking that if I could be so permitted, over there on that spot I would build a secret pavilion, a palace unknown to the outside world. The sheer rock walls of this hidden place lend themselves to the structure of a columned pavilion. The outer columns would stretch higher than the inner columns. To the right of the far end of the pavilion, I would build a tall tower through which the rain that runs off the mountain would descend into a fountain. Maryeta, here in this hollow mountain would rise a pavilion and tower that show to what *Beauty* truly aspires. It would be a place where one could fittingly thank the heavens for the manifold blessings given to us."

"The brilliant young sculptor is exactly right," affirmed Maryeta placing the hands of Elyir in hers. "For the building of a great pavilion this place lends itself perfectly. I can right now picture in my head its rising columns."

That same day Lockshray began to plan the new garrison. Now that the stranded Egyptians knew where their future was to lie, the tasks that waited could be well organized. First would be built corrals and stables to protect the invaluable livestock. Stone barracks would be made large enough to house four hundred men. Plans for food granaries were drawn up.

Lockshray soon discovered that Elyir could not only sculpt, but that he had a gift for visualizing from beginning to end the construction process. The slender young Phoenician knew which steps the builders could accomplish at the same time, and what next steps in the construction must follow. Elyir's uncle, Merlew, had the uncanny ability to know ahead of time when something would not work. Merlew's innate understanding of the strength needed in a foundation, wall, corner, or column, saved Elyir untold headaches. Under the guidance of Merlew, the indispensable job foreman, five of every eight men busied themselves with construction.

One of every eight sailors was assigned to security. Sentries were posted not only about the entrance to the stronghold, but on corners of the wide plain that opened to the west and north. The remaining two of every eight men were assigned to cutting timber, plowing, planting, weeding crops, and tending to the cattle and horses as they grazed along the banks of the river that flowed outside the hollow mountain. Because of the prescient knowledge possessed by Chief Cali about when and where to plant seeds, the onset of the rainy season coaxed many seeds of maize to shoot upward.

The rapid progress of the construction projects astounded the chief. He found it difficult to believe that a barracks for four hundred men, what he called a big village, could be built in the passage of two moons.

"Lockshray, I discovered the secret of your building so fast. Your Egyptian tribe teaches you how to organize many things at once. I do not hunt and farm at the same time. If I hunt, that is all I do. You plan out ten things to accomplish at the same time. Before you finished the corral and the living quarters for your men, you began to build granaries, a guard house, and a cistern tower. Egyptian people are very smart in the head!"

"Cali, about the Egyptian people you are right," answered Lockshray. "We were born to build very big things. Before we are finished, from these canyon walls you will see us cut huge stones and stack them on top of each other to rise to the sky."

The Egyptian captain insisted that everyone take ownership of their duties and responsibilities. When complaints were voiced that Elyir and Merlew were not Egyptians, Lockshray reminded his men that Egypt was very far removed from the hollow mountain, and that in this new place everyone was to be treated the same. Elyir, Merlew, and even Lockshray counted on the respect accorded to the intimidating aspect of Abel to help reform attitudes of men with proclivities to grumble and complain about the orders they were given.

When baskets of food appeared on a knoll outside the stronghold, the chief's wife always knew who had sent the food.

"This pattern of basket weaving is from my mother's people that live isolated. I am proud that their food comes quietly from so far away to help our new neighbors."

"Did you know, Lockshray, that our people make bets about what crazy thing you will next do?" offered Chief Cali with a smile. Natives continued to be astonished by the doings of the strange men and beasts that had come to dwell in their land.

CHAPTER 35

FOOD AND RACES

Maryeta decided that she had a knack for cooking. The girl's sense of smell was acute. She liked blending root, leaf, and blossom savors to achieve just the right taste, and with new recipes she was adventurous.

While enjoying the aromas of the kitchen, Chief Cali and Benilvina liked to watch Maryeta cook. Comfortable in his position as emissary to the Egyptians, Cali would offer pointed comments. "The men who help you cook do not do it right. Women are better at cooking. I do only four things. I hunt, fight, eat, and sleep."

"Actually, my husband is most practiced at disappearing. Our men use any excuse to depart our village and not come back until the hard work of farming is done."

"Maryeta needs better help to prepare food. I go to find her help." That said the chief rose, stretched his back and limbs, and walked out of the hollow mountain.

"You see that, Maryeta? Now I will not see my husband for many days." The chief was indeed slow to return. But with him when he did return were five maidens.

"Among all my relatives," Cali informed Maryeta, "these young ladies cook best!" The quality of the meals served to sailors made to be farmers, carpenters, and stone masons improved noticeably. Along with the more flavorful cuisine, sailors could not help but notice that the native cooks happened also to be pretty.

"You there! Quit flirting with that sailor! Agghh! Instead of just keeping my cooks in line, I am supposed to be running a kitchen. And even with more kitchen help I still do not have any time for myself." Maryeta was little pleased that without exception the native maidens had developed favorites among the men.

"Cooking for four hundred men is too hard work!" declared one afternoon Maryeta to Cali and Benilvina sitting close by. "I deserve a break from my kitchen. It would be nice if Matron Lorial, Peli, and Briarburr came here to visit me while I cook, just like you two and Winfray do. But they do not, and that is wrong of them. Well, since the three horned horses want to be left alone, I will go find Lyons, Elyir, and Abel. At least they are still fun."

She handed her apron to a surprised Cali. "You are now in charge!" With that gesture Maryeta was from the kitchen gone. Cali began to happily order about the cooks.

Games

"So this afternoon Maryeta took a well-deserved break from cooking," commented Merlew to Lockshray, Abel, Elyir, and Jomain upon finishing his supper. "Hmph! Just like Maryeta, the men slow their pace."

"That is because during the passage of more than two moons they have worked every day, nonstop," answered Lockshray putting down his plate.

"When the soldiers and unicorns in the army of Fahseed bickered and shirked more than they trained, Abel organized a day of games," commented Jomain. "That one day break revitalized our training camp, and united the entire army, even the unicorns and horses."

"Because I ostensibly had big arms, which of course I do not," commented Elyir, "Abel singled me out to take his bet on the race that Lyons had the good luck to win. Still, I would rather not stop our work. We do accomplish something each day, albeit less than I want." After frowning and thinking more, Elyir changed his mind. "*Well...* at that I suppose I can agree that from their hard work the men deserve a break."

"What say you, Lockshray, that a day be set aside for races, wrestling, and stone throws?" inquired Abel. "Even if the prizes are of little value, they provide recognition, the right to brag about being the fastest or strongest."

Afternoon rains did not threaten on the day of the games. When a host of natives joined the Egyptians and the few Phoenicians gathered on knolls overlooking the course, the competition was immediately expanded to also include athletes among the native men, women, and youths. The chief's face glowed every time an acquaintance, friend, or relative showed well in an event.

"Your people, Chief Cali, run fast," said Lockshray joining to congratulate his friend.

"And Maryeta is so fast she could outrun even me!" The tone of the chief's voice changed to serious. "The members of my tribe show today that they accept the presence of the strange men in our land. With their own eyes my people see that your sailors mean no harm to us. You do not use your metal points and horses to steal from us or pillage our villages. Since you came to our place of mountains, our enemies have not bothered us. My people dare to hope that your presence in this valley will finally bring peace to our land." Cali took a step closer to Lockshray and said quietly, "But, I do not understand how you control your men better than I do mine. My warriors are too independent minded. I tell them what to do, and then they each decide whether to go along with my idea... *or not.*"

"As for me," replied Lockshray, "I think the army in my homeland of Egypt insists too much on obedience. I do not mind if my soldiers voice honest differences with me on how to build our garrison. I like it when their ideas are better than mine, or better than Elyir's."

"Did you notice that Maryeta won the two races she entered?" commented Abel upon joining Cali and Lockshray. "She sprints fast. On top of that she possesses the endurance to run far. Climbing so many trees as a child toughened her arms and legs, and made her to become a fine athlete."

"I just had an idea!" exclaimed Cali with his eyes widening. "The final foot race will be between Maryeta and the big men of the newcomers. The race will be done my way, the hunter way."

After calling together Elyir, Merlew, Abel, Lockshray, Lyons, and Maryeta, the chief proceeded to explain the rules of his event.

"Since my sister shoots arrows better than me, she alone will represent our family, and I will cheer her on."

"All right, Lyons, this chief agrees that it is best not to have the two winners be from the same family."

"Being as well family, when both Merlew and I won the race it would offend the others." That said, Elyir waved goodbye to Cali.

"Lyons and Elyir are now off the hook, but you four... *must stay!*" Cali handed his beaded and feathered rabbit hide to a young brave. The hide was stretched onto a rounded willow shoot, and then tied between two tree branches. Thirty paces in front of the target were placed four bows and four quivers with arrows. A dozen children were sent two hundred paces away to there stand in a small group.

"At my signal sling your quiver over your shoulder, grasp your bow, grab an arrow, shoot, and hit the target," instructed Cali. "Once your arrow penetrates through my rabbit skin, run fast to circle the children. Hit the target twice more, and with bow in hand circle twice more the children. To honor my rabbit skin that has for many years protected me, you must hit the target and after run three times. The first to hand me their bow, *wins.*"

"But there is a nuisancing breeze, and it has been too long a time since I shot arrows," demurred Merlew. "Can I at least practice for a while?" That request was dismissed with a laugh by Cali.

"This is a race for our leaders. I am only a girl."

"No Maryeta, a cook for so many men has the most important work. If the men do not eat they do not build. And you are no longer a girl, but a maiden." For all four remaining contenders no excuse could be found to not comply with Cali's orders.

The chief waved for the competition to begin. Grabbing quivers and bows, three men quickly sent unlucky arrows at the rabbit skin. A second volley flew. Again none of the three arrows hit the target.

A calm Maryeta found the arrow she wanted, drew her bow, waited for the right slip of breeze to steady the target, and flew the arrow point through the rabbit skin. Running at an easy pace she was off to circle the group of marker children that enthusiastically urged on her feet.

The arrows of Abel, Lockshray, and Merlew finally hit the target. Racing against each other the three men overtook Maryeta, barely beating her back to the target. Abel quickly sent four more arrows that missed the target above, below, right, and left.

"Arrgh! With this tricky breeze I overcorrect my shots!"

Arrows of Lockshray and Merlew as well missed the target.

Again the girl carefully selected the arrow she wanted, drew her bow, relaxed the string, and drew again. Holding her breath she sent her second arrow through the rabbit skin. A second time ran Maryeta toward the group of children hollering for her to run even faster.

Abel's arrow a second time achieved the target, as did soon after the arrows launched by Lockshray and Merlew. The three men caught up with Maryeta as she was aiming her third arrow.

As before the unwinded girl took her time, measured the breeze, and for a third time hit the target with the first arrow sent from her bow. The Phoenician's first arrow hit a feather hanging down from the pelt. His second was too high. His third and fourth arrows missed right and left. When Abel's fifth arrow hit dead center he was off in pursuit of Maryeta, again with Lockshray and Merlew close on his heels. Finding themselves winded, the three men could not this time catch a girl running as fast as her legs would carry her. Gasping for breath, Merlew handed his bow to Cali and placed second. Lockshray placed third.

"Thank heavens I placed no worse than fourth," said a winded Abel smiling slyly.

Set upon the shoulders of Abel the winner was paraded to cheers... from everyone.

Lockshray had the champions of all the events assemble in front of the spectators. Whether strong in arms, fleet afoot, or possessing stamina to run long the winners big and small were with claps and shouts applauded. Not one fight erupted among tough Egyptian sailors drinking fermented fruit juice.

"How did you do that?" inquired Cali upon finding Maryeta. "Not even I could have three times hit the target with my first arrow."

"I sent my mind back to a time when Lyons taught me to shoot rabbits in the forest. My brother always told me that I had to think like a rabbit, wait until the rabbit was still and at rest, draw my bow ever so slowly, and picture in my mind the arrow flying through the air. My eyes waited for the rabbit skin to think that it was hidden well, so nobody could see him. Only then did I let fly my arrow."

Later that night Maryeta gave a big hug to the neck of a seated Abel.

"What was that for?"

"I know that the great soldier with both sword and bow was today a gentleman. You let me to win."

"For my sake I only wish that were true. If I heard it said once, I heard it said fifty times that I let a girl to beat me. This has to be the most embarrassing day of my life."

"Well looking at it that way, it would have been more embarrassing if you had placed behind both me *and* Lyons."

"Ahh, yes. Lyons is the fastest runner in our garrison. He may also be the best archer, err second best archer after you." At that comment the girl reached to squeeze the hand of Abel.

Easy smiles were the next day worn on the faces of stone masons at work. In spite of the good-natured ribbing he continued to endure, the smile worn by the Phoenician lieutenant was grand.

CHAPTER 36

NEWNESS IN THE SECRET PAVILION

One night everything for Peli changed. The camp awoke to find that in a secluded recess of the slowly rising pavilion a little filly had to the world presented.

"The foal is perfect," observed Lorial. "The coat of the darling little filly is pure as driven snow, and her tiny stub of a horn is precious. Peli, you and Briarburr should be so proud of the precious magical life you brought into this new land."

Briarburr had eyes only for the mare and her foal. It was as if his full time job was to observe to grow breath by breath the foal he claimed as his own. The little filly was soon bounding about the hollow mountain getting the full attention of men, horses, cows, and Maryeta's black dogs.

"With the touch of your horn please spark the gift of the uniform animal language to my black dogs," requested Maryeta of the matron unicorn. "They will then be the best company for the new foal that loves to chase after them."

"I am sorry to disappoint you, Maryeta, but our code prohibits friendship with non-unicorns. The uniform tongue has only rarely been bestowed on humans that possess not only intelligence, but innate goodness."

"But my dogs rescued you from mean wolves," responded the girl. "They are both smart and good-hearted."

"Your black dogs have also nipped too many times my hooves."

"But... that was only in play," responded Maryeta with a sigh.

"Your secret pavilion gave birth to magic!" exclaimed Lockshray upon approaching Elyir. "What can be more auspicious for our future?"

"I will have the spot where the filly came into this world to be marked with a sculpture of the foal," responded Elyir. "The size of the statue will measure exactly her size on the day she was born."

It became time for Briarburr to pull himself away from his mare and foal and exercise his legs; for that purpose served the weight of a rider. After a long run Lyons dismounted to walk beside his blackmaned friend.

"Young man, there is something on my mind. You have a solitary quality to your personality, as do I, and we both have often felt ourselves to be alone in this world. But you have your sister and your grandfather, and now the foal has given me a family of my own. If at some future time I again come to shed the blood of an enemy, how can that now fit the image of a unicorn sire? How do I change from a war unicorn, to a father and husband unicorn?"

"Thinking back, because I carried the burden of Maryeta's safety on my small shoulders I could not just be a little boy. For me the forest was a daunting place.

Can you believe that I still have nightmares where I have to snatch my sister back from tree branches that grab her away from me? The burden of responsibility for my smaller sister forever changed me. I do not know that I would want to become a father, and have again the charge of a defenseless little one. What I am trying to say, Briarburr, is that I am not the right person to give advice on being a good father unicorn. Hah! But I would have slept better in the forest had I known that you were keeping the wolves away from Maryeta and me.

"But rather than cause you to worry about your new responsibilities, I need to encourage you. The blackmane will be a *wonderful* unicorn sire. And your foal will come to inherit the courage of both her sire and dam. With the blood of the blackmane and the winged horse flowing in her veins, she is bound to become a magnificent unicorn mare. I dare say that she will one day come to be the matron of a unicorn clan." The two walked on in silence.

"Your look, Lyons, has become more serious."

"Thinking on what it must mean to be a parent, something else occurs to me." Placing his hands on the unicorn's cheeks, Lyons looked into the eyes of Briarburr.

"My grandfather many times asked himself how a poor villager that had to affect that his grandchildren did not exist, could be mother and father to Maryeta and me. Just as Fahseed's role in our lives was not traditional, so your role in your foal's life may not be natural in the unicorn way. But the only thing that mattered to my sister and to me, and what will matter to your foal, is to know... *love*.

"I want to have someday written on my tombstone... *Lyons felt loved*. The love of my grandfather, my sister, you, and Abel means everything to me. So, Briarburr, if a war unicorn can do no more than to make his foal know and feel that she is loved, you will have done your part as her sire."

"You encourage me, Lyons. Whether in large, or small ways, I will show love to Peli and my foal."

"Beyond doing that, Briarburr, try not to worry about what tomorrow presents to you as a sire." A unicorn horse and a boy that together shared the blessings of deep and long friendship, returned at sunset to the canyon of the secret pavilion.

"In two or three more moons the construction of most things here will be finished," commented Lockshray one evening to Abel, "excepting of course for the pavilion palace. That will take Elyir maybe even a lifetime to complete. Seriously Abel, for Elyir's ideas which all the time become more grandiose, the pavilion may never come to be finished."

"About that you may not be mistaken. I have noticed that rather than Prow Mountain, sailors begin to call this place Pavilion Mountain."

"My sailors understand that the pavilion that Elyir and Merlew are slowly raising will be marvelously transcendent."

"Even I can see that the pavilion palace will come to be extraordinarily beautiful. Err, Lockshray, my thoughts return to Spire Mountain. The time will soon come to secure blue gold for the swords and armor of your men, and for me to return to Phoenicia. In that regard, it was smart to take advantage of Jomain's blacksmithing skills."

"Thank goodness Jomain completed the smelter and forge. Under his tutelage the repair of bent and damaged weapons and armor has been taught well to his apprentices. But for now there is no rush to mine the blue gold. Since we are now able to defend well our stronghold, I expect no enemy to worry me for a long time. Who would dare to confront my Egyptians secured in this protected place? Abel, you must with me stay one more moon. By then Peli's foal will have grown legs strong enough to travel to the unicorn hold."

CHAPTER 37

A TWENTY HORSE CAVALRY

Not many days after Lockshray reassured Abel about the safety of the pavilion stronghold, a sentry arrived on horseback to report that an army had entered the valley of the secret pavilion. The faces and arms of twenty five hundred warriors were smeared bright with war paint. Pursuing the same stream that Lockshray's hungry sailors had before followed, the intruders had begun to slowly and methodically move down the far side of the valley, ravaging villages in each canyon they entered.

"The arrogant northern tribes banded together to here bring even more warriors," reported a crestfallen Chief Cali to Lockshray and Abel. "My enemies before attacked during the dry season. It is outrageous that they now come to attack us in the wet season when our fields of maize stand tall. By destroying our crops they weaken us with hunger."

"Cali, this valley is now become my home," answered the Egyptian captain. "The same as you, I cannot have my crop of maize to be destroyed. I will fight at your side." Upon hearing that, with no more words spoken Chief Cali was gone.

"In this hollow mountain I have too many mouths to feed," lamented Lockshray to Abel. "Within these rock walls my sailors are made safe only so long as last my scant food supplies. My granaries are almost empty. Because I spent too much time building, instead of arming my men with the blue gold, my soldiers are not prepared and our stronghold has become a trap."

Not waiting for his fields of maize to be found, Lockshray led Briarburr and a twenty horse cavalry to the other side of the valley. Before the entrance to the canyon of Benilvina and Cali, the Egyptian captain would confront and harass the advancing enemy. Lockshray was confident that his horses and the blackmane were superior weapons against warriors on foot. The words he addressed to his cavalry were meant to not only clarify military tactics, but also to instill confidence.

"Until my infantry and Chief Cali's braves arrive to join the fight, our cavalry must keep the enemy off balance and halt their depredations against peaceful villages. Learning how to stop our charging horses will delay our foes and cost them valuable time. The blue gold swords of Abel, Lyons, Maryeta, and Jomain will anchor the center of our line of cavalry. Use the magic swords to reflect sun into the faces of the war chiefs. Let them learn quickly that blue gold magic is powerful. To take full advantage of Briarburr's gift to deflect flighted arrows and thrown spears, the blackmane will move about where he is needed.

"Look to each other! Bring rescue to any rider that becomes entangled and overwhelmed! Do not let yourself, nor any of us, to become surrounded! Fight for our secret pavilion, and for our friends Chief Cali and Benilvina!"

The enemy army stopped its advance. Pointing upward, enemy braves stood transfixed at the approach of a horse on wings.

"I could not, Briarburr, remain behind," neighed Peli in greeting. "I must fight for my stallion and my foal. If we do not stop this invasion, on some future day our foal will be sacrificed like a lamb led to slaughter. Your magic gift will protect me from spears and arrows. And my wings will shield the stallion that I love from the hatred that burns in the eyes of our enemies."

"While I am a war unicorn, you are a new mother horse with soft wings. I beg you to return to our foal. The meaning of my life is that I cannot risk... *losing you.*"

"You forget that my wings are long-practiced in the defense of unicorn mares. When I need my feathers to harden, they obey me. Today two magical horses, one with a black mane and the other with wings, are going to put on a show for the intrepid Lockshray." Waiting for nothing more to be neighed, Peli lifted up to circle above Briarburr.

Heat fused into magical rays borne of the sun, singed painted faces and painted arms. Had it not been for the earnestness of a life and death struggle, the sight of enemy chiefs hopping about in order to not be burned by reflected magic, would have been comical.

When Briarburr jerked downward his head, fifty arrows fell to lodge in the ground before him. At full speed the blackmane hit the line of the enemy. While his big hooves slugged and stomped, around him he felt wind to swirl as Peli's wings beat hard against warriors on one, and then on his other side.

"As she inflicts so much damage, how do her soft feathers not tear apart?" muttered the blackmane amazed at the force of Peli's fight. Seeing terror fill the eyes of warriors running away from Peli, a new thought came to Briarburr's mind. "It is as she said. Her love for our foal, and for me, has gifted Peli's wings the hardness of stone. She has discovered the true strength of her magical gift."

The assault of twenty cavalry horses wreaked panic among clumped warriors terrified to see huge four-legged beasts bear down on them. Unfortunately for Lockshray's cavalry, when warriors filled with fear fell back, a new wave of the enemy took their place. Soon after crumpling inward, the forward arc of the invading force was reinforced.

"From their many casualties the enemy learns!" yelled Abel. "Their line spreads out to encircle us!"

"If we run from this battle the enemy will never stop their pursuit!" shouted Lockshray. "Form into a half-moon!" The small cavalry would flex as they must, and as a last resort make the ends of their half-moon formation extend and join together to better defend each other's backs.

"Stand in our midst, Briarburr! Deflect over our heads their spears and arrows so that their own weapons inflict damage upon themselves! Peli must stop any hole that breaks open the containment of our defense!"

The ears of the blackmane detected the sound of myriad arrows splitting the air. The movement of his head swayed those arrows upward to clear the encircling horsemen and after fall into one or the other side of the enemy.

"They suffer terrible losses!" exclaimed Maryeta to Lyons. "Why do they continue to fight?"

"The enemy treats life meanly," answered Lyons. "The opportunity of plunder presents to their lives value unequaled."

"Brother, so long as Briarburr stands, you and I will hold out!" exclaimed Maryeta. "The noble unicorn gave everything for us, for Phoenicia, and for the white herd. We will not let him to fall before we do."

Doing his utmost to redirect arrows and spears away from Lockshray's horses and riders, the unicorn with a black mane jumped and twisted everywhere about his body. With such rapid revolutions of hooves a normal stallion would have lost his balance, not so Briarburr.

When her wounded mare collapsed beneath her, Maryeta became separated from Lyons. Seeing her plight, the Phoenician lieutenant wheeled his horse to break through the warriors contending with the girl's sword. Reaching his arm to hers, he swung Maryeta behind his saddle. Until she regained the protection provided by Briarburr and Peli, the magic forged into her blue gold blade and the swordsmanship taught by Cavour could not be dissuaded.

Briarburr's muscles weighted so heavy he wondered that he could lift more his hooves. It became impossible for the blackmane to turn aside every arrow and spear launched at his confederates, and at himself. Bleeding from his neck, the faltering unicorn stallion leaned into the horse mounted by Jomain.

"I lose the magic wanted by my horn."

"The brave life of Briarburr cannot end in this fight against marauders!" exclaimed the blacksmith.

Caught in a Vice

"Look Blackmane!" exclaimed Jomain. "From out of the canyon they cross the stream!"

As they broke upon the west flank of the enemy force, the shouts of Cali's allied warriors came to drown out all other sounds. Because they did not this time fight alone, and because they fought knowing that their allies commanded fierce four-legged beasts, the spirits of Cali's warriors soared in bravery. Honoring the unpainted faces of their Egyptian allies, Cali's warriors wore no war paint.

The sound of drums signaled that the Egyptian infantry was soon to enter the battle.

"I have many times commanded soldiers in battle," addressed Winfray the infantry. "I always go at the front. Some of you are more sailors than soldiers. No matter our experience in war or our place of birth, today every man of us fights for our friends. This powerful wedge of Egypt will strike and divide the enemy."

"Master Winfray, for a soldier not Egyptian you have mettle!" exclaimed one of the oldest sailors. "I will make sure our plucky Phoenician does not today fall!"

Slashing swords and crashing their bodies into painted warriors, almost four hundred foot soldiers proved to be a fearsome battering ram. With every step fought forward by Egyptian infantryman, the center of the enemy force compressed. The entrance of Cali's warriors from the west, coupled to the arrival of the Egyptian infantry from the east, clamped enemy warriors in a vice. Made tight, the vice severed in two the column of raiders.

The time happened in the battle that everything changed. Fronted by a company of horse soldiers, and with their middle constricted by Chief Cali and Winfray, enemy warriors did not wait for their chiefs to tell them what next needed to be done. One after another painted warrior gave up the fight. With suddenness incomprehensible to the twenty horsemen that had struggled on the field of battle for what seemed time unending, the fight broke off.

The thousand enemy warriors found below the pincer of Cali's braves and Winfray's infantry came to be made prisoners. The body language of the prisoners indicated they had confidence of good treatment. There was value to be gotten in the trade of one set of prisoners for hostages previously taken.

The remaining part of the army of painted warriors that had transgressed the valley before Prow Mountain, fled north. Behind them in hot pursuit pushed Cali's warriors.

Safeguarded

"Abel, when we were surrounded with nowhere to turn," observed Lockshray, "I questioned whether I should have held off my cavalry attack until Cali's warriors and my infantry were joined to the fight. Against so many enemies it was reckless of me to risk twenty precious horses and the irreplaceable Briarburr."

"How else, Lockshray, could be quickly stopped the slaughter of native villagers?"

"I did consider using our twenty horses as bait to lure the warriors away from Benilvina's canyon."

"A few warrior chiefs would have perhaps swallowed the proffered bait, but too many of the enemy would have stayed behind to enter and destroy the home of Cali and Benilvina. You could not abandon the woman that with baskets of maize rescued our column from starvation. You rightly counted on the strong magic of Briarburr. Peli joined us, and was today magnificent.

"The recklessness of Lockshray in today's battle will give birth to a legend. Cali's people will long sing of the valor of the twenty horse soldiers. Because of your willingness to risk everything in battle, because of what we this day accomplished with numbers so small, many years will pass before an army of painted warriors dares to again trespass the valley of Prow Mountain."

"For that, Abel, I will thank the heavens." The Egyptian captain dropped to his knees and raised arms upward in thankfulness. With open hands held high,

Abel joined his friend in silent thanks for aid and rescue come at the hardest time of the fight.

"Fellow helper from Phoenicia," said Lockshray relaxing his arms. "We from across the sea, and natives from these mountains, fought as one. Today the heavens look down on you, Cali, Winfray, and me as brothers."

"Why do we not, Lockshray, tire of war against enemies that flow the same red color in their veins? After living my life in the middle of the fray, I have come to think of the men I attack with a sword as little children fathered by the same creation."

"When I was young, Abel, I knew that the odds for my long survival as a soldier were small. For that I valued little myself, and had no thought for my enemy being a person just like me. But come this far in life, I with you conclude that war wastes the precious blood of men that to someone are brothers, sons, and fathers."

Wood was brought. Reflecting diminishing sunrays from his magic sword, Lyons lit a fire next to where reposed Briarburr and Peli. Nearby rested Cali, Lockshray, Abel, and Maryeta. The wings of Peli did not stop caressing the blackmaned unicorn's many bloody cuts.

"I do hate the loss of your mount, Maryeta. I know that you were very attached to that mare."

The princess did not answer Abel. Wiping tears from her eyes, she turned to instead comfort the winged horse. "Joined to the love you bear, the touch of your wings will with precious magic heal the sire of your foal."

Rising to stand, Cali began to dance a circle around the black marked unicorn, the winged horse, and the fire. As he revolved his body to the beat of drums marking rhythm to the mood of a victorious evening, his steps were light. Concluding his dance the chief sat down cross-legged.

"For the joy of this day's deliverance my spirit moved me to dance. My enemies that before took turns raiding our villages came this time all together. With the help of two magic horses, Lockshray's cavalry, and four hundred foot soldiers on one battlefield were defeated all my enemies. For my youngest daughter I will trade a captured chief. With her hands tied, Jewelelk was from me taken. With hands untied, Jewelelk will now return to her father. I have enough prisoners, with many important chiefs among them, to redeem every one of my relatives held captive in the north.

"My enemies run for their lives. For three days my warriors will pursue and take more broken-spirited prisoners. The clans of my tribe will now heal from the despair of long defeat. In these mountains we will be a new nation, a tribe confident of its future. I go now to walk among the campfires of my people." After taking a few steps Cali turned to exclaim, "The three arrows Maryeta sent from her bow made my rabbit skin to become for me... an even greater charm!"

"The hammers and chisels?" inquired the Egyptian captain of a soldier standing nearby.

"As you ordered, Sir. The men brought them in their belts and pouches."

"I will wager that more than one of our enemies suffered blows from a soldier holding a sword in one hand, and a hammer in the other," offered Lyons.

"Tomorrow my infantry and cavalry will also chase northward the enemy warriors," said Lockshray to those with him. "Hostages taken will be handed over to Cali. As my men follow after the enemy their other purpose is to regain Spire Mountain. The cloaks of my soldiers will carry magic ore back to Prow Mountain. The smelter and forge built by Jomain will soon refine and fashion the priceless gold into swords and armor. My sailors will also mine the weight of fifty men for Abel to carry back to Phoenicia. One hundred Egyptians, this time walking in high spirits, will transport the blue gold down to the Phoenician barge."

"Ahem, I did at that promise your grandfather that I would bring you two... *back to him,*" said Abel turning to Lyons and Maryeta. "Fahseed will be overjoyed to once more hold his grandchildren in his arms."

"I am grown too big for Grandfather to lift me up like he used to," replied Lyons.

Maryeta did not react as Abel expected. She began to sob. "Wuahh, wuanhh... I cannot leave Peli. If she here stays with the white herd... I must... with her stay."

"After the stormy times of a life spent protecting unicorn mares and foals, the unicorn hold would present to me a welcome safe haven," neighed Peli in reply. "I want to be a mare dwelling secure with her foal amidst the white herd. But Briarburr will never by the unicorns be welcomed. To them he is no longer a unicorn, but a war horse. And after today's battle, the unicorns will as well see me to be a war horse.

"I must... do what... I never imagined I could do. In the keeping of Lorial I will leave behind my foal. Taking my place, the matron will become the mare of my foal. That is the only way my little one will have a chance to know a life woven into the wondrous clans of unicorns. With Maryeta, Lyons, Abel, Winfray, Jomain, and the blackmaned unicorn that now commands my heart, on the barge returning to Phoenicia will I also be found."

"I will also miss deeply our foal. But that you, Peli, are to remain at my side is at the same time wonderful for me to learn."

"For now, Briarburr, I am going to be happy that soon in Prow Mountain we, along with Maryeta and Lyons, will be reunited with our foal."

No soldier or warrior could the next night be found where had been waged the *Battle of the Twenty Horse Soldiers.*

CHAPTER 38

PROMISES

Having broken off their pursuit of enemy warriors, Lockshray and Abel regained Spire Mountain.

During their second visit to the canyon whose rock walls shined with magic, Egyptian sailors neither suffered hunger nor witnessed violent dissension among their officers. Once more made to be miners, Lockshray's men rapidly procured the blue gold required for their swords and armor, as well as the blue gold to be freighted on Abel's barge to Phoenicia.

Burdened by cloaks made heavy with magic ore, one hundred men and ten horses commenced the long walk toward the anchored Phoenician barge. Together Lockshray and Abel watched the column begin the descent to the coast.

"It is time, past time, that I return to my barge. You know, Lockshray, whenever I think of the shine that I will soon glimpse in the eyes of my loyal sailors, my mood improves."

"My spirit, Abel, was one hundred times lifted by your confidence in me. Taking a stand against the formidable Admiral Boschene... *scared me*. Never before had I done anything of the sort. You were the first to believe that in spite of the challenge of Boschene's arrogance and enmity, I could command, and command well."

"More than fearing Boschene, you were afraid of not doing the right thing for the four hundred Egyptian sailors left behind with you in this land. The mark of a true commander is that he always puts his men first."

"With magic gold set in the hold of your barge, and two magic equines as passengers, the omens for your voyage are favorable. I trust that you will not follow Boschene's example, but will instead return by sailing the northern half of the circle that reconnects with the sea before Phoenicia."

"I will follow your counsel, Lockshray. It is logical to expect that the westward winds that brought us here return eastward in a circular pattern."

"That makes sense, Abel. Prevailing wind patterns going opposite directions cannot at the same time coexist in the same part of the sea."

"On our return voyage we will sail upon new islands. I look forward to the exhilaration that comes with voyage under new skies. Who knows? By the time we reach Phoenicia I may have learned to like being the commander of a barge."

The two hesitated to part.

"What new adventures await you in Phoenicia?"

"I will help Briarburr to keep removed from trouble the one clan of unicorns that remained behind in Phoenicia. And I can unfortunately predict that there will be more battles to fight against fearsome Hittites come down from the north."

"If you do not halt the Hittite march southward, they will soon come to plague my Egypt."

"Phoenicia will long remain friends with the great land of Egypt. Speaking of which, do you believe Boschene's barge has now found its way safely back to the pharaoh?"

"I *am* confident, Abel, of your safe return to Phoenicia. With regard to Boschene, neither my head nor my heart reassures. The admiral inflates himself with arrogance, and in so doing gives bad orders. To be honest, I fear that the blue gold on Boschene's barge will arrive at a place not pertaining to Egypt. You and I both know that Boschene always intended to keep some of the magic gold for himself. Maybe fate will favor Boschene, so that in some far land he keeps for himself all the blue gold salvaged from his final shipwreck."

"Boschene does at that too suddenly find shore in a storm."

"Thinking more on it, Abel, many men on Boschene's barge may live longer than does their commander. I do not doubt that Boschene will soon find his luck has changed."

"And it was Lockshray that started his downturn. Your standing up to the admiral changed his destiny."

"No, Abel, the wreckage of two magnificent barges against a benign beach changed irretrievably his luck from good to bad."

"It will take your column at least fifteen days to reach my barge," said Abel bringing the conversation back to the work ahead.

"At least, Abel, the travel will be mostly downhill."

"A few more days will be spent loading the blue gold and securing the decks against wind and waves. Lockshray, upon your return to Prow Mountain tell Briarburr and Peli that in twenty or twenty five days I will be watching for them as I sail south along the coast. I expect some morning to see Briarburr and Peli, with their mounts Lyons and Maryeta, trotting along a beach in the direction of my vessel. Once they are safely on board, I will turn my barge toward the morning sun and begin in earnest the return voyage to Phoenicia."

"Your message will be given, Abel."

"It will take your men and horses more than thirty days to go to the coast, and then return to the pavilion stronghold."

"For that do not worry, Abel. The permission you gave for Elyir and Merlew to remain as my chief builders was more than adequate compensation for the transport of gold to the coast. Soon enough four hundred Egyptians will be reunited in the hollow mountain."

"You know, Lockshray, I cannot quit thinking how saddened Briarburr and Peli will be to leave behind their little filly in the care of Lorial. Briarburr's friendship for the Phoenicians, and now for the Egyptians, has cost him much. He is rejected by unicorns that were it not for the blackmane's courage, would still be hunted in Phoenicia. His participation in the defense of the valley before Prow Mountain quitted him of any remaining expectation for acceptance by the white herd. I hope that Briarburr and Peli find peaceful purpose, and that a new foal will someday come to bless their union."

"I *promise* that I will not forget you, Lieutenant Abel."

"Nor I you, Lockshray."

"Perhaps your long delay here, with me, makes Jomain and Winfray to wonder if you are in fact returning with them to your barge."

By a horse intent on catching up with the departed column, Lieutenant Abel was carried quickly away.

The Pavilion Mountain

Some days after departing the canyon of blue gold, Lockshray's main force was once again found in the pavilion stronghold. Hammers were soon heard to pound blue gold, tin, and copper in the manufacture of armor and weapons.

One afternoon Elyir, Merlew, and Lockshray together observed construction work on a front corner column of the pavilion.

"I agree with Merlew," said Lockshray. "The background of a large sky diminishes the way corner columns are by our eyes seen. Set against the perspective of towering cliff walls and blue sky, the corner columns should be made a little wider in diameter. If not, there will be the illusion that the corner columns appear to be thinner than the inner columns."

"So it shall be done," answered Elyir.

"Permit me to mention another matter," petitioned Merlew. "It is an issue far more serious than by how much of a fraction to augment the width of a corner column. While I was guarding the entrance tunnel, after our cavalry and foot soldiers had departed to do battle, a thought occurred to me. If, heaven forbid, we had lost our battle to the invader we few that had remained behind in this stronghold would have found ourselves helplessly trapped.

"While only a handful of soldiers can prevent an entire army from entering our stronghold, in a long siege the small size of the entry tunnel becomes a trap. A platoon of enemy warriors placed in the tunnel could prevent our entire force from breaking out of the stronghold. We need that a second way be made for Egyptians to escape from this hollow mountain, if flight were the only way left to save them."

"I little like to hear you say that I selected a garrison stronghold that can become a trap," replied Lockshray furrowing his brow. "Still, Merlew, I guess you tell me what I already know. Something must be done. I will have you two consider how we can build a stairway up and out of this sunken canyon."

The uncle and nephew skilled at building, nodded heads at each other.

Sporting a smile even grander than usual, the chief came to visit Lockshray and Elyir. He brought the welcome news that young men from the mountain tribes wanted to help build the pavilion palace.

"The young and stalwart Lockshray fought bravely for us. He brought to my people new courage that regained their freedom. In exchange, my people will for him build."

"Well chief," replied Elyir with a smile, "the young native men that help us build are in for a long haul. It could take twenty years to finish the pavilion."

"Only twenty years, Elyir?" interjected a grinning Lockshray. "Knowing you as I do, I think it could take thirty years for you to complete a pavilion palace that meets your high expectations."

"Of course I will take the time needed to get it right. Remember that Merlew says it takes twice as long to unbuild errors in the stonework, as it takes to do it correctly the first time."

"Anyway, Elyir," added the Egyptian captain, "because I do not wait for the pharaoh's navy to soon retrieve us, we have lots of time to dedicate to a construction project."

As they worked together Egyptians began to learn words in the language of their neighbors, and natives began to use words unique to the Egyptians. Little by little two languages grew closer to each other.

Briarburr, Maryeta, and Lyons watched the foal bare her teeth as she chased after five black dogs become her particular playmates. When stone masons reached out to pet the foal, she shied away refusing to let be stroked her hide. Within her was an innocent part she would guard and keep independent of cajolery.

"Hmph! You told me once that your five dogs would have a purpose. Sister, the purpose of your black dogs has now been revealed. It is to *amuse* the foal."

"Hah! About that, brother, you are right," responded Maryeta. "The foal is so lovable. But why does she not let me come close to her? I love her sire and mare, and I perfectly love the rambunctious little filly."

"Let me tell you about my foal," interjected the blackmane standing close by. "She wants to do everything by herself. Her legs grow faster than the rest of her. Perhaps someday she will become the best friend that a human person can have. It will simply take some time for her to grow through and beyond her young self."

"I admit that I would rather see the foal wild and independent, like I was as a little girl, instead of tame and docile. Given the chance everyone here would spoil the foal and that would ultimately do her no good. Still, I hate that I will not be afforded the chance to know friendship with this very special filly when she is grown big and has learned to do fantastic magical things."

"At least my sister and I can always rub the shoulders of her sire, this stout stallion standing with us. And that is a very worthy consolation."

Remembrance

With one wing at her side and the other resting on the back of Briarburr, Peli stood one day staring at the fall of water that plummeted down the rock wall located close by the site of the pavilion palace. Briarburr's hooves pointed the opposite direction toward the entranceway to the stronghold.

"Look Lyons!" exclaimed Maryeta walking with her brother toward Peli and Briarburr. "They are positioned exactly as they stood on the day we first saw them. We were only children then. We were so astonished to see a unicorn and a winged horse, that we fell out of a tree."

"How well do you two remember that day so long ago?" inquired Lyons come to stroke the face of Briarburr.

"Like it was yesterday," neighed Peli. "While my eyes were fixated on something magical that I felt behind the waterfall, Briarburr noticed you two up in a tree."

"Your crash down from the tree spooked me," neighed Briarburr.

"This is the second time I have overheard that story told," interjected the approaching Elyir. "You know what? This day you have inspired me. Along with a tower containing a huge cistern to supply water during the dry season, at the place where the water cascades down I will build a pool to remind me of what you just recalled. Into two great stones set in the midst of the pool I will sculpt the placement at this moment of Briarburr and Peli. Statues of a blackmaned unicorn and a winged horse will forever preserve the memory of the time Briarburr and Peli first beheld two orphans in a forest."

"That is splendid," offered Lyons. "The best part is that channeling the fall of water into a tower, building a pool, and sculpting stone statues of a life sized unicorn and a winged horse will only extend five more years the pavilion construction project."

"About that Lyons is not wrong," responded Elyir nodding his head. "Ahead of me is now to be done... *even more work.*"

CHAPTER 39

CEREMONY IN THE PAVILION

B riarburr, Peli, the foal, Matron Lorial, Maryeta, and Lyons walked side by side toward the tunnel that led out the pavilion stronghold. Their serious demeanor and the tone of their farewells made it clear that the royal youth and the unicorns had chosen this day to forever depart the hollow mountain. As the news of their departure spread, a commotion began.

"You cannot yet depart Prow Mountain!" exclaimed Elyir planting himself before Briarburr. "Before you leave us, you must give me a few moments of your time."

"But, why do we need to tarry?"

"Trust me, Briarburr. Not without good reason would I ask you to grant me this favor. We were planning something bigger, but given your rush to leave, a small ceremony will have to do. The dais of the pavilion palace is practically finished. Follow me there." Upon arrival, Lockshray, Cali, and Merlew were found to be awaiting the unicorns and their two friends.

"Come, Lorial, to stand before me," said Lockshray. "Great dame unicorn, the flowers Merlew holds represent our esteem for the purity of your heart. We will never forget your kindness toward us." A garland of pink, purple, and red flowers was by Cali placed on the matron's neck. Woven green fronds secured in place the huge garland. Strings of yellow flowers were made to trail on each side of Lorial.

"You are next, Maryeta," continued Lockshray with his face spread in a big smile. "Your encouragement led Peli's wings to the canyon of blue gold. Your words of motivation brought the winged horse to discover this hidden canyon where Elyir now builds this fabulous pavilion. As the commander of Prow Mountain, with all my heart I thank you for the defense given by your blue gold sword in the battle against painted warriors. With the help of his uncle Merlew, your dear friend the artistic Elyir has fashioned something for you to wear on very special occasions. On the front of this blue gold diadem is etched an image of what the pavilion palace shall come to be. Notice how the fluted columns raise high."

"The pavilion's columns will sustain the crowning architrave and triangular cornice," interjected Elyir.

Lockshray placed the diadem on Maryeta's brown hair colored rich by flowing auburn tresses. When the princess bowed gracefully, the perfectly fit diadem did not fall from her head.

"I will much mourn the loss of the princess from our kitchen," added Chief Cali.

"Come forward, Prince Lyons," continued Lockshray. "Wielding your marvelous blue gold sword, your untiring arms helped to make safe our home in this new land. And I will never forget that your conversation about guardian lions hastened the discovery of Shining Canyon and its deposit of blue gold."

Moving to stand next to Lockshray, Elyir made the presentation.

"These braces that I fashioned of purest blue gold, shall protect from future blows in battle, the forearms of Lyons. Etched into each brace is your namesake, a lion." After Elyir adjusted their tightness, the youth held up his arms to display the beauty of the golden braces.

"Come forward Peli and Briarburr." The Egyptian captain proceeded to hug the two unicorns, but of course was not permitted to show affection to the foal standing next to her mare.

"Peli's wings... *entered first* the Shining Canyon of blue gold, and as well... *entered first* this hollow mountain," spoke next Merlew. "I have been many times told that her wings after provided rescue to every soldier in the twenty horse cavalry." The hands of Merlew caressed the gift he was about to present. "Made sheer, lithe, and diaphanous this halter decorated in blue gold reflects the love, beauty, and friendship that to us you have shown. Holding to your forehead a magical medallion, that like Maryeta's diadem depicts the pavilion's future columns, the interwoven strands of magic blue gold shall make more powerful the wings of Peli."

"None of us will ever forget the intrepid blackmaned unicorn that anchored our cavalry in the *Battle of the Twenty Horse Soldiers*," said Lockshray as he placed a halter on the stallion. "On your forehead now rests a medallion fashioned out of blue gold that depicts the rock prow of our mountain stronghold. By the way, Briarburr, I am very proud of Merlew's workmanship in the making of these blue gold halters."

Two unicorns displayed bows, made by shining halters to be even more elegant.

"Now I can offer one assurance. If after two or three moons of usage the diadem, forearm braces, or halters do not fit you exactly right, if they do not feel completely comfortable, come back to Prow Mountain and Elyir and Merlew will be most glad to adjust them for you."

Thinking on how difficult it would be to ever again return to Prow Mountain, now that Abel's barge was soon to travel back the immense ocean, the face of the usually solemn Briarburr broke out in longish smile.

The small ceremony ended, Briarburr's procession made its way out the tunnel that entranced the canyon stronghold. Maryeta mounted Peli and Lyons mounted Briarburr. A unicorn matron, winged horse, unicorn stallion, and one foal turned and reared a hoofed salute. Joining them, the Prince and Princess of Phoenicia waved farewell to Lockshray, Cali, Elyir, Merlew, and five black dogs found standing at the entrance to Prow Mountain.

With the foal stationed between Peli and the matron, four magic equines loped toward the west. They stopped for the night at a sentry post provisioned with maize, flatbread, and plentiful grazing.

Lyons, Maryeta, and the equines continued early the next morning toward the western edge of the valley that spread wide before the hollow mountain.

Following at midday the turn of the river southward, the small procession left forever behind Prow Mountain and its secret pavilion.

The path taken along the river came to a narrow bottleneck set between high cliffs. Natives had there gathered to bid farewell. Children reached hands to touch the unicorns and their magic halters. To the dismay of the youngsters, the foal was determined to stay hidden between Peli and Matron Lorial. Amidst the exuberant crowd, mounted on horseback waited Chief Cali and his wife Benilvina. Seated on a third horse was a young maiden.

When his ears alerted to the sound of distant hoof beats, Briarburr turned his head. Down the path just traveled, trotted the horse of Lockshray.

CHAPTER 40

JEWELELK AND LOCKSHRAY

"I will show Lockshray the best way to travel to the hold of the unicorns!" exclaimed the chief.

"Because my wife loves to ride, she also goes with us. Hmph! I need Briarburr to spark the uniform tongue to my daughter!" So it was done.

"Maryeta, this is my Jewelelk who was long held captive," said Benilvina grabbing the hand of her daughter. "Our youngest is a beautiful jewel with heart strong like a great elk. Her captors did not dare to offend me with ill-treatment of Jewelelk. Having inherited my strong will, not even our terrible enemies could diminish her spirit. She insisted to see for herself the splendor of the tall volcano that stands against the unicorn hold."

"I will also see the beauty of the white herd," added Jewelelk smiling wide at Maryeta.

"I am to finally enjoy some girl talk!" responded Maryeta.

"Harr! Lockshray does not know he is to marry! My little Jewelelk is going to be his wife!" At that spontaneous comment the natives crowded around the chief broke into laughter.

"I forbid my father to say that! Released from long captivity, I will not now become captive to any man, least of all to one I do not even know. Besides, he is not one of our people. As he approaches, I can see that the color of his skin is different."

"My child, in your captivity you learned that it is not the color of one's skin that determines the value of a man or woman, it is the trueness of the heart that lies beneath the skin. The strong chief of his people, Lockshray is like a brother to me. It is right for such a powerful man to marry the daughter of the greatest chief in these mountains... that being me! Harr!"

"Hmph!" retorted Benilvina. "If Jewelelk does not marry the man she wants, she will every day make her husband to suffer."

"Dear wife, you know that I want only for our daughter to know happiness."

Once the Egyptian captain gained his friends, the unicorns, horses, and riders continued on their journey. As they threaded along the banks of the river, the height and breadth of Prow Mountain came into full view.

"Because the place of our garrison forms a prow made of two enormous mountain slabs," said Lockshray to Cali, "it ever reminds me of the incredible Egyptian voyage made across the endless sea."

"I will talk to my friend about something else, something that is for you serious."

"And because in this country there is found no man wiser than Chief Cali, I promise to listen carefully to his words."

"It is a simple thing, Lockshray. Ahem... I have arranged for you to marry my daughter Jewelelk, the pretty young woman that with us rides."

Lockshray could not believe what his ears had heard. After glancing at the chief's daughter he replied, "I cannot take a wife. After all, I am a military man. It is not fair for a woman to marry a man one day destined to perish in battle."

"Even for a soldier, a wife keeps warm the bed of her husband. My daughter is courageous, honest, and strong. She will make you the best wife." The other riders had of course overheard. Newly provoked, Jewelelk contradicted the words of her father.

"Quit saying that! I will marry the man I choose. He will have to be a perfect man. For no less will I settle."

"Daughter," answered Benilvina, "in these mountains a perfect man cannot be found. If you insist on finding a perfect husband, then you had better marry him the same day you meet him, before you discover what flaws he has."

"Even the father of Jewelelk has one or two imperfections. Harrgh!"

"My husband has exactly five imperfections, and many times I have counted all five in the same day."

It came time to camp. The magical horses grazed while a meal was prepared, and by a fire shared. Across the night sky, stars made shimmering their appearance.

Cali Thief

About the ebbing campfire five blankets for six people were unrolled; Cali and Benilvina would share.

"Where is my blanket? Father, you *took* my blanket!"

"Daughter, your mother is cold and I feel chilled down to my bones. We two need your blanket more than you do."

"You already have one! Now I have none!"

"For my daughter that is not a problem. Lockshray sleeps under a big blanket that has room for two. I ask my daughter to visit with him, talk to him. If only for the sake of your father, get to know him a little."

"Enough of your tricks! Give me back... *my blanket!*"

While the chief pretended to snore, his daughter tried to pull her blanket away from him. For all his snoring and all Jewelelk's strength, Cali held tightly the two blankets in his possession.

"All right, I will this night sleep beside my mother." Jewelelk nestled in. "I need more blanket. Father, you have too much blanket about you, and I have next to none!"

The maiden sat up, reached over, and with the bottom of her fist clunked her father on his head. "I do not like the way the Egyptian captain looks. He has scars on his arms. If I set my mind to it I can get a man with smooth skin, even the best looking."

"Tell me wife," inquired the no longer snoring chief, "is there any other man so brave and noble as Lockshray?"

"No man that I know. Only my dear husband comes close."

"It is kind of Jewelelk to not mention the scar I wear on my cheek, the new one I earned in the last battle," responded Lockshray pulling tighter his blanket. "Cali is indeed a fearsome warrior. I am glad that on that day he fought as my friend."

Rolling onto his other side the sea captain muttered to himself, "After so many years of battle, it would not be easy to unlock tenderness from the heart of Lockshray."

"While Lockshray may be expert in war, that does not make him expert in love," replied Jewelelk frowning.

With her mouth tucked under her blanket Maryeta began to giggle. Her brother rolled over and elbowed his sister.

"Ouch!"

"Get to sleep, sister. Tomorrow we have a long ride ahead." That said Lyons pulled tight his blanket.

"Squeeze closer, Mother, to keep me warm."

In sleep that night old Chief Cali wore a broad smile.

Although morning air felt crisp, Jewelelk awoke warmed. Sometime in the night the blanket of the Egyptian captain had been spread to cover her.

Three days later the procession of Cali, Lockshray, Benilvina, Jewelelk, Lyons, Maryeta, four unicorns, and four horses drew close to a tall conical volcano. Over and over Maryeta allowed that the volcano had to be the most majestic that anywhere existed.

"The base looks to be perfectly round. See how huge is the start upward of the volcano. Small in size, the summit is as well, formed perfectly. The snow that covers the top of the cone is pure as a white sea bird, or the hide of a unicorn." Maryeta looked at Briarburr and added, "Err, that is the hide of an... *all white* unicorn."

"Nothing else in nature has the majestic symmetry of a high volcano," responded Jewelelk.

The friendship of the two young ladies continued to blossom. The next morning they jointly petitioned to climb high enough the side of the volcano to look out upon the blue sea. Briarburr neighed that his muscles would relish a hard climb. Peli likewise said that her wings could benefit from the challenge of upward flight. After climbing higher all afternoon, the little procession found itself at a place that offered a clear view of the wide sea.

Surveying the panorama of the watery expanse, the heart of Jewelelk was much moved. "In color the sea is a second sky. How I envy you, Maryeta. You will soon sail upon endless beauty."

At the sight of something extraordinarily lovely Maryeta's emotion was to laugh, jump up, and shout out loud for joy. So upon dismounting Maryeta, laughed, jumped, and shouted, "Hahah! I do so love the sea! I want to live the rest of my life on a boat!"

"Over there is the hold of the unicorns," neighed Lorial pointing her horn. "The dwelling place of the white herd is given to both the beauty of the sea and the majesty of the volcano."

"Has the sky ever been so clear?" neighed Peli flapping her wings in the cool breeze rising up the side of the volcano. "Truly we are traveling through a marvelous natural chamber."

"That is it!" exclaimed Lockshray. "I just realized what Elyir has in mind to do. He will make the pavilion palace to be his... *room of beauty.*"

That evening five blankets were once again placed by a fire that flickered high up the side of the volcano. Since it was still early, Benilvina grabbed the arm of her husband and said softly, "You and I will tonight enjoy the stars. It will be romantic." The two walked into gathering darkness.

"Will you walk with Maryeta, Lyons, and me?" said Lockshray turning to Jewelelk. "The night up here is special. Even the air feels different. I have never seen the stars cover above in such splendor."

"Oh... all right. We had better make sure that my parents do not get themselves somewhere lost."

Silence ensued until Lockshray broke it. "There is nowhere I would rather be this night than walking here with my companions Lyons and Maryeta, and with the daughter of my valiant friends Chief Cali and Benilvina."

"My sister and I are more than just your companions, Lockshray, we are your... *great friends,*" rejoined Lyons.

"I have the opinion that Lockshray likes Jewelelk," chimed in a giggling Maryeta. "And even though she will not admit it, I think Jewelelk likes the Egyptian captain. After all, Lockshray is the most trustworthy and courageous man I know, err, that is after my brother... and Abel. I just wish that Abel would not continue to sport so much anger against his head. I am tired of seeing him bald. And I wish my black dogs were right now here with me. I miss them."

"Well, at that, Abel does nourish his beard," responded Lyons.

"Both on his chin and top, he would look better if he cut his beard and let grow the hair on his head."

"Come with me, Maryeta," said Lyons grabbing the hand of his sister. "I want to show you something."

Left alone with Jewelelk, Lockshray reached out his hand. After a moment of hesitation she consented to place her hand in his.

"I want to correct something unfair that I said before, I find you passably handsome. I know that you are very brave. It is the first time that I ever heard my father suggest that someone is more courageous than he himself. And it was... kind of you the other night to give me your blanket. I am sure that without a blanket you suffered from the chill. Perhaps, I misjudged you, Lockshray." Her voice softened, "No blanket was in captivity given to me. I hated every day of my imprisonment. I know that you had much to do, had everything to do, with my being again made free."

"I am sorry you were taken captive."

"My heart... was never taken captive. Each day and night of my bondage I guarded well my heart, so well that even now I am afraid to give any man its key."

"It is right for you to be careful of love," replied Lockshray tightening his grip on the maiden's hand. "If

I were given that key," Lockshray turned and looked the maiden full in her eyes, "your heart would never more be unlocked from mine."

Eyes opened wide, Jewelelk returned the gaze of the Egyptian captain.

Cold night air embraced the volcano. The teeth of Chief Cali began to chatter as he lay under stars that sparkled a delicate satiny light. With a quick motion he yanked the blanket from off his daughter.

"Father, I thought you were over this nonsense."

"On this volcano the nights are twice as cold. Daughter, do not forget that it was your idea to come to this high place."

"No, father, it was Maryeta's idea to come here. I only seconded her idea."

"Besides, daughter, I know that you and Lockshray are meant to talk to, and get to know each other."

A silence ensued. Enjoying to unfold the continuing drama between Chief Cali and his favorite daughter, Maryeta put her hand over her mouth in the hope that no one would hear her muffled giggles.

Jewelelk stood up and made a show of stomping off. She shortly returned carrying a branch. "All right. As nothing more than his friend, for I do feel friendship for him, I will share the blanket of the Egyptian captain. This boundary stick will rest between us." Lockshray drew his blanket over the young woman and her stick.

"Do not worry for anything, Daughter. Your mother's eyes will be wide open all night. The slightest sound and..." His own snoring interrupted the words of Cali.

Lockshray did not at first say anything. His gaze rested long on the maiden. Making his blanket to cover only the maiden he spoke four words that warmed her heart, "You are most lovely."

In the misty light of early morning Benilvina noticed that her daughter, still blanketed, hugged the back of Lockshray for warmth. The chief's wife smiled when she saw that an arm's length distant from where slept her daughter, rested unblanketed the boundary stick.

The volcano was left behind.

Lorial scrambled up the side of a hill. This time her effort was rewarded. In the distance the matron glimpsed yearling colts frisking about. Appearing no larger than small flecks of white, foals reclined sunning themselves. Close by their napping foals, mares grazed peacefully.

"From here we cannot see the waterfall," observed the unicorn matron. "In my mind I picture it to be the most beautiful part of my new home."

"Lorial," neighed Peli softly, "placed between the sea, the forest, and the volcano, the future home of my foal is wondrously beautiful."

Peli nuzzled her foal. "*Aneighlee*...that is the new name I give to my young filly that will soon noisily neigh in the lee side, the sheltered side, of a beautiful volcano. Now tell me, Aneighlee, what do you think of the place where you will grow up playing with foals your age?"

The little unicorn began to race about copying the frolic of the yearlings she saw far below her.

Lorial led downward into a canyon graced by the benevolent meandering of a stream. The matron unicorn soon found herself stepping onto a beach of whitish sand. Eight unicorns and horses in an expedition come from Prow Mountain, were off running.

CHAPTER 41

A SALUTE TO BRIARBURR

"I go to see the waterfall of the new hold," that neighed, Peli was aflight with Maryeta. Upon glimpsing the oncoming horse wings, young unicorns jumped about with excitement.

"Run to your clan, Lorial," neighed Briarburr. "This is your moment of triumphant return." With the little foal at her side, Lorial galloped toward the hold. Finding their matron returned back to them safe and sound, unicorns ran toward her neighing excited greetings. Clinging to the matron's side, the foal was unwilling to be nuzzled by the strange unicorns come to be all about her.

Peli and Maryeta flew in return direction toward Briarburr, Lockshray, Lyons, Cali, and his family. When something caught Peli's eye, her wings carried her upward so that her eyes could penetrate farther the distance.

"We saw a sail!" exclaimed Maryeta landed back to the ground. "It has to be the barge that bears my name. Is not that wonderful!"

"Because we relished the climb of the volcano, Abel got the jump on us," observed Lockshray to Cali. "Briarburr does not now have to gallop up the coast; to him Abel has come." The sails of the Phoenician barge came into full view.

When Peli glimpsed Lorial and Aneighlee standing high on the beach with heads turned in the direction of the oncoming barge, she neighed to Briarburr, "Aneighlee clings to Lorial. My foal will not long remember... that I am her mare."

"Our foal will always know that you are her mare," replied Briarburr nuzzling with tenderness the cheek of his mate. "Lorial will not let her to forget. Our foal will also remember that I am her sire. Little Aneighlee knows more than we think she does. She even understands that while for her own good she stays behind, we are to leave and never return. Darling Peli, the foal clings to the matron to protect her little heart from breaking."

A beach made wide by the receding tide came to be lined with curious unicorns watching the approach of the Phoenician barge. With heads arched high, eight unicorn matrons stood before their respective clans.

Less than half a league off the unicorn beach the barge dropped anchor.

"Captain Lockshray... I am afraid... that I will never see you again." As he neighed farewell to a man that had always shown him kindness, Briarburr's voice choked, "A strong soldier... you are a man most dear to me."

"By me the blackmane is profoundly loved," answered the captain.

Gaining control over his emotions Briarburr neighed simple farewells to Lockshray, Cali, Benilvina, and Jewelelk. Together their four mounts reared front hooves, while at the same time neighing their unending friendship with the blackmaned unicorn stallion. To her friends Peli also neighed farewells.

By feelings overcome, and so unable to speak words of goodbye, the princess sank her face into the mane of Peli and began to bawl. Seated on Briarburr, the prince pointed his left arm toward Lockshray, and placed his right hand over his heart in a signal of love.

Four riders sat straight and tall on their horses as they watched depart from their lives, for all time, the blackmane, the winged horse, Prince Lyons, and Princess Maryeta.

When his heart told an illustrious chief that he must at this moment dance, Cali dismounted. Shuffling his feet and turning himself about, he chanted in loud voice:

Briarburr Blackmane, the Gatherer of the Phoenicians!
Briarburr Blackmane, the Stronghold of the Egyptians!
Briarburr Blackmane, the Spear of Mountain Warriors!

A Last Farewell

Changing its mind, the tide commissioned gently rolling waves to climb back the beach.

In the softening light of a descendant sun Abel flashed his magic sword in welcome to the oncoming Briarburr, Peli, Lyons, and Maryeta. Standing in chest high water halfway between the barge and the unicorns lining the beach, Briarburr and Peli together neighed one last time to their foal. Upon seeing Aneighlee pedal hooves upward in return salute, Peli's eyes filled with tears.

Moving to the water's edge Lorial reared hooves upward and neighed in full voice, *"Briarburr Blackmane, Defender of the White Herd!"* Then a wondrous thing happened that Briarburr and Peli would never forget. Each and every unicorn in the clan of Lorial reared high and neighed feelingly, *"Briarburr Blackmane, Defender of the White Herd!"*

For the very first time, Briarburr neighed in return his love for the herd of pure white unicorns.

Seven clans of unicorns stepped forward to stand in a line with the clan of Lorial. Spread wide along the beach, every unicorn in the white herd neighed in unison:

Briarburr and Peli, Defenders of the White Herd!
Briarburr and Peli, Defenders of the White Herd!

As with a wing she caressed his neck, Peli gave witness to eight unicorn clans that her love would ever after protect the blackmaned unicorn stallion. The unicorns lining the beach saw that Briarburr would never again be alone.

Turning to look one last time in the direction of the horses she had travelled with, Peli was pleased to see Jewelelk clutching the arm of Lockshray. Sharing their future together, her life would become his, and his hers.

Into rising waves galloped the blackmane and the winged horse. Lifting up on wings, Peli soon descended hooves onto the deck of the barge. Briarburr leaped long and high to land hooves beside his mate. Once the feet of Lyons slid to the deck he placed an arm around the shoulders of his sister.

As the sun's decline began to lengthen shadows over the unicorn hold found in the lee of a majestic volcano, billowing sails carried away the Phoenician barge.

"Unicorn horns shine on the beach!" exclaimed Maryeta. "Each one is bathed in blue luminescence!" A sheen of blue light had spread up and down the beach of the unicorn hold.

"Their horns shine like sentinels on guard to protect us," offered Abel. "By the light of magic we are bid farewell and safe voyage."

"Eight clans of unicorns are now contained entire in the virtue of nature," added Maryeta. "The noble magic horses will walk each new day in the sunlight of hope." Glancing at Briarburr and Peli the girl exclaimed, "Your gold halters shimmer the light of blue diamonds!"

CHAPTER 42

PROW MOUNTAIN AND PHOENICIA

Prow Mountain came into the view of the four riders. Thinking about the protection the redoubt offered to the Egyptians, Jewelelk posed a question to Lockshray. "Like your sailors, do the unicorns feel truly safe in this land?"

"Because too many unicorns were in past years slaughtered, it will take much time for the terror of their persecution to be forgotten. Now that I think about it, between Prow Mountain and the unicorn hold I will post sentries. You can be sure, Jewelelk, that your father will as well be watchful for any wishing harm to come to the unicorns."

"About the safety of the unicorns Lorial is optimistic," offered Cali. "She told me that for a thousand years to come the unicorn hold will stand firm and out of harm's way."

"Good," responded a satisfied Jewelelk. "The fierce northern tribes must never be permitted to covet the horns of the unicorns."

"Uh, what... Darling, I am sorry. More than listening I was looking at you. Every day I notice more *my gemstone*. Hmm. Thinking about Lorial's thousand years of unicorn peace, I should be very pleased that a dynasty of Egyptian pharaohs for that long endured."

"Now that the matron unicorn and the foal are safely returned to the white herd, what are your plans during the next moons?" inquired Cali of Lockshray.

"We keep building. Elyir is an enormously talented architect. And his uncle is a true genius. Merlew makes sure that Elyir not only builds, but that he also takes the necessary time to sculpt and coax beauty from slabs of rock. The building of the pavilion palace is not just for the sake of beauty. Reminding them of their country Egypt the monument gives purpose, meaning, and hope to the lives of my sailors. In that regard every stone must be cut and laid with care."

"Even I can see that were Merlew not making sure that work gets done properly, Elyir would be lost," observed Cali. "Just like you and me, Merlew and Elyir make a good team."

"Let me also say, Chief, that the blue gold must be kept safe. I will shut so tight the Shining Canyon that no one more comes to mine again the mountain of spires."

"What if ten years from now I require a blue gold head band?"

"Do not for that worry, Cali. A way will be thought of to allow me to obtain enough blue gold to satisfy my friend's desire."

"The Egyptian captain will protect well his new lodging in this land."

"To ensure peace there is no alternative but to remain vigilant. In this place I dare hope with Cali to grow old. I here serve my men, the white herd... *and you.*"

The horses of Cali and Lockshray slowed to trail behind Benilvina and Jewelelk. "Only to you, Lockshray, will I admit my former wrong-headedness. Before you came to these mountains I lost heart and let myself be pushed around by my enemies, and even by rival chiefs within my tribe. When to my valley you came, I again saw how a true chief must act. Taking heart, I returned to my old self. With you at my side I gained victory over my enemies to the north. Now my enemy will be anyone that seeks to harm the Egyptian captain. Errhrmm... now that I think about it, I do have a favor to ask of you. I want be a chief that wears a blue gold breastplate. Sun reflections will make me shine so much that my wife will again see me as young Chief Cali."

"My last store of blue gold ore will be fitted to the chest of Chief Cali."

Upon hearing that Cali shouted, "I am to wear a breast plate made of the magic gold!"

The chief's wife reined her horse to a stop. When her husband caught up with her she leaned over and embraced him warmly. "Cali, a chest plate of blue gold will make you the best dressed husband in all the land!"

Lockshray, Cali, Benilvina, and Jewelelk gained Prow Mountain.

The Pavilion

Even though she did not know, he knew it too well to ever forget. On that long ago morning when they had first met outside the gates of the garrison of Vylas, he had fallen in love with Maryeta. When his words that day swore an oath of loyalty to Fahseed, his heart declared his love for Maryeta. During the voyage of the unicorns, as he and Maryeta everyday talked of the beauty of sky and sea, his love for her had grown. Still, he had never found the courage to tell her that she filled his heart.

His uncle that memorized constellations and named each bright light twinkling in the night heavens, said that some great hand had hung each star in its place. To Elyir, Maryeta was like a heavenly star placed... out of his reach.

Elyir's ideas were not like his uncle's made of numbers, but of pure feeling. Because there was no compromise with his undying love for Maryeta, the only way forward for Elyir was to subjugate the longing of his heart. Now that she was gone forever, he knew what remained for him to do. It was something Elyir had known since he first entered the hollow mountain. He would make the pavilion to be his new love. Elyir called it the secret pavilion, not because its foundation was laid in a secret canyon, but because the rising palace concealed the secret of his love for Maryeta. The airy and columned pavilion, that would a thousand years endure, was for the slender artist and sculptor the embodiment of Maryeta's loveliness.

Elyir's pavilion would be built tall with clean, fluted lines. The capitals crowning the columns would display carvings of unicorns. Just as he had beheld from afar the unbounded innocence and loveliness of Maryeta, so the open roofed pavilion's double rows of columns would reach upward toward the beauty and purity of the stars.

The entrance side of the pavilion would be capped with a long square beam, an architrave. Above the beam would rest a frieze of carvings with sun symbols from Egypt, images of horns of unicorns, and engraved depictions of magic swords. The triangular cornice crowning the entrance would tell the story of the voyage of the unicorns to their new home. Ambulatory walkways would flow harmoniously between each side's outer and inner columns. In the apse at the far inner end of the columns was already built a raised dais from which height a leader, or orator, could be both seen and heard.

On some days the ideas that tumbled through the head of Elyir were so compelling that he lost his appetite and forgot to eat. As Lockshray would sacrifice his body on the field of battle, Elyir would sacrifice his strength to build a great work of art, a magnificent pavilion palace rising in the recess of a lost canyon.

Elyir had before wanted his life to always know Maryeta's beauty and companionship. In the elaboration of his architectural jewel he would ever after see and feel her beauty. The secret pavilion that consumed his thoughts would for the remainder of his life be his room of disciplined love.

The true secret of the hidden pavilion was that it was a love story carved in stone, the story of Elyir's love for a beautiful princess that to him became lost.

The Maryeta Sails for Phoenicia

"Beyond sight on the starboard side is an island that shows no signs of human persons," neighed Peli to Abel upon alighting back on the barge. "It has grass, fruits, and roots to eat; a stream of fresh water cuts across the beach. The island is luxuriant."

"So long as I can count on your winged eyes to survey about us, and can count on dolphins to each day provide me escort, I command very well this barge."

On a following evening a reflective Maryeta stroked the side of the unicorn stallion. "You know I think a lot about the end of our voyage. What will Briarburr do upon his arrival in Phoenicia?"

"Come to mean life itself to me, I will always keep Peli at my side. Each morning when I awake and see her wings, I tell myself that they are the most exquisite and welcoming sight my eyes have ever seen."

"Because Briarburr loves them, I too have grown to cherish the wings that before kept me apart from unicorn mares, and so burdened my heart. My wings are now cherished by the stallion that possesses my heart. You must stop me from getting too emotional... *say something* Maryeta."

"Since we left Phoenicia I have grown taller. It gives me pleasure to think that Grandfather's eyes will light up the moment he sees how much I have grown. His eyes have always shown that he loves me very much. Heheh! I am his favorite granddaughter!"

"I heard that! And you are his *only* granddaughter," responded Lyons newly aroused from his thoughts. He walked over and joined his sister and friends.

"My brother was meant to hear that."

"Yes, sister, as his younger grandchild you are the most loved. As for me, once back home I will rest for a whole moon. I will after pledge myself to the army. Since I already know to do soldiering, that makes sense to me. Because I so often chased rabbits as a child, I am a fast runner. And thanks to the training of Cavour, I will be the *best* swordsman in my battalion."

When Abel felt a fresh breeze waft over his cheeks he glanced upward at billowing sails straining taut their lines. He reminded himself that the voyage home to Phoenicia had begun well. Relaxing his features he offered, "It becomes my turn to say something. In the space of two moons I hope to enter our native sea. Within three moons I hope to report the success of our voyage to the king. I cannot wait to hear Fahseed tell me that our cargo of blue gold will signify the long survival of Phoenicia."

"But I am the one that most looks forward to seeing King Fahseed!" exclaimed Winfray joining to the conversation of his friends. "His pronouncement of *pardon*... will to my ears be the sweetest word."

Loyalty Unrebukeable

On another evening as twilight approached, Maryeta teased, "Abel, when my grandfather sees you he will be too shocked to say anything, except to ask what happened to your head? He will next comment that with all that new grown hair, your head looks to be twice as big as before."

"So my secret is out. People will know that I used to wear a shaved head so that its abnormal watermelon size would not be so obvious."

"I was teasing. You surely know, Abel, that I like you better with hair growing on your head. I cannot wait to see how you look when your hair is one hand long. Lots of girls will think you a handsome man."

"Including... you?"

"*Of course* including me." Reaching out to grab hold a big hand she asked, "Why are you become so serious?"

"Maryeta, my thoughts range ahead. I want King Fahseed to be proud of my workmanship in the far land where is now established the unicorn hold." Abel lowered his head as if to study the gentle swells of the sea.

"At the command of Baltric, I did wretched things. To lessen the pain I felt for following his unjust orders, I drank much. I looked upon myself as chief among rogues. I now ask myself how does one reconcile a journey through life that sows both bad and good. I hope, Maryeta, that your grandfather will think only on this new chapter of my life lived with you, your brother, Winfray, Jomain, Peli, and Briarburr. I hope to hear the king say to me, Lieutenant Abel, your loyalty to Phoenicia is... *unrebukeable.*"

Seeing a tear roll down his cheek, the princess squeezed tight the unsmall sides of the lieutenant.

"Dear Abel, neither my father nor I can forgive you. You are the one that has to forgive yourself. Still, I will be there to help you heal. As children, you and I both suffered terrible loneliness. Now you have me, and I have you. Letting your hair grow out signifies that you are become changed from the man that you were."

"Maryeta, I also fear what the king will answer when I ask for your hand."

"My grandfather likes you. While I can barely remember my real father, did you know that Winfray has become almost like a father to me?"

"His heart is kind and his smile is infectious. We all have seen that with you he is very special."

"And while at Prow Mountain, he loved to play with my dogs."

Many days passed at sea on board the *Maryeta*. One evening as they often did Lyons, Peli, Briarburr, Jomain, and Winfray joined Abel and the princess to watch the sun's decline over rippling waves adorned by subtle shades of silver and gray.

"Do you know, Sir," said Maryeta as she took the hands of Winfray, "that I have thought much about the time I begged my grandfather to spare the life of Roward. I was sure that I was right about showing mercy to him. Hmph! I now think of Roward by the name of *Froward*, one that is disposed to disobedience. My grandfather will be upset to learn of Froward's treachery."

"Dear girl," answered Winfray, "never question the nobility of petitioning mercy in lieu of pursuing vengeance. After all, it was your petition for mercy that also saved me. Even though it did not change the heart of Roward, yours was an act most noble." Hearing that said, a beaming princess grabbed again the hands of Winfray.

"I, for one, will not mention to anyone in Phoenicia the details of the demise of the former Lord Froward," offered Jomain.

"It just occurred to me that Winfray should be given a new name," interjected Maryeta. "For his heroism leading the Egyptian infantry into battle, he has earned it. The colors of this seascape inspire me." She turned to address the former overlord. "I shall call you *Windray*. You will for me be the pure light of a sunray that walks on a clean wind."

"So then, Maryeta, I shall no more be the fray that was part and parcel of my old name. I shall henceforth be known only as... Windray."

"Your future life shall be carried forth *above the fray*," added Jomain.

"Errm, I now think on something else," said Maryeta placing two fingers over her lips to muffle a laugh. "Upon our return to Phoenicia the only other head in the whole world that will be so large as yours, Lieutenant Abel, will be the head worn on the shoulders of Boschene as he hears the pharaoh laud him for bringing back to Egypt a barge laden with magic gold."

"A small voice inside tells me that the ears of Boschene will no more come to hear his pharaoh's praise," neighed Briarburr. "That little voice tells me that the final destination of Boschene's barge... is not to be Egypt."

"Having by now suffered enough from him, I do not believe that the crew of Boschene any longer obeys their admiral's commands," agreed Lyons. "Before reaching the port of Egypt, the admiral's sailors will surely have mutinied."

"*Yeeaarrhehheh,*" neighed Peli laughingly. "I can imagine that right now Admiral Boschene finds himself stranded and alone. He is such a poor navigator that he will not have the foggiest idea where exactly he finds himself to be. Just as he did not voluntarily choose to search for the lost and lame Lorial, I for one will not search for Boschene. If he is lost, let him remain so."

"Peli, you do not often speak your mind," commented Abel as he reached to stroke the neck of the winged horse. "But when you do, you speak it... *clearly.*"

"Do you think the great pharaoh will be content that you bring home the precious blue gold to Phoenicia," inquired Maryeta of Abel, "while Egypt receives nothing back from across far seas, not even the return of the pharaoh's investment in three great barges?"

"I hope," interjected Lyons, "that the ruler of Egypt sees things clearly enough to know to place blame for the disaster, only on Admiral Boschene."

"Someday the pharaoh will find the service of Boschene to be... *rebukeable,*" concluded Abel.

CHAPTER 43

THE PHARAOH WAITS

On a day about work and not pageantry, the pharaoh sat on his throne with thighs and waist tied simply in cotton cloth. His seat provided a view of a large construction project in the desert.

"So again today comes no news of my barges laden with the magic gold?"

"Majesty," Ambassador Adolfo bowed low as he replied, "I was told by a trusted source returned last night from the Phoenician court, that while the king was settling land disputes..."

"What land disputes?"

"Highness, when were defeated the petty despots that before ruled Phoenicia many claims arose to take back lands that had been previously dispossessed by the overlords."

The pharaoh waved his hand as if the disputes were of no consequence.

"While so occupied a messenger was received by King Fahseed. The message conveyed that the unicorns in the one clan remaining in Phoenicia had become very active and energetic with moods exultant. That activity was taken to be a sign that the one Phoenician barge, that accompanied our three great barges carrying unicorns, now returns to Fahseed. Along with blue gold treasure, the war unicorn with black markings that so impressed

Boschene and I with his display of magic, was said to be on the returning barge."

"Then Admiral Boschene will soon enter my port with three barges weighted heavy with magic gold."

"Ahem. King Fahseed was said to have made the same observation. The answer given to him was that according to sentient unicorns, the Egyptian barges are not now found in return to our sea."

"*What?* How can that be? My barges are many times larger and stronger than the small Phoenician vessel. Six hundred superb Egyptian sailors man the oars of those three vessels. No navy has ever triumphed over one of our massive war barges. If anything, it should be the Phoenician lieutenant and his few sailors that do not return."

"The unicorns sense that only one barge now returns to our sea. That barge was said to be not yours."

"Then it is my right to intercept the Phoenician barge and claim for Egypt the blue gold it carries. What ships has our navy that can be dispatched to search for the Phoenician vessel?"

"Our war barges are so great in size that their sails would be seen by the Phoenician vessel long before the sails of their small barge were by us sighted. Intercepting the Phoenician barge would be made more difficult if the magical unicorn on board sensed danger and alerted to the approach of our formidable war barges. If the unicorn discerned our presence, the Phoenician vessel would change course to avoid us."

"Then we will station war barges off the Phoenician coast and intercept the Phoenician barge before it enters its home port." That said, the pharaoh looked hopefully to his brother the ambassador.

"Phoenician vessels every day enter and depart their port," answered Adolfo. "Upon being informed of our designs, Fahseed would interpret them as an act of war."

"You are well-aware, Adolfo, that I cannot now afford a war with the upstart and dogged Phoenicians. My hands are full with the Nubians, the Assyrians, the Mesopotamians, and the blasted pirate dogs that sail from lands on the northern reaches of my sea. What then do you suggest I do?"

Adolfo took three steps forward so that his back was to the pharaoh, and gazed at the enormous pyramid rising ever higher in the distant desert.

"Let us be confident that if any vessel returns it will be commanded by Admiral Boschene. After all he is your brother, and mine."

"You are my one true brother. He is but one of my half brothers. In truth, father liked him far more than I do. Boschene is more true to himself than to me."

"Highness, Boschene has many times told us that he is the most gifted admiral in the world. It is impossible that a decrepit Phoenician barge with a crew of only forty sailors returns, and Boschene's great barges do not."

Adolfo moved to again stand behind the throne. In a low voice he said, "More than anything else, King Fahseed is a general that knows how to command. He would fight hard to protect Phoenicia. But, perhaps there is another solution to this problem. Sire, you have many times cursed the upstart pirate vessels. What if the Phoenician barge were to be found not by Egyptian war barges, *but by pirates loyal only to you?*"

Chapter 44

Pirates

"Where travel this night your thoughts?" inquired Abel joining Windray at the rail.

"In fifteen days these benevolent winds should bring our barge to Phoenicia. There I have a pardon to obtain. I much want, Lieutenant, to be again a free man. We cannot now let anything prevent us from receiving welcome by Fahseed."

"Have you observed, Windray, that both Briarburr and Peli grow restless. While their change in disposition is subtle, I do notice it. Not knowing the cause of what bothers them, they cannot neigh to me what it is."

The next morning Jomain climbed down from the lookout perch at the top of a mast to apprise Abel, "It seems that a ship follows us. The curious thing is that it is flashing sun reflections. Can it want for us to wait for it?"

"Already slowed by the weight of the blue gold cargo, when so close to our native land we cannot slow more. If we sail on and a Phoenician vessel catches up to us, no harm is done. But, what if it is an Egyptian vessel that follows us? If our barge falls into the hands of Boschene's confederates, our right to the blue gold will in nothing be honored. No, Jomain, we do not for anything slacken our sails."

"Yesterday it was one," informed Jomain. "Today, Lieutenant, *three* vessels follow us, or pursue us if you want to look at it that way."

"So the sun flashes you mentioned yesterday were call signals to the other two ships. Still, because independent-minded pirates do not often sail in convoy, I do not take these to be ordinary raiders. Keep a close eye on the pursuing vessels, and perhaps you will come to identify them. But before you again climb the mast, you and I are going to talk with Briarburr and Peli."

"Yes, Abel. Briarburr and I both sense that some danger is to befall us. The ships behind us do not feel right to me."

"Perhaps Peli can fly ahead and request the king to send ships to reinforce us," offered Jomain.

"I will not abandon my Briarburr. If this vessel is to face a fight, my wings shall in that conflict find use."

"And there is not time enough for ships to sail out from the Phoenician port to meet us before we are intercepted," neighed Briarburr.

"Nor would I have our pursuers upon seeing Peli in flight, learn so soon that her wings provide strategic advantage to our barge," added Abel.

That night the lanterns of three ships flickered in the distance. When the next morning Lieutenant Abel saw that the three vessels following the *Maryeta* had become four, and had drawn closer, he became deeply worried.

"Windray, please tell me that the ships following us are Phoenician."

"I think not, Lieutenant. Since the sails of each vessel are colored separate and hung distinct, they look to be true pirate ships. They cleverly delayed their assault on the *Maryeta* until all four ships came to sail abreast."

"Our sails are trimmed taught and my sailors can row no faster. We need for the magic of unicorns and blue gold to help protect us. Although we require perhaps ten more days to reach our port, under no circumstance will any of the treasured gold be jettisoned to secure us more speed."

When on the following morning the *Maryeta* ran only a half league ahead of four vessels in pursuit, a council of war was called.

"It is clear that the ships closing on us are to soon attack," declared Abel. "Odds of four against one in nothing favor us. I cannot believe that pirate captains can be as disciplined and perseverant as display our pursuers. Something is not what it seems."

"How can they know of our precious cargo?" inquired Maryeta. "If our hold carried ordinary commerce, we would be a poor choice for the expenditure of so much effort by four ships to capture us."

"From a now returned Boschene they have learned of the blue gold we carry," offered Jomain. "I can think of no other way that pirates, if they are real pirates and not Egyptian vessels in disguise, could know anything about the blue gold. If our pursuers only pretend to be pirates, the purpose of the deceit is to have King

Fahseed not blame Egypt for seizure of blue gold that rightfully belongs to Phoenicia."

"Had Egypt received the blue gold carried on Boschene's vessel," observed Windray, "the pharaoh would see himself as invincible and hence welcome war with Phoenicia. I think that Boschene has not yet refound Egypt, and never will. However, by some manner of divination, or soothsaying, the pharaoh has learned that the *Maryeta* carries blue gold. Faced with the failure of Boschene, the pharaoh cannot risk open war with Phoenicia, but will take in stealth what is not his."

"Let us for now infer that Egypt is behind the intended robbery of our cargo," said Abel. "To carry out their subterfuge, we can also surmise that no Phoenician witness to the theft will be permitted to survive. We find ourselves in a fight not just for the precious gold, but for our very lives."

"As a ruler you had much experience in war," offered Jomain. "Tell us, Windray, how to prepare for the battle that comes."

"Blue gold swords in the hands of Lyons, Maryeta, Jomain, and Abel will assuredly inflict much damage on those that attempt to board us. Fortunately for us, the pirates cannot burn, or ram and sink our barge because that would forfeit them the treasure they seek. The requirement that they capture intact our barge provides leeway for the working of unicorn magic. Our strategy of defense must center on our two unique weapons, Briarburr and Peli."

"My magic gift will turn away arrows and spears in flight," neighed Briarburr.

"I could ascend on wing and attempt to light enemy sails ablaze. But, unfortunately my short horn does not spark hot like Briarburr's."

"It is worth a try," responded Abel. "Still, it must be done at night when Peli is by darkness protected. Our rowers will expend their utmost strength and effort so that we are not overtaken before nightfall. You know, I am beginning to feel better about our chances. Although the pirate vessels number four to one against us, by them the *Maryeta* will not be easily subdued."

Lyons, Maryeta, Windray, Jomain, and Abel joined turns at the oars. As night descended the moon and stars came to be shrouded behind high clouds. The lanterns of one pirate vessel, the fastest under sail of the four, loomed close behind the *Maryeta*.

"She... is... gone," neighed Briarburr.

In the distance began a commotion, and shouting was heard. In light-flickered flight the flame of a ship lantern moved upward.

"In her teeth Peli grabbed the handle of an oil lantern!" yelled Jomain from atop the mast. "The flame descends to set an enemy sail afire."

The main sail of the barge closest in pursuit of the *Maryeta* burst into flames.

"My wings are unhurt," neighed Peli as she lit down beside Briarburr.

"Are you certain that no spear or arrow pierced your flesh or damaged your wings?"

"The astonished pirate sailors could have right away wounded me, but perhaps thinking that I was a ghost they hesitated. The aft lantern that I closed my teeth upon was brimmed full of oil. I climbed upward, and then protecting the flame with one wing, I dived at the sail. The dry fabric became kindling for the lantern's flame. The mast itself began to burn."

It was not long before Peli redirected her neighs, "Lieutenant, shall I attack the next boat in line?"

"Attack instead the farthest in the line of pursuers. Perhaps the sailors on the most distant vessel do not yet understand what inflamed the sail of the lead barge in their convoy. Go only if you are confident that you will return unharmed." Peli was again aflight.

The crew of the *Maryeta* peered anxiously into darkness. Long moments passed before was heard faint shouting from afar. For the second time a main sail burst into flame. Once more Peli returned safely to the *Maryeta*.

The lanterns aboard enemy vessels were snuffed out. Four enemy ships became enveloped in darkness.

When the new light of morning revealed two pirate ships in close pursuit, Abel asked for a reconnaissance flight of Peli mounted by Lyons.

"No one else flies with Peli, but me!" insisted Maryeta.

Abel was reluctant to send the princess that now commanded his dreams, on a flighted mission full of risk. But Maryeta's obstinacy gave Abel no choice but to relent in the matter. Soon the flying horse and her mount were returned to the *Maryeta*.

"What, Princess, did you find? Are they real pirates?"

"I think not Abel... at least not all of them. Clad differently than the common sailors, the dress and aspect of the officers is Egyptian. Lieutenant, the two vessels damaged last night by Peli are again with sail. By nightfall they will have caught up with the two close vessels that trail us."

"So, the danger has not lessened," said Abel with a look crestfallen. "The Egyptians will tomorrow have not two, but all four vessels to attack us. It will be much harder to again surprise them with Peli's wings. Archers will be perched about their masts, and they will tonight leave no lanterns unguarded. Although the bravery of Peli bought us precious time, we must ready ourselves to withstand a grievous assault upon our barge."

The new sun witnessed a line of four pirate vessels bearing down upon the *Maryeta*. Without neighing a word, Briarburr jumped into the sea and swam toward the closest privateer. While he swam, his horn swerved arrows away from his body. Peli was off in flight.

"She will bother the pirate ships," said Abel. "For the benefit of Briarburr, she makes of herself a distraction."

"We knew she would protect her mate," added Windray.

"Join with Lyons and me!" exclaimed the princess to Abel and Jomain. "At this close range, our magic swords can direct hot fire into enemy sails."

Four blue gold swords boiled sunlight against the sail of the closest enemy vessel. The sail began to kindle flames. As they scrambled to collapse the burning main sail, pirate sailors lost track of the swimming unicorn.

Briarburr placed his horn against the hull of the close enemy vessel, and sparked it into flame. Darting about as a decoy, Peli's wings distracted sailors and forbad them to contend with Briarburr. A second set of flames willed by Briarburr spread along the hull of the pirate vessel.

Four magic swords shifted sun reflection to the main sail of the second closest enemy vessel, the one that Briarburr now swam toward. Again while he swam his horn swerved arrows and spears to fall harmlessly into the drink. When the point of his horn attached a second time to a hull, a second hull became inflamed. Once more the hard pounding wings of Peli created a diversion. The enemy barge found not only its sail aflame, but also flames leaping up from its hull. An exhausted Briarburr returned to the *Maryeta* and clambered aboard. Peli landed hooves beside the blackmane.

The two undamaged pirate vessels closed one on each side of the Phoenician barge. On the starboard side of the *Maryeta* waited a unicorn, winged horse, Windray, and half the Phoenician crew ready to engage the enemy. On the port side waited Abel, Lyons, Maryeta, Jomain, and twenty more heavily armed sailors. The two enemy vessels simultaneously joined to the *Maryeta*.

Briarburr and Peli jumped to land onto the starboard enemy barge. In support of the unicorns, Windray and the Phoenician sailors that trespassed the pirate vessel fought with double the conviction of their numbers. Enemy sailors were pushed, kicked, and butted into the sea.

Bolstered by the devastating work of the four blue gold swords wielded by Maryeta, Lyons, Jomain, and Abel, the allied blades of Phoenician sailors withstood every attempt to be boarded on the port side of the *Maryeta*.

When the victorious Briarburr and Peli changed to the second enemy vessel, final resolution came to the fight. With crews bleeding and broken, two enemy vessels floated helpless in the water.

On the third morning following the defeat of four pirate barges, the ever alert Jomain was the first to glimpse the approach of a fleet of small vessels sailing westward; with the fishing boats sailed a barge.

"Unicorns alerted Grandfather that our barge neared Phoenicia!" exclaimed Lyons. By fisherman from Phoenicia, and a barge commanded by Cavour, the *Maryeta* had at last been made safe.

Clad in an elaborate purple robe, King Fahseed waited at the great wharf for the mooring of a vessel that had traveled to the ends of the world and back. With him were Elyeazar and Colyado. The king and his two blacksmith friends learned that Egypt had employed pirates to intercept the *Maryeta* and steal Fahseed's three great treasures, two substanced by his own flesh and blood.

CHAPTER 45

INTRIGUE IN NEW BIBLOS

"I wish that my grandfather could have seen the feats of Peli and Briarburr," offered Maryeta seated with Lyons and Fahseed at the supper table. "Their hooves, horns, and wings brought victory over four pirate ships commanded by Egyptian officers."

"So then, Granddaughter, I raise my cup to the heroism of the blackmane and the winged horse." Fahseed beamed as he added, "And a second toast to a princess grown more lovely. Why, just on this very day of your long-awaited return to me, more than one told me that my granddaughter is the prettiest maiden in the land."

"That is not so," answered Maryeta. "And exaggeration does not become a king. Lyons fought very bravely against the pirates. With his sword Lyons has become unbeatable."

"Excellent," responded Fahseed nodding his head. "By the way, Maryeta, I named our capital New Byblos. I once told you and Lyons that we would someday live as a real family in Byblos; we do that now in *New Byblos*. The name of our isolated village, the place where you and Lyons befriended Briarburr, lives on in our prosperous new capital city."

"Grandfather, the people drop the word new... and simply call our capital *Byblos*. That is not right, for there is only one Byblos. It is the place where innocence, love, and truth made to happen a miracle."

"No matter, Maryeta. Our little village is nothing compared to the great city that grows without the walls of my palace. Dear girl, the important thing is that you and Lyons are returned to me."

"When did you start to so expertly trim your beard?" inquired Lyons leaning in to look closely at the chin of his grandfather. "Hmph! I liked it better when it was scruffy looking."

"But Lyons, people tell me that my beard looks ten times better than before," responded Fahseed whisking fingers through his beard. "Trimmed every third day by the best barber in the land, it *should* look very nice. And I especially like that the scissoring is free of charge."

Three moons after the return of the *Maryeta*

The king sat at the large table in the palace entertaining his two grandchildren, Abel, Windray, Cavour, and his blacksmith friends Colyado, Elyeazar, and Jomain.

On the king's lap rested his magic sword. He held it up and kissed the sword's handle. "I continue glad to have this blade returned to me."

"You do know, Grandfather, that it was that sword in the hands of Abel that made it possible for Maryeta and I to come back to you."

"And I remind you, Lyons, that it was me that early-on recognized the valor of Lieutenant Abel. He made me petition him several times before he finally changed his allegiance to me."

The king motioned his sword to the pile of blue gold ore, displayed for all to see on the floor of the great room.

"Every day the mound grows smaller... as more ore is transformed into swords, shields, and armor destined to make our army invulnerable. Hmph! You know I will hate to see the day come when no more blue gold piles on the floor of this great room. I confess that I have become strangely drawn to its lustrous magic."

"Your grandfather is much changed," muttered Jomain seated next to Lyons. "Showered with all manner of flattery and gifts, he has come to think very highly of himself. He likes that wealthy and powerful men come to the palace to ask for your sister's hand."

"This, Jomain, cannot continue," replied Lyons squirming uncomfortably in his chair. "You, Maryeta, Abel, Windray, and I did not travel to the ends of the earth so that Grandfather would become the subject of... *flattery*."

Lyons pushed his chair back from the table and rose to his feet. "Grandfather, I have something to say to you."

"I am entertaining our guests. These men are like family to me. My grandson and I can talk later."

"Grandfather, since your guests are as you say, *family*, what I have to share can be heard by everyone here. Lieutenant Abel is like a brother to me. He has proven himself loyal to you and to Phoenicia. Without his bravery, the blue gold that you so love would not have found its way back across the far sea to pile here in the great room of your palace. My sister, your granddaughter, is in love with Lieutenant Abel and he with her. Of course this you know already. I ask that you, this night, give them your blessing in marriage."

"Come now, Lyons. Maryeta can have her pick of any number of... *rich princes*. Your sister is very beautiful. She has fought bravely with a magic sword. She rides a winged horse. Like her there is no other princess. For that, Maryeta is much desired by every royal house. In comparison, what prominence and wealth can Abel offer to her?"

"Without finding the opportunity, I have long wanted to ask for Maryeta's hand in marriage," said Abel risen to his feet. His eyes moistened and his cheeks flushed. He breathed deeply so that he would not be seen to cry.

"King Fahseed, you trusted me to take your two wonderful grandchildren across far seas to lands unknown. For their very lives you made me responsible. It was to me that you entrusted your blue gold sword, a magic blade with value beyond reckon. How can you not enough trust me to marry Maryeta, the young woman that I love more than life itself?"

Maryeta moved to clasp her hands around a hand of Abel's. Seeing the intimacy shared by the two, Fahseed was momentarily taken aback. Regaining composure, the king smiled kindly at his granddaughter and said, "My dearest Maryeta, you

417

are... you are *too young* to marry. Wait a few years. Take your time to consider."

In tears, Maryeta ran out of the banquet hall of the palace. Head bowed and shoulders slumped, Abel next left the room. Without excusing himself, Fahseed rose to his feet and abruptly left the table. His manner of departure was not to be disputed with.

"Never before have I seen the eyes of Abel to well up in tears," said Lyons. "Not even when the sword of Cavour cut deeply the lieutenant as he rescued me in battle." Upon observing the youth despondent, the diplomatic Colyado moved to sit by the prince.

"Come over here Elyeazar, Cavour, and Windray," insisted Jomain. "Including this noble prince and Colyado, we six have a problem to solve. Let us put our heads together and come up with a solution... *to heartbreak.*" On the opposite side of the table one blacksmith and two former overlords pulled up chairs.

"The prince is well-persuaded of this love?" inquired Colyado.

"Who better than me to know my sister's heart? Ever since we were children alone in the forest, Maryeta and I have been inseparable. How can I not desire to see her happy? To each one of you the heart of Abel is intimately known. Whether here, or in the far land across the immeasurable sea, at the side of Lieutenant Abel we six have fought for life itself. The true and correspondent hearts of Abel and my sister are meant to be given to each other."

"Fahseed talks much about royal suitors for his granddaughter," said Elyeazar. "Do any of you believe that is the true motivation for his refusal to give Maryeta his blessing to marry Abel? I, for one, do not for a moment believe it."

"Hmph, perhaps Elyeazar is right," responded Jomain. "It may be that our old friend cannot bear the thought of Maryeta ever leaving his side. Princes that marry stay behind. Princesses depart to the land of the prince they marry. Since her return, Fahseed every day dotes on Maryeta."

"My sister should not be made to fill the empty place left in the heart of Grandfather, when my mother to him became lost."

"Whether the king does not want Abel for Maryeta's husband, or whether Fahseed wants to keep her forever close to himself, or for both reasons our leader is wrong," said Windray. "Our precious Maryeta has her own life to live."

That said, the face of Windray gave birth to a small smile that slowly spread. Seeing that, Jomain commented, "I believe a thought has just occurred to Windray that we should all like to hear."

"Since you asked, something does occur to me. What if in this matter the hand of Fahseed were to be forced? What if Maryeta were to feign agreement to go very far away, with let us say an unworthy, even contemptible prince? Fahseed would surely come to his senses and accept Lieutenant Abel as a better son-in-law alternative than maybe never seeing again his granddaughter, or finding her become unhappily married. Friends, can we among us invent a prince... *more clown* than royal?"

"You know what, Windray? Your idea... is brilliant. It just might work," agreed Jomain.

Cavour rose and began to mutter as he paced back-and-forth beside the table. "Hmmm... let me think... who... no... no... ah... yes... *right!* Hah! A candidate for royal clownage does occur to me. I am thinking of the scion of Mesopotamia. By more than one ambassador I have been told that Crown Prince Rimush is a person reprehensible. Now that I think on it, I was told by someone that knows the prince only too well that Rimush is shallow, arrogant, willful, cowardly, and in every way the exact opposite of Abel."

"Hah!" responded Jomain clapping his hands. "And now at war with Mesopotamia, the Egyptians would much disapprove of a marital union between Phoenicia's royal house and the throne of their powerful enemy. Perhaps Fahseed's friend Ambassador Adolfo of Egypt might play a role in the drama that we together may be about to present in the palace. You know, I like nothing better than to watch the acting out of a good piece of drama. In that regard, the palace would provide a *marvelous* stage on which to perform."

"I cannot even guess how far distant is found Mesopotamia," offered Lyons. "Grandfather would absolutely hate to see Maryeta to be gone so far away. Not to mention that I also would miss her... *terribly*."

The Clown Prince

"What we say here must remain among only ourselves," said Jomain as he motioned for the chairs to be brought closer together. "Should news of this subterfuge reach the ears of Fahseed, it would lead to disaster for all of us. And Lyons, that includes you as well.

"This is how our plan can unfold. The king must be convinced that it would be to his advantage to invite young Prince Rimush to the palace to woo Maryeta. Now then, Cavour, I have recently come to know a close cousin of the ruler of Mesopotamia. It so happens that this cousin of Prince Rimush works in our capital city as an actor. Because it would not suit for his royal relatives to know that he is working in a theater frequented by common people, the actor goes by an alias. His real name is Naram.

"As it happens, Naram lives very near to where I live. He entertains the children of my neighborhood by acting out stories and legends of magic lamps and flying carpets. You all know that I love to listen to stories that present the opportunity for me to laugh. Naram is so entertaining that I can listen to him all evening.

"We have developed confidence in each other. For example, I know that Naram despises every one of his relatives that now rule in his country. That, by the way, lends support to what Cavour said about the character of Prince Rimush. Acquainted as I am with Naram's acting and storytelling skills, I am certain that he could persuade Fahseed to invite the young Mesopotamian prince to the palace of Pho..."

"But a *huge* problem stands in our way," interrupted Elyeazar. "The initiation of this royal courtship requires that a suitable gift must be delivered to the ruler of Mesopotamia. The giving of a gift is a ceremonial bribe intended to convince the family of Rimush that Fahseed is indeed serious in this matter of matrimony. Become notoriously miserly with his treasury, our king will not himself pay for the bribe. He will say that given the compelling beauty and desirability of Maryeta, there is no need to send a gift. But, the king will at the same time know that upon the visit of Rimush to his palace, the Prince of Mesopotamia would in turn shower Fahseed with very valuable gifts."

"That part of the gift giving, and know that I say this without intending offense," added Jomain nodding toward Lyons, "would heartily meet with our king's approval."

"Hmph! Made too rich too suddenly, my grandfather knows not how to truly value wealth. By the way, we do not have to worry about Prince Rimush swallowing the bait. The prospect of marrying a stunningly beautiful princess who possesses a magic sword and rides a flying horse, would prove irresistible to a self-centered royal scion."

"Errhmm," having cleared his throat Cavour said quietly, "some of you may remember that Fahseed took my treasury. But as I just now... happen to recall... below the floor of my old garrison one chest of gold remains buried still. Because of its size, that box contains quite a lot of gold. Thinking back on it... I decided to keep that chest intact in the event that there should arise an unforeseeable future need by my king."

"That is perfect," affirmed Colyado. "All six of us will escort Naram to the palace to plant in the ear of Fahseed the idea of Maryeta's matrimony to Rimush. Then it will be the supposedly wealthy Naram that travels to Mesopotamia, and on behalf of our king offers Cavour's chest of gold as the preliminary gift in the negotiations. Of course the chest will be made a little less heavy by the cost of Naram's finery, and the expense of travel back to his homeland."

"I promise you that upon his return to Mesopotamia, my friend Naram will put on a real show!" quipped Jomain.

The drama quickly began to unfold. Within fifteen days of the onset of the conspiracy, the accomplished actor Naram had convinced Fahseed that an alliance with Mesopotamia would thwart the pharaoh's territorial designs on the southern half of Phoenicia, and more than that, the new alliance would vastly increase the prestige of both Phoenicia and its king.

Fahseed very much liked the idea that as an enticement to the royal house of Mesopotamia, the *supposedly* fabulously wealthy Naram would by himself finance the dowry of a chest full of gold. When Naram unconditionally agreed to the request that Rimush should think the gold chest came from the king himself, Fahseed decided he had just acquired a new best friend.

Three moons after the birth of the conspiracy elaborated by six men seated at a table, the palace in New Byblos received Prince Rimush.

Strangely enough to those who knew her well, Maryeta seemed to be much taken with as Lyons called him, *Clown Prince Rimush.*

With Colyado, Elyeazar, Jomain, Windray, Cavour, and Lyons in attendance in the throne room, Maryeta confirmed her intention.

"Almost three moons ago I made you promise that if I did not marry Lieutenant Abel, I could marry whichever prince I wanted. So, Grandfather, I choose Prince Rimush. Why, for the opportunity he gives me to be his queen, I absolutely *love him!*"

The heads of six attendant men nodded immediate agreement to the words of Maryeta.

"Granddaughter... to my ears that is... well I guess that is good news. My dearest Maryeta, you know how much I should hate for you to depart my palace. Nevertheless my advisers, all of them mind you, tell me that an alliance between Phoenicia and Mesopotamia carries great advantages for me. With you as the future queen of Mesopotamia, the league of our two countries would be forged strong as iron. That said, I cannot tell you how much I will hate to see you travel from me... *so far away.*"

Naram on Stage

The evening of the betrothal banquet came. With the exception of Abel, the close friends of the king were all in attendance. In the place of honor next to the king sat the visiting Prince. Opposite Rimush, at the king's left hand side sat Maryeta. Sitting on the other side of the Mesopotamian prince, the *new best friend* of Fahseed began to play the leading role in the final act of the drama. It was a part in a real-life play that Naram relished.

"This wine, Great King Fahseed, is absolutely... *exquisite!*" began Naram. "I must refill the cup of the illustrious Prince Rimush! Drink up, my Prince! Does not Phoenicia compare well to our magnificent country?" Ever so slightly the young foreign prince nodded his head in agreement.

"Hmm, well, Naram, just remember that Phoenicia is less than a tenth the size of my country of Mesopotamia. My two great rivers several times surpass the size of all the rivers found here. Tell us how much greater is my country's trade with the east compared to all the trade of this country."

"Many, *many* times greater, my prince!" responded quickly Naram.

"So as you of course know, Cousin Naram, I am here *only* because the princess is incredibly beautiful. Maryeta will be the wife that I love."

"Is not my future husband, the prince I have come to love so much, very young to be already married?" responded Maryeta feigning surprise.

"The first wife of Rimush was only twelve when she married my cousin," answered Naram for his prince. "If I recall correctly, at that time my beloved prince was himself only thirteen. You see, Maryeta, every ruler wants to give our illustrious prince... a wife. That is how lesser countries buy favor with the great kingdom of Mesopotamia. But, of course, I am not now suggesting that the Kingdom of Phoenicia is a lesser country. Ahem. Princess Maryeta will be the fifth wife of Prince Rimush, but of course the one most beautiful."

With notable flair Naram filled again the cup of his prince.

"Hmph! Prince Rimush, I insist that you find me to be the wife most dear to your heart." That said, the frown left her brow and Maryeta's tone became more enthusiastic.

"Dear, dear, Rimush, I cannot wait to see your great palace with its wondrous gardens. Grandfather, you must promise to come often to look upon the fabulous gardens of my sweet Prince Rimush. The trip there and back will take you less than three moons to complete. And while you are away, you can leave the matters of the Kingdom of Phoenicia in the hands of Cavour. He is a serious man. I find that for such a powerful man, Cavour is refreshingly honest. Grandfather, is not it wonderful that General Cavour is by all regarded to be a statesman most capable?"

"Hmph. Yes, Maryeta. Cavour *is* very capable. But, I will confess that I know next to nothing about the famous gardens found in the capital city of Prince Rimush. And somehow Naram overlooked telling me that the prince had already a wife, errhmm... *wives.*" Fahseed glanced coldly at his new best friend. "I thought that my granddaughter would alone bear the children of Rimush."

A smile spread to possess the face of Naram as he cajoled, "Prince Rimush, be so kind as to tell the king how many children you now have."

"Four... or five."

"Did not you complain to me that at last count it was seven?" corrected Naram. "But of course about that I must be mistaken. Hah! What is certainly true is that in his loins my prince is lucky! A toast to Prince Rimush the... *ladies' man!*"

Amidst thick silence cups were raised. While again being made to have his cup replenished, Rimush said something to Naram that was intended more for the ears of Maryeta.

"You of course know, Cousin, that I shall treasure a child of Maryeta's. And I shall proudly wear the magic sword of Princess Maryeta while I take her child for a ride on the winged horse. Everyone will be impressed when from the sky my blue gold sword flashes sunrays down into the courtyard of the palace. Hahah! My sword reflections will light afire one of the palace's priceless carpets!"

"That reminds me," interjected Maryeta, "of when Lyons, Abel, Jomain, and I flashed sunrays to set fire to the sails of pirate ships. Prince Rimush, I shall be proud to see my future husband use my magic sword in battle. Living in the lap of luxury, I will have no more need of the blue gold sword fashioned by my grandfather in the humble village of... *Old Byblos.* So then, I suppose my magic sword will to me become," she sighed long, "only a shiny ornament."

"One of many, my dear!" responded Rimush.

"It pains me to hear you say that, Maryeta. Remember that you yourself, your brother, three stalwart friends found seated here, and I together made your precious magic sword."

"I will clarify something for King Fahseed," offered Naram. "My prince intended no insult by speaking lightly of the magic that you forged. You must understand that Prince Rimush does not himself brandish a sword to commit acts of bravery. And that is through no fault of my... *brave prince!* The mother of Rimush has forbidden that her son's royal blood be chanced in battle. To be sure, that would be an unforgivable waste of the matchless royal talent of Prince Rimush. Although to be fair, I will tell you that my prince has used a sharp sword to behead a few of his mother's enemies. Hahah! Rimush even chopped off the heads of two of my own brothers. And, of course in that he was absolutely right to so do. Come to think of it now, Maryeta's magic sword would make easier the prince's decapitation of his numerous royal relatives fallen from favor."

"An idea just occurred to me," exclaimed Prince Rimush clapping his hands. "The princess can ride the winged horse in the marriage procession, and I can ride the war unicorn... err... Burrbriar."

"The unicorn's name is... *Briarburr*," said the king.

The prince smirked, raised his glass to the king, and added, "*Whatever...*" Upon being patronized, those gathered at the banquet table could not help but notice Fahseed stir uncomfortably in his chair.

"Prince Rimush, I trust that my granddaughter will next year return to visit me. Perhaps your mother will also accompany her?"

Sporting a smile meant to ingratiate, the prince looked in turn at each person gathered at the table in expectation of their approval. Unusually large smiles were returned to Rimush.

"I cannot imagine that the princess would ever desire to return to this, errm, let us be honest... backward land," said Rimush. "Father-in-law, once your daughter has seen the great capital of Mesopotamia made each year more wealthy by trader caravans come from the east, she will choose to never again leave my city. Oh, and my mother would never consent to travel so far to this... not very large palace. Hahah! I can hear her telling me that in your palace there would not be room enough to house even half of her multitude of servants."

Having clarified the greatness of his realm for the benefit of those seated on all sides of him, Prince Rimush once again smiled big while hitting his cup to the table for more wine.

After filling the cup of his prince, Naram leaned forward to say something that everyone caught. "The prince is simply informing you, King Fahseed, that his mother is kept far too busy to travel to your court."

"How lucky is the mother of my prince to have a multitude of servants! Can my sweet prince even believe that in my father's palace I have fewer than ten? How many servants will I have in your palace?"

"Just imagine, Maryeta! My bride will have fifty servants to wait on her hand and foot!"

When the king buried his head in his hands, all eyes at the table came to be upon Fahseed. After rubbing his belly the king pushed back his chair.

"I am unfortunately become indisposed," said Fahseed. "This night I have drunk too much wine. I will now sadly remove myself to my quarters."

"Has my father-in-law's stomach for long been acting up?" inquired Rimush.

"For the last while it does seem to," replied the king. "Funny. When I was a rough and ready soldier my stomach never used to bother me. Hmph, I cannot even recall how many battles I fought with what was then a tight waist."

"Be glad, Fahseed, that your future son-in-law can handle his wine better than you," came the parting words of Rimush lounging comfortably in his chair. "Hah! I will make sure that at my wedding feast you shall drink too many cups of the best wines found in all of Mesopotamia!"

Naram rose, smiled big at his prince, and raised his glass, "Another toast before the king departs the table! We drink in honor of my unrivaled Prince Rimush, who will carry to the very distant land of Mesopotamia his brand new bride to be." He turned to look Fahseed in the eyes, "The beautiful, sweet, innocent, and incomparable Princess Maryeta."

With not another word said to Prince Rimush, or to anyone else, Fahseed left the banquet table. After nodding his head to Naram, Elyeazar, Jomain, Cavour, Windray, and Colyado, Lyons followed after Fahseed. He found his grandfather in his private quarters sitting with his head hung down.

"Rimush is a... *total disaster!*" The eyes of the king grew large as he added, "Good heavens, Lyons! What in blazes happened to Maryeta on the voyage to the unicorn hold? She now acts nothing like her real self. Blast! I have never once heard my granddaughter to lie, but tonight she lied about her servants. In my palace your sister has not a single servant... because *she refuses* to have servants!"

"My sister did not exactly lie. Maryeta said she has less than ten servants, and speaking precisely, that is not incorrect."

"Well, Lyons, what about me? Did I to myself lie? What possessed me to consent to the marriage of my precious granddaughter to a prince without any discernible virtue, whose only advantages are his wealth and power? How did judgment and reason so easily abandon me? Blast it all! I fear that I myself have begun to act like that spoiled and worthless Prince Rimush. Imagine that! The humble blacksmith that liberated his village from the tyrant Baltric has sunk to the level of... *Prince Rimush the Imbecile!*

"And now having given Maryeta my word of honor, I am to lose the apple of my eye to an insolent prince with many wives already... who of real life knows nothing. Confound it! If I keep my word to Maryeta, and this marriage proceeds, I will be made miserable. If I go back on my word I will break her heart, and so lose her love and respect. And Lyons, I cannot tell you how much I dread someday meeting the prince's mother!"

Grown taller than his grandfather, the kind smile of Lyons angled down.

"It really is a shame that it is too late for you to convince my sister to marry not Prince Rimush, but to instead marry the man she used to love, and I think deep down in her heart loves still.

"Grandfather, you must know that when you forbade Maryeta to marry Lieutenant Abel, her heart broke. After the loss of her dream of a future life lived with the brave and true Abel, Maryeta gave up. She obediently did what you thought best for her; she found a rich prince. I, for one, am glad that Abel is not remotely like Prince Rimush.

"Against Vylas and Cavour in the *Battle of the Unicorn Stallions*, you commended Abel for saving my life. In the *Battle of the Twenty Horse Soldiers* fought across the far sea, Abel saved Maryeta's life. Perhaps you can recall a time when Abel also saved your life in battle?"

"That more than once did Lieutenant Abel."

Lyons pulled from his coat a letter bearing the seal of the pharaoh. "Oh, err, Grandfather, here is something come for you from your friend Ambassador Adolfo."

"Well then, open it. Right now I need some good news to improve my mood." Lyons read silently the letter.

"Grandfather, this news is not good, but contrariwise very troubling. Ambassador Adolfo writes that a royal matrimonial union between Phoenicia and Mesopotamia will assuredly bring to our land war with Egypt."

"Blast and Ruin!" exclaimed Fahseed slumping down more. "Bring me wine... a lot of wine!"

"But Grandfather, I thought your stomach was upset."

"I told you to bring me wine!" No sooner had Lyons poured then Fahseed drained his cup and flung it across the room.

Finally made calmed, the king turned to Lyons, "You are more son to me than grandson. I ask you what... what have I done to deserve this catastrophe?"

"For fifteen years Maryeta and I were your anchors in a stormy life. We were your fixed star. Upon sending us far away you felt both guilty for promulgating our departure, and for becoming by us abandoned. I know that you every day tormented yourself with the thought that you would never again find me, and especially Maryeta, returned to you. In worry and long frustration, from yourself you went astray. Dear Grandfather, I will not permit you to again be swayed by the false winds of fear, vanity, and great power."

As he reached out to grasp the hands of Lyons, tears formed in the eyes of Fahseed. For the first time Lyons had the thought that his grandfather had come to look... *old.*

"Your eyes tell me that something more weighs on your mind," said Lyons.

"Son, it has come time for me to confess to you that I am a murderer. For years my transgression has eaten away at my heart. In fact, I am a... *double* murderer."

"That cannot be, Grandfather."

"Unfortunately, Lyons, it is so. I need to get this off my chest before it destroys not only me, but my relationship with Maryeta and you.

"It happened after you were by Cavour gravely wounded in the *Battle of the Unicorn Stallions*. I found myself to be in a desperate sword fight with Lord Auldham. My blue gold sword could against Auldham make no headway. When Abel sounded his horn that help was on the way, everyone looked to where the line of unicorns fast approached the battlefield.

"When Auldham turned to watch the compelling sight of a charging line of magnificent unicorn stallions, he lowered his sword. Because at that moment the battle was for all purposes finished, like my opponent I should have lowered my sword as well. I did not. Instead, I ran through the defenseless Auldham. Other than to reclaim my pride as a swordsman, I had no reason to end the life of Auldham.

"Surely you remember Lord Cavour telling you how fine a man was his friend Auldham. So, you see Lyons, in killing a defenseless man with a true heart, I became a murderer. Even worse, knowing that I had done wrong I could have right away called for unicorns to heal Auldham and save his life. That, I deliberately chose not to do. For twice over murdering the same good man, I fear that I shall be forever... *cursed*."

"Even in battle, murder is always gravely wrong, but now that you have confessed your transgression the healing can begin."

"I learned that lesson from Maryeta, *and from you,* when on the battlefield I wanted to behead Windray after his defeat. Would that I had learned it before committing a double murder."

"Grandfather, it is fully within your power to each day do good things for one person or another. Let *that* be your penance."

CHAPTER 46

ADMIRAL BOSCHENE FURIOUS

Back at their beach camp, the limping Lufflol and Altber collapsed exhausted frames onto ground. The two Egyptian ship captains found themselves more haggard and hungry than when three days previous they had left behind their admiral to undertake a scouting mission.

"What *took* you so long?" barked Boschene.

"Can you believe that like two children at play we fell out of a tree?" replied Altber. "For that injury our return here was made slow and painful."

"The fault was mine," offered Lufflol. "Because of my short stature I climbed a tree to study better the lay of the land. I insisted that Altber join me in the branches. Attempting to see more, I leaned too far out and lost my footing. When Altber tried to restrain my fall, I unfortunately carried him down with me."

"The worst of it is that I limp because Lufflol fell on me."

"That you limp from the hurt of a fall matters nothing to me," groused the admiral. "Just tell me what manner of island this is."

"We climbed the high and densely treed promontory that you see in the far distance," said Lufflol seating himself on a fallen log. "From a tall tree on that height we observed that on three sides of us sweeps the sea. On the fourth side extends an endless expanse of forest and winding rivers."

"So I am stranded on... a large island," answered Boschene crossly.

"Not exactly. Altber and I concluded that the peninsula we find ourselves walking on is a part of a mainland, a piece of a continent."

"You two idiots are again wrong!" Boschene's thoughts strayed to once more rail at the seamen who had abandoned him to this place. "How dare sailors cast me off... *my own ship!* When the pharaoh hears of the treason and treachery of my sailors, our divine ruler will have every one of them tortured. After their bodies are made lifeless, they will be dismembered so that they can never enter the afterlife."

"Where is your horse?" inquired Altber. "At least the mutineers let you keep your horse. That is something."

"After bucking me off, that damned animal ran off down the beach!"

"The beast will try to return to the unicorns," mused Altber. "As we are stranded on the mainland, the admiral's horse just might succeed."

"We came upon a destroyed village," informed Lufflol. "The fire was recent. That means that not far from here are found hostile natives."

"It is urgent that we escape this dangerous place," continued Altber. "A boat must be built, provisioned with food, and by us sailed back to Egypt."

"Never tell me what to do! I will first find my sailors and make them pay for their crimes against me!"

"Admiral, nearly every one of your sailors was beaten by the lash," interjected Lufflol. "They were every day dying. With nothing but a vast sea in wait of them, they could not longer bear both starvation and your harsh discipline. The survivors in your crew decided to save their lives the only way they knew how. With the rebellion of your barge crew, that chapter is now over and done with. You have to face the facts, Admiral. You will never find the mutineers, or the cargo of precious blue gold."

"You dare, Lufflol, talk to me like that?"

"It has never been my desire to offend my Admiral. I before prided myself on my obedience to your every order. But like your crew, I have nothing more to lose by speaking now my mind."

"Against current and wind your men rowed hard day after day until they could not any more do so," concurred Altber with what Lufflol had just said. "You should have listened to Captain Lockshray and taken the northern route back to our sea. Thanks to your bad navigation, in this dangerous and unknown land the three of us now find ourselves... *lost and forsaken.* If not by starvation, our deaths will be brought by poison tipped arrows. For once in your illustrious life, Admiral Boschene, you should listen to something I say. Let us build the biggest boat that we can manage, and as best we can find our way eastward to Egypt."

With the back of his hand Boschene wiped at tears as he collapsed down on the sand. He sobbed, "What... unhnn... about... unhnnn... *the blue gold?*"

"Sir," continued Altber, "somewhere into this vast continent has vanished the blue gold. Perhaps in this land of mountains and jungle the gold will be used to build a great temple to the Egyptian Sun God."

"All right... all right... you two win. Using our swords for tools we will build a boat. But it will not be easy for our blades to carve pieces of trees and branches into ship boards." After glancing teary-eyed at Altber and Lufflol the admiral sighed deeply.

"Lockshray is to blame for my being found here stranded. I should have killed him that day on the beach when he first raised his voice against me. By the time we reached Shining Canyon, it was too late. There Lockshray commanded four hundred, and I only one hundred commanded. I also blame the blackmaned unicorn. And I blame the winged horse.

"And yes... I blame my half brother Ambassador Adolfo. He never liked me. When Adolfo told the pharaoh that the voyage of the unicorns must be undertaken, the ambassador knew that one way or the other, *he would win.* If I returned with the magic gold Egypt would be much strengthened, and his insistence that the voyage be made would be much praised. If I did not return to Egypt, well then for Adolfo so much the better. He would be forever rid of me." More for his own benefit than that of the two officers with him, Boschene added, "Just remember one thing. The people of Egypt... *love me.*"

With a look disconsolate the admiral spoke on, "If the currents take our boat empty of blue gold back to Egypt, because of my royal birth I will be returned some measure of power. If the currents take our boat back to the west, I will find where Lockshray builds in the mountains, and there force myself to make amends." Wanting to be alone with his thoughts, the admiral walked away from his two officers.

"Did we just witness a high man change himself to be no more arrogant and haughty?" asked Altber of Lufflol.

"About that we shall soon see."

CHAPTER 47

EPILOGUE: A ROYAL WEDDING

Unicorns liked to neigh that *Wittanorr*, the name of their new home, signified the place of white unicorns and gold colored sand. However, the sand layering the beach before the unicorn hold was colored more white than gold.

The Wittanorr unicorns came to relish a natural setting favored by warm sunshine, lush forest, broad beach, and a luxuriant waterfall. When at nightfall unicorns turned behind the falling cascade to enter the large cool cavern where sleep was easily obtained, they felt themselves to be truly at home.

The volcano looming high above Wittanorr had come to be regarded as the sentinel protector of the hold. However, as a precaution learned from long struggle on the other side of the sea, unicorn stallions marched guard along the river bank demarking the landed western limit of Wittanorr.

The fast growing foal of Peli remained inseparable from Matron Lorial. Because there was no horse reason to do so, no unicorn thought to inquire of Lorial the progeny of the perfectly formed and perfectly colored foal. Every time her thoughts returned to the fearless sire of Aneighlee, Matron Lorial's face lit in a long smile. With her most guarded thoughts the matron could not help but wonder if the black markings of Briarburr, or the black color that swathed the underside of the wings of Peli, would on a future day present themselves in new foals carrying the bloodlines of Aneighlee.

"As she every day watched the noisy and mischievous foal grow bigger, the matron began to hope a strange thing for Peli's filly. The matron wanted to live long enough to see the birth of a black marked unicorn blessed not by war, but by the peace and safety of the unicorn hold.

Walking one day on the beach of Wittanorr, while her ward was at play with other colts, Lorial saw in the distance a horse she recognized in spite of his being gaunt, matted in burrs and brambles, and limping badly. The matron rushed hooves to nuzzle the visitor.

"Welcome to the hold of the unicorns," neighed Lorial to a horse that had before been her companion.

"*Nyerrrhhunhhunh...* at last I am made safe," grunted the horse formerly ridden by Admiral Boschene.

"I come to think that the admiral no more commands a war barge of Egypt," responded Lorial. "Poor, miserable, Boschene. *The unjust are ever reserved for judgment.*"

As Lorial's thoughts wandered back to the time when she had previously known the now exhausted and hurt horse, she was reminded of the day she promised to help repay a debt owed for the deliverance of the unicorns. However, she had not helped to find the blue gold. Moreover, as a proper unicorn she had declined to participate against marauding warriors in the *Battle of the Twenty Horse*

Soldiers. So just what had she done? How had she helped with... anything? Lorial hrrrruummed a long horse sigh. Finally, her countenance brightened.

"I now know how to keep my promise. I will to Briarburr and Peli repay my debt by being the best grandmare in the white herd. I shall spare no effort to ensure that Aneighlee one day becomes a great unicorn mare. The blackmane and the winged horse gave to their filly the legacy of unicorn belonging and fellowship. They did this knowing that the white herd would never accept a black marked unicorn or a winged horse that had fought at the side of valiant men.

"I solemnly vow that I will never let Aneighlee forget that her sire and mare loved her enough to spare her danger, fighting, and war. I will instruct Aneighlee to guard that knowledge of great sacrifice, and to pass it on to the foals that she will someday bear. That is how I will keep the promise that I still owe for the deliverance of the white herd.

"More than any other unicorn, I will have Aneighlee's heart to fill and grow large. And, if the mane of Aneighlee someday becomes spotted in black roots, I shall love her even more."

A Princess Wed

The royal boulevard was thronged to overflowing. Children wanting to glimpse the bride and groom crowded everywhere about. The only thing wished for by one child and another was that the sky had broken out in sunshine instead of presenting fluffy white clouds.

A prancing unicorn with tautly muscled flanks and shoulders, and a mane colored black, came into view. On his head fit a finely made halter that dazzled in blue gold magic. Seated upon the unicorn's back, the groom led the wedding procession. Riding first was symbolic of his new responsibilities. He would on this day commit to love and protect his bride for as long as he lived. His love for her would be pledged to be greater than his love for himself, greater even than his love for his own flesh. If misfortune someday came to pass, he would starve himself so that his bride might eat.

Holding a large satin pillow upon which rested two magic swords, Lyons followed after the groom. The sword blades were crossed to symbolize two bodies interjoined to become one. That he followed close after the bridegroom symbolized his pledge to become brother to the man to be wed to his sister.

Pacing in step with one another followed ten army captains. With points shining of blue gold, their spears bent in salute to the royal couple. Behind the ten officers followed an honor guard comprised of one hundred sailors. The twenty drummers that came next kept perfect time with the tun, tun, and tun of each other.

With his royal crown cradled in the crook of a bent arm, following after his sailors walked with notable solemnity the king.

The most honored guest of the celebration came last. Seated on the back of a winged horse whose head wore a halter glowing the color of blue diamonds, rode

Princess Maryeta. As she watched lead her onward the grandfather that for long years had protected her from a wicked overlord, she knew this would be the last time Fahseed would have the preeminent role in her life.

Children gasping *ohhs* and *ahhs*, and giggling and laughing, spread a path of flower petals before Peli. For the beauty of flowers spread before her hooves, the *thank you* returned by the winged horse was to begin to prance proudly and rhythmically to the tunning of the drums, all the while holding high and still her head.

Worn delicately on the bride's hair was a sparkling diadem said to have come from very far away. Some thought that the luster of the diadem made the tresses of the princess look reddish, others thought auburn, and others thought the sheen of the diadem colored her hair more brown.

As the winged horse pranced, her sides and rear quarters were caressed by the gold colored train of the bridal gown. The wedding dress of royal Phoenician purple was at Maryeta's neck and down her arms, embroidered with interlaid strands of magic blue gold threads. Drawing across her chest and thinly down her sides, the white parts of the bridal dress were decorated with blue gold lacing that gleamed communicant with hidden sunlight. The smile that glowed on the face of the bride made her look to be... more than happy.

On this day made more loving grandfather than king, Fahseed waited before the steps of his palace to help dismount a bride that was to him more daughter than granddaughter. Even though she had wanted a celebration less of royalty than of a common girl that had a thousand times climbed her favorite tree, a purple carpet was extended for Maryeta's feet to climb the steps of a palace whose pillars were entwined with brightly colored flowers that numbered beyond count.

Expectant silence spread over the crowded plaza.

As she walked stairs upward the princess paused and turned her head. The warmth of her smile penetrated into every corner of the plaza. Whether standing close or far-off, those gathered saw that on this her special day the princess was the very picture of earthly beauty.

Maryeta had persuaded, rather insisted that Fahseed privilege to officiate at the ceremony a man whose life she had once saved, a man whose inspiration had once helped her to surmount a crisis. The king neither understood nor liked that a man formerly condemned to hard labor was granted such a rare and precious honor. Nevertheless, it was Windray who presided over the occasion.

Standing on the great porch of the palace Windray raised his arms for silence. In loud voice a pardoned overlord began speaking words that told of the gift of unity between a man and a woman.

"This day happens the miracle of two lives made joined in one. This marriage is a resplendent gift brought about by the magic of unicorns and blue gold. When the purity and innocence of Briarburr and Peli fused with the truth and verity of blue gold, wondrous magic penetrated and filled the hearts of the bride and groom, and the miracle of perfect love was born."

Windray paused to smile kindly at the groom.

"By the winds of new love the dust from former paths has been carried away. Along with the departed dust, the previous paths walked by this man have now vanished into forgottenness."

Windray took two hands, one big and one small, in his.

"A shared new road paved in tenderness and growing endearment will from this day onward be walked together by Princess Maryeta and her husband."

It was not long before Windray pronounced the couple married. He gave his blessing, "May two kindred minds and spirits know companionship and lasting beauty that through each shared day grow more compelling. I give reverence to the life that will unfold before you. May your love for each other increase evermore eternal. By the grace of the heavens above, I bless and magnify your union."

When the bride and groom kissed, the great plaza of New Byblos broke out in cheers that for a long time seemed would never come to an end.

Upon descending the steps leading from the palace, the bride and groom were greeted by very many well-wishers including as many men as women, as many children as grownups, as many not poor... which on this occasion was *everyone*. For on this heartfelt and glorious day in New Byblos no man, woman, or child felt himself or herself to be poor.

After helping his bride to remount Peli, the groom remounted Briarburr.

Everyone crowding the plaza before the palace sought to touch the hem of Maryeta's magical wedding dress, or to feel pure magic from the touch of a horse's wing, or to stroke the black mane of a magical and storied unicorn.

With suddenness the sun pried open a blue pocket in a sky painted over in pure white clouds. Sunrays made to glitter the descent of fine drops of rain. Taking the refreshment of rain drops as a propitious sign, the bride reached to hold the hand of her groom.

"Darling, this reminds me of once upon a far time in a forest," said Maryeta feeling raindrops glance against her cheeks. "I was running free when a surprising sun made every drop of rain to sparkle."

When Maryeta smiled the bridegroom glimpsed an innocent little girl whose heart brimmed over with delight at seeing a thing enchantingly beautiful, like a cascade of falling water framing for the first time ever a blackmaned unicorn and a winged horse.

The radiance of Maryeta's eyes made to part Abel's heart.

The third heart parted most by happiness on a long ago day made dazzling and beauteous by the miracle of true love, beat fast in the breast of Fahseed.

The hearts of Lyons, the blacksmiths Colyado, Elyeazar, and Jomain, the former overlords Windray and Cavour, and not least of all the heart of the actor Naram, beat triumphant.

THE END

G. D. Hanson

ABOUT THE AUTHOR

G. D. Hanson taught at Auburn and Penn State Universities. His academic degrees are from Dartmouth College and the University of Minnesota. Married, he and Isabel reside in South Dakota and Costa Rica.